ENEMY IN SIGHT!

Also by
ALEXANDER KENT

★

TO GLORY WE STEER
FORM LINE OF BATTLE!

ENEMY IN SIGHT!

*

ALEXANDER KENT

THE
COMPANION BOOK CLUB
LONDON AND SYDNEY

This edition is published in 1971 by
The Hamlyn Publishing Group Ltd,
and is issued by arrangement with
Hutchinson & Co. (Publishers) Ltd.

Made and printed in Great Britain
for the Companion Book Club
by Odhams (Watford) Ltd.
Standard 600771377
Deluxe 600871371
8.71

No captain can do very wrong if he places his ship alongside that of an enemy.

HORATIO NELSON

1. A Time for Parting

THE TALL WINDOW of the Golden Lion Inn which faced south across Plymouth Sound shivered violently in its frame as another freak gust speckled the glass with drizzle and blown spray.

Captain Richard Bolitho had been standing with his back to a blazing log fire, his hands behind him, as he stared unseeingly at the bedroom carpet, and the sudden flurry of wind made him look up, his mind dragging with the mixed emotions of urgency and a new, alien sense of apprehension at leaving the land.

He crossed quickly to the window and stood looking down across the deserted roadway, the shining cobbles and the grey tossing water beyond. It was eight o'clock in the morning, but being the first day of November was still almost too dark to see much more than a blurred grey panorama through the dappled glass. He could hear voices beyond the bedroom door, the sounds of horses and wheels in the yard below, and knew that the moment of parting had almost arrived. He stooped over a long brass telescope which was mounted on a tripod by the window, no doubt for the benefit of inn guests or the amusement of those who saw the passing ships-of-war as nothing more than things of beauty or momentary distraction. It was strange to realize that 1794 was drawing to a close, that England had been at war with Revolutionary France for nearly two years, and still there were many people who were either indifferent or totally unaware of their peril. Perhaps the news had been too good, he thought vaguely, and certainly this year had gone well at sea. Howe's conquest, the Glorious First of June as it was now called, Jarvis's capture of the French West Indian islands, and even the taking of Corsica in the Mediterranean should have meant that the way was already opening up for total victory. But Bolitho knew better than to accept such ready judgements. The war was spreading in every direction, so that it seemed as if it would eventually engulf the whole world. And England, in spite of her ships, was being forced back further and further upon her own resources.

He eased the telescope carefully to one side, seeing the serried whitecaps cruising across the Sound, the wedge of headland and the hurrying ranks of leaden clouds. The wind was freshening from the north-west and there was a hint of snow in the air.

He held his breath and steadied the glass on a solitary ship which lay far out, seemingly motionless and making the only patch of colour against the bleak sea.

The *Hyperion*, his ship, was waiting for him. It was hard, no impossible, to picture her as the battered, shot-scarred two-decker he had brought to Plymouth six months earlier after her desperate fight in the Mediterranean following Hood's failure to hold and occupy Toulon. Six months of pleading and bribing, of bullying dockyard workers and watching over every phase of the old ship's repairs and refit. And she *was* old. Twenty-two years had passed since her good Kentish oak had first tasted salt water, and almost all the time she had been in continuous commission. From the freezing misery of the Atlantic to maddening calms in the Indies. From the broadsides of the Mediterranean to patient blockade duty off one enemy port or another.

When she had been docked Bolitho had seen weed nearly six feet long scraped from her fat bilges. No wonder she had been so slow. Now, outwardly at least, she looked a new ship.

He watched the strange silvery light play across her tall side as she swung heavily at her anchor. Even at this distance he could see the taut black tracery of her rigging and shrouds, the double line of gun-ports, the small scarlet rectangle made by her ensign as it stood out in the freshening wind.

Once it had seemed as if the refit, the work and delays would never end. Then in the last few weeks she had returned to the waiting sea, her rigging had been set up, her seventy-four guns replaced, the deep-bellied hull filled with stores, provisions, powder and shot. And men.

8

Bolitho straightened his back. Six months was a long while to be away from her natural element. This time she would not be returning with the seasoned, well-disciplined company he had taken command of sixteen months ago, most of whom had been aboard for four years. In that time you could expect even the dullest landsman to find his place in things. But those men had been paid off. Not to a well-earned rest, but scattered to the demands of an ever-growing fleet, leaving him with only a few of the senior ones who were needed to deal with the ship's more intimate repairs.

For weeks his new company had been gathered from every available source. From other ships, the port admiral, and even the local Assizes. At his own expense, but with little hope, Bolitho had sent handbills and two recruiting parties in the search for new men, and had been astonished when some forty Cornishmen had arrived on board. Most were landsmen, from farms or the mines, but *all* were volunteers.

The lieutenant who had brought them aboard had been full of compliments and something like awe, for it was rare indeed to volunteer to leave the land for the harsh discipline and hazards of life in a King's ship.

Bolitho could still not believe that these men actually *wanted* to serve with him, a fellow Cornishman, one whose name was well known and admired throughout their native county. He was completely baffled by it and not a little moved.

Now that was all in the past. Crammed within the one-hundred-and-eighty-foot hull his new company was waiting for him. The man who, next to God, would control their lives. Whose judgement and skill, whose bravery or otherwise would decide whether they lived or died. The *Hyperion* was still some fifty short of her six hundred complement, but that was little enough in these hard times. Her real weakness lay in the immediate future, the days when he would have to drive every man in order to weld them all into one trained community.

He came out of his brooding thoughts as the door opened, and when he turned he saw his wife framed in the entrance. She was dressed in a long green velvet cloak, the hood thrown back from her rich chestnut hair, and her eyes were very bright, so that he suspected the tears were only just held in check.

He crossed the room and took her hands. It was still difficult to understand the good fortune which had made her his wife. She was beautiful and ten years younger than he, and as he looked down at her he knew that leaving her now was the hardest thing he had ever done. Bolitho was thirty-seven years old, and had been at sea from the age of twelve. During that time, as he survived both hardship and danger, he had often felt something akin to contempt for the men who preferred to stay in the safety of their homes rather than sail in a King's ship. He had been married to Cheney for five months, and now he understood just how agonizing such partings could be.

During the long refit she had never been far from his side. It had been a new and devastatingly happy time, in spite of the ship's needs and the daily work which took him to the dockyard. Mostly he had spent his nights ashore with her in the inn, and sometimes they had gone for long walks above the sea, or had taken a pair of horses as far as Dartmoor. That was until she had told him she was going to have his child, when she had laughed at his immediate concern and protective uncertainty.

He said, 'Your hands are like ice, my dear.'

She smiled. 'I have been down in the yard telling Allday how to unpack some of the things I have prepared for you.'

Again the tilt of the chin, the slight quiver in her lip. 'Remember, Richard, you are married now. I'll not have my captain as thin as a rake for want of good food.'

From the stairway Bolitho heard Allday's discreet cough. At least he would be with him. His coxswain, the man who, next to his old friend Herrick, probably knew him better than anyone.

He said quickly, 'Now you *will* take care, Cheney?' He squeezed her hands tightly. 'When you get back to Falmouth there will be plenty of friends if you need anything.'

She nodded, then reached out and touched his white-lapelled coat and rested her fingers on his sword hilt. 'I will be waiting for you, my dear Richard.' She dropped her eyes. 'And if you are at sea when our child is born you will *still* be with me.'

Allday's stocky figure rounded the side of the door. 'The

barge is waiting, Captain. I've stowed all the gear as ma'am ordered.' He looked at her admiringly. 'And never fret, ma'am, I'll take good care of him.'

She gripped Bolitho's arm fiercely and whispered, 'See that you do. And pray God will keep both of you safe!'

Bolitho prised her fingers away and kissed her gently. He felt wretched and wished he had words to make the parting easier. At the same time he knew that there were no such words, nor ever had been.

He picked up his gold-laced hat and tugged it down across his forehead. Then he held her in his gaze for a few more seconds, feeling their pain, understanding their loss, and then without another word turned and strode to the stairs.

The landlord bowed as he crossed to the main doors, his round face solemn as he intoned, 'Good luck, Cap'n! Kill a few o' they Frogs for us'n!'

Bolitho nodded curtly and allowed Allday to wrap the thick boat-cloak around his shoulders. The landlord's words were meaningless, he thought. He probably said exactly the same to the endless procession of captains and sea officers who stayed briefly beneath his roof before returning to their ships, some for the last time.

He caught sight of himself in a wall mirror beside the ostler's bell and saw that he was frowning. But what a difference the past six months had made. The realization made him stare at himself for several moments. The deep lines around his mouth had faded, and his tall figure looked more relaxed than he could remember. His black hair was without a trace of grey, in spite of the fever which had nearly killed him between the wars, and the one lock which still curled rebelliously above his right eye made him look younger than his years. He saw Allday watching him and forced a smile.

Allday threw open the doors and touched his hat. 'It seems like a long while since we were to sea, Captain.' He grinned. 'I'll not be sorry to leave. The Plymouth wenches are not what they were.'

Bolitho walked past him and felt the rain across his face like ice rime. He quickened his pace with Allday striding comfortably behind him. The ship was lying a good two miles offshore, both to take advantage of the wind and tide and to deter any would-be deserter. The barge crew would have a hard pull to reach her.

He paused above the jetty stairs feeling the wind swirling around him, the land beneath his feet, and knowing as he always did that he might never set foot ashore again. Or worse, he might return as some helpless cripple, armless or eyeless, like so many who thronged the waterfront taverns as reminders of the war which was always present, even if unseen.

He turned to look back at the inn and imagined he could see her in the window.

Then he said, 'Very well, Allday, call the barge alongside.'

Once clear of the jetty wall the oars seemed to make the boat skim across the low cruising whitecaps, and as Bolitho sat huddled in his cloak he wished that he had a whole ship's company like these bargemen. For they were his original barge crew, and in their white trousers and check shirts, with their pigtails and tanned faces they looked every inch the landsman's idea of British sailors.

The barge's motion became heavier as it plunged clear of the shore, and Bolitho settled down to watch his ship as she grew slowly out of the haze of spray and drizzle until the towering masts and yards and the neatly furled sails seemed to fill the horizon. It was a normal illusion but one which never failed to impress him. Once, when a mere child, he had gone to join his first ship, of similar size to *Hyperion*, but in those tender years she had seemed even larger and more than a little frightening. As this ship must now seem to the newly gathered men, he thought, both the volunteers and those pressed from safer lives ashore.

Allday swung the tiller and guided the barge past the high bows so that the gilt figurehead of Hyperion, the Sun God, seemed to reach with his trident right above their heads.

Bolitho could hear the twitter of pipes carried on the wind, and saw the scarlet-coated marines already mustered by the entry port, the blue and white of the officers and the anonymous press of figures beyond.

He wondered what Inch, his first lieutenant, would be thinking about this moment of departure. He wondered, too, what had made him retain the young lieutenant when plenty of senior ones had been ready to take such a coveted appointment. Next in line to a ship's captain there was always the chance, even the hope, that promotion would come by that captain's sudden death or advancement to flag rank.

When he had taken command of the old seventy-four, Bolitho had found Inch as the fifth and junior lieutenant. Service away from the land and often far from the fleet had guided the young officer's feet up the ladder of promotion as one officer after the other had died. When the first lieutenant had taken his own life, Bolitho's friend, Thomas Herrick, had been on hand to take over, but now even he had left the ship with a captain's rank and a ship of his own. And so, Lieutenant Francis Inch, gangling, horse-faced and ever-eager, had got his chance.

For some reason, not really understood by Bolitho himself, he was being allowed to keep it. But the thought of taking the ship to sea as second-in-command for the very first time might make him view his new status with misgivings and no little anxiety.

'Boat ahoy?' The customary challenge floated down the ship's side.

Allday cupped his hands. '*Hyperion!*'

As the oars were tossed and the bowman hooked on to the chains, Bolitho slipped out of his cloak, and clutching his sword to his hip jumped quickly for the entry port. And he was not even breathless. He found time to marvel at what good food and regular exercise ashore could do for one so long cramped and adjusted to shipboard life.

As his head came above the coaming the pipes broke into a shrill twitter, and he saw the sharp jerk of muskets as the marine guard came to the present.

Inch was there, bobbing anxiously, his uniform soaked with rain so that Bolitho guessed he had not left the quarter-deck since first light.

The din ceased and Inch said, 'Welcome aboard, sir.'

Bolitho smiled. 'Thank you, Mr Inch.' He looked around at the watching men. 'You have been busy.'

Inch was peering at the barge and was about to call to its crew when Bolitho said quietly, 'No, Mr Inch, that is no longer *your* work.' He saw Inch staring at him. 'Leave it to

13

your subordinates. If you trust them they will come to trust you.'

He heard heavy footsteps on the damp planking and turned to see Gossett, the master, plodding to meet him. Thank God he at least had been aboard the ship for several years.

Gossett was huge and bulky like a barrel, with a pair of the brightest eyes Bolitho had ever seen, although they were usually half hidden in his seamed and battered face.

'No complaints, Mr Gossett?'

The master shook his head. 'None, sir. I always said the old lady'd fly along once she got rid of 'er weed.' He rubbed his massive red hands. 'An' so she will if I 'ave any say.'

The assembled company were still crowded on the gangways and deckspace, their faces pale when compared with Gossett and Allday.

This should have been the moment for a rousing speech, a time to bring a cheer from these men who were still strangers to him and to each other.

He lifted his voice above the wind. 'We will waste no more time. Our orders are to join the blockading squadron off Lorient without delay. We have a well-found ship, one with a fine history and great tradition, and together we will do our best to seal the enemy in his harbours, or destroy him should he be foolish enough to venture outside!'

He leaned forward, resting his hands on the quarterdeck rail as the ship lifted ponderously beneath him. It was amazing, but some of the men were nudging each other and grinning at his empty words. In a few months they would know the true wretchedness of blockade duty. Riding out all weathers with neither shelter nor fresh food, while the French rested in their harbours and waited in comfort for a gap in the British chain of ships when they might dash out, hit hard and return before any offensive action might be taken against them.

Occasionally a ship would be relieved for re-provisioning or serious repairs and another would take her place, as *Hyperion* was now doing.

He added briskly, 'There is much to accomplish, and I will expect each one of you to do his best at all times to become proficient at whatever task he is given.' Here, some of the older men grimaced. They knew it would be gun and sail

14

drill under an officer's pocket-watch until their captain was satisfied. In this sort of weather it would not be comfortable work, especially for the men who had never been afloat before.

Bolitho let his eye stray to the opposite side of the quarter-deck where Inch and the other four lieutenants stood in line by the rail. In the hectic days leading up to and following the *Hyperion*'s recommissioning he had had less time than he would have wished to get to know his new officers. The three junior ones seemed keen enough but were very young and with little experience. Their uniforms shone with newness and their faces were as pink as any midshipman's. The second lieutenant, however, a man named Stepkyne, had qualified as a master's mate aboard an East Indiaman and had found his way in the King's service when appointed to a cumbersome storeship. It must have cost him much hard work and bitter experience, to attain commissioned rank, and as he stood swaying easily on the *Hyperion*'s deck Bolitho could see the tense lines around his mouth, an expression bordering on resentment as he glanced sideways at young Inch.

Beyond the lieutenants were the ship's six midshipmen, again very young, but obviously excited at the prospect of what was for most of them a first voyage.

Captain Dawson stood with his marines, heavy-jowled and unsmiling, with his lieutenant, Hicks, an incredibly smart but vacant-looking young man, by his elbow. Bolitho bit his lip. The marines were excellent for forays ashore or the cut and thrust of close action. But they offered little help in the matters of driving a ship of the line under full sail.

He felt the wind swirling damply around his legs and added shortly, 'That will be all for now.' He nodded to Inch. 'Prepare to get the ship under way, if you please.'

Bolitho caught sight of Joshua Tomlin, the boatswain, by the entry port, his sharp eyes moving quickly across the men nearest him. Tomlin was another of the original company, a squat, massively built man, almost as broad as he was tall, and extremely hairy. When he smiled, which was often, he displayed a fearsome and maniac grin, having had both front teeth knocked out by a falling block many years before. He was known for his patience and his rough good humour, and Bolitho had never yet seen him strike a man in anger, which

15

was unusual in his trade. But it would take more than his store of tolerance to remain calm with his new collection of hands, he decided grimly.

Pipes shrilled again and the decks came alive with stamped-ing feet as the men ran to their stations, urged on by kicks and curses from harassed petty officers who had not yet had time to memorize the names of their own divisions.

Bolitho touched Inch's arm and drew him aside. 'The wind has backed a point.' He glanced meaningly at the mast-head pendant. 'Break out the anchor at once and send the hands aloft.' He saw his words causing havoc on Inch's horse-face and added quietly, 'It will be better to get the new people aloft now and have them spaced on the yards *before* you pass your orders. We do not want to have half of them dropping to the deck with the port admiral's glass on us, eh?' He smiled and saw Inch nod doubtfully.

He turned his back as Inch hurried to the quarterdeck rail, his speaking-trumpet at the ready. He wanted to help him, but knew that if Inch could not take the ship to sea from a wide and comfortable anchorage he might never have the confidence to move alone again.

'Stand by the capstan!'

Gossett crossed to Bolitho's side and said impassively, 'We'll have snow afore the week's out, sir.' He winced as one of the men at the capstan bars skidded and fell in a welter of arms and legs. A petty officer lashed out with his rattan, and Bolitho saw the lieutenant in charge turn away with embarrass-ment.

Bolitho cupped his hands. 'Mr Beauclerk! Those men will work together if they have a shanty to bite on!'

Gossett hid a grin. 'Poor fellows, they must find it strange, sir.'

Bolitho breathed out tightly. Inch should have seen to it earlier. With *Hyperion*'s sixteen-hundred-odd tons tugging on the cable it needed more than brawn to turn the capstan. The fiddle's plaintive notes were almost lost in the wind, but as the first pawl clinked home on the capstan Tomlin roared, 'Now, me little sweethearts! Let's give them soft-bellied buggers in Plymouth a sight and sound to remember, eh!'

He threw back his head and opened his mouth, so that one

of the watching midshipmen gasped with awe, and then broke into a well-tried shanty.

Bolitho looked up to watch the men spreading out along the massive yards, black and puny against the sky like so many monkeys.

Then he took a glass from Gascoigne, the signal midshipman, and trained it towards the shore. He felt a lump in his throat as he saw her green cloak framed in the distant window, a patch of white as she waved towards the ship. In his mind's eye he could picture what she was seeing. The two-decker, swinging already on her shortening cable, the figures clinging to the yards, the activity around the forecastle where already more men were standing by the headsails.

'Anchor's hove short, sir!'

Bolitho met Inch's eye and nodded. Inch lifted his trumpet. 'Loose heads'ls!'

A quick glance at Gossett, but there was no need to worry there. The master stood by the big double wheel, his eyes moving between the helmsmen and the first strips of canvas which even now were flapping and cracking in the wind.

'Lay a course to weather the headland, Mr Gossett. We will lie as close to the wind as we can in case it backs again directly.'

'Up an' down, sir!' The cry almost lost in the wind.

Inch was nodding and muttering to himself as he moved restlessly across the quarterdeck.

He yelled, 'Loose tops'ls!'

The great sails billowed and thundered wildly as the cry came from forward, 'Anchor's aweigh, sir!'

Bolitho gripped a swivel gun for support as, freed from the land, the *Hyperion* swung dizzily into a deep trough. There were a few nervous cries from aloft, but nobody fell.

'Lee braces there!' That was Stepkyne's voice carrying without effort above the din of wind and canvas. 'Jump to it, that man!' He was pointing angrily. 'Take his name!'

Clank, clank, clank went the capstan, the hidden anchor swinging below the surface like a pendulum. But the *Hyperion* seemed to care nothing for the confusion and frantic activity about her decks and yards. She showed a strip of bright copper as she tilted heavily into the choppy water, throwing the spray high above her beakhead so that the gleaming Titan seemed to be rising from the sea itself.

Inch came back wiping his face. 'Sir?'

Bolitho eyed him gravely. 'Get the courses on her.' He looked up at the masthead pendant as it streamed almost abeam and as stiff as a lance. 'We'll have the t'gallants on her directly once we've cleared Rame Head.'

The helmsman intoned, 'Sou'-west by south, sir! Full an' bye!'

Bolitho felt the deck tilting steeply as the old ship gathered the wind into her spreading canvas. She must make a fine sight now, he thought vaguely. Topsails and courses set and hard-bellied like pewter in the dull light, the yards braced round to take maximum advantage of the wind which was ruffling the blurred headland like wet fur.

The anchor was clear of the water now and already being hauled towards the cathead.

And still the men sang, some glancing across their shoulders as the green headland sidled so quickly into the mist of rain and spray.

'I knew a lass in Portsmouth town,
Heave, my bullies, *heave*!'

How many sailors had sung as their ships had slipped into the Channel, how many on the shore had watched moist-eyed or grateful, or just thankful for being spared similar hardship? When Bolitho raised his glass again the land had lost all individuality. Like its memories and hopes it was now so distant as to be unreachable. He saw some of the younger men staring across the gangway, one of them actually waving, although the ship must be all but invisible by now.

He thought suddenly of Herrick. When he had been his first lieutenant in the little frigate *Phalarope*. Bolitho frowned, when was that? Ten, no twelve years ago! He started to pace slowly along the weather side as his mind went back over the years. Thomas Herrick, the best subordinate he had ever had, and the best friend. He had said in those far-off times that he had looked forward to a command of his own more than anything else. Until it became a real possibility. He smiled at the memory, and two midshipmen seeing his face exchanged awed glances as their captain paced back and forth apparently oblivious or indifferent to the shouts and scurrying figures around him.

Now Herrick *had* that command. Better late than never, and more than richly deserved, even if she was the old sixty-four, *Impulsive*. Herrick would be joining the squadron, too, when his ship was overhauled at Portsmouth.

He heard Inch stammering with anger as a man caught his foot on a hatch coaming and slithered into a master's mate, bringing him down with a crash on the tilting deck.

It was hard to realize that when he met Herrick again it would all be different. Two captains with individual problems and not the common bond of keeping one ship alive. Herrick always had such a questioning mind and a complete understanding of what Bolitho needed.

Bolitho shut the thought from his mind. It was pure selfishness to wish Herrick here with him.

He looked at Inch and asked mildly, 'Are you satisfied?'

Inch stared round anxiously. 'I—I think so, sir.'

'Good. Now turn the hands to and put extra lashings on the boats. It will keep them from mooning at the bulwarks until England is out of sight.'

Inch nodded and then grinned awkwardly. 'It was not too badly done, sir, I thought?' He dropped his eyes under Bolitho's stare. 'I—I mean . . .'

'You wish to know what I think of your efforts, Mr Inch?' Bolitho saw Gossett keeping his face like a mask. 'I thought that considering only half of the men on each yard were doing more than holding on for their lives, and taking into consideration there was a five minute interval between each mast, I would say it was a *fair* beginning.' He frowned. 'Do you see it so, Mr Inch?'

Inch nodded humbly. 'Aye, sir.'

Bolitho grinned. 'Well, that *is* something, Mr Inch!'

Gossett called, 'Ready to alter course, sir!'

The headland, and indeed most of the shoreline, had disappeared into the grey murk, but the wind was as steady as ever, whipping the crests from the waves and cascading spray above the weather rail like tropical rain.

'Bring her up a point, Mr Gossett. We will wear ship in four hours and run with the wind in our coat-tails!' He saw Gossett nod cheerfully. 'We may have to reef before much longer, but I imagine you want to see how she behaves under full canvas?'

He looked at Inch. 'I am going to my cabin. I am sure you do not need me for the moment?' He turned and walked quickly towards the poop before he could reply. Inch had got over the first part quite well. It was only fair to give him his head in open water without his captain watching every move and decision. And Gossett would be quick to see if anything really serious was about to happen.

He saw some of the unemployed seamen watching him as he ducked below the poop and made for his cabin. First impressions were all important and he had to appear quite unconcerned even though he was straining his ears to listen to the creak and whine of shrouds and stays as the ship plunged her way indifferently almost into the teeth of the wind. Faintly he heard Tomlin bellow, 'Not that 'and! Yer *right* 'and, I said! The one you fills yer face with!' A pause. ' 'Ere, let me show you, you clumsy maggot!' Bolitho half smiled. Poor Tomlin, it was starting already.

A marine sentry snapped at attention outside the stern cabin, his eyes unblinking beneath his shako. Bolitho closed the door and leaned his back against it, thankful to be alone for just a few precious moments.

For the remainder of the forenoon and well into the afternoon watch, the *Hyperion* drove steadily down channel, her yards bending like great bows as she heeled to the blustering offshore wind. Bolitho spent more time on the quarterdeck than he had first intended as one crisis after another called him from his cabin. Inch had managed to set the topgallants, and under the great pyramids of straining canvas the ship was heeling over at an almost permanent angle, so that working aloft seemed even more hazardous than before to the men on the lee side. Looking down from their dizzy perches the ship appeared to have shrunk in size, while below them there was nothing but the angry wavecrests creaming and spitting from the labouring hull. One man clung to the fore topgallant yard and would not move at all. Or rather he could not, and his fear was greater than that of an enraged bosun's mate who clung to the mast cursing and threatening, all too aware of his opposite number on the mainmast who was calling insults to the delight of his nimble-footed topmen.

Eventually Inch sent a midshipman who had already displayed a great agility aloft to fetch the wretched man down, and Bolitho had come on deck just as both had arrived on deck breathless and gasping with exertion.

Lieutenant Stepkyne had yelled, 'I'll see you flogged for that, you gutless dolt!'

Bolitho had called, 'Bring that man aft!' Then to Inch, 'I'll not have a man terrified to no good purpose. Get one of the older hands to go aloft with him now.'

As the man in question had stood shivering below the quarterdeck ladder Bolitho had asked, 'What is your name?'

The man had muttered thickly, 'Good, sir.'

Stepkyne had been plucking at his belt with impatience and had said quickly, 'He's a fool, sir!'

Bolitho had continued calmly, 'Well, Good, you must go back to that yard *now*, do you understand?' He had seen the man peer upwards at the foremast again. The yard was over a hundred feet above the deck. 'There's no shame in fear, lad, but there's danger in showing it.' He had watched the mixed emotions on the man's pinched features. 'Now off with you.'

The man went, and Inch had said admiringly, 'Well, that was something, sir.'

Bolitho had looked away as the frightened seaman commenced to climb up the vibrating ratlines. 'You *lead* men, Mr Inch. It never pays to torment them.' To Stepkyne he had added, 'We are still shorthanded and need every fit man we can get. To flog that one senseless seems rather pointless, wouldn't you agree?'

Stepkyne had touched his hat and strode forward again to supervise his men.

To Inch, Bolitho had continued, 'There's no easy way. There never was.'

At six bells it was time to wear ship and the whole business started all over again. Dazed and bruised, with bleeding fingers and faces tight with strain the new men were led or dragged out along the yards to shorten sail, for the wind was freshening every minute, and although the land was only ten miles abeam it was hidden in mist and spray.

Bolitho made himself stay silent as he watched the frantic efforts to obey his orders. Time and time again some men had to be shown what to do, even had halyards or braces put into their hands while Tomlin and his assistants scampered from one piece of confusion to another.

Then at last even Gossett seemed satisfied, and with the men straining and sliding at the braces the *Hyperion* turned her bows to the southward, the wind battering across her quarter with relentless force so that two additional men had to be sent to the wheel.

But she was enjoying it, Bolitho thought. Even shortened down to topsails she was leaning forward and down, plunging her bowsprit towards the invisible horizon in great sweeping thrusts as each successive roller cruised against her fat flank and then broke high over her tumblehome in a welter of frustrated spray.

He gripped the hammock nettings and looked astern, even though he knew there was nothing to see. But somewhere back there was the rugged coast of Cornwall, with his own Falmouth a bare twenty miles to westward. The big house below the bulk of Pendennis Castle would be waiting for Cheney's return. For the birth of their child which he would not see for some time to come.

Another wave roared hissing over the weather gangway, and he heard Gossett murmur, 'A second reef'll be needed shortly, I'm thinkin'.'

Pipes shrilled as the watch below was dismissed at long last, and Bolitho said, 'Keep me informed.' Then he made his way aft once more.

The big stern cabin looked warm and friendly after the windswept quarterdeck. The deckhead lanterns swung in busy unison and cast strange shadows across the green leather chairs and the bench seat below the windows, the old polished desk and table which gleamed in the lamplight like new chestnuts. He stood by the broad windows staring at the distorted panorama of leaping waves and flying spectres of spray. Then he sighed and sat down at his desk and looked at the pile of papers which his clerk had left for his inspection. But for once he found he had no stomach for it, and the realization troubled him.

The door opened silently and Allday padded into the cabin, his stocky body appearing to lean at a grotesque angle on the tilting deck.

Allday studied him sadly. 'Begging your pardon, Captain, but Petch, your servant, says you've not eaten since you came aboard today.' He ignored Bolitho's frown. 'So I've taken the liberty to bring you some game pie.' He held out a plate which he had covered with a silver lid. 'Your good lady gave it to me special for you, Captain.'

Bolitho did not protest as Allday laid the plate on the slanting desk and busied himself with the cutlery. Game pie. She must have packed it while he was getting dressed that morning.

Allday pretended not to notice the look on Bolitho's face and took the opportunity to retrieve his sword from a chair and hang it in its place on the bulkhead. It shone dully in the spiralling lanterns, and he said quietly, 'It'd not be the same without it now.'

But Bolitho did not answer. That sword, his father's and his father's before that, was something of a talisman, and a ready topic of lower-deck conversation whenever Bolitho's exploits were being discussed. It was part of him, part of his background and tradition, but at this moment he could think of nothing but what he was leaving behind. Even now the horses would be trotting along the road from Plymouth. Fifty miles to Falmouth where his housekeeper and his steward, Ferguson, who had lost an arm at the Saintes, would be waiting to greet her. But *he* would not be there. Above the hiss of spray against the windows, the creak of timbers and the over-riding boom of canvas he imagined he could hear her laugh. Imagined perhaps he could feel her touch, the taste of her freshness on his lips.

Oblivious to Allday he opened the front of his shirt and looked at the small locket around his neck. In it was one lock of her hair, a talisman better than any sword.

The door opened and a sodden midshipman said breathlessly, 'Mr Inch's respects, sir, and can he have permission to take in a second reef?'

Bolitho stood up, his body swaying to the steady roll. 'I'll come.' Then he saw Allday and gave a small smile. 'There is little time for dreaming, it seems.' He followed the midshipman's envious stare and added, 'Or for game pie either!'

Allday watched him go and then covered the plate with the silver lid.

He had never seen him like this before and he was troubled by it. He looked across at the sword as it swung from its hook, seeing again that same blade gleaming in the sunlight as Bolitho had stormed the French battery at Cozar, had charged across the bloodsoaked planking of an enemy ship, had done so many things so many times. And now Bolitho seemed changed, and Allday cursed the mind which had despatched *Hyperion* to blockade duty and not to a place to do battle.

He thought too of the girl Bolitho had married. They had even met for the first time aboard *this* ship. He stared round, finding it hard to believe. Perhaps that was what was lacking. She had been part of the ship, had known danger and terror when the old hull had quivered to the broadsides and the scything winds of death. Bolitho would be thinking that too, he decided. Thinking and remembering, and that was bad.

Allday shook his head and walked towards the door. It was bad simply because they all depended on him more than ever before. A captain had no one to share his sadness and nobody to share his blame should he fail.

He walked past the sentry and climbed through a small hatch. A yarn and a glass with the sailmaker might shake him out of his troubled thoughts, he decided. But he doubted it.

2. Broad Pendant

RICHARD BOLITHO finished writing his personal log and leaned back wearily in the chair. Even in the sealed cabin the air was chill and damp, and the leather of his desk chair was clammy to the touch. Around him the ship lifted, paused and then staggered forward in a savage corkscrewing motion which made even thinking an effort of will, yet he knew if he returned to the windswept quarterdeck he would find no peace for more than a few minutes.

He stared through the thick glass of the stern windows,

although they were so caked with salt and running spray it was only possible to tell day from night. It was close on noon, but could have been any time. The sky was either black and starless, or like now, the colour of slate. And so it had been as one day followed another and while the *Hyperion* drove further and further to the south-east, deeper into the Bay of Biscay.

He had been quite prepared for the discomfort and boredom of blockade duty, and when on the second day out from Plymouth the masthead lookout had sighted ships of the squadron he had already decided to make the best of it. But as he should have known well enough after nearly twenty-five years at sea, nothing in the Navy could ever be taken for granted.

His orders had stated that he was to join the flag of Vice-Admiral Sir Manley Cavendish, K.B., and take his place with all the other weather-beaten ships, the constant vigilance of which could decide the fate of England, and thereby the whole world. Off every French port these same ships rode out storms or tacked wearily back and forth in a never-ending patrol, while closer inshore, and sometimes within range of enemy batteries, sleek frigates, the eyes of the fleet, reported every movement of shipping. They gathered information from captured coastal craft, or impudently sailed almost into the French harbours themselves in their ceaseless search for intelligence.

Since Howe's victory of the Glorious First of June the French had shown little inclination for another major clash, but Bolitho, like any other thinking officer, realized that this uneasy calm could not last. Only the Channel lay between the enemy and a full scale invasion of England, yet until the French could muster a powerful fleet that same strip of water might just as well be an ocean.

In the great naval ports of Brest and Lorient the French ships of the line were unable to move without being seen and reported by the patrolling frigates, while in every harbour on the west coast, down as far as Bordeaux, other ships waited and watched for a chance to slip out and hurry north to join their consorts. One day soon they would make a break for it. When that happened it was essential that news of the enemy's movements was carried swiftly to the heavy squadrons, and more important still, interpreted correctly so that action could be taken to engage and destroy them.

Under the flagship's lee Bolitho had stood in silence watching the flags soaring up the big three-decker's yards, the frantic efforts of Midshipman Gascoigne and his signal party to keep pace with acknowledgements. It had been then that he had received his first inkling all was not as he had expected.

Gascoigne had yelled, '*Flag* to *Hyperion*. Stand by to receive orders and despatches!'

Inch had looked as if he was about to voice a question but had held his tongue. The two days out from Plymouth had been difficult ones for him. Within hours of turning south the wind had mounted to something approaching gale force, and under close-reefed topsails, with a fierce quarter-sea making the ship stagger and roll drunkenly from one trough to the next, Inch had been beset with demands and chaos from every side. Many of the new men were almost helpless with seasickness, and most of the others kept continually at work splicing rigging, which like all new cordage was taking this first real strain badly, and the rest were led or driven back and forth either trimming sails or standing relays at the back-breaking work of pumping bilges.

More than once it had been all that Bolitho could do to refrain from interfering with Inch's efforts, yet at the same time he knew that he was solely to blame. Inch was too inexperienced for his work, that was quite apparent now, but if Bolitho showed his true displeasure it might finish Inch for good. Not that Bolitho need say anything. It was quite obvious from Inch's unhappy features that he knew his own shortcomings well enough.

The next signal from the flagship had been brief.

'Prepare to receive Flag Captain.'

It was customary for captains to report in person to receive fresh orders when joining a squadron, although in cases of really bad weather for the sealed bag to be drifted across from ship to ship on a grass line. But this time the admiral was apparently sending his own captain.

The barge which had brought the flagship's captain across the choppy water had been almost swamped before it eventually hooked on to the main chains, and the thickset officer in his sodden boatcloak had hardly glanced at the side party and saluting marines as he had seized Bolitho's hand and growled, 'For God's sake let us go below!'

Once within the big cabin the visiting captain had come straight to the point.

'I've brought you fresh orders, Bolitho. You are to continue to the south-east and join the inshore squadron of Commodore Mathias Pelham-Martin. My admiral detached him and his ships some weeks ago for duty off the Gironde Estuary. You'll find a complete list of ships and requirements in your new orders.'

He had spoken quickly, almost offhandedly, but Bolitho had been aware of a warning sensation at the back of his mind. Pelham-Martin. The name had been instantly familiar, yet at the same time he had been unable to recall any sea officer, commodore or otherwise, who had distinguished or shamed himself enough to warrant this special visit by the flag captain.

The other man had said abruptly, 'I do not like deceit, especially with a fellow captain. Things have been very bad between my admiral and the commodore. Pelham-Martin, as you will discover, is a difficult man to serve in some ways.'

'This bad feeling. How did it come about?'

'It all happened a long while ago, really. During the American Revolution. . . .'

Bolitho's mind had suddenly cleared. 'I remember now. A British colonel of infantry surrendered to the Americans with all his men, and when some of our ships arrived with reinforcements they sailed right into a trap.'

The flag captain had grimaced. 'The colonel was Pelham-Martin's brother. I do not have to tell you who the officer was who commanded the ships, eh?'

A midshipman had appeared at that moment. 'Signal from flagship, sir! Captain to return on board forthwith.'

Bolitho had understood fully at that moment what the visit had really meant for him and his ship. No admiral could voice a lack of confidence to a captain newly joining his command. But through a fellow captain it was just possible to show his displeasure and his uncertainty.

The flag captain had paused by the cabin door, his eyes searching.

'I know your record, Bolitho, and so does Sir Manley Cavendish. When news was received that you were joining the squadron he told me that you were to be sent to Pelham-Martin's sector to the south-east. You are well remembered for your part in the St Clar invasion last year, although you got precious little credit for it. The commodore's squadron is a small one, but its work and vigilance could prove to be vital. Your viewpoint and presence there could help to break this stupid feud.' He had shrugged heavily. 'This is between ourselves naturally. If a word is voiced to me that any suggestion of mistrust or incompetence was made, I will of course deny it!' Then with another quick handshake he had left the ship.

Now, sitting at his littered desk, Bolitho found it hard to believe such bitterness could have been allowed to jeopardize the efficiency of the hard-pressed ships and their weary companies. That meeting with the flagship had been four days ago. While the *Hyperion* had plunged further to the south-east and her company had fought half-heartedly against seasickness and bad weather alike, Bolitho had studied his orders carefully, and during his lonely walks on the quarterdeck had tried to estimate their true meaning.

It seemed that Pelham-Martin had three ships of the line and three frigates under his command, as well as two small sloops-of-war. One of the former would be sent to England for overhaul and repairs as soon as she was replaced by *Hyperion*, so it was a very small force indeed.

But properly deployed it could be well placed to watch over any sudden movement by enemy vessels. It was known that several large French ships had slipped past Gibraltar and had already found their way into the Bay of Biscay. It was equally well known that although Spain was now an ally of England, it was more from necessity than any real friendship or co-operation. Many of those French ships must have sailed close inshore around Spain, and some might even have hidden in Spanish ports to avoid being attacked by British patrols. To join the bulk of the French fleet any such ships would probably make first for the Gironde or La Rochelle to receive their orders overland, and then take the first opportunity to follow the coastline to Lorient or Brest.

There was a tap at the door and Midshipman Gascoigne stepped over the coaming. 'Mr Stepkyne's respects, sir, and we have just sighted a sail to the east'rd.'

'Very well. I shall come up.'

Bolitho watched the door close and rubbed his chin thoughtfully. Whatever the rights or wrongs of the matter, he would not have long to wait now.

He stood up slowly and reached for his hat. He felt the locket rubbing against his chest and thought suddenly of Cheney. He had written a letter to her and sent it across with the flagship's captain for the first homebound sloop. There had not been time to change any of it and she would still believe him to be off Lorient. Not that another two hundred miles made much difference, he thought vaguely.

As he walked to the quarterdeck he saw the officers stiffen into awkward attitudes of attentiveness, and guessed that prior to his appearance they had probably been in deep discussion about the distant ships.

Bolitho looked up at the hard-bellied sails and the whipping tongue of the masthead pendant. The canvas was stiff with rain and salt, and he felt a moment's pity for some of the men who were working high above the swaying hull. The wind was almost directly astern and the sea had changed to an angry panorama of short, steep crests, which gleamed like yellow fangs in the harsh light. There was no horizon to speak of, and although he estimated they were within twenty miles of the coast there was nothing to be seen.

He took a glass from a midshipman and trained it slowly across the nettings. He knew the others were watching him as if to gauge his reactions, and perhaps their own fate, but kept his face impassive as he picked out the first misty pyramid of sails. He shifted the glass very slightly and waited as the *Hyperion* sidled into a deep trough and then smashed indifferently across another cruising bank of wavecrests. There was a second ship, and possibly a third.

He closed the glass with a snap. 'Lay her on the larboard tack and prepare to shorten sail, Mr Stepkyne.'

Stepkyne touched his hat, 'Aye, aye, sir.' He rarely said much, unless to use his tongue on some clumsy or careless seaman. He seemed unwilling or unable to share either confidence or casual conversation with his brother officers, and Bolitho knew as little about him now as on the first day he had met him. For all that, he was a very capable seaman, and Bolitho had been unable to find fault with any task he had carried out.

Even now he was rapping out orders, his hands on his hips as he watched the men being roused once more to man braces and halyards.

Bolitho shut Stepkyne's cold efficiency and Inch's bumbling efforts from his mind. If the weather moderated, just for a few days, even Inch would get a chance to drill the hands to better results. He said curtly, 'Steer east by south, Mr Gossett.'

The masthead lookout's voice called faintly above the cracking canvas, 'Three sail o' th' line, sir!' A pause while every unemployed eye peered aloft at the tiny figure outlined against the racing clouds. 'Leadin' ship wears a broad pendant, sir!'

A shoe scraped on the deck and Bolitho saw Inch hurrying towards him, some biscuit crumbs clinging to his coat.

He touched his hat. 'I am sorry to be late on deck, sir.' He glanced round anxiously. 'I must have fallen asleep for a moment.'

Bolitho studied him gravely. He would have to do something about Inch, he thought. He looked desperately tired, and there were dark shadows under his eyes.

He said quietly. 'You may call all hands now, Mr Inch. We will be up with the squadron directly and may have to wear ship or heave to.' He smiled. 'Commodores are no different from admirals when it comes to immediate requirements.'

But Inch merely nodded glumly. 'Aye, aye, sir.'

Slowly but surely the other ships grew out of the tossing murk until they stood in line, hulls shining with spray, their reefed topsails straining and gleaming like pressed steel in the blustering wind.

They were all seventy-fours like *Hyperion*, and to a landsman might look as much alike as peas in a pod. But Bolitho knew from hard experience that even ships launched side by side in the same dockyard could be as unalike as salt and wine, just as their individual captains might choose to make them.

Gossett, who had been studying the leading two-decker, said absently, 'I know the commodore's ship well enough, sir. She's the *Indomitable*, Cap'n Winstanley. I fought alongside 'er in '81.' He glanced severely at Midshipman Gascoigne. 'You should 'ave seen 'er and reported earlier, young gentleman!'

Bolitho studied the leading ship through narrowed eyes as flags broke from her yards, and after what seemed like mere seconds the whole line tacked slowly round until the *Indomitable* was running almost parallel with *Hyperion* and barely two cables distant. Even without a glass it was possible to see the great streaks of caked salt and sea slime around her beakhead and bows, while as she plunged heavily into a shallow trough her lower gunports were momentarily awash. But her sail drill and manœuvring were impeccable, and behind him Bolitho heard Gosset murmur, 'Cap'n Winstanley 'as the feel of the old lady well enough.' From him that was praise of the highest order.

This time Gascoigne was ready. As more balls soared up the *Indomitable*'s yards and broke stiffly to the wind, he yelled, '*Flag* to *Hyperion*. Captain repair on board forthwith!'

Bolitho smiled grimly. No doubt the commodore was impatient to hear what his old enemy had said about him.

'Heave to, if you please. Call away my barge.'

He stared at the leaping wavecrests and imagined his bargemen cursing the commodore for his early summons.

With the hands straining at the braces and the sails cracking and booming like cannonshots the *Hyperion* swung slowly and unwillingly into the wind, while Tomlin bellowed lustily at his boat-handling party to sway Bolitho's barge up and clear of the nettings. One of the steadying lines from the barge caught a young seaman round the throat and he fell heavily against some of the men at the main topsail brace. For an instant there was complete confusion, with the spray-swollen rope screaming out through its block, and bodies falling and scattering like puppets until a bosun's mate hurled himself into the mass of shouting and cursing men and checked it himself.

Stepkyne, who was in charge of the main deck, seized the unfortunate seaman and yelled at him, their faces only inches apart. 'You stupid, whimpering bugger! I'll teach you to behave!'

The seaman held up his hand to his throat which had been flayed raw by the steadying line. 'But, sir, I couldn't help it!' He was almost weeping. 'Worn't my fault, sir!'

Stepkyne seemed beside himself. Had the bosun's mate not intervened the confusion might have caused a disaster, especially to the men working aloft on the topsail yard, but with the weight of the boat on one end of the line and the strength of several bargemen on the other, the man was lucky not to have lost his head.

Inch gripped the quarterdeck rail and shouted above the wind, 'Fend off that boat! And you can dismiss that man below to the surgeon, Mr Stepkyne!'

The wretched seaman scurried for the hatch but Stepkyne stood his ground, his eyes blazing as he stared up at the quarterdeck. 'Need never have happened! If these men had been properly drilled that fool would have seen the danger in time!'

Allday called, 'Barge is alongside, Captain!' But his eyes were on Inch and Stepkyne.

Bolitho ran quickly down the quarterdeck ladder and said coldly, 'When I return I will see you in my cabin, Mr Stepkyne. When an order is passed you will do well to obey it without question, do you understand?'

He kept his voice low, but knew the damage was done. Stepkyne was wrong to question Inch, let alone criticize his actions. But Bolitho knew too that his anger was justified. Inch should have checked each man before allotting him his station. Especially new and untried ones.

More than anything else he blamed himself for allowing Inch to remain as first lieutenant.

Touching his hat briefly he lowered himself through the entry port, and after waiting a few seconds jumped outward and down into the pitching barge.

As the boat pulled clear of the side, Bolitho did not look back. It would all be waiting for him when he returned, by which time he must decide what action to take.

Captain Amelius Winstanley was ready to receive Bolitho at

the *Indomitable*'s entry port, and even before the trilling pipes had fallen silent he stepped forward and gripped his hand and wrung it warmly with obvious relief.

'A man after my own heart, Bolitho!' He was grinning as Bolitho endeavoured to straighten his cocked hat and readjust his sword. 'I never could take a bosun's chair up the side of a strange ship m'self either!'

Bolitho recovered his breath and tried to ignore the rivulets of water which were running down his chest and legs. The barge had made a rough passage to the flagship, but the last part had been by far the worst. As the *Indomitable*'s towering side had lifted and rolled above them he had stood swaying in the sternsheets, his teeth gritted to control his impatience and apprehension as the bowman made one frantic attempt after another to hook on to the ship's main chains and secure the madly tossing boat. Once, when an anxious Allday had reached up to steady his arm he had rasped, 'I can manage, damn you!' And it was perhaps his coxswain's obvious lack of confidence in his ability to jump the wide gap to the ship's side which had finally decided him to decline the offer of a bosun's chair. It was far safer, but Bolitho had always considered it undignified when he had watched other captains swaying above a ship's side, legs spiralling, while seamen busily manipulated guide lines as if they were handling so much cargo.

But it had been a near thing this time. His sword had tangled between his legs, and for a brief moment as the barge had dropped beneath him he had seen the water swirling to pluck him from the ship's side and had heard Allday call out with alarm.

Soaked and angry, Bolitho managed to pull himself up to the safety of the entry port, and as the pipes shrilled in salute and the side party stiffened to attention he glanced quickly at their wooden expressions, expecting to see amusement or disappointment that he had not indeed fallen, if only to provide a ready topic of gossip for the lower deck.

Winstanley guided him to the quarterdeck, his resonant voice held down with obvious effort. He was a giant of a man, loose limbed and outwardly ungainly, but gave an immediate impression of great competence. His face was toughened and seamed from countless voyages, but his small twinkling eyes and the mass of crowsfeet around them gave an equal impression of a ready sense of humour.

The captain of a flagship, even that of a lowly commodore, needed all of that and more, Bolitho thought grimly as he squelched up the ladder and into the shelter of the poop.

Winstanley was saying gruffly, 'I was watching your ship through my glass. She looks a mite different from the last time I saw her. Like new she is.' He glanced up at the commodore's broad pendant which streamed stiffly from the masthead. 'The *Vectis* will sail for Plymouth now that you've arrived to relieve her, and after that it'll be my turn.' He gripped Bolitho's arm as they approached the stern cabin. 'Next to me you're the senior captain, so I've no doubt *Hyperion* will wear *his* pendant in due course.'

He must have seen the question on Bolitho's face for he said quickly, 'I'll speak with you later. Pelham-Martin is no man to keep waiting.'

He opened the door and Bolitho followed him into the cabin, his hat jammed beneath his arm, and conscious of the wet footmarks across a rich, pale coloured carpet as he approached a littered table which was arranged to one side of the stern windows.

The commodore was seated comfortably at a high-backed chair, seemingly relaxed in spite of the slow, sickening motion around him. He was incredibly broad, but as he got slowly to his feet Bolitho sensed something like shock when he realized that Pelham-Martin was extremely short and his effort at standing made little difference at all. All his bulk seemed to go into his breadth, like Tomlin, the *Hyperion*'s bosun, but there the similarity ended. He had a round, pale complexioned face and his fair hair was cut in the newly fashionable short style. But whereas it may have suited the Navy's younger bloods, it merely made the commodore's head appear even smaller when compared with the great bulk beneath it.

'Welcome, Captain.' His voice was smooth, even gentle. 'You must have made a quick passage.' His eyes moved calmly over Bolitho's bedraggled appearance, but he did not remark on it. Then he waved to some chairs and pointed to a silver wine casket which swung gently from the deckhead. 'A drink, perhaps?'

Across his bulky shoulder Winstanley gave the merest shake of his head and Bolitho said, 'No, thank you, sir. Not for the moment.'

He saw Winstanley relax slightly and noticed that Pelham-Martin was smiling. He was grateful for Winstanley's warning, yet at the same time he was irritated at being put to some private test for the commodore's own purpose.

'Well, I expect you have read all the available reports, Bolitho. Our duty here is to patrol the approaches to the Gironde Estuary and stop any shipping entering or leaving. I have made a signal to *Vectis* to sail for Plymouth for repairs. She lost her mizzen in a great gale some two weeks back, and spare spars are in great demand here. In a few months' time we will be joined by two more sail of the line, and by then we should know what the Frogs intend to do, eh?' He leaned back comfortably and smiled. He looked more like a rich merchant than a sea officer, Bolitho thought vaguely.

He heard himself say, 'The French will be out before that, sir.'

Pelham-Martin's smile stayed fixed on his small mouth. 'You say so? Where did you gather this information?' He leaned forward slightly. 'Has the admiral been keeping something from me then?'

Bolitho smiled. 'No, sir. But I have been reading all the available reports, and I consider that the French will have to break out soon if they are to be of any use to their cause.'

Pelham-Martin nodded slowly. 'That is a masterpiece of self-deception, Bolitho.'

He waved one hand towards the windows and through the salt-stained glass Bolitho could see the next ship astern throwing the spray across her bows, yet giving the impression of ponderous indestructibility.

The commodore added calmly, 'These ships will prevent any such foolishness.' He seemed to become impatient and dragged a chart from beneath some leather-bound books. 'We are here,' he stabbed the chart with one pink finger, 'and I have placed the two frigates, *Spartan* and *Abdiel*, on the southern approaches to warn of any attempt by the enemy to cross into this area from Spanish waters.' The finger moved towards the rambling coastline above the Gironde. 'Here I have deployed my third

35

frigate, *Ithuriel*, in the exact area to see and report any French attempt to leave Bordeaux for the north.'

Bolitho looked up. 'And the sloops, sir?' Again a quick shake of the head from Captain Winstanley, but Bolitho's anger at Pelham-Martin's easy dismissal of his ideas had thrust caution at one side.

'Sloops?' Pelham-Martin nodded gravely. 'You have *indeed* read your reports, Bolitho.' The smile vanished. 'I have despatched them to Vigo for, er, extra stores.'

Bolitho looked away. It was incredible. Vigo, on the north-west coast of Spain, was over four hundred miles away. Further from the Gironde Estuary than Plymouth itself!

The commodore's hands began to tap a slow tattoo on the edge of the table. Like two smooth, pink crabs. He asked quietly, 'You seem to disapprove?'

Bolitho kept his tone level. 'The frigate *Ithuriel* is all alone so close inshore, sir. And the other two frigates are too far to the south'rd to assist her if she is attacked.'

Pelham-Martin eyed him for several seconds. '*Ithuriel's* captain has my orders, my *orders*, d'you understand, to close the squadron the moment he sights any sign of activity.' The smile came back slightly. 'I understood that you had been a frigate captain, Bolitho? Surely you do not deny the *Ithuriel's* captain the chance to prove his worth?'

Bolitho said flatly, 'I think he would stand no chance at all, sir.'

Winstanley shifted on his chair. 'What Captain Bolitho means is . . .'

Pelham-Martin lifted one hand. 'I *know* what he means, Winstanley! Not for him the business of blockade, dear me, no! He wants to drive headlong ashore and seize some wretched ship for prize money, no doubt!'

'No, sir.' Bolitho gripped the arms of his chair. He had made a bad start. Worrying about Inch and Stepkyne, his near fall into the sea from his barge under the eyes of the squadron had pared away his normal reserve when dealing with senior officers. 'But I do believe that unless we know exactly what we are blockading we can never take steps to deal with whatever ruse the French will employ.'

The commodore stared at him. 'My orders are to patrol this

36

area. That is what I *am* doing. Really, Bolitho, I do not know what you were told aboard Vice-Admiral Cavendish's flagship, but I can assure you we are well aware of the task entrusted to us here.'

'I did not go aboard the flagship, sir.' Bolitho saw a quick flash of surprise in the other man's eyes before the shutter dropped again. He added quietly, 'My orders were sent across to me.' It was a lie, but only half a lie.

But the effect of it was instantaneous and more than surprising. Pelham-Martin dragged a gold watch from his straining waistcoat and said, 'Please me by going on deck, Winstanley. Just make sure that all my despatches were sent across to the *Vectis* before she left the squadron, eh?' As soon as the door closed behind the other captain he continued evenly, 'I am sorry if I seemed unwilling to listen to your appraisal of our situation here, Bolitho.' He smiled and lifted a decanter from the silver casket. 'Some brandy, eh? Took it from a French coaster a week ago.' He did not wait for a reply but poured it liberally into some glasses which had been concealed below the table. 'The fact is, I do not always see eye to eye with Sir Manley, you know.' He watched Bolitho above the rim of his glass. 'It is a family matter, a deeply rooted dispute of some standing now.' He wagged the glass. 'Not unknown in your family too, I believe?'

Bolitho felt the brandy burning his lips. It seemed as if his brother's memory, his disgrace to the family name would never be allowed to die. And now Pelham-Martin was using it as a comparison with some stupid feud caused by his own brother's cowardice, or whatever it had been which had caused him to surrender without first warning the ships coming to relieve and sustain his soldiers.

The commodore nodded gravely. 'Of course, *my* brother did not actually desert his country, but the end result is the same. He was trying to save his men from useless slaughter.' He sighed deeply. 'But history only judges results and not intentions.'

Bolitho said flatly. 'I am sure that neither the vice-admiral nor you would jeopardize efficiency over this matter, sir.'

'Quite so.' Pelham-Martin was smiling again. 'But as his junior I have to be doubly careful, you understand?' His tone hardened. 'And that is why I obey my orders, and nothing more.' He paused before adding, 'And so will *you*!'

The interview was over, but as Bolitho rose to his feet Pelham-Martin said easily, 'In any case, this tiresome duty will give you ample opportunity to drill your people into shape.' He shook his head. 'The sail handling was, to say the least, very poor indeed.'

Bolitho stepped from the cabin and breathed out very slowly. So this was how it was to be. Outwardly everything perfect, but as far as initiative and closing with the enemy were concerned, their hands were to be well tied.

On the quarterdeck Winstanley greeted him with a relieved smile. 'Sorry about the warning, Bolitho. Should have told you earlier. The commodore likes to get officers in their cups before he starts his interviews. A nasty little habit which has cost more than one of 'em a quick passage home.' He grinned. 'Not me of course. He needs a good old salthorse to run his ship.' He gripped Bolitho's arm. 'Just as he'll need you before we're done, my friend!'

Bolitho smiled. 'I am afraid I needed no drink to irritate him.'

Winstanley followed him to the quarterdeck rail and together they stared across at the *Hyperion* as she swayed heavily on the steep offshore swell.

He said, 'I agree with everything you said about the frigates. I have told him my views repeatedly, yet he still believes the real threat is from the south.' He shook his head. 'But if he is indeed wrong then he will have more than an enraged admiral to contend with.' He added grimly, 'And so will we!'

The wind had eased slightly during the interview and Bolitho had little difficulty in boarding his barge. On the way back to his ship he thought back over every word Pelham-Martin had uttered, and over those he had not spoken.

As he climbed through the entry port he found Inch waiting for him and realized with a start that while he had been contemplating the commodore's strategy the small drama of Inch's clash with Stepkyne had faded from his mind.

He said curtly, 'Get the barge inboard and prepare to wear ship, Mr Inch.' He unclipped his swordbelt and handed it to Petch, his servant. Then he dropped his voice and added,

'I would suggest that you go around the upperdeck yourself while you have time.' He held Inch's eyes with his own. 'Better to be sure now than sorry later.'

Inch nodded, his face so full of gratitude that Bolitho felt ashamed for him, and for himself. He had fully intended to give Inch the greatest reprimand he could muster, and in his heart he knew that it was probably doing him a disservice by not doing it. But after the commodore's attitude to his superior and the danger it could entail for all of them, he could not bring himself to break Inch's last strand of self-confidence.

Even as the barge swung dizzily above the larboard gangway Gascoigne called, '*Flag* to *Hyperion*! Take station astern of column!'

'Acknowledge!' Bolitho clasped his hands behind him. Astern of column, he thought bitterly. *Vectis* had already slipped away into the drizzle and mist, and now there were just three ships, and they too distant from the enemy to do much good. Somewhere, far beyond the flagship was one solitary frigate. He could pity her captain.

The pipes shrilled and men swarmed to their stations, as if each one was fully aware of the flagship's nearness, more so perhaps of their own captain's displeasure.

But in spite of the clumsiness and expected confusion amongst some of the hands the manoeuvre was completed without further incident. The *Hyperion* went about, and showing her copper in a steep swell tacked round to take station astern of the other seventy-four, *Hermes*, so that to an onlooker, had there been one, there was nothing to show that a new sentinel had arrived, nor that one was already making full sail for England and a momentary rest from blockade.

Eventually Inch crossed the quarterdeck and touched his hat. 'Permission to dismiss the watch below, sir?'

Bolitho nodded. Then he said, 'In future, Mr Inch, be firm when you are giving your orders. Whether it be to those who know better or merely *think* they know better. Then they will have confidence in you.' The words stuck in his throat as he added, 'Just as *I* have confidence in you.' He turned on his heel and walked to the weather side, unable to watch Inch's pathetic determination.

Inch gripped the quarterdeck rail and stared blindly at the milling seamen around the foot of the foremast as they were relieved from duty. He had been dreading Bolitho's return, not because he was going to be told of his failures, for he was better aware of them than anyone. But because he had caused Bolitho displeasure and disappointment, and *that* he could not bear. To Inch's simple mind Bolitho was more like a god than a captain. If hero-worship was a driving force then Inch possessed it more than a will to live.

He pointed suddenly and called, 'That man! Come now, you can do better than that!'

The seaman in question looked up guiltily and then turned back to his work. He did not know what he had done wrong, and in any case he was doing his task the only way he knew. Nor could he possibly realize that to the first lieutenant he was just a misty blur, an outline amongst many as Inch stared along the length of the labouring ship seeing his own future come alive once more.

Gossett, writing on his slate beside the helmsman, glanced across at him and then at the captain as he strode up and down, head lowered in thought, his hands behind him, and gave a slow nod of understanding. Poor Inch, he thought. Some captains he had known would never have bothered with an officer like him. But Bolitho seemed to care about everyone. When they failed him he seemed to feel the blame himself, yet when he succeeded he always appeared to share the rewards with them. The old master smiled to himself. Equality, that was the word. It suited Bolitho right well. *Equality Dick*. His features split into a broad grin.

Bolitho paused at the end of his walk and said sharply, 'Mr Gossett, there are six midshipmen aboard this ship whose instruction in the arts of navigation was due to commence some fifteen minutes ago to my reckoning.'

Gossett touched his battered hat, but could not stop grinning. 'Aye, *aye*, sir! I will attend to it immediately!'

Bolitho stared after him. It was not like Gossett to daydream.

He recommenced his pacing and returned to his thoughts. No doubt they would all have time for daydreaming under Pelham-Martin's broad pendant, he decided.

3. Deception

AS DAYS DRAGGED into weeks it seemed to Bolitho as if
there was no limit to the merciless cruelty of wind and sea, and
the whole world appeared to have shrunk to the inner confines
of the ship's hull and the wave-dashed upper deck. Neither
was there any let-up in the commodore's orders. Day after day
the three ships tacked back and forth in every conceivable
kind of weather which the Bay of Biscay could offer. Short,
gusty winds would change to the full force of an Atlantic gale
within minutes, and as seamen struggled aloft again and again
to fight the icy, frost-hardened canvas station-keeping became
a nightmare. For days on end the three ships might ride out a
storm under reefed topsails, and when visibility returned they
would be greeted by a whole stream of urgent signals from
the *Indomitable* to regain formation and begin all over again.

There was no longer any seasickness aboard the *Hyperion*,
and when they were released for brief spells from work on
deck the hands slumped into their cramped hammocks like
dead men, grateful only for the warmth of the other bodies
swinging around them as the ship smashed on through the
angry offshore currents and screaming winds.

But hardly an hour seemed to pass before the pipes were
shrilling again and the cry, 'All hands! All hands! Aloft and
reef tops'ls!' would be passed from hatch to hatch.

To prevent the ship's company from giving way completely
to despair Bolitho used every available opportunity to keep
them occupied. Gun drill was carried out whenever possible,
with the starboard side competing against the larboard. The
gunners from the lower battery had to take turns on the main
deck for as yet the weather had been too rough to open the
lower ports.

When Bolitho made his regular weekly inspections throughout the ship he was moved by the wretched conditions of the
men who lived on the lower gundeck beside and between the
thirty twenty-four pounders they would service in action.
With the ports sealed and the ship rolling heavily it was like a

scene from hell. Some three hundred men lived, ate and slept there, and even allowing for one watch being on deck, the atmosphere was sickening. The foul stench of bilge mixed with packed humanity and clothing which was never able to dry was more than enough for the most hardened seaman.

Three weeks after joining Pelham-Martin's command they lost a man overboard, a young seaman who had been pressed in Devon. He had been working on the forecastle with the bosun's party when a great wave had reared high above the jib boom and had hurled him clean over the rail like a piece of canvas. For a few moments he had clung, kicking to the nettings before another bursting wave had torn him away and carried him screaming down the ship's side.

It had been blowing a gale at the time and it was impossible to heave to without danger of dismasting the ship. Not that there would have been any point. By the time a boat could have fought its way clear of the side there would have been no chance of finding the man in that tossing wilderness. But it made a great impression throughout the ship which even the toughened acceptance of more seasoned men could not dispel.

It had been the ship's first death since leaving Plymouth, and with the weather driving the ship inwards upon her own resources it seemed to hang on the crowded messdecks like a threat. There had been much the same atmosphere over the first flogging, too. A seaman had somehow managed to break into a spirit store, and without telling any of his companions had found a quiet corner deep in the ship's hull and got raving drunk. He had emerged during the first watch, stark naked and had capered around the darkened deck like an insane ghost screaming taunts and curses at anyone who tried to overpower him. He had even managed to fell a petty officer before others succeeded in hurling him to the deck.

The next day, while the ship wallowed heavily in a rain squall, Bolitho had the hands called aft to witness punishment, and after reading the Articles of War ordered the bosun's mates to carry out the award of thirty lashes. By any standard it was a lenient punishment in the Navy's harsh code of discipline. Breaking into the spirit store was bad, but striking a petty officer was liable to court martial and hanging, as everyone knew well enough.

Bolitho had found no comfort in awarding the minimum punishment. Even the fact that the petty officer had agreed to say he had not in fact been struck at all was no compensation for the flogging. Punishment at any other time was necessary, but it had seemed to him as he had stood by the rail with his officers and the marine drummer boy's sticks had beaten a slow roll between each swishing crack of the cat-o'-nine-tails across the man's naked back, that the whole ship had enough to bear without any extra misery. It had somehow been made worse by the rain, with the watching ship's company huddled together for warmth, the scarlet line of marines swaying to the deck's uneven roll, and the writhing figure spread-eagled on the gratings, gasping and sobbing as the lash rose and fell in time with the drumbeats.

Occasionally a sloop would seek out the small squadron with despatches from the fleet or stores brought from Vigo, and when weather permitted the commodore would summon his captains aboard the flagship while he read out his own formal report in their presence before signing it, and then to Bolitho's astonishment, asking each of the three captains in turn to sign it also.

He had never heard of such a thing before, but he could tell from the wooden faces of his two companions that they were quite used to Pelham-Martin's strange whim. It was increasingly obvious that the commodore had no intention of leaving a single flaw in his plan to keep the vice-admiral's criticism or possible displeasure at bay by causing his three captains to be implicated in everything he did. So far of course he had done nothing at all, except abide by the letter of his orders. Patrol and blockade, and nothing more.

Whenever Bolitho was called aboard the *Indomitable* he found Pelham-Martin to be a lavish entertainer. The sloops which came and went from Vigo apparently kept him well supplied with choice wines, and what was more important as far as Bolitho was concerned, a small link with the outside world.

The last occasion Bolitho visited the flagship was on Christmas Day. Curiously enough, the weather moderated to a slow north-westerly breeze and the sea eased out its lines of cruising wavecrests into a deep, sullen swell. The *Hyperion*'s upper deck became crowded with figures as they stared at the grey, undulating water and at the other ships as if for the first time. As well they might, for during the eight weeks since joining Pelham-Martin's command the weather had never eased for more than an hour at a time.

Bolitho was irritated at having to visit the flagship. Christmas under these conditions would be wretched enough for his company without his leaving as if to enjoy himself at the commodore's lavish table. The *Hyperion's* fresh food had long since gone and the Christmas dinner for the lower deck was a strange concoction of hot beef hash well laced with rum, and doubtful-tasting duff, which Gilpin, the one-eyed and villainous-looking cook, assured Bolitho 'would set their hearts all aflame.'

But Bolitho knew that the visit to the flagship was not merely for good cheer. A sloop had appeared at first light, using the light airs to dash down on the slow moving two-deckers like a terrier after three ponderous bullocks. She was not one of Pelham-Martin's sloops, but from the main squadron off Lorient, and by the time Bolitho had thrown on his dress coat and called away his barge he saw the sloop's gig already alongside the flagship.

Upon arrival aboard the *Indomitable* he found Pelham-Martin in a very jovial mood. In the great cabin Winstanley was quite expressionless, and Captain Fitzmaurice of the *Hermes* looked openly dismayed.

The news from Lorient was unsettling. Vice-Admiral Cavendish had despatched two frigates to patrol close inshore to check upon any sign of change or movement amongst the mass of anchored shipping within the port. It was a routine task, and one to which both frigate captains were well accustomed. But as they closed the shore their masthead lookouts had reported the startling news that instead of being in ordinary as before, the French ships of the line had their yards crossed, and to all appearances seemed fewer in number. So some must have slipped out through the blockade.

The sloop's commander had not been prepared to add much to this news until Pelham-Martin insisted he should take some of his brandy. The young officer's tongue, thus loosened, told the commodore that in addition to all this both frigates had

44

only just missed being overwhelmed by four French ships which had apparently dashed out of Belle Ile and had almost caught the two scouts on a lee shore.

Pelham-Martin's eyes glistened with tears as he laughed, 'You see, Bolitho! I *told* you this would happen! These hit and miss affairs are no use for blockade. Patience and a show of strength is all we need.'

Bolitho asked quietly, 'Did the sloop bring any new orders, sir?'

Pelham-Martin was still chuckling. It seemed he could have not been more pleased if the fleet had won a great victory, instead of his old enemy having allowed the French to prepare for sea without being discovered.

He said between chuckles, 'Sir Manley Cavendish requires a full report of French men-o'-war in this area, their state of readiness and so forth.' He made it sound so trivial that Bolitho imagined for an instant he had missed something. But Fitzmaurice's grim face told him otherwise.

Pelham-Martin laid one hand on Bolitho's sleeve. 'Never fear, we will send a report in good time.' He cocked his small head on to one shoulder and smiled gently. 'You can close inshore tomorrow, Bolitho, and make contact with *Ithuriel*. How does that suit you, eh?'

The commodore had arranged a grand meal in his own cabin for the three captains, after first writing a brief acknowledgement for the sloop to carry back to Vice-Admiral Cavendish. He had obviously been sorely tempted to add something in the nature of a sarcastic condolence, but even he knew that such wording would be taken as what it was, an open sneer at Cavendish's misfortune.

All through the meal Bolitho fretted and fumed at the delay. There might be a few ships near the Gironde Estuary, and again there could be a possibility of taking some action against them. If there was nothing of value he might even use his brief freedom from Pelham-Martin's apron strings to sweep further along the coast, for information if nothing better was at hand.

Pelham-Martin was obviously well connected, he thought. Throughout the meal he tossed off names and titles of people he knew, of affairs at Court and in Parliament, and if only half true it was no wonder to Bolitho he had been able to survive his admiral's hostility.

He had a maddening way of simplifying or ignoring any sort of danger from the gathering French ships, but at the same time there was something almost likeable about him. Out of his own pocket he had paid for fresh fruit to be sent from Vigo, enough for every man aboard the three ships under his immediate control.

As Bolitho peeled an orange and listened to Fitzmaurice retelling in detail the last moments of Howe's victory on the First of June, he thought of Falmouth, and wondered if Cheney was thinking of him, if the old grey house was covered in snow, if his child would be boy or girl. He did not care which, so long as she was happy.

Eventually, and thankfully, it was over, and Bolitho returned to his ship without further delay. Surprisingly it seemed very quiet, and but for the duty watch the main deck was completely deserted. Only from the wardroom was there any sound of gaiety, and that merely a deep bass voice raised in some sentimental song beloved of sailors, which obviously belonged to Gossett.

Inch was waiting to receive him, and said in reply to Bolitho's question, 'Most of our people have turned into their hammocks, sir.'

Bolitho nodded. After weeks of hardship and wet misery the good hot food and extra rations of spirits would leave little room for further celebrations.

'Good. We will leave them in peace, Mr Inch, until it's time to call the watch on deck.'

He looked suddenly at Inch's drawn face. 'Have you dined well today?'

Inch shuffled his feet awkwardly. 'I've had a lot to do, sir.'

Bolitho studied him with fresh understanding. Of course Inch would never join in with the others with his captain away in the flagship. He had a sudden picture of Inch bobbing and scurrying from deck to deck, making sure that everything was well. Doing his best.

He said abruptly, 'Come aft, Mr Inch.' He walked towards the poop, adding, 'We will leave the squadron at first light tomorrow and make visual contact with the *Ithuriel*.' He

46

nodded to the marine sentry and led the way into his cabin where Petch was screwed up into a tight ball against the bulkhead, fast asleep.

Bolitho grinned and unbuckled his sword. 'A drink with me, Mr Inch.'

Inch took off his hat and clasped it between his hands as he stared round the cabin, probably remembering those other days when he had been a mere fifth lieutenant and Bolitho had come aboard to take command and carry them through one battle after another.

He blurted out suddenly, 'I—I got engaged to be married, sir, when we were at Plymouth.'

Bolitho poured two full measures of claret. 'Then I am glad to drink your health, Mr Inch.'

Inch dabbed his mouth and held the glass up to a lantern. 'Daughter of a doctor, sir. A very fine girl.' He nodded. 'I hope to marry when we put back to England.'

Bolitho looked away, remembering suddenly how much a part Inch had played in his life since he had taken command of the old *Hyperion*. He had even been there in church to see him married to Cheney.

He turned and said quietly, 'I wish you every success. It is another good reason to do well and gain advancement.' He grinned. 'A command of your own, eh?'

Inch looked at his feet. 'I—I hope so, sir.'

Bolitho had already had quite enough to drink and eat aboard the flagship, but at the same time the thought of being alone, cut off from the rest of the ship by the bulkhead and the marine sentry, was more than he could bear. Not tonight, of all nights. He walked across the cabin and shook the servant by his shoulder. As Petch staggered to his feet Bolitho said, 'We will have some more claret. And I think some of that excellent cheese which my wife sent aboard.'

Inch said, 'She'll be thinking of us tonight, sir.'

Bolitho stared at him for several seconds without speaking. Of us. That was what Inch had said, and he was right. He of all people must remember what she had meant to the *Hyperion* when she had taken passage aboard. When she had served the wounded while the timbers had quaked to the broadsides above her.

He replied quietly, 'I am sure she will.'

As Petch busied himself at the table Inch watched Bolitho, hardly daring to blink in case he should miss something. He could not recall having seen him like this before. He was sitting on the bench seat below the windows plucking absently at the lock of black hair which Inch knew covered the livid scar from some past action, and although his eyes were on Petch they were unseeing and distant, and somehow defenceless. It was like a discovery or an intrusion, and Inch knew he would always remember it, and keep it to himself.

Even before there was a hint of grey in the sky all hands were called, and with topsails and courses filling and cracking to a moderate wind the *Hyperion* headed away from her two darkened consorts. As the seamen moved briskly at halyards and braces Bolitho stood by the quarterdeck rail, very conscious of the changed atmosphere which the brief freedom from Pelham-Martin's supervision had brought. For the first time in two months since they had left Plymouth Sound he heard the topmen calling and chattering as they worked busily above the vibrating yards, and he could hear the shriller voices of midshipmen who were urging their men in some unofficial and dangerous contest, their behaviour hidden from their superiors by the dark sky and spreading sails above and around them.

Only a few seemed listless and with little to say, and Bolitho guessed that the icy dawn air, in competition with the previous day's rum-soaked food, was to blame rather than any lingering resentment.

He shivered and walked quickly to the compass. In the feeble binnacle light he could see the card swaying but steady. North-east by north. With luck they would close the lonely *Ithuriel* by noon. If there was nothing to report there might still be time to make use of this rare freedom to sail further north and beyond the estuary. For in spite of the commodore's confidence and his obvious belief that any possible prize or blockade runner would appear from the south where he had placed his other two frigates, Bolitho knew from experience that the French were rarely obliging when it came to assisting their own defeat.

Inch crossed the deck and touched his hat. 'Shall I set the t'gallants, sir?' He, too, sounded crisper and more alive again.

Bolitho shook his head. 'You may send the hands to breakfast, Mr Inch. They've worked hard and will have gained healthy appetites in this keen air.' He wondered briefly if salt pork and iron-hard biscuits would throw half the seamen into a wave of nausea but added, 'We'll get more canvas on her as soon as it's daylight.' He nodded to Inch and then made his way aft to the cabin.

He threw his threadbare seagoing coat on to a chair and seated himself at his desk. Petch had laid out a plate and some steaming coffee, and was busy with his master's breakfast in the adjoining pantry. Even Petch seemed to have got used to Bolitho's habit of eating from his desk rather than the dining table.

But Bolitho enjoyed sitting with nothing but the great glass stern windows between him and the open sea. Sometimes he could shut the ship and her teeming company from his thoughts and just stare out and away to nothing. It was a complete delusion, but it was some comfort when he most needed it.

Today it was still too dark to see much beyond the ship's white bubbling wake as it surged clear of the rudder. But he was momentarily content. The ship was alive again, and anything, *anything* was better than doing nothing. He pitched his ear to the sounds and strains around him. The vibrating rumble of steering gear, the sluice and thunder of water against the hull, and above all, the great sighing moan of wind through rigging and shrouds as the ship gathered it to her own resources and drove on towards the invisible land.

Petch laid his breakfast on the desk and stood back to watch Bolitho's reactions.

A slice of fat pork, fried pale brown with biscuit crumbs. Two ship's biscuits liberally spread with thick black treacle, and the coffee. It was a spartan enough dish for a captain of a King's ship, but after Pelham-Martin's rich table it was somehow welcome and reassuring.

But it was all too good to last. Later as he walked slowly on the quarterdeck watching the hands busy with holystones

49

and swabs and the marines going through their mysterious ceremonies of musket drill and inspection, Bolitho had the feeling that things had changed.

Gossett called suddenly, 'Wind's veerin', sir!'

Bolitho squinted up at the masthead pendant. Perverse as ever the Bay's weather was changing against him, and already the topsails were shaking and banging with nervous disarray.

He said, 'We will alter course two points. Steer north-east by east.'

Stepkyne was officer of the watch and looked as if he had been drinking heavily the day before.

'Midshipman of the watch! Pipe the hands to the braces, and lively with it!'

Even as the ship wallowed round on to her new course Bolitho knew it was not going to be enough. The wind was still veering and losing some of its strength, and the masthead pendant, instead of standing out stiffly was cracking and curling like a coachman's whip.

Gossett plodded to his side and murmured, 'We'll 'ave to tack, sir.' His palm rasped across his jowl. 'By my way o' thinkin' the wind'll be blowin' right offshore afore the watch changes.'

Bolitho eyed him gravely. Gossett was rarely wrong about the elements.

'Very well. Lay her on the larboard tack. We will have to beat well to the north'rd of the estuary if we are to find *Ithuriel* today.'

He smiled at Gossett, but inwardly he was angry and disappointed. But as the wind went round still further he knew there was nothing else for it. By two bells of the forenoon watch the wind had steadied to the north-east, some ninety degrees from its original bearing. So instead of driving comfortably to some point where they could sight and signal the frigate, they must claw their way well north of the estuary in order to take what small advantage there was from the wind's lessening power.

Inch crossed the deck and said, 'It'll take hours before we can go about again, sir.' He, too, sounded disappointed.

Bolitho watched the yards creaking round and felt the ship cant heavily as she swung across the wind, her sails flapping and billowing before filling again to lay her over still further to follow the endless ranks of small, leaping white horses.

'We will make up for it later.' He controlled his own irritation and added shortly, 'This is an excellent chance to exercise the lower battery, Mr Inch.'

He walked aft and peered at the compass. North, north-west. Well at least it would allow the lower gundeck to exercise without being swamped through the open ports. Some ventilation would not come amiss either to drive away the damp and the foul air from the ship's deep hull.

It took another six hours to make good the enforced alteration of course, and by the time the *Hyperion* was running south again, carrying every stitch of canvas to receive the indifferent offshore wind, the daylight was already beginning to fade.

Bolitho was walking back and forth at the weather side when the masthead lookout suddenly broke into his brooding thoughts.

'Deck there! Sail fine on th' larboard bow!'

Bolitho glanced at the masthead pendant. There was no point in altering course. It would take more precious time, and there would be no light at all within an hour. They would pass the frigate some two miles abeam, and that would suffice to read her signals.

He lifted his glass and peered across the nettings. He could not see the distant ship, for her shape was well merged with the dull grey blur which he knew to be the French coast. He looked aloft again and bit his lip. Up there, swaying comfortably on his dizzy perch, the lookout would be able to see her quite well, and more important, the lay of the land beyond.

He made up his mind. 'I'm going aloft, Mr Inch.' He ignored the quick exchange of glances, but concentrated all his will on climbing out on to the weather shrouds and slowly step by step up the quivering ratlines. Ever since he had been a midshipman Bolitho had hated heights, and each time he had found himself forced to make such a climb he always expected he would have outgrown such a stupid fear. But it was not so, and with gritted teeth, his eyes fixed firmly towards the swaying topmast, he continued to climb higher and higher. Up and around the maintop, where two startled marines were cleaning a swivel gun, and gritting his teeth still harder to control the rising nausea as he felt the pull of his weight against his fingers while his body hung outwards on the futtock shrouds. But with more eyes fixed upon him than the approaching frigate, he could not take the easier passage of the lubber's hole.

When at last he reached the crosstrees he found a grizzled, pigtailed seaman already moving aside to give him room to sit down. Bolitho nodded gratefully, as yet unable to regain his breath. For a few moments he sat with his back against the trembling mast while he groped for his slung telescope and tried not to look down at the deck so far below him.

He heard Midshipman Gascoigne yelling, 'She's made the recognition signal, sir!' Inch must have said something, for seconds later the arranged acknowledgement broke in a bright rectangle from the main topsail yard.

Bolitho trained his glass and saw the sleek frigate swooping across the lens, the spray lifting above her bows in one unbroken curtain. He forgot his discomfort as he remembered his own service in frigates. Always on the move, with the dash and excitement which only such graceful ships could give. He pitied her captain's lonely vigil here. Back and forth, day after day, with nothing to show for it. A ship of the line was bad enough in these conditions, but within *her* sleek hull it would be a living nightmare.

He dragged the glass away from the other ship and swung it across the darkening spit of headland to the north of the estuary. A few pale patches, probably coastguard houses, he thought. Above the distant offshore current they appeared to be moving and the sea to be still. He lowered the glass and wiped his eye with his sleeve. He heard Inch's voice carried by the wind. 'Captain, sir! *Ithuriel* has nothing to report!'

By waiting for the mizzen topsail to flap momentarily in the falling wind it was possible for Bolitho to see the shortened figures standing on the quarterdeck, their faces pale blobs against the worn planking. He could see Gascoigne, his signal book flapping in the breeze, and Stepkyne with his glass on the frigate as she cruised past on the opposite tack. Even the ship looked small and compact, so that it was hard to accept that six hundred human souls lived out their lives within her fat hull.

He thought, too, of the frigate's wretched conditions. One of a chain of ships, weatherbeaten and dependent on their own resources, yet essential if the enemy was to be contained within his harbours.

Bolitho swallowed hard and seized a backstay. He could not face another long climb, even downwards, so watched by the lookout with something like awe he swung from the crosstrees, and holding his breath made his way to the quarter-deck by a faster, if less dignified method. He arrived panting on deck, conscious of the grinning seamen around him and of the pain in his legs where the thick stay had seared through his skin in the speedy and heart-stopping descent.

He said stiffly, 'Before the light goes I will make a signal to *Ithuriel*.' He beckoned to Gascoigne. 'I've forgotten her captain's name.'

Gascoigne was still gaping as if he could not believe a captain could behave in such an odd manner. Then he opened his book and stammered, '*Ithuriel*, 32, Captain Curry, sir!'

It would sound trite to wish him a good New Year, Bolitho thought, but it would be better than nothing.

Stepkyne said, 'Well, they've kept her smart enough, in spite of the damn weather.'

Bolitho took Gascoigne's big signal telescope and lifted it above the nettings. The frigate was on the *Hyperion*'s larboard quarter now and he could see the huddled figures on her quarterdeck below the tattered remnant of her ensign. He blinked his eyes rapidly to clear them from strain. He was mistaken. He *had* to be.

His voice was still calm as he snapped, 'Make this signal, Mr Gascoigne. *Hermes* to *Ithuriel*. Good luck.'

He ignored the startled look on the midshipman's pale face and rasped, 'That's right. I said *Hermes*!' Then he added, 'Thank you, Mr Stepkyne.'

Nobody spoke. Those standing near Bolitho even averted their eyes as if unable to watch his madness.

Gascoigne said in a small voice, 'She's acknowledged, sir.'

Bolitho looked away. 'Lay her on the starboard tack, Mr Gossett. We will steer due west.' Then as the pipes twittered and the men ran to the braces he added harshly, '*Ithuriel* is a thirty-two-gun frigate, gentlemen. That ship is a thirty-

six! And only a Frenchman would fail to see *we* are not the *Hermes*!'

They were all staring at him now. 'Mr Stepkyne saw it first, even though he did not recognize fully what he had discovered. She is *too* smart, too clean after weeks of blockade duty!'

Inch said, 'What does it mean, sir?' He seemed stunned.

Bolitho watched the yards swinging and the sails filling again to the wind.

'It *means*, gentlemen, that *Ithuriel* has been taken. That explains how those people knew our recognition signals.' It was amazing how calm he sounded. He could not understand it, when every fibre in his body was crying out for them to understand, as he did. He saw Allday leaning against a nine-pounder, staring astern at the frigate as she sidled once more into the haze of spray and growing darkness. He would know how Bolitho felt. He had been aboard his ship, the *Phalarope* when she had been attacked by an American privateer. That, too, had been a British frigate taken as a prize.

Bolitho asked slowly, 'Why should the French bother with such a deception? They have taken a good frigate, so why keep it a secret?'

Gossett said, 'Seems to me, sir, that they got summat to 'ide.'

Bolitho showed his teeth in a smile. 'I believe so, Mr Gossett.' He looked up at the flapping pendant. 'There is no time to inform the squadron, even if we could find them.' His tone hardened. 'As soon as it is dark we will go about and work to a position north of the estuary again. I have no doubt the frigate's captain, whoever he is, will anchor for the night. He will know it to be unlikely for another ship to come from the squadron for days, even weeks maybe.' He tried to keep the bitterness from his voice. If Pelham-Martin had concentrated his three frigates, and if possible the sloops as well in a tight arc around the patrol area and within visual distance of one another, this could never have happened. He continued in the same flat tone, 'We will close the shore as near as we are able. When the first daylight appears I want to have the wind-gage.' He glanced coldly at the nearest guns. 'This time I will do the talking first. And with *authority*!'

As the banks of cloud closed across the horizon and plunged the sea into total darkness Bolitho still paced the quarterdeck. He was soaked to the skin with spray but did not even feel it. He was seeing that frigate again, feeling the arrogance of her captain as he had signalled to the two-decker. And it had been such a *close call*. He felt the anger twisting in his stomach like fire. Another few minutes and they would have parted. *Hyperion* would have informed the commodore there was nothing unusual to report, and he would have been more than willing to accept it.

And the frigate? He paused in his pacing so that the helmsman's eyes blinked anxiously in the compass light as Bolitho stared unseeingly through him. She would be able to tell her masters that the English were deceived. He frowned. But to what purpose? He continued his pacing, aware of nothing but his thoughts and what they could mean for him, and his ship.

Hyperion could have dismasted the frigate with one ill-aimed broadside as they had passed. Suppose she was no longer on her station when dawn came? Pelham-Martin would not even have the satisfaction of knowing an enemy ship had been destroyed when he wrote to Cavendish with the admission of *Ithuriel*'s capture.

Pelham-Martin would not be in any mood to shoulder the blame alone either, Bolitho decided grimly.

But there had to be a reason for the Frenchman's actions. There *had* to be.

At length, worn out and suddenly ice cold, he said wearily, 'I will go to my cabin, Mr Stepkyne. Call me half an hour before the morning watch, if you please.' He took Inch by the arm. 'Pass the word that I want all hands roused at that time. They will be fed and ready for whatever we must do when light returns.'

As he walked into the darkness of the poop he heard a voice mutter admiringly, 'Cool as a shark's belly, that one! Sees a bloody Frog under his guns an' don't turn a hair!'

Then Gossett's bass voice. ''Old yer yap, damn you! You'll find plenty o' time for noise when the guns begin to crack around yer ears!'

Bolitho entered his cabin and slammed the door. For a

few moments he stood quite still, his shoulders pressed against the bulkhead as he stared emptily at the swinging lanterns.

Gossett knew well enough. Less than a quarter of the company had set foot aboard a ship before, let alone known the horror of an enemy broadside.

He closed his eyes tightly and tried to clear his mind of doubt. There was no choice, nor had there been from the moment he had seen through the frigate's calm deception.

And it had nearly worked, that was the worst part in some ways. In spite of all his experience and training he had only seen what he had *expected* to see. The frigate's captain had gambled on this, but he must have known the consequences for failure, must have found each minute like an hour as the *Hyperion* had surged by within two miles of him.

Whatever it was the French were hiding it must be very worth while. Surprisingly the realization steadied him, and later when Petch padded into the cabin with some coffee he found Bolitho sprawled on the stern bench, his face relaxed in sleep.

Petch was a simple soul, and when he told some of his friends that their captain was so self-assured he was fast asleep already, the tale gained much in the telling.

Allday heard the story and said nothing. He knew Bolitho better than any of them, and guessed that like himself he had probably been thinking of that other time, so many years ago, when a similar ruse had all but cost him his life, and his ship.

Allday examined his heavy cutlass in the dim light of a shaded lantern. If there was going to be a fight, the *Hyperion*'s raw company would need more than confidence. A whole lot more!

4. A Name to Remember

'CAPTAIN, SIR!'

Bolitho opened his eyes and stared for several seconds at Inch's anxious face. He had been dreaming. There had been some sort of green field with an endless flowered hedgerow, and Cheney had been coming down the road to meet him.

He had been running, and so had she, yet they never seemed to draw nearer to one another.

'Well?' He saw Inch pull back nervously and added, 'I'm sorry. Is it time?'

Inch nodded, the lantern above the bench seat throwing his face into half-shadow. 'There's a mist coming offshore, sir. It's not much, but Mr Gossett says it could make the final approach more difficult.' He jumped aside as Bolitho swung his legs over the side and began to pull on his coat.

Bolitho's mind was quite clear now. 'What is our approximate position?'

Inch pouted. 'Ten miles nor' nor'-west of the headland, sir.'

'I'm ready.' Bolitho took a last glance around the cabin and then extinguished the lantern.

On the quarterdeck it was very dark, and only when Bolitho looked up did he realize the extent of the mist. It was moving quite fast, so that the sails were still drawing well, but above the mainyard he could see nothing at all, as if some giant hand had sheared away the remainder of sails and spars.

Stepkyne spoke from the darkness. 'Galley fire doused, sir.'

There was an air of nervous expectancy on every side, but Bolitho forced himself to ignore the others as he walked aft to the compass again.

'Alter course two points. Steer sou'-east!' He held up his hand. 'Make as little sound as possible!'

He crossed to the weather side and peered at the nearest sails. It was a pity he could not reduce the spread of canvas, he thought. The *Hyperion* was creeping very slowly down the enemy coast, and at first light any vigilant sentry might be quick to see the ship's topgallants and sound an alarm before Bolitho could cross the last stretch of water and place himself in the best position to find the frigate. But if he was to have enough speed and manœuvrability to catch the frigate before she could show him her stern, he had to be ready.

He made up his mind. 'Hands to quarters, Mr Inch. No piping or any excitement. Just pass the word, and then clear for action.'

If anything it made the business of getting the darkened ship ready for action all the more unnerving. Shadows flitted back and forth, while from below decks came muffled thuds and bangs as screens were removed, lashings cast off from guns, and officers spoke in fierce whispers as they sought out and checked their own men. And all the while the *Hyperion* was gliding through the long tentacles of mist like a phantom ship, her sails wet with spray and drizzle, her rigging and spars creaking as the hull countered the swift current and the lookouts strained their eyes into the unbroken darkness around them.

Bolitho gripped the nettings and watched the mist sifting through the mainshrouds, like pale liquid, before another clammy gust of wind across the ship's quarter drove it lifting and swirling towards the open sea. Behind him he could hear Captain Dawson speaking with his marines, the occasional click of steel or squeak of equipment as they swayed together in a close-ordered square across the quarterdeck. In the drifting mist their uniforms looked black and their white crossbelts stood out with startling clarity.

Inch appeared, puffing and sweating. 'Ship's cleared for action, sir.'

Bolitho grunted. What sort of a fool would he look if the *Hyperion* found the sea empty when daylight came? Any sort of confidence he had managed to build up amongst the barely trained seamen would soon be lost when the word went around that the captain was frightened of his own shadow.

Any other time he might have waited. Experienced men could load and run out, reload and keep on firing while all around them was lost in a nightmare of deafening explosions and screaming men, and if necessary they could do it in total darkness. He thought of all these men now, crouched behind sealed ports, ears cocked to every sound, hearts pounding, and grateful of the darkness if only to hide the fear from their companions. It was not worth the risk. If it came to a choice he would rather his men should laugh behind his back than die because of his conceit.

'Very well, Mr Inch. You may pass the order to load.'

As Inch beckoned urgently to a midshipman Bolitho recalled the other times when he had sailed into action. Every gun double shotted and loaded with grape for good measure for that first devastating salvo. But with half-trained men fumbling

58

in the gloom of the 'tween decks it would be inviting disaster. It took experience to gauge those methods. One wrong charge and a gun would explode, killing its complete crew at the very least.

The wind eased slightly, and in the sudden stillness he heard the patter of feet across the sanded decks as the little powder monkeys scampered from gun to gun with the charges newly drawn from the magazine, where Johns, the gunner, in his sparkproof felt slippers would be standing in the one place from which there was no escape should the ship take fire in action. Thank God he was an old hand and unlikely to dwell too much on the skill of those he was supplying from his magazine.

Gossett called, 'By my reckonin' we are runnin' about three miles abeam the 'eadland, sir.' He coughed. 'O' course, with this current an' the mist, it's a mite 'ard to be sure.'

'All guns loaded, sir!'

Bolitho held his watch against the compass lamp. It should be getting light now. He looked around quickly. Was it in fact brightening slightly, or were his eyes so used to the gloom that the nine-pounders on the lee side appeared black and stark against the bulwark?

He wished he could take one further look at the chart, but there was no more time left. He tried to picture it exactly as he had last seen it, to memorize and recall the headland and the sheltered water beyond, the soundings and shoals, the deep water, and the swirling current which could turn any foolhardy approach into total ruin.

'Starboard a little!' He stood beside Inch at the quarterdeck rail, his telescope across the weather side as the wheel creaked over.

'Steady as you go!' He could hear Inch breathing noisily, and level with his waist saw one of the quarterdeck gunners kneeling at the breech of a nine-pounder, naked to the waist in spite of the freezing air, a cutlass thrust carelessly through his belt, the hilt black against his bare spine. The length of the man's pigtail told Bolitho he was no novice, and he hoped that at every division of guns there would be a few—other than the petty officers in charge—who would bring stability and order when the time came.

59

Someone dropped a rammer on the main deck, and when he darted an angry glance forward he realized with a start that he could see the forecastle and the web of rigging around the bowsprit and jib boom beyond. But as the ship regained her personality from the fading darkness the mist appeared to grow thicker and whiter, until at length *Hyperion* seemed to be floating helplessly abeam, the illusion made more complete by the speed with which the wet mist passed through and around the shrouds.

Bolitho said suddenly, 'Get aloft, Mr Gascoigne. You've a sharp pair of eyes.'

As the midshipman hurled himself up the ratlines, Inch said, 'We could miss the frigate, sir.'

Bolitho saw the main topsail shake in a down eddy, and in those brief seconds noticed a faint patch of blue. Above the mist the sky was already clearing. Bright and cold, which was just as well.

Blocks and halyards clattered nervously, and Gossett murmured, 'Wind's freshenin', sir.'

It was very slight, but enough. All at once the mist was breaking up and thinning into low lying vapour, and even as Gascoigne's shrill cry came down to the waiting men, Bolitho saw the other ship's outline.

'Frigate fine on the starboard bow!' Gascoigne was yelling with excitement. 'At anchor, sir!'

Inch stared from the other ship to Bolitho, as if unable to believe either.

Bolitho watched the frigate impassively as her outline hardened against the mist which was already passing her and drifting towards the open sea. There was the headland, blue-grey in the dawn light, and although it was still impossible to see the other side of the estuary he knew he had calculated correctly, and could almost find pity for the first man aboard the frigate to see the slow moving *Hyperion*. Placed between him and safety she would look like a messenger from hell itself, he thought, with her gently flapping topsails and topgallants, her courses clewed up, and that gold-faced, hard-eyed figure-head pointing his trident as if to steer the ship straight on his victim.

Across the strip of swirling water Bolitho heard the sudden

blare of a trumpet. A mile yet separated the frigate from the two-decker, but even if she cut her cable it would take time to drive the men to quarters and raise enough canvas to beat clear. Above his head Bolitho heard the topsail billowing like subdued thunder as the ship glided clear of the headland's shelter. The frigate would not get that time.

He gripped the rail and shouted, 'Listen to me!' The men at the guns and braces tore their eyes from the frigate and stared aft as one. 'That is a French ship yonder, and I intend to engage her.' Someone cheered, but fell silent under his captain's unsmiling stare. 'If we can take her as a prize all well and good. But if not we will destroy her!' He let his words sink in and then added, 'But do not be deceived by her appearance. She can still give a good account of herself, and I have seen as many men die from over-confidence as from the enemy's accuracy!' Then he smiled, in spite of the steel-hard tension in his stomach. 'Do your best, lads! For the ship, and for England!'

He turned back to the nettings as cheers broke out along the lines of guns, to be taken up by the men on the lower deck, until the whole ship was alive with yells and cries of excitement.

Bolitho said quietly, 'Let them cheer, Mr Inch. At least it might unnerve the Frogs, eh?'

Nearer, nearer, and all the while Bolitho watched the confusion aboard the rudely awakened frigate, as first a flapping jib and then the foretopsail appeared, before a lookout called down, 'She's cut 'er cable, sir!' Another yelled, 'E's 'oistin' 'is colours!'

Bolitho watched as the Tricolour broke from the frigate's gaff. Her rightful flag this time. Anyway, it was quite obvious he was not going to give in without a fight.

'Run out, Mr Inch!'

A whistle shrilled, and as the port lids were raised the waiting muzzles raced each other down the tilting deck until the *Hyperion* showed her full broadside to the French ship like a double line of black teeth.

Stepkyne was standing at the foot of the foremast, his sword drawn, his eyes towards the quarterdeck.

On the forecastle Lieutenant Hicks of the marines waited

beside the two massive carronades, while the bulk of the red-coats had broken from their neat square to deploy along the poop and quarterdeck nettings, their long muskets already trained on the approaching ship.

'Larboard your helm!' Bolitho held out his hand as if to control his ship. '*Steady*, lads!' He watched the jib boom settle in line with the frigate's foremast, until it seemed as if the other vessel was already pinioned on it like a giant tusk.

'*Steady!*' His heart was thumping against his ribs, and he could feel the dryness on his lips like salt. 'Stand by, Mr. Gossett!'

The enemy captain had probably intended to turn away and run for it. He would not be able to pass the *Hyperion*'s massive armament unscathed, but once in open water could outsail her within minutes.

Bolitho knew that to every captain the enemies were the 'ifs' and the 'whys'.

Why had the lookout not seen the *Hyperion* earlier? Or *if only* the mist had not prevented her being sighted, *if* Bolitho had misjudged his blind approach, and *if only* the sail could have been loosed just a few minutes quicker. All that and more would be flashing through the Frenchman's mind as he stared now at the gleaming two-decker as she drove straight at the heart of his own command.

There was no time to run for it. To expose his unprotected stern to those twenty-four pounders would be the end without firing a shot in reply.

Almost dejectedly the frigate's yards swung round, her larboard guns already running out as she prepared to accept the challenge.

Bolitho snapped, '*Now!*'

Gossett bellowed, 'Helm a-lee!'

When the double wheel went over, the yards were already creaking round, and as he steadied himself against the rail Bolitho saw the bowsprit swinging further and further, the impetus of wind and rudder turning the old ship to run all but level with the enemy.

'Fire as you bear!'

He watched Stepkyne run to the forward twelve-pounder

and crouch beside the gun captain, staring through the open port as the ship wheeled ponderously beneath him and the French frigate glided across the muzzle.

'*Fire!*' He sliced the air with his sword, and down the length of the main deck gun captain after gun captain jerked his trigger line, and the sea faded in a great wall of billowing brown smoke, the air torn apart by the detonations.

Bolitho yelled, 'Again, lads!' He wiped his streaming eyes and felt the deck quiver to the squeal and rumble of trucks as the first guns were sponged, loaded and run out once more.

'*Fire!*' The smashing explosions shook the hull like earth tremors, and when the quarterdeck nine-pounders hurled themselves inboard on their tackles Bolitho saw the frigate's foretopmast quiver and then stagger drunkenly into the smoke.

He shouted, '*Reload*, damn you!' Some of the men had left their stations and were capering and cheering through the choking smoke as they tried to see the extent of their bombardment.

'Larboard your helm!' He saw the smoke gush and writhe in long yellow tongues as the Frenchman fired for the first time.

The balls were puny by comparison, but Bolitho felt them strike hard into his ship's hull and shouted, 'Close the range, Mr Gossett!'

The main deck gunners had stopped cheering, and as Step-kyne dropped his sword and the guns hurled themselves inboard again, many must have been surprised that a mere frigate could hit back and survive such punishment.

A ball crashed into the starboard gangway and a man fell shrieking, a jagged wood splinter driven into his back like an arrow. Some of his companions left their gun to help the writhing figure towards the hatch but Bolitho yelled, 'Get back to your station!' Another ball ploughed through an open port and smashed into the hesitant seamen like an axe. One second a group of dazed, confused men. The next there was a tangle of limbs and blood which seemed to be everywhere amongst the thrashing remains.

Bolitho tore his eyes away and noticed that the frigate's

maintopmast had vanished also, and when a freak wind drove away the smoke he saw what his broadsides had done.

Her sails were in ribbons, and the low-lying hull was battered almost beyond recognition. Here and there a gun still fired, but as *Hyperion's* lower battery roared out across the narrow strip of water Bolitho saw the blood seeping from the frigate's scuppers, watched ice-cold as corpses fell from the splintered tops and yards to join the flotsam and wreckage which floated unheeded between the two ships.

Great pieces of the Frenchman's bulwark and gangway were flying skyward, and even without a glass Bolitho could see the carnage strewn around the littered deck, like the interior of a slaughterhouse.

He snapped, 'Cease firing!' As silence fell over the dreadful scene Bolitho stared at the frigate with something like dismay. Then he cupped his hands and yelled, 'Strike your colours! *Strike!*'

The frigate might still be repaired and used to replace *Ithuriel*. A prize crew could take her to Plymouth or Cadiz, where her papers and documents would yield further information about her.

Below his feet he felt the deck murmuring to the rumble of guntrucks as the men completed reloading before running out once more to face the enemy across less than seventy yards of water.

No guns fired from the frigate, but there was a sudden rattle of musketry from her poop, and a marine beside Inch threw his hands to his face and screamed like an animal as the blood gushed between his fingers. He was still screaming when he was seized and dragged below to the surgeon.

Gossett took off his hat and stared at a gobbet of blood which had splashed it like a cockade. He said, 'The Frog cap'n still 'opes 'e can slip past us, sir.'

Bolitho peered forward above the crouching gun captains. It was true. Following the frigate in a wide arc, the *Hyperion* was now pointing straight at the opposite headland. He would have to go about soon, and that would enable the Frenchman to slip past.

The Tricolour still flapped from the gaff, and the musketry was a clear answer to his plea to end the one-sided fight.

Yet he could not give the order to fire. Without leaning out over the nettings he could picture that double line of guns, with each port filled with watching eyes and a gaping muzzle. Every gun aboard the frigate's engaged side was either up-ended or smashed, and she was already so low in the water that she could not last much longer without more men to assist her. He could not let her escape, nor could he risk his own men's lives in an attempt at boarding. The French captain must be a fanatic. He smiled half to himself, and the naked-backed seaman at his side seeing the curve of his lips shook his pig-tailed head in wonderment. But Bolitho's smile was one of pity and sadness. He was remembering himself as a young frigate captain matched against a ship of the line. The 'ifs' and 'whys' had been on his side that day, or maybe he had just been lucky, he thought dully.

Two feet hit the deck with a loud crash, and for a moment he imagined a wounded man had fallen from the yards. But it was Gascoigne. Bolitho had forgotten all about the young midshipman until this moment.

'Well, boy, why have you left the masthead?' It was a stupid question, but it was giving him a few more seconds to think and decide what to do.

Gascoigne rubbed his sore hands. 'Couldn't make myself heard, sir.' He swung his arm towards the estuary. Beyond the sandbars and the remnants of offshore mist Bolitho saw the dark outline of land and the once busy waterway to Bordeaux.

He blurted, '*Masts*, sir! The mist is so thick up there I couldn't see too much, but masts there are and plenty!' He recovered himself and blushed. 'Three or four ships, sir, and coming our way!'

Bolitho saw Inch's face across the boy's shoulder. 'Now we know, Mr Inch!' He walked to the rail and pointed at Lieutenant Stepkyne. 'Go along each gun in turn. I want every ball to hit!' He looked impassively at the slow moving frigate. There were sandbars beyond her, and *Hyperion* was near the centre of the main channel. 'I want her sunk where she is *now*, Mr Stepkyne.' He removed his hat and did not even flinch as a musket ball struck a nine-pounder and whined away over the poop.

Stepkyne walked to the first gun. A midshipman stood at the main hatch ready to pass the word to the lower battery, so that each weapon would have a twin for the final act.

'Fire!' Bolitho looked away as the frigate's mizzen fell in a great welter of fractured spars and tangled rigging.

'Fire!' A whole section of the main deck erupted in splinters, amidst which corpses and dying men were thrown about like bloodied rag dolls.

In between each remorseless pair of explosions he could hear men screaming and sobbing, as if the ship herself was pleading for mercy. He gripped the rail, willing the frigate to sink and end the slaughter.

'Fire!'

Bubbles were already churning the bloodstained water around the ship into a miniature whirlpool, and here and there a despairing survivor was leaping overboard, only to be carried away on the swift current.

Gossett said thickly, 'She's goin', sir!' He was looking at Bolitho as if seeing a stranger.

Two last shots bellowed from the *Hyperion*'s ports, and as the order to cease fire reached the lower battery Bolitho said harshly, 'We will wear ship, Mr Gossett!'

He tores his eyes from the shattered, listing hull and looked at Gascoigne by his side. 'You did well, my lad.'

He tried to smile but his lips felt frozen. Even Gossett thought he had slaughtered helpless men to no purpose. He snapped, 'Carry on!'

Sails slapping and cracking to the fresh wind, the ship swung her stern slowly across the wind. Bolitho waited, counting seconds, then said, 'Steer nor' nor'-west.'

Gossett faltered under Bolitho's eyes. 'Beg pardon, sir, but we'll need to 'ead more west'rd to clear the 'eadland.'

Bolitho ignored him. 'Shorten sail, Mr Inch. We are going to anchor directly.'

If he had uttered some dreadful obscenity he could not have caused greater consternation.

He did not wait for anyone to speak. 'Mr Gascoigne has seen what that frigate was hiding from us. And why it was necessary to take the *Ithuriel* before she could warn us.' He pointed across the starboard quarter. 'There are ships putting to sea, gentlemen! There is no frigate for us to send to the commodore for help, and *we* do not have the speed for such business.' He looked around their tense and shocked faces. 'We will anchor in the centre of the channel.' He turned his head to watch as the frigate dipped and rolled over in a great welter of bubbles and swirling wreckage. 'Any large ship must pass us. The other channel will be blocked by the wreck.'

Inch said in a small voice, 'But we are alone, sir!'

'I know that!' He softened his tone slightly. 'Pelham-Martin may send someone to see what we are about.' He looked away. 'In the meantime we must do all we can to stop or cripple as many as we are able!'

Then he walked back to the rail and stood in silence as the ship glided purposefully towards the first headland. He could feel no anger at Pelham-Martin's foolish optimism or the hopelessness of the next few hours. Below deck some of the men were cheering again, as if they had just won a great victory. The ship was all but unmarked, and but for the bright splash of blood below the nettings, they could have been at manoeuvres.

Inch said wearily, 'Shall I stop them cheering, sir?'

Bolitho stiffened as a lookout pealed, 'Two ships on the starboard quarter, sir!'

Inch stared fixedly at the topsails of the leading vessel. They were moving above the low bank of mist, detached and impersonal, and all the more threatening.

Bolitho replied at length, 'Let them cheer.' He raised his voice above the din. 'Helm a-lee!'

Slowly the *Hyperion* swung into the wind.

'Tops'l clew lines!'

The bowsprit was seeking the land again. Bolitho gripped his hands behind him to control his rising despair.

'Let go!'

As a shaft of watery sunlight painted the topmast of the leading ship like a golden crucifix, the last of the mist cleared from the sea as if a curtain had finally been lifted.

All cheering aboard the *Hyperion* ceased, and over the whole ship there was a silence you could feel.

Bolitho lifted his glass and studied the approaching vessels. The first was a two-decker, so too was the second. Rounding the side of a jutting spur of land came the third, her hull shining as she swung slightly in the current. A three-decker with a vice-admiral's command flag at the fore. Bolitho tried not to lick his lips. It was hopeless. No, it was worse even than that.

He wondered briefly what the leading captain must be thinking at this moment in time. At last the order to sail had been given. The watching English frigate had been overpowered before the alarm could be passed, and after months of waiting, the French were on the move again.

There was the open sea, with a bright if blurred horizon as the prize.

But alone in the centre of the channel was a single ship, anchored and ready for a fight to the finish.

Allday crossed the deck and held out Bolitho's sword. As he clasped the belt around his waist he said quietly, 'It's a fine day for it, Captain.' Their eyes met as he added, 'First really good one since we left England!'

There were, as Gascoigne had indicated, four French ships in all, and as the minutes dragged by it seemed to the watching British seamen that the whole channel was filling with sails and masts.

Bolitho made himself walk aft to the poop ladder where Roth, the *Hyperion*'s fourth lieutenant, was standing as if mesmerized beside his nine-pounders. Roth had proved to be a competent officer and quick to learn the implications of his first appointment to a ship of the line. But as he stared at the oncoming ships his face was the colour of parchment.

Bolitho said evenly, 'Should I fall, Mr Roth, you will assist the first lieutenant on the quarterdeck to the best of your ability, do you understand?' The man's eyes moved and settled on his face. 'Stay with your guns, and give your people every encouragement, even if . . .'

He swung round as Inch called hoarsely, 'The leading ship's dropped anchor, sir! By the living God, so has the second one!'

Bolitho thrust past him and climbed into the mizzen shrouds. It was incredible, but true. Even as he watched he saw a feather of white spray beneath the bows of the stately three-decker, and knew that she, too, had followed suit. The last ship was too well hidden by her consorts, but he could just make out the flurry of activity on her yards as first one then another sail vanished as if by magic. The French had chosen the last and only place to anchor in safety. The widest part of the channel, before the treacherous sandbars which guarded the final passage to the open sea.

He swung himself back to the deck, only half hearing the excited shouts and the incredulous voices from the lower gundeck as word flashed through the ship that the French had anchored rather than fight.

Inch asked, 'What d'you make of it, sir?' He stared at Bolitho as if to find an immediate answer. 'Surely they're not afraid of *one ship*?'

'I think not, Mr Inch.'

Bolitho stared up at the men on the *Hyperion*'s yards who minutes earlier had been taking in sails and preparing to face death in one last hopeless fight. Now they were cheering, and some were waving towards the anchored French ships and yelling insults and jibes, their voices cracking with derision and relief at this unexpected reprieve.

But it was strange. Bolitho walked away from his chattering officers and stared towards the nearest headland. Maybe the French had already sent for help elsewhere. Heavy artillery from Tochefort perhaps? He dismissed the idea instantly. It was close on thirty miles by road, and by the time guns had been properly sited where they had the slightest chance of hitting the anchored *Hyperion*, anything could have happened. The wind might back within the hour, and the French admiral was not to know that help was not already on the way for the one solitary ship which blocked his escape. Whatever he was going to attempt, he must do it quickly.

Bolitho said, 'Send extra lookouts aloft, Mr Inch. They may sight a sail to seaward, and theirs or ours, I wish to know immediately.' He checked him in his stride. 'And tell our people to keep silent! There's more to this than I like, and I want them to be prepared to fight at a moment's notice!'

Half an hour dragged past with the anchored ships swinging calmly at their cables, separated by some two miles of rippling water, which in the harsh light shone like crumpled silk.

'Deck there!' The lookout's voice made more than one man start with alarm. 'Boat shovin' off from the French flagship!'

Bolitho studied the boat through his glass and then said, 'Flag of truce, Mr Inch. Stand by to receive it alongside, but watch out for tricks!'

It was just a small gig, and as it moved briskly towards the *Hyperion*'s bows Bolitho heard several shouts of surprise from the anchor party and some marines who had been covering its swift approach with a swivel gun loaded with canister.

Inch came aft at the run.

'Sir! There's a British officer on board! The oarsmen, too, are some of our people!'

Bolitho tightened his jaw to hide his sudden apprehension. 'Very well. Be on your guard!'

The gig hooked on to the main chains and the seamen at the entry port fell back in silence as a lieutenant in a torn and smoke-stained uniform climbed up through the boarding nets and made his way aft, looking neither right nor left until he had reached the quarterdeck. He saw Bolitho and crossed the last few feet of deck, his shoes dragging as if he could no longer bear the weight of his limbs.

When he spoke his voice sounded dull and devoid of life. 'Lieutenant Roberts, sir.' He tried to pull back his shoulders as he added. 'Of His Britannic Majesty's Ship *Ithuriel*!'

Bolitho said quietly, 'Come to my cabin, Mr Roberts, if you have some message for me.'

But the lieutenant shook his head. 'I am sorry, sir. There is no time. I was paroled to speak with you and then return without delay.' He swayed and almost fell. '*Ithuriel* was taken by the frigate which you have just destroyed, sir. We were investigating some luggers when she bore in from seaward. It was a clever trap, and even the luggers were filled with armed men. We were dismasted and then boarded within an hour, and my captain was killed.' He shrugged. 'I gave the order to strike. No choice or chance seemed left open to me.' His eyes suddenly clouded with despair and anger. 'Had I known what would happen, I would have let every one of my men die fighting!' He was shaking violently and tears ran down his grimy cheeks as he said in a choked voice, 'The French admiral wishes me to say that unless you weigh and put to sea at *once*,' he paused, suddenly aware of the watching faces around him, 'he will hang every one of *Ithuriel*'s people here and now!'

Inch gasped, 'Good God, that's not possible!'

The lieutenant stared at him, his eyes dull with fatigue and shock. 'But it is, sir. The admiral's name is Lequiller, and he means what he says, *believe* me!'

A gun boomed dully across the inlet, and then as two small, twisting shapes rose kicking and jerking to the mainyard of the French flagship the *Hyperion*'s hull seemed to quiver to a great groan of horror which came from the watching seamen and marines.

The lieutenant said desperately, 'He will hang two men every ten minutes, sir!' He seized Bolitho's arm and sobbed, 'For God's sake, there are *two hundred* British prisoners in Lequiller's hands!'

Bolitho released his arm and tried once more to mask his feelings from those around him. The cold inhumanity, the very horror of the French admiral's ultimatum had made his mind swim with both fury and sick despair. As he glanced along the crowded main deck he could see his own men standing back from the guns, staring up at him or at each other, as if too stunned to move. They had been prepared to fight and die, but to stand by and watch a slow, merciless execution of helpless prisoners had broken their spirit with no less effect than the greatest broadside ever fired.

'And if I obey his demand?' Bolitho forced himself to watch the lieutenant's misery.

'He will land *Ithuriel*'s people and send them under guard to Bordeaux, sir.'

Again the gun echoed and re-echoed across the water, and Bolitho turned to hold and keep the picture in his mind. So that he would never forget it. Two small, writhing shapes. What must those men have thought as they had waited with the halters around their necks? *Hyperion* would have been the last thing they saw on earth.

Bolitho gripped the lieutenant's arm and thrust him to the quarterdeck ladder. 'Go *back* to the flagship, Mr Roberts!'

The man stared at him, his eyes blinded with tears. 'You mean you *will* sail, sir?' He seemed to imagine he had misheard for he tried to seize his hand as he continued in the same broken tone. 'You'll retreat for the sake of our men?'

Bolitho turned away. 'Put him in his gig, Mr Inch, and then have the capstan manned and prepare to get under way!'

He saw Gossett watching him, his face filled with concern and understanding. 'Lay a course to clear the headland, if you please!' Bolitho could not face him, nor could he meet Inch's eyes when he hurried back to his place by the rail.

The men had to be pushed and driven to their stations, as if dazed by what was happening. The older and more experienced ones could only stare aft at their captain's slim figure, surrounded yet quite alone, as he stood watching the French ships, for they knew the enormity of his decision, and what it could mean.

But Bolitho saw none of them, and was barely conscious of the confusion and barked orders as hands manned the capstan bars and the topmen swarmed up the ratlines, some still wearing cutlasses with which they had been ready to fight and die.

The gig was pulling back to the French ships as fast as it could against the stiff current, and Bolitho clenched his fingers until the nails bit into his flesh as the gun fired yet again and two more bodies swayed up to the flagship's yard.

The French admiral had not even waited for the gig to return. He had kept to his timing. Had kept his word.

The gig vanished beyond the anchored ships and then Gossett murmured, 'One of 'em's shortenin' 'er cable already, sir!'

From forward came the cry, 'Anchor's hove short, sir!'

Inch stepped forward to ask permission to get under way, but saw Gossett's grim face and his quick shake of the head. So he turned on his heel and yelled, 'Carry on! Loose tops'ls!' Even when he lowered his speaking trumpet towards the deck Bolitho showed no sign of hearing or of taking his eyes from the enemy ships.

'Man the braces! Lively there!' A rattan cracked across a man's shoulders, and from forward came the call, 'Anchor's aweigh!'

Slowly, even reluctantly, the *Hyperion* went about and gathered way, the watery sunlight touching her spreading and bellying canvas like silver as she heeled to the offshore wind.

Bolitho walked to the weather side, his eyes still on the ship. Lequiller. He would remember that name. *Lequiller*.

A master's mate knuckled his forehead. 'Beg pardon, sir?'

Bolitho stared at him. He must have spoken aloud. He said, 'There will be another day. Be quite sure of that!'

Then he climbed up the poop ladder and said shortly, 'You may dismiss your men, Captain Dawson!'

When the last of the marines had clumped past him he started to pace the small deserted deck, his mind empty of everything but that one name.

It was all he had. But one day he would find him and know him, and when that time came there would be neither pity nor quarter until the memory of those small, wretched corpses was avenged.

5. The Chase Begins

FIVE DAYS after the *Hyperion* had rejoined her two consorts Bolitho was sitting in his cabin, his breakfast untouched, the coffee cold in its cup as he stared listlessly through the stern windows at the empty horizon. He could not recall any days so long or so devoid of purpose, and he knew that his own uncertainty was shared by the whole ship, like a sense of foreboding.

When he had boarded the *Indomitable* within minutes of taking station astern of the other ships he had been conscious of nothing but a sense of failure, and when he had been ushered into the commodore's great cabin he had listened to his own voice as he had made his report, more like a detached on-looker than one who was not only directly involved but also a possible culprit for the chain of events which had followed his retreat from the estuary.

Pelham-Martin had heard him out without a word or an interruption. In fact, looking back Bolitho could recall no expression or reaction of any sort which he could recognize as either anger or apprehension. He had merely said, 'Return to your ship, Bolitho. I will draft an immediate report for Sir Manley Cavendish's attention.'

Again like an onlooker, Bolitho had paced his quarterdeck while signals had broken from the commodore's yards, and for a few hours at least there had been every sign of urgency and purpose. Fortunately, both sloops had returned to the small squadron during *Hyperion*'s brief absence, and as one sped northwards to seek out the vice-admiral's ships, the other had gone about and headed in the opposite direction to recall the two remaining frigates.

But as day followed day with nothing to break the waiting and uncertainty Bolitho knew that a new show of force was less than pointless. The stable door was still open, but it was unlikely there were any more large ships waiting to test the strength of the commodore's vigilance.

Over and over again he asked himself what he could have done. What he *should* have done. If he had stayed offshore to shadow the emerging French ships Pelham-Martin would have remained in ignorance. But by returning immediately to the squadron he had allowed the enemy to escape. To vanish into thin air as if they had never been.

The third course he had rejected without hesitation, but as he fretted and brooded in his imposed isolation he could no longer see even that one act in its true value. Humanity and honour were seen quite differently in the cold austere atmosphere of a court martial assembly. It was ominous that for once Pelham-Martin had not required anyone to witness his report or to know its content.

Several times he had started to write another letter to Cheney. To prepare her for news which at any time could bring her nothing but despair. If Pelham-Martin had worded his report to place the full responsibility on *Hyperion*'s captain, then it would not be long before Falmouth would learn of Bolitho's disgrace, with all the terrible consequences which would follow.

He sat up as a voice called, 'Deck there! Sail on th' weather bow!'

He made himself remain seated at his desk until a midshipman brought the news formally that a ship had been sighted to the north-west. Then, in spite of his mounting anxiety, Bolitho pulled on his coat and made his way slowly to the quarterdeck.

Inch hurried to him. 'She's a frigate, sir!' He watched Bolitho's face worriedly. 'She'll be bringing despatches, sir?'

'Maybe.' Bolitho sensed Inch's concern and added quietly, 'Have no fear. Your part in all this is made quite clear in my log.'

Inch took a pace forward. 'I'm not worried about that, sir! It's just, just . . .'

Bolitho eyed him calmly. '*What* is it?'

Inch squared his narrow shoulders. 'It's so damned unfair, sir! We all think the same!'

Bolitho watched the gulls lifting and diving above the lee gangway. They were foolish enough to make the long flight from land. There was little enough to eat for the ship's company.

Then he said, 'You will not discuss these matters of conjecture in the wardroom, Mr Inch. You may be required to assume command at any time, for any one of a hundred reasons. To open your heart too much might render you vulnerable when you can least afford it.' He saw Inch's crestfallen expression and continued, 'But thank you all the same.'

When the frigate drew closer it was soon obvious that she carried more than mere despatches. As she shortened sail and went about to drive straight for the slow-moving two-deckers Bolitho saw that she wore a vice-admiral's flag at her foremast, and knew from the sudden flurry of signals that Sir Manley Cavendish had arrived in person to pronounce verdict and penalty with the least possible delay.

Midshipman Gascoigne yelled, 'General, sir! Heave to!'

As officers and seamen scampered to their stations he added breathlessly, '*Flag* to *Hyperion*. Captain repair on board in thirty minutes!'

'Acknowledge.' Bolitho looked at Inch. 'Heave to and then call away my barge.' He tried to appear relaxed under the eyes around him. 'It will give me time to change into my dress coat.'

While the ship laboured and swayed in the light wind and Petch busied himself laying out clean shirt and best uniform, Bolitho glanced around the cabin, thinking momentarily of all the dramas and hopes it had witnessed, and would see again. From here captains had gone on deck to die in battle or triumph against one of a dozen of England's enemies. Had left to be promoted or to witness a flogging, to offer help to a ship in distress, or merely to watch the passing beauty of some particular cloud or seascape. It was strange that the same ship which might bring fame and fortune to one, could bring ignominy and disaster to another.

He pulled his neckcloth tight and saw Petch watching him anxiously. He was probably already wondering if by this time tomorrow he would be serving a new master.

Inch stepped into the cabin. 'Barge alongside, sir.' He paused before adding, 'The commodore's already gone over to the frigate, sir.'

Bolitho held out his arms, for his heavy, gold-laced coat with the white lapels. The one which Cheney admired so much. It was what he had expected. The two senior officers would need privacy for their own confrontation, he thought grimly.

'Very well, Mr Inch. I'm ready.'

He paused as Petch fumbled with the swordbelt about his waist and then walked quickly to the door.

A great silence seemed to hang over the upper deck as he strode towards the entry port. It was strange to realize there were still so many faces he did not know or recognize. Given time he would have changed that. He looked up at the great web of rigging and the sails which flapped loosely in the wind. Given time, a lot of things might have been different.

The pipes twittered and the marines presented arms as he swung himself outboard and down to the pitching barge below.

He sat stiffly in the sternsheets as the oars picked up the stroke and sent the boat scudding towards the distant frigate. It was then that he noticed every one of his bargemen was dressed in his best checked shirt and Allday was wearing a brass buttoned coat he had not seen before.

Allday kept his eyes on the frigate but said softly, 'Just to show 'em, Captain. So they'll all know how *we* feel!'

Bolitho gripped his sword-hilt and stared fixedly above the seamen's heads. He could not even find the words to speak. Did not trust himself to reply to Allday's simple loyalty.

The bowman made fast to the chains, and without waiting

for Allday to r:se to his feet Bolitho hauled himself up the frigate's side and raised his hat to the quarterdeck.

For a moment he looked across at the ship he had just left. Then he straightened his shoulders and nodded curtly to the frigate's young captain.

'Lead the way, if you please.'

The frigate's stern cabin was low-beamed and spartan after that in a ship of the line, but to Bolitho was instantly familiar. When he had taken command of a frigate for the first time he had thought his quarters palatial when compared to a small sloop, but now as he ducked his head beneath the deck beams he was equally conscious of the lack of space, made more apparent by the three figures arranged around it.

Vice-Admiral Sir Manley Cavendish was thin and grey haired, and although his features were tanned and weathered, his cheeks looked sunken, and beneath his resplendent dress coat his breathing seemed quick and shallow. Bolitho knew him to be in his sixties, and the fact he had not set foot ashore for more than a few hours during the past two years could have done little to help his obvious poor health. But there was nothing feeble about his voice, and the eyes, close set above an imperious nose, were as bright and searching as any lieutenant's.

'Punctual at least, Bolitho!' He eased himself painfully in his chair. 'You had better sit down. This may take some time, and I am not in the habit of repeating myself!'

Bolitho found a chair, conscious the whole time of Pelham-Martin's heavy bulk seated against the opposite side, his pink hands gripped together across his waistcoat as if to hold himself motionless in his enemy's presence. The other occupant was a flag lieutenant, an expressionless young man who stared straight at an open log book, his pen poised like a sword above an empty page.

Cavendish said, 'I have read the reports, and I have considered what can be done. What must be done.'

Bolitho glanced at the pen. It was still motionless.

'I have spoken with your Commodore and heard all that has happened, both before and after the loss of the *Ithuriel*.' He leaned back and eyed Bolitho stonily. 'Altogether it is as melancholy as it is dangerous, but before I make my final decision I would like to hear if you have anything to add to your, er, assessment of the situation.'

Bolitho knew that Pelham-Martin was staring at him, but looked straight at Cavendish. 'Nothing, sir.'

The flag lieutenant studied him for the first time. Then Cavendish asked calmly, 'No excuses? No blame to be laid elsewhere?'

Bolitho pressed his spine against the chair, holding back the sudden flood of anger and resentment. 'I acted as I thought fit, sir. It was my responsibility and I chose what I thought . . .' he lifted his chin slightly, '. . . what I *think* was the only course open to me.'

The pen scratched busily across the paper.

The admiral nodded slowly. 'If you had stayed to fight you would have forfeited your ship, and maybe six hundred men. You say you were prepared so to do?' He crossed his fingers and watched Bolitho's face for several seconds. 'Yet you were *not* prepared to risk the lives of others already lost to us through fault or negligence, eh?'

Bolitho replied, 'I was not, sir.' He listened to the busy pen and felt his body relax for the first time. He was condemning himself, but could do nothing to prevent it. Not unless he was prepared to slander Pelham-Martin, or to denounce an action he still believed to be right.

Cavendish sighed. 'Then that is all there is to be said on the matter.' His head twisted sharply as he stared at Pelham-Martin. 'Do you wish to make any comment?'

'Captain Bolitho was detached from my supervision, sir.' The commodore was speaking quickly, and against the harsh light thrown through the stern windows his round face was shining with sweat. 'But I am sure, that is, I *feel* under the circumstances he acted as he thought fit.'

Cavendish glanced at his flag lieutenant. It was just a brief moment, but Bolitho thought he saw a flicker of contempt in those cold eyes.

Then he said, 'I have already told your Commodore what I intend, but as you are directly concerned I will give you the bones of my conclusions.' He turned over some papers on the desk and added curtly, 'Four ships avoided my squadron off

Lorient, as you are no doubt well aware. Now more have escaped through your own patrols. You think maybe there is no connection?' He tapped the papers with his small wizened hands. 'I have had every frigate alerted, questioned every available source, yet there is not one single sign of these ships!' He slapped his hands hard on the desk. '*Not one sign!*'

Bolitho watched him evenly. It was hard to see where this was leading. Did Cavendish intend to place the whole blame on Pelham-Martin, and thereby on him?

The vice-admiral snapped, 'Tell me, Bolitho, during the past few days since this misfortune, have you at any time wondered at the French admiral's brutality?'

Bolitho replied, 'He could have fought my ship, sir. We would have given a good account of ourselves, but the end would have been inevitable. It was four to one against, and my people are still new to warfare for the most part.'

Cavendish's grey head bobbed impatiently. 'Well, don't sit there muttering, get on with what you're thinking, dammit!'

'He could not have expected defeat, sir.' Bolitho took a quick breath. 'Therefore he must have feared damage to spars and sails.' He looked squarely into the other man's eyes. 'I believe he must have intended to make a long voyage and not just a quick attack on our ships.'

Cavendish glared at him. 'Thank you. The only useful piece of news to come out of all this is that you discovered the name of the French admiral. Lequiller is no clumsy peasant left over from the Revolution. He has an excellent record in battle. He commanded a frigate in the West Indies and fought us time and time again.' His eyes fastened on Bolitho. 'He helped to form and train the American privateers whom you at least will know were more than effective against us there.'

Bolitho felt dazed. There was still no mention of recriminations, and it was obvious from Pelham-Martin's expression that *he* had already suffered under Cavendish's tongue.

Cavendish was saying. 'Once it was sufficient to see a flag to know your enemy. But this is a new form of war, and we must live by new methods. Now we must learn to know the man beneath that flag, to study his background and his motives, if we are to survive, let alone win a victory which will last. Admiral de Villaret Joyeuse commands the French fleet at Brest. Even now he is mustering ships and men for a final thrust to overthrow both our fleet and our country. He is a dedicated and intelligent man, and if he has entrusted this Lequiller with a special task, then it must be of some value, and Lequiller worthy of it!'

Bolitho thought suddenly of the signal gun, of the men dying before his eyes like felons on a gibbet.

Cavendish eyed him dispassionately. 'Maybe Lequiller is using new methods, too.' He shrugged with sudden impatience. 'But I am more concerned with his intentions. I believe that by now he will have joined with other ships and is heading westward across the Atlantic. That would be the only explanation for my patrols failing to sight him.'

Bolitho said, 'The Caribbean, sir?'

'I think that is the most probable destination.' The vice-admiral turned towards Pelham-Martin. 'And what is your opinion, if any?'

Pelham-Martin came out of his thoughts with a jerk. 'Maybe he intends to attack the islands taken from the French by Sir John Jarvis, sir?' He dropped his eyes under Cavendish's fierce stare.

'He'd need a force three times the size to make that possible!' Cavendish leaned back in his chair and closed his eyes. 'During the American Revolution Lequiller was often sighted in the southern Caribbean. He would have made good use of his time there to make friends and to store his intelligence for some later time.'

Bolitho said slowly, 'Most of the islands there are either Spanish or Dutch, sir. They are of course our allies, but it takes little to change sides with the war going as it is.'

Cavendish opened his eyes and watched him bleakly. 'True. There is little likelihood of the Dutch staying on our side if their own homeland is finally overrun by the common enemy.' He shrugged. 'And as for the Spanish, well they are of little help to our cause as it is. They are still brooding over Gibraltar perhaps, or dreaming of past glories.'

'Then, sir, I would suggest that Lequiller has another motive.' Bolitho tried to picture the sprawled line of islands which ran from east to west above the great mass of the southern Americas. It was almost as if he was thinking aloud.

'To remain our ally Spain needs to stay rich. Much of her wealth comes from the Americas. One such convoy of gold and silver plate is enough to sustain her for a whole year, maybe longer.'

Cavendish's cold eyes gleamed. 'Exactly! Also, if it fell into enemy hands it would be more use than ten regiments, as Lequiller must know better than most!'

Pelham-Martin said uneasily, 'It might take months to find Lequiller and bring him to action, sir . . .'

He got no further. For once Cavendish seemed unable to contain his dislike in front of his subordinates.

'Don't you *ever* see beyond your quarterdeck? If Lequiller can cause havoc with the Spanish and Dutch trade and supply routes there will be many who will see it as a sign for the future. God knows we are stretched thinly enough now. How long do you think our naval supremacy will last with the whole world against us?'

The anger seemed to tire him and he added wearily, 'Yours is the fastest ship available, Bolitho, that is until the others have returned from overhaul. I have told your Commodore to shift his pendant to *Hyperion* at once. Together with the two frigates you will sail for the Caribbean with all haste. *Indomitable* and *Hermes* with the sloops will follow you, but I want you there *as soon as possible*, is that clear?'

Pelham-Martin heaved himself to his feet. 'I should like to return to my ship, sir. There are things I must attend to.'

Cavendish remained seated. 'The French fleet will be out soon, and I cannot spare another frigate for your use.' He added in a sharper tone, 'Nor can I go with you myself for the same reason. I want Lequiller found and his ships taken or destroyed. I will have my written orders sent to *Hyperion* within the hour, *by which time* I will expect you ready to proceed. You will sail first to the Dutch island of St Kruis. It has a good harbour and is well placed for you to watch over the neighbouring islands. It is less than a hundred miles from the mainland and Caracas where most of the plate and bullion is loaded for shipment to Spain.'

He gave a curt nod of dismissal as the commodore left the cabin. Then almost to himself he said, 'It is quite a task which I have given him, Bolitho. One which requires each captain

81

to think for himself, yet work in a team. Blockade is only half an answer. It postpones rather than decides, just as it punishes the weak and the innocent along with the guilty. The only way to win this war is to meet the enemy ship to ship, gun to gun, and man to man!'

He sighed and seemed to relax slightly.

'Is your ship ready, Bolitho? God knows she should be after a six months' refit.'

'I was fifty men under complement when I recommissioned, sir, and I lost ten killed in battle with the frigate.'

The vice-admiral's eyes clouded over. 'Ah yes, the frigate. I am glad you were able to avenge *Ithuriel*.' His tone hardened. 'Well, I can spare no men for you. You must obtain them as best you can.' Then he heaved himself to his feet and stared at Bolitho searchingly. 'I knew your father, and I am aware of your record. But for that, and the fact you dropped anchor *before* Lequiller's ultimatum, I might have found you guilty of cowardice.' He shrugged heavily. 'In any case, no matter what I might have believed, the Articles of War make small allowance for past achievements or private confidences. Forty years ago they shot Admiral Byng for making a mistake. They would think very little of hanging a mere captain if the example should serve to encourage others to greater efforts!'

Surprisingly, he smiled and held out his hand. 'Go to your ship, and good luck. We are now in 1795. It could be a profitable year for our cause. Or it could be a disaster. You belong to a generation of sea officers who are the right age and in the right time to avert the latter.'

Bolitho could find no other answer than, 'Thank you, sir.'

Cavendish suddenly became grave and severe. 'I hear you have married?' He glanced at the old sword on Bolitho's hip. 'I recall your father wearing that. Maybe your son will carry it one day.' He followed him to the door, adding quietly, 'See that it goes to him with the same honour it came to you, eh?'

Bolitho walked on to the quarterdeck, his mind in a whirl. It was the same scene as when he had come aboard, yet so very different. Even the air tasted cleaner, and it was all he could do to stop himself from running down to his barge.

The frigate's captain was waiting beside the entry port and

glanced at him curiously. 'Will you have any mail for me to take, sir?'

Bolitho stared at him. 'Yes. I will send it across directly.'

The sudden implication of the question brought him back to reality. He had worried about being so far from Cheney. Now he was going to the other side of the Atlantic. It was close on five thousand miles to that part of the Caribbean. It could be months, even years before he returned. If ever.

He touched his hat and climbed down to the barge.

Allday studied his grave features. 'Back to the ship, sir?'

Bolitho looked at him and then smiled. 'There's nowhere else to go.'

As the boat pulled strongly towards the *Hyperion* he tried to apply his mind to all the countless details and alterations he would have to make in his plans and daily routine. There were problems and shortages, and not least of his worries would be having Pelham-Martin as his constant companion.

But again and again his thoughts returned to the house in Falmouth, the feeling of distance mounting up and up, until it seemed like part of another world.

Allday rested his fingers on the tiller and kept an eye on the stroke oar. During Bolitho's stay with the vice-admiral Allday had not been idle. A frigate was too small and cramped to hold an important secret, and the lower deck always knew about a change of plans almost as soon as the wardroom.

The Caribbean again, he thought. And all because of that bloody-minded Frog admiral who had hanged helpless prisoners. It would mean sun and sweat, rancid water, and the constant threat of disease. It might mean a whole lot worse before they were done, he decided.

Then he studied the set of Bolitho's shoulders and smiled slightly. But at least they still had the captain with them. And to Allday, that was just about all that really mattered.

Lieutenant Inch sat awkwardly on the edge of a chair, his hat crushed between his knees as he listened intently to Bolitho's news. Bolitho said, 'So you see, it seems as if your marriage will have to be postponed for a while?'

Inch nodded, his face screwed into a mask of concentration as if to memorize every word.

'You may inform the officers of the destination and possible purpose, but *I* will tell our people as soon as I have a spare moment.'

Bolitho heard the bellow of orders and scrape of feet on the gangway, and guessed that the last of the commodore's personal possessions were being hauled aboard.

He added, 'Pelham-Martin is used to a smart ship, Mr Inch. Even at short notice he will rightly expect the proper honours.'

Inch came out of his thoughts with a jerk. 'I have told Captain Dawson, sir. The guard and bandsmen are already assembled.'

'Good.' Bolitho glanced round the cabin. He had already had his own things removed to the chartroom, and Pelham-Martin would enjoy the comfort of these quarters. And the view from the stern windows, too, he thought sadly.

He continued, 'As soon as we get under way I want to see the purser. A full and detailed account of fresh water and lime juice will also be required. It may be months before we can expect to replenish stores with fresh food and fruit, and some of our people will find it hard enough without being plagued with scurvy or worse.'

Inch stood up, his thin body swaying loosely to the uncomfortable motion. 'I am very sorry, sir, but I neglected to tell you. We have a new midshipman aboard.'

Bolitho stopped leafing through his neatly written orders and stared at him. 'Did he fall from heaven, Mr Inch?'

The first lieutenant flushed. 'Well, sir, when you were aboard the admiral's frigate I was so troubled that I forgot about it. He was sent across from the frigate with some mail and medical stores. He is straight out of Plymouth, and never before in a King's ship.'

Bolitho leaned back at the desk. 'Well, one more midshipman will be very useful later on, no matter what experience at his disposal.'

There was a loud thud from the main deck and Tomlin's voice shattered the air with a stream of curses.

'Very well, Mr Inch. Send the young gentleman in, and then go and watch over the commodore's possessions, eh?' He smiled dryly. 'It would be an even worse beginning if *they* were damaged.'

84

He turned back to his orders again, thinking of what lay ahead, and of the remarks Vice-Admiral Cavendish had privately voiced to him.

New methods, and a new type of sea officer. It was strange but true that men like Rodney and Howe, names once revered throughout the Navy, were now openly criticized by younger and more zealous officers. Like the young Captain Nelson whom Bolitho had seen over a year back off Toulon, whose personal initiative and daring had taken Bastia from under the very noses of the French army.

At the right age and at the right time, Cavendish had said. Bolitho shut the desk drawer and locked it firmly. We shall see, he thought.

There was a hesitant tap at the door, and when he swung round in the chair Bolitho saw the new midshipman standing uncertainly at the far end of the cabin.

'Come over here so that I can see you.' Bolitho could hardly spare the time to meet the newcomer, but knew from bitter experience what it was like to join a ship already in commission, alone and with no familiar faces to ease the first jolts and scrapes.

The boy stepped forward and halted within feet of the desk. He was tall for his age, slim and dark eyed, with hair as black as Bolitho's. He had a wild, restless appearance about him, which reminded Bolitho of an untrained colt.

He took the heavy envelope from the midshipman's hands and slit it open. It was from the Port Admiral at Plymouth, with the bare facts of the approved appointment to the *Hyperion*. The boy's name was, it appeared, Adam Pascoe.

Bolitho looked up and smiled. 'A fellow Cornishman, eh? How old are you, Mr Pascoe?'

'Fourteen, sir.' He sounded taut and on guard.

Bolitho studied him. There was something strange about Pascoe, yet he could not place it. He noted the poor quality of the boy's uniform coat, the cheap gilt on his dirk.

Pascoe did not falter under his scrutiny but dived one hand inside his coat and produced another letter. Quickly he said, 'This is for you, sir. I was told to give it to no one else.'

Bolitho slit open a crumpled envelope and turned away slightly. It was common enough to get a private letter under these circumstances. An unwanted son being sent away to sea, a request for special privilege, or merely a fond mother's personal plea for his care in the world she could never share.

The paper quivered in his fingers as he gripped it with sudden force. The letter was from his own brother-in-law, Lewis Roxby, Falmouth landowner and magistrate, and married to Bolitho's younger sister. The sprawling writing seemed to swim as he read the middle paragraph for the second time.

When the boy came to me for my protection it was of course necessary to investigate the value of documents he brought with him. There is no doubt that the claims made on his behalf are genuine. He is the son of your late brother Hugh. There are letters from him to the boy's mother, whom it appears he had some intent upon marrying before he quit the country. He never saw his father of course, and lived until recently with his mother, who was little more than a common whore to all accounts, in the town of Penzance.

There was more, quite a lot more, all of which spoke of excuses and reasons for getting the boy away from Falmouth without delay.

Bolitho swallowed hard. He could well imagine the consternation the boy's sudden appearance must have caused. He did not really like Roxby, nor could he ever understand his sister's choice for a husband. Roxby loved a good rich life, with all the hunting and bloodsport he could find to fill his day with others of the county whom he might consider as his equals. The thought of being involved with a re-born local scandal would be more than enough to move him to write this letter and send the boy packing to sea.

He turned and looked again at the young midshipman. Letters of proof, Roxby had said. But just to look at him should have been enough. No wonder he had seemed strange. It was like looking at himself as a boy!

Pascoe met his gaze, his expression drawn between defiance and anxiety.

Bolitho asked quietly, 'Your father, boy, what do you know of him?'

'He was a King's officer, sir, and was killed by a runaway horse in America. My mother often described him to me.' He faltered before adding, 'When she was dying she told me to make my way to Falmouth and seek your family, sir. I—I know my mother never married him, sir. I have always known, but . . .' His voice trailed away.

Bolitho nodded. 'I understand.' What a lot had been left unsaid. How the boy's mother had managed to keep and clothe him, to protect him from the truth that his father had deserted the Navy and had fought against his country, spoke volumes, and moved Bolitho to say, 'As you must know, your father was my brother.' He looked away and hurried on, 'And you lived in Penzance, you say?'

'Yes, sir. My mother was sometimes a housekeeper for the squire. When she died I walked to Falmouth.'

Bolitho studied his face thoughtfully. Twenty miles on foot, alone and with no knowledge of what might be waiting for him in a strange town.

The boy said suddenly, 'Aunt Nancy was most generous, sir. She took care of me,' he dropped his gaze, 'while they were looking into things.'

'Aye, she would.' Bolitho recalled his sister with sudden clarity, how she had nursed and mothered him when he had lain half dying with fever after his return from the Great South Sea. She would look after the boy better than anyone, he thought.

It was strange to realize that all these years he had been living a bare twenty miles from Falmouth, and the house which, if not for this cruel twist of fate, would have been his own property one day.

Pascoe said quietly, 'When I was in Falmouth, sir, I went to the church and saw my father's plaque there. Beside all those others . . .' He swallowed hard. 'I liked that, sir.'

There was a tap on the door and Midshipman Gascoigne stepped carefully into the cabin. Gascoigne was seventeen and the ship's senior midshipman. In the coveted post of looking after the *Hyperion*'s signals, he was next in line for promotion to acting lieutenant. Also, he was the only midshipman who had been at sea before in a King's ship.

He said formally, 'Mr Inch's respects, sir, and the barge is putting off from *Indomitable* with the commodore on board.' His eye strayed to the new midshipman, but did not even flicker.

Bolitho stood up, groping for his sword. 'Very well, I'll come directly.' He added sharply, 'Mr Gascoigne, I will place Mr Pascoe in your charge. See that he is allotted a station and keep a careful eye on his progress.'

'Sir?' Gascoigne looked inscrutable.

Bolitho hated favouritism of any kind, and despised those who used it to grant or receive advancement or special treatment.

But it seemed little enough now. This poor, wretched boy who was grateful for a chance to make good when he was entirely blameless for the fate which had left him without a father or his proper name, was now in his ship, and from what he could gather from Roxby's letter, likely to have nowhere else to go in the whole world.

He said calmly, 'Mr Pascoe is my, er, nephew.'

When he looked again at the boy's face he knew he had been right.

Unable to watch the torment in his dark eyes a moment longer he added harshly, 'Now be off with you! There's more than enough work as it is!'

Minutes later as he stood by the entry port to receive the commodore, Bolitho found himself thinking of what the boy's arrival might come to mean. As he glanced casually at the other officers he wondered just how much they knew or considered their captain's background and the one flaw in his family's record.

But their expressions were mixed. Excitement at the voyage ahead, troubled by the thought of leaving someone dear even further astern, the faces were as varied as their owners. Maybe they were just relieved at being spared from the boredom of blockade, and did not yet fully comprehend the enormity of the ship's true mission. The sudden change of orders seemed to have driven the horror of the hangings, the sharp and fierce clash with the frigate from their minds. Even the handful of seamen killed in the one-sided fight, who had been buried at sea almost before their blood had been scrubbed from the planking, appeared to have faded in memory. Which was just as well, he thought grimly.

As Pelham-Martin's cocked hat appeared up the side and the pipes squealed and the marines' drums and fifes broke into

Heart of Oak, Bolitho momentarily thrust his personal hopes and misgivings to the back of his mind.

He stepped forward, removing his hat, knowing from the uplifted eyes of a small sideboy that the broad pendant had broken from the masthead at exactly the right moment, and said formally, 'Welcome aboard, sir!'

Pelham-Martin clapped on his hat and peered around at the watching figures. He was perspiring freely, and Bolitho could almost taste the brandy on his breath. Whatever Cavendish had said to him privately had certainly moved Pelham-Martin enough to fortify himself well before coming across to his new flagship.

He said shortly, 'Carry on, Bolitho.'

Then followed by Petch he waddled aft to the quarterdeck ladder.

Bolitho looked at Inch. 'Get the ship under way, if you please.' He glanced aloft at the new pendant. 'The wind has backed a trifle, I think. Make a signal to the frigates *Spartan* and *Abdiel* to take station as ordered.' He watched Gascoigne scribbling on his slate, the flags dashing up to the yards. He saw, too, that Pascoe was with Gascoigne, his head bent to catch what his senior was telling him. At that moment the boy looked up, and across the hurrying seamen and jerking halyards their eyes met.

Bolitho nodded curtly, and then gave a brief smile. When he looked again the boy was hidden by the afterguard as they clumped to the mizzen braces.

He said, 'We will steer west-south-west, Mr Gossett.'

Later, as the *Hyperion* tilted steeply to the wind and more and more canvas blossomed and thundered from her braced yards, Bolitho walked on to the poop and stared astern. The other two-deckers and the vice-admiral's frigate were already lost in a misty haze, and of France there was no sign at all.

Inch came aft and touched his hat. 'It'll be a long chase, sir.'

Bolitho nodded. 'Let us hope it may also be a fruitful one.' Then he crossed to the weather side and retreated into his thoughts again.

6. A King's Officer

FOR THREE WEEKS after leaving the rest of the squadron the *Hyperion* and the two frigates drove south-west, and later when the wind backed perversely and mounted to a full gale, due south under all sail which it was safe to carry.

Then, as January drew to a close, they picked up the north-east trade winds and headed out on the longest and final leg of their voyage. Three thousand miles of ocean, with nothing but their own meagre resources to sustain them.

But as far as Bolitho was concerned the weather for the first part of the voyage had been a welcome ally. Barely an hour passed without the hands being called to reef or trim the sails, and the ship's company had found little time to brood over their unexpected isolation and the great breadth of ocean which greeted their tired eyes at every dawn.

And in spite of the hardships and privations, if not because of them, he was pleased with the way his men were shaping up. As he stood by the quarterdeck rail and watched the hands toiling with holystones and swabs he saw the obvious changes which had come about. Gone were the pallid skins and haggard faces. The bodies were still lean, but it was a tough leanness born of hard work and sea air, and they performed their daily tasks without the need of constant guidance or harrying. Of course the weather had a lot to do with it. All the colours were different. Blue instead of dull grey, and the rare clouds fleecy and unreachable as they glided across the clear sky towards an horizon which always seemed as hard and as bright as a sword blade.

While the *Hyperion* took full advantage of the friendly trades so she, too, altered her appearance accordingly. Now in a full suit of light sails to replace the thick heavy-weather canvas, she seemed to lean forward and down across the endless panorama of glittering whitecaps, as if she was glad to be throwing off the bleak monotony of blockade duty and eager to reach beyond the sea's edge, and beyond that.

He lifted his telescope and moved it slowly above the nettings until he found the tiny pyramid of sails far out on the starboard bow, a mere flaw on the horizon to show that the frigate *Abdiel* was on her proper station. The other frigate, *Spartan*, was some twenty miles ahead of her and quite invisible. He closed the glass and handed it to the midshipman of the watch.

At moments like these it was hard to believe he was not still in sole command. Pelham-Martin rarely seemed to come on deck, and remained aloof and unreachable in the stern cabin for most of the time. He would grant Bolitho a brief audience every morning, listen to his comments or ideas, and then confine his comments to, 'That seems quite a good plan.' Or, 'If you consider that to be in the best interest, Bolitho.' It was as if he was saving himself for the real task which still lay ahead, and was content to leave local affairs to his captain.

Up to a point it suited Bolitho, but as far as the true depth and meaning of Pelham-Martin's orders were concerned, he was in complete ignorance.

The commodore still seemed unwilling to place any value on the selection of captains for certain tasks, and left it completely to Bolitho's own judgement, even though he was a stranger to the squadron. Bolitho thought about the far off *Spartan* and how Pelham-Martin seemed almost surprised to learn that he already knew her young captain. But it was only mild surprise and nothing more. He appeared to hold personal relationships at arm's length, as if they were of no importance at all.

Bolitho started to pace slowly up and down, thinking back over the years, to all the faces and memories which made up his service at sea. The *Spartan*'s captain for instance. Charles Farquhar had once been a midshipman under him, and he had been the first to see his value and promote him to acting lieutenant. Now, at twenty-nine, he was a post-captain, and with his aristocratic family background and a long line of naval connections, it was likely he would end his career as an admiral and a very rich man. Curiously, Bolitho had never really liked him, but at the same time had recognized right from the start that he was both shrewd and resourceful, just as he was now said to be something of a tyrant when it came to running his own command.

But the *Spartan* was the leading ship, and upon her captain's first quick judgement could depend the success or failure of whatever Pelham-Martin might intend.

When he had mentioned to Pelham-Martin that Farquhar had once been a fellow prisoner aboard an American privateer the commodore had merely said, 'Very interesting. You must tell me about it sometime.' As he paced busily back and forth Bolitho found time to wonder what Pelham-Martin's reaction would be if he ever discovered that Bolitho's captor had been his own brother!

Inch hovered nearby, trying to catch his eye.

'Well?' Bolitho faced him abruptly, shutting the commodore's strange attitudes from his mind. 'What can I do for you?'

Inch said, 'Gun drill, sir?' He pulled out his watch. 'I am hoping we may do better today.'

Bolitho hid a smile. Inch was so serious these days, but a great improvement as a first lieutenant.

He replied, 'Very well. They still take too long to clear for action. I want it done in ten minutes and not a second more. And there are also too many delays in loading and running out.'

Inch nodded glumly. 'I know, sir.'

Bolitho half turned as a burst of laughter floated down from the main shrouds. He saw three midshipmen racing each other for the top; one of them he recognized as his nephew. It was strange that in a crowded ship they rarely seemed to meet. It was even harder to enquire of his welfare without appearing to show favouritism, or worse, mistrust.

He said distantly, 'You know my standards. Clear for action in ten minutes or less. Then three broadsides every two minutes.' He eyed him calmly. 'You know it. Make sure *they* know it too!' He walked back to the weather side adding casually, 'I suggest you give one gun to the midshipmen this morning. It will keep 'em out of mischief, and more to the point will make our people all the more keen. It does them good to know they can beat an officers' crew in timing and efficiency.'

Inch nodded. 'I'll attend to it directly . . .' He flushed with embarrassment. 'I—I mean *at once*, sir!'

Bolitho continued his pacing, his jaw aching as he tried to stop the grin from spreading across his face. It was just as if Inch was trying to mould himself on his captain, even to the way he spoke.

At two bells precisely he left the quarterdeck and made his way aft to the cabin. Much as usual he found Pelham-Martin seated at the table, a silk napkin under his chin while he consumed a final cup of coffee after his late breakfast.

He said, 'I have sent the hands to gun drill, sir.'

Pelham-Martin dabbed his small mouth with a corner of the napkin and frowned as the deck trembled to the rumble of gun trucks and stamp of feet.

'So it would appear!' He shifted his bulky frame on the chair. 'Is there anything else to report?'

Bolitho eyed him impassively. It was always the same. 'We are steering west-south-west, sir, and the wind is steady as before. I have set the royals on her, and with luck we should reach St Kruis in three weeks.'

Pelham-Martin grimaced. 'You sound very confident. But of course you know these waters well.' He glanced towards the litter of papers and charts on the desk. 'I hope to God there is some news awaiting us at St Kruis.' He scowled. 'You never can tell with the Dutch, of course.'

Bolitho looked away. 'It cannot be easy when you know your own homeland is being conquered sir.'

The commodore grunted. 'That is not my concern. The point is, will they help us?'

'I believe so, sir. The Dutch have always been good friends, just as they have been honourable and courageous foes.'

'Maybe.' Pelham-Martin pulled himself on to his short legs and moved slowly up the tilting deck. At the desk he fiddled with the papers and then said bitterly. 'My orders give me no real indication of what I am to expect. No sort of guide . . .' He broke off and swung round as if expecting criticism· 'Well? What do *you* think?'

Bolitho said slowly, 'I think we must try and inspire some confidence, sir. Be one move ahead of Lequiller's ships and foresee whatever he tries to do. He will use his strength whenever he can to force others to help and supply him. But at the same time he must realize that his squadron is vulnerable

93

and will want to use it without delay and to the best effect.' He crossed to the charts. 'He will know that he is being chased, and will therefore have the advantage.'

Pelham-Martin leaned heavily on the desk. 'I know that, dammit!'

'It will be necessary to seek him out, to prevent him from carrying out his intentions, *before* he can act.'

'But in the name of heaven, man, do you know what you're saying?' He sounded shocked. 'You are actually suggesting that I should sail to some mark on a chart and merely sit and wait?'

Bolitho replied calmly, 'A chase is always a chase, sir. I have rarely known one group of ships to overhaul another without some piece of extreme luck. To catch a shark you must have a suitable bait, one so rich that even the wiliest cannot resist it.'

Pelham-Martin rubbed his chin. 'Treasure ships. You are speaking of those?' He walked unsteadily across the cabin. 'It is a terrible risk, Bolitho. If Lequiller intended to attack somewhere else, and we were watching over some ships at the other end of the Caribbean,' he shuddered, 'it would be *my* responsibility!'

Perhaps the commodore was only now beginning to realize the full implication of his task, Bolitho thought. Reaching St Kruis without delay was not even a beginning. There were countless islands, some almost unknown except to pirates and renegades of every kind. And Lequiller's past experience would have taught him about many of them, of places to hide and water his ships, where he could glean information and sow unrest, and always he had the vast sea areas at his disposal in which to vanish at a moment's warning.

Bolitho could almost feel sorry for Pelham-Martin's dilemma. It was likely that Cavendish had already been reprimanded for his failure to contain the French ships in port. It was even more likely he would soon use Pelham-Martin as a ready scapegoat if anything further went wrong.

And yet there was equally great scope in the neatly worded orders. Given the same chance, Bolitho knew he would have jumped at the opportunity of conquering Lequiller and defeating him on his own terms.

There was a tap at the door and Inch stepped over the coaming, his hat under his arm.

'*Well?*' Bolitho sounded irritated. In another minute it was possible, even likely, that Pelham-Martin would have confided in him further.

Inch swallowed. 'I am sorry to disturb you, sir.' He looked at Pelham-Martin.

The commodore sank on to a chair and waved one hand. 'Please carry on, Mr Inch.' He sounded almost relieved at the interruption.

Inch said, 'Mr Stepkyne wishes to award punishment, sir. But under the circumstances . . .' He looked at his feet. 'It is Mr Pascoe, sir.'

Pelham-Martin said mildly, 'Hardly an affair for your captain, I would have thought?'

Bolitho knew there was much more behind Inch's words. 'Send Mr Stepkyne aft, if you please.'

Pelham-Martin murmured, 'If you would rather dispense judgement elsewhere, Bolitho, I shall of course understand. It is difficult when one has a relative, no matter how harmless, aboard one's ship. It is sometimes necessary to show bias, eh?'

Bolitho looked down at him but the commodore's eyes were opaque and devoid of expression.

'I have nothing to hide, thank you, sir.'

Stepkyne entered the cabin, his dark features unsmiling but composed.

Inch said, 'It was nothing really, sir.' He added firmly, 'During gun drill one of the seamen got his foot crushed when they were running out a twelve-pounder. All the midshipmen had taken turns as gun captain, and Mr Pascoe refused to run out his gun until the man on the other team was replaced. He said it would be an unfair advantage, sir.'

Stepkyne kept his eyes on a point above Bolitho's shoulder. 'I ordered him to carry on with the drill, sir. There is no room for childish games in matters of gunnery.' He shrugged, as if it was too trivial to discuss. 'He was unwilling to attend my order and I took him off the gun.' His lips tightened. 'He will have to be punished, sir.'

Bolitho could feel the commodore watching him, even sense his amusement.

'Is that all that happened?'

Stepkyne nodded. 'Yes, sir.'

Inch stepped forward. 'The boy was provoked, sir. I am sure he meant no real harm.'

Stepkyne did not flinch. 'He is no boy, sir, he is to all intent an officer, and I'll have no insolence from him or anyone else who is my junior!'

Bolitho looked at Inch. 'In your opinion, did Mr Pascoe show any insubordination?' His tone hardened. 'The *truth*, Mr Inch!'

Inch looked wretched. 'Well, sir, he did call the second lieutenant a damned liar.'

'I see.' Bolitho locked his fingers behind his back. 'Who heard these words, apart from you?'

Inch replied, 'Mr Gascoigne and, I think, your coxswain, sir.'

Bolitho nodded coldly. 'Very well, Mr Inch, you may award punishment.'

The door closed behind them and Pelham-Martin said cheerfully, 'Well, that was no threat of mutiny, eh? Anyway, a few cuts with a cane never hurt anyone, did it? I lay odds that you kissed the gunner's daughter across the breech of a gun in your youth.'

'Several times, sir.' Bolitho eyed him coldly. 'But I do not recall that it did me any good either!'

Pelham-Martin shrugged and got to his feet. 'That's as may be. Now I am going to lie down for a while. I have a lot of thinking to do.'

Bolitho watched him go, irritated with himself for displaying his concern, and with Pelham-Martin's lack of understanding.

Later as he sat in the small chartroom toying with his midday meal he tried to concentrate his thoughts on the French ships, to go over what he had gleaned from the commodore's brief confidences and then place himself inside the mind of the enemy commander.

There was a rap on the bulkhead and he heard the marine sentry call, 'Midshipman of the watch, sir!'

'Enter!' Without turning Bolitho knew it was Pascoe. In the small cabin he could hear his quick breathing, and when he spoke, the pain in his voice.

'Mr Roth's respects, sir, and may he exercise the quarterdeck nine-pounders?'

Bolitho turned in his chair and studied the boy gravely. Six strokes of the bosun's cane would always be hard to take. Tomlin's arm was like the branch of a tree, and Pascoe's slim body was more bones than flesh. In spite of his better judgement Bolitho had been unable to stay away from the cabin skylight when the brief punishment had been carried out, and between each swish of the cane across the boy's buttocks he had found himself gritting his teeth, and had discovered a strange sense of pride when there had been not one cry of pain or complaint.

He looked pale and tight-lipped, and as their eyes met across the chart table Bolitho could almost feel the hurt like his own.

As captain he had to stay aloof from his officers, but was expected to see and know everything about them. They must trust and follow him, but he should in no way interfere with their duties when it related to matters of discipline. Unless . . . The word hung in his mind like a rebuke.

'You must understand, Mr Pascoe, that discipline is all important in a ship-of-war. Without it there is no order and no control when it really counts. At this moment you are at the bottom of a long and precarious ladder. One day, perhaps sooner than you realize, it will be your turn to award punishment, maybe decide upon a man's very life.'

Pascoe remained silent, his dark eyes fixed on Bolitho's mouth.

'Mr Stepkyne was right. Gun drill is a contest, but it is no game. The whole survival of this ship and every man aboard will depend on her guns. You can navigate a ship from Plymouth to the ends of the earth, and some may say you have done well. But until you have laid her beside the ship of an enemy and the guns are calling the tune, you will know how thin is the margin between success and failure.'

Pascoe said quietly, 'He said my father was a traitor and a rebel, sir. That he'd suffer no argument from another one in his own ship.' His mouth quivered and his eyes filled with angry tears. 'I—I told him that my father was a King's officer, sir. But—but he just laughed at me.' He dropped his eyes. 'So I called him a liar!'

Bolitho gripped the edge of the table. It had happened, and it was his fault. He should have guessed, have remembered that Stepkyne was also from Falmouth, and would certainly have heard about his brother. But to use his knowledge to get his own back on a boy too young and too ignorant of life at sea to understand the full importance of drill was despicable.

He said slowly, 'You took your punishment well, Mr Pascoe.'

'Can I ask you, sir?' Pascoe was staring at him again, his eyes filling his face. 'Was it true what he said?'

Bolitho stood up and walked to the racks of rolled charts. 'Only partly true.' He heard the boy sob behind him and added, 'He had his own reasons for acting as he did, but of one thing I can assure you. He was a brave man. One you'd have been proud to know.' He turned and added, 'And I know he would have been proud of you, too.'

Pascoe clenched his fists at his sides. 'I was told . . .' he faltered, floundered for words. 'I was always told . . .' It would not come.

'When we are children we get told many things. As Mr Stepkyne said, you are an officer now and must learn to face reality, no matter in what shape it comes.'

As if from far away Pascoe said brokenly, 'A traitor! He was a *traitor!*'

Bolitho studied him sadly. 'One day you will learn to understand, as I did. I'll tell you about him later, and then perhaps you will not feel so bitter.'

Pascoe shook his head so that his hair fell forward over his eyes.

'No, sir, thank you. I *never* want to know. Never want to hear of him again.'

Bolitho looked away. 'Carry on, Mr Pascoe. My compliments to Mr Roth. He can exercise his guns for one hour.'

As the midshipman hurried from the cabin Bolitho still stared at the closed door. He had failed. Given time he could have repaired some of the damage. He sat down angrily. Could he? It was unlikely, and it was stupid to delude himself. But as he thought of Stepkyne's cold accusations and the boy's tormented features, he knew that he must do something.

When he went on deck to watch the drill he saw Gascoigne

move to Pascoe's side and put one hand on his shoulder. But the boy shook it off and turned away from him. It had gone even deeper than Bolitho had feared.

Inch crossed the deck. 'I am sorry, sir.' He looked miserable.

Bolitho did not know if he was speaking of the boy or of his own new discovery about Bolitho's brother. He kept his face impassive as he replied. 'Then let us exercise the quarter-deck guns, Mr Inch. Otherwise we may all be sorry before we are much older.'

As the whistle shrilled for the drill to commence Bolitho walked to the weather side and stared up at the pendant. Wherever he went, no matter what he did, his brother's memory always seemed to hang over him. And now another, one less able to deal with it, had been damaged even more by what should have been left hidden in time.

Some of the gunners seeing his expression worked even faster at their drill. And Inch who stood with his hands clasped behind him as he had seen Bolitho do so often, watched his face and wondered. He could cope with his own shortcomings now for he knew and recognized them. But Bolitho's frown made him feel uneasy and vaguely apprehensive.

Perhaps it was better not to know your captain beyond his protective aura of command, he thought. A captain must be above ordinary contacts, for without some protection he might be seen as an ordinary man.

Bolitho's voice shattered his thoughts. 'Mr Inch! If you are quite ready to begin, I would suggest that you stand clear of the guns!'

Inch jumped backwards, grinning with something like relief. This was the Bolitho he understood, and he no longer felt quite so vulnerable.

Four weeks later as the *Hyperion* laboured uncomfortably in a light north-easterly the *Abdiel* signalled that her lookouts had at last sighted the island of St Kruis. Bolitho received the news with mixed feelings, and found little consolation in achieving a perfect landfall after crossing several thousand miles of ocean without meeting a single ship, friend or enemy. He knew they could have reached their destination days, even a week, earlier but for Pelham-Martin's infuriating inability to keep to a set plan, his apparent unwillingness to make and act on earlier decisions. Off Trinidad, for instance, the *Abdiel* had sighted a solitary sail hull down on the horizon, and after passing a signal via her to the *Spartan* to rejoin her consorts, Pelham-Martin had ordered an alteration of course to intercept the unknown ship. It had been near dusk as it was, and Bolitho had guessed that the sail belonged to one of the local trading vessels, for it was unlikely that Lequiller would dally so near to a Spanish stronghold.

When they resumed their original course after failing to find the ship, Pelham-Martin's dilatory and hesitant mind had caused yet another long delay while he had drafted a despatch to be carried by the *Spartan*. Not to St Kruis, but far to the south-west, to the Spanish Captain-General at Caracas.

Bolitho had stood beside the desk while Pelham-Martin had sealed the heavy envelope, hoping even to the last that he could make the commodore change his mind.

The *Spartan* was more use probing ahead of her two consorts than carrying some wordy and unnecessary message to the Spanish governor. The Spaniards had never been renowned in Bolitho's experience for keeping silent, and the news would soon spread far and wide that English ships were moving into the area, and there were always spies in plenty to pass such intelligence to the quarter where it would really count.

And unless Pelham-Martin was prepared to fight, with the larger part of his force still days or even weeks away, he was giving away information which could do little but harm.

But about the *Spartan* Pelham-Martin was adamant. 'It is a matter of common courtesy, Bolitho. I know you show little faith or liking when it comes to the Spaniards. But I happen to know that the Captain-General is a man of high birth. A gentleman of the first order.' He had regarded Bolitho with something like pity. 'Wars are not just won by powder and shot, you know. Trust and diplomacy play a vital part.' He had held out the envelope. 'Pass this to *Spartan* and then resume course. Signal *Abdiel* to remain on her present station.'

Captain Farquhar must have been as relieved as he was surprised at his new mission. Almost before the boat had cast off from the *Spartan*'s side to return to *Hyperion* the frigate's sails were spreading and filling and her low hull alive with sudden activity as she went about and headed away from the other ships.

But now at last St Kruis had been reached. As the harsh midday sunlight slowly gave way to the mellow orange glow of evening the *Hyperion*'s own lookout reported sighting the ridge of pointed hills which cut the small island in half from east to west.

Bolitho stood at the quarterdeck rail and raised his glass to study the purple hazy outline as it rose slowly above the darkening horizon. There was not much to know about St Kruis, but what there was he had collected in his mind like a picture on a chart.

It was some twenty miles by fifteen, with a spacious protected bay on the south-east corner. The large anchorage was in fact the main reason for the Dutch seizing the island in the first place. It had been used constantly by pirates and privateers as a base while waiting to dash out on to some unsuspecting West Indiaman or galleon, and the Dutch had occupied the island more from necessity than of the need to extend their colonial possessions.

According to Bolitho's information St Kruis boasted a governor, and some form of defence force to protect the island from attack and to make sure that the mixed population of Dutch overseers and imported slaves could carry on their affairs without interference.

He rested his palms on the rail and looked down at the main deck. Both gangways were crowded with seamen and marines, all peering beyond the slowly corkscrewing bows towards the blurred smudge of land. How strange it must appear to so many of them, he thought. To men used to green fields or town slums, to the crowded world of between decks, or those snatched from their loved ones by the impartial pressgangs, it would seem like another planet. After months at sea on bad food and in all weathers they were coming to a place where their own familiar problems were unknown. The old hands had told them often enough of such islands, but this was a visible part of the sailor's world, which by choice or enforcement they had now joined.

The bare backs and shoulders of the seamen were getting tanned, although some showed savage blisters from working aloft in the relentless glare. But he was thankful that blisters were the worst part of it. With a new ship's company under these conditions many a man's back might have been marred with the cruel scars of the cat.

There was a heavy step at his side and he turned to see the commodore staring along the upper deck, his eyes all but hidden in puckered flesh as he squinted against the dying sunlight.

Bolitho said, 'Unless the wind drops we will anchor tomorrow morning, sir. There is a two-mile shoulder of reefs on the eastern side of the bay and we will have to tack from the south to avoid them.'

Pelham-Martin did not reply immediately. He looked calm and more relaxed than Bolitho had yet seen him, and seemed in good humour.

He said suddenly, 'I have been thinking for some time that all this fuss may be without any justification, Bolitho.' He nodded ponderously. 'Yes, I have been thinking a great deal of late.'

Bolitho kept his lips straight. Pelham-Martin had spent more hours in his cot than on his feet throughout the voyage, and thinking or not, he had often heard his snores through the chartroom partition.

Pelham-Martin continued, 'Lequiller's mission could have been merely a catspaw. To draw more ships from the blockade, from Ushant and Lorient, so that the whole fleet could burst out and make for the English Channel.' He eyed Bolitho cheerfully. 'That would be a slap in the face for Sir Manley, eh? He would never live it down!'

Bolitho shrugged. 'I think it unlikely, sir.'

The smile vanished. 'Oh, you never see these things properly. It needs vision, Bolitho. Vision and an understanding of men's minds!'

'Yes, sir.'

Pelham-Martin glared at him. 'If I had listened to you we would have been involved with goodness knows what by now.'

'Deck there! *Abdiel*'s going about, sir!'

Pelham-Martin snapped, 'If he asks permission to enter harbour tonight, tell him it is denied!' He walked with heavy tread towards the poop ladder. 'We will enter together, with my flag leading.' Over his massive shoulder he added irritably, 'Frigate captains! Damned young puppies, I'd call them!'

Bolitho smiled grimly. Captain Pring of the *Abdiel* could just manage to reach an anchorage in spite of the fading daylight. If *Hyperion*'s stores and water supplies were low, his must be almost completely gone. And he would know that once the two-decker had dropped anchor she would take precedence over all his own requirements. Bolitho could recall without effort an occasion when he had commanded a thirty-two gun frigate and had been made to idle outside port while three ships of the line anchored and stripped the local merchants and chandlers bare before he was allowed to take his pick of the frugal remains.

Midshipman Gascoigne was already in the mizzen shrouds, his glass on the distant frigate. As she swung gracefully across the wind her topsails caught the sunset, so that the straining sails shone like pink seashells.

Some of the seamen on the quarterdeck had heard the commodore's last remarks and were grinning as *Abdiel*'s flags broke from her yards.

An old gun captain with a pigtail down to his waist growled, 'Serve 'em roight, I says! Let 'em bide their time an' give us a chance with they coloured lassies!'

'*Abdiel* to *Hyperion*. Gunfire bearing west by north.'

Gascoigne's voice reached many of the men on the gangways and a great murmur of excitement and surprise made the commodore pause at the top of the poop ladder as if he was suffering a seizure.

Bolitho snapped, 'Acknowledge!' To Pelham-Martin he called, 'It must be an attack on the harbour, sir!'

'*Abdiel* requests permission to make more sail, sir!' Gascoigne's eyes flitted between his captain and the commodore's portly figure framed against the darkening sky.

Pelham-Martin shook his head. 'Denied!' He almost fell down the last two steps in his haste to reach Bolitho's side. '*Denied!*' He was shouting, and seemed more angry than anything else.

Bolitho said, 'I agree, sir. Ships powerful enough to attack a defended harbour would make short work of her frail timbers.' He held back at what he was really thinking. That if *Spartan* was still in company things might have been very different. Two fast frigates swooping in from the open sea could cause some havoc before taking advantage of the growing darkness. But alone it was asking too much of *Abdiel*'s captain, and it would take *Hyperion* hours to reach a position of any advantage. By which time it would be dark and too hazardous to close the land.

Pelham-Martin spoke rapidly. 'Signal *Abdiel* to take station to windward.' He watched the flags dashing aloft. 'I must think.' He rubbed one hand across his face. '*I must think!*'

'*Abdiel*'s acknowledged, sir!'

Bolitho saw the frigate's yards bracing round as she started to swing back towards the *Hyperion*'s quarter. He could imagine her captain's disappointment. He said, 'We can work to the sou'-west, sir. By first light we will be in a better position to surprise the attackers.'

Pelham-Martin seemed to realize that countless eyes were staring up at him from the crowded main deck. 'Get those bloody people to work! I'll not be gaped at by a lot of damned idlers!'

Bolitho heard the sudden air of activity and bellow of orders. Pelham-Martin was just filling in time. The emotions which flooded across his face were proof enough of his inner confusion.

He said in a more controlled tone, '*Indomitable* and *Hermes* might be here within days. With their support I can give a better account, eh?'

Bolitho eyed him gravely. 'They could just as easily be delayed for weeks, sir. We cannot take the chance, or the risk.'

'Chance? Risk?' Pelham-Martin was speaking in a fierce whisper. 'It is *my* head on the block! If I close and give battle and we are overwhelmed, what then, eh?'

Bolitho hardened his voice. 'If we do not, sir, then we could lose the island. Our ships would not have to be beaten in battle. They could be starved and parched into submission!'

Pelham-Martin searched his face, his expression both desperate and pleading. 'We can sail for Caracas. The Spanish might have ships to assist us.'

'It would take too long, sir, even if the Dons have ships there and are willing to help us. By that time Lequiller will have taken St Kruis, and it would need a fleet to drive him out, and at a great cost.'

The commodore swung away angrily. 'Lequiller! That's all you think about! It might not even be him!'

Bolitho said coldly, 'I don't think there is much doubt about that, sir.'

'Well, if you hadn't let him slip through your fingers, if you'd held fast instead of weighing anchor, all this might never have happened.'

'And let those prisoners hang, sir?' Bolitho watched the massive shoulders tense. 'Is that what I *should* have done?'

Pelham-Martin faced him again. 'I am sorry. I was over-wrought.' He spread his hands. 'But what can I do with only one ship of any size?'

'You have no choice, sir.' He kept his voice quiet, but could not hide his anger. 'You can fight, or you can remain a spectator. But if you decide the latter, the enemy will know that he can do as he likes. And our friends here will also know it.'

Pelham-Martin looked at him, his face in shadow as the sun's dying rays disappeared beyond the horizon like the tails of a comet. 'Very well.' He still waited, as if listening to his own words. 'I will do as you suggest. But if we fail, Bolitho, I will not suffer the consequences alone.' He turned and walked aft to the cabin.

Bolitho stared after him, his face set in a frown. If we fail there will be nobody left to argue the rights or wrongs of it, he thought bitterly.

Then he sought out Inch's lanky shape by the rail. 'Mr Inch, show a shaded stern lantern for *Abdiel*'s benefit. Then you may take in the courses and reef down for the night.' He listened to Inch passing his orders and raised his glass to peer beyond the dark mass of rigging and shrouds.

The island had vanished in the gloom, but so too had any sort of gun flashes. The enemy would have to wait for dawn now.

Inch came aft at the trot. 'Anything else, sir?' He sounded breathless.

'See that our people eat well. We may have to forgo breakfast tomorrow.'

Then he crossed to the weather side and watched the frigate's ghostly outline until she, too, was hidden from sight.

7. Action This Day

BOLITHO closed the chartroom door and walked swiftly on to the quarterdeck, pausing only beside the dimly lit compass to see that the ship's head was still pointing almost due north. For most of the night the preparations for battle had gone on without a let up, until as satisfied as he could be Bolitho had called a halt, and the hands, tense but exhausted, had curled up beside their guns for a few hours' rest.

As he crossed the quarterdeck Bolitho felt the light breeze cold and clammy through his open shirt, and wondered how long it would hold when the sun lifted above the horizon once more.

Inch said, 'Good morning, sir.'

Bolitho stared at his pale shape and nodded. 'You may load and run out now, but pass the word for as little noise as possible.'

As Inch craned over the rail to pass his orders he looked up towards the sky. It was much lighter than when he had been on deck half an hour earlier. Now he could see the tightly spread nets which Tomlin and his men had hauled above the decks during the night to protect the gunners from falling spars, when before they had been merged with the sky. Towards the eastern horizon the last stars had vanished, and some small, isolated clouds had their bellies touched with the colour of salmon pink.

He took several deep breaths and tried to ignore the squeak of trucks and the dull thuds of guns being hauled up to the open ports. Unlike his men, he had not slept, and even during the last half hour he had filled in his time by making himself shave by the light of a small lantern. He had twice cut himself, so great was his inner tension, but he had known that if he did not occupy himself fully his nerves would be in an even worse state. It was always the same. The doubts and anxieties, the fear of failure and the dread of mutilation with its attendant horrors under the surgeon's knife, all these things lurked at the back of his mind like spectres, so that as he shaved he had needed all his strength to hold the razor steady.

Now the waiting was almost done. There, black across the bows and stretching away on either hand was the island, and he no longer needed a glass to see the faint necklace of white feathers which marked the sea's breaking over the reefs.

Hyperion was close hauled on the starboard tack with her topsails and topgallants braced hard round to take maximum advantage of the low wind. All the courses were clewed up, for these large sails were always a fire risk once the fighting started. Inch straightened his back as a voice called up from the main deck.

'All run out, sir.'

Like Bolitho and the other officers he was stripped to shirt and trousers, and there was a slight tremor in his voice which could have been either excitement or because of the chill air.

'Very well. Send a midshipman to inform the commodore.'

Several times while he had been shaving Bolitho had paused to listen through the partition. But for once he had heard no gentle snores. Pelham-Martin must have been lying in his cot fretting and pondering, without even the ship's affairs to occupy his mind.

Gossett blew his nose into a large red handkerchief, the noise shattering the silence like a musket shot. He muttered humbly, 'Pardon, sir.'

Bolitho smiled. 'We may need all your wind for the sails later on.'

Some of the marines at the nettings chuckled, and Bolitho was glad they could not yet see his face.

Inch said, 'What are the Frogs up to, I wonder?'

'They are quiet enough at present.' Bolitho watched the small, white-crested waves cruising slowly down on the ship's weather beam. He could see them stretching away much further now, and when he shifted his eyes forward he saw that the land had taken on a harder outline, so that it appeared to be right on top of the bows. It was a normal illusion at first light, but nevertheless they should sight something soon.

Hyperion was driving as close to the reefs as she dare to give maximum advantage when the time came to turn and head either across or into the bay itself.

A lot depended on the island's defences. No ship was a match for a well-sighted shore battery, but you could never be sure. Bolitho recalled how he and Tomlin had been the first men up the cliff when he had successfully overpowered the French battery at Cozar in the Mediterranean. It *could* be done with enough determination.

Inch called, 'Good morning, sir!'

The commodore walked stiffly to the rail and sniffed the air. Bolitho studied him in the strange half-light. He was wearing a long blue watch coat which came almost to his ankles, and was without a hat or mark of rank of any sort.

He would be sweating hard when the sun reached him, he thought. He felt a touch of compassion when he considered the reason for this strange garb. Pelham-Martin was a very large man, a big enough target for some French marksmen without drawing attention to himself by showing his proper uniform.

He said quietly, 'Soon now, sir. The wind is steady from the nor'-east, and until we close right inshore we shall have enough power in our sails.'

Pelham-Martin sank his small head firmly into his collar. 'Maybe. I don't know, I'm sure.' He moved slightly to one side and lapsed once more into silence.

Bolitho was about to speak to Inch when he saw the lieutenant's eyes light up like twin furnaces. Even as he swung round he heard a violent explosion rumble across the open water and saw a tall column of flames leaping skyward, the sparks breaking away and rising hundreds of feet in the air.

Inch gasped, 'A ship! She's afire!'

Bolitho narrowed his eyes, picturing for the hundredth time the bay as he had expected it would look. The ship which was now burning so fiercely above her fiery reflection was a small one, and somewhere on the *Hyperion*'s starboard bow.

There were shots, too, puny and sporadic, and he guessed the enemy were using boats to slip closer inshore under cover of the remaining darkness. Maybe the ship had been fired by accident, or perhaps the raiders just wanted to inflict as much damage as they could before hauling off again.

Another explosion roared dully over the water, but this time there was no flash, nor any indication of bearing or distance.

'Ah, 'ere she comes!' Gossett lifted his arm as the sun raised itself slowly above the sea's edge, thrusting shadows aside and painting the endless patterns of wave crests with pale gold.

'Deck there! Two ships on th' lee bow!' A startled cry and then, 'Belay that! Thar's another close inshore, sir!'

But Bolitho could see them well enough now. In the Caribbean there was little break between night and day, and already the sunlight had changed the island's rough outline into purple and green, with a sliver of gold to mark the crest of the nearest hilltop at the far side of the bay.

The first two were ships of the line, sailing slowly on the opposite tack, almost at right angles to his own course and barely two miles clear. The third looked like a frigate, and a quick glance at her sails told him she was anchored close under the western headland.

Anchored? His mind brushed away doubts and apprehension as the realization came to him. The enemy must have fired the anchored ship inside the bay as a diversion.

On the opposite side of the protected anchorage where the main shore battery was said to be sited, the attackers had launched a full-scale assault, the defenders momentarily distracted and off guard. In the early hours it would not be too difficult, he thought grimly. It was human enough for men to find comfort from others' misfortunes, even their own comrades', if it meant being spared from attack.

And while the awakened gunners watched from their battery walls, the raiders would have landed stealthily from boats and scaled the headland from the other side.

Pelham-Martin said in a tight voice, 'They have sighted us!'

The leading French ship was already signalling her consort but as the frail sunlight lifted over the sheltered water of the bay and across the white painted houses at the far end, neither vessel showed any sign of altering direction or purpose. The first shock of seeing the *Hyperion*'s topsails emerging from the half light must have been eased when the enemy realized she was accompanied by a solitary frigate.

Bolitho felt the sun's weak rays touching his cheek. He

could continue across the enemy's bows and into the bay, but if the French seized the battery their own ships could sail after him with impunity. Yet if he stayed clear, they would withdraw into the bay anyway and prevent even a large force from following.

He glanced at the commodore, but he was still staring at the French ships, his face a mask of indecision.

Inch murmured, 'Two seventy-fours, sir.' He, too, glanced at Pelham-Martin before adding, 'If they reach the other side of the bay they'll have the advantage, sir.'

Bolitho saw some of the seamen by the braces craning to stare at the French ships. They looked perfect and unmarked by the island's gunners, and seemed all the more menacing because of their slow approach. Sunlight glanced on levelled telescopes from the leading ship's poop, and here and there a figure moved or a pendant whipped out from a masthead as if lifted by some force of its own.

But otherwise the ships glided across the small whitecapped waves slowly and unhurriedly, until it seemed as if *Hyperion*'s jib boom would lock into the leading Frenchman's like two mammoths offering their tusks for combat.

On the main deck, the tension was almost a physical thing. At every open port the men crouched at the guns, their naked backs shining with sweat while they waited for the first hardening line as a target crossed their sights. Each hatch was guarded by a marine, and aloft in the tops the marksmen and swivel gunners licked their lips and screwed up their eyes as they sought out their opposite numbers across the shortening range.

Pelham-Martin cleared his throat. 'What do you intend?'

Bolitho relaxed slightly. He could feel the sweat running down his chest and the heart's steady beat against his ribs. The question was like the opening of a dam. The removal of a great weight. For one moment he had feared Pelham-Martin's nerve had failed and that he would order an immediate withdrawal. Or worse, that he would drive at full speed into the bay, where the ship could be pounded to fragments at the enemy's leisure.

'We will cross the enemy's bows, sir.' He kept his eye on the leading ship. The first sign of extra sail and the *Hyperion* would never be in time. It would mean either a collision or he would have to wear ship and present an unprotected stern to a full French broadside.

Pelham-Martin nodded. 'And into the bay?'

'No, sir.' He swung round sharply. 'Starboard a point Mr Gossett!' In a quieter tone he continued, 'We will wear ship once we pass her and engage her larboard side.' He watched his words playing havoc on the commodore's face. 'With luck we can then cross her stern and pass between both ships. It will mean losing the wind-gage, but we can give both of them a good raking as we come through.' He grinned, and could feel his lips drying with the effort. But Pelham-Martin *had* to understand. If he tried to change the manœuvre halfway through it would be disastrous. He looked again at the French ships. Half a mile at the most now separated the leading one from his guns. It would be disastrous anyway if the enemy dismasted him at the first encounter.

The French frigate was still anchored, and by using a glass Bolitho could see her boats plying back and forth to the headland, and when he saw the smoke rising from the top of the slope he knew that the loud explosion must have been some sort of bomb to breach the battery wall or ignite a magazine.

He felt Pelham-Martin's hand on his arm. 'Sir?'

The commodore said, 'Signal *Abdiel* to engage the frigate!' He wriggled his shoulders beneath the heavy coat. '*Well?*'

'I suggest she stays to windward, sir. Until we start our attack. If they suspect for one moment we are not trying to seek the protection of the harbour, I fear we may be out-manœuvred.'

'Yes.' Pelham-Martin stared fixedly at some point above the headland. 'Quite so.'

Bolitho tore his eyes away and hurried to the opposite side to watch the leading ship. He thought suddenly of something Winstanley had said when he had first gone aboard *Indomitable* to meet the commodore. *He'll need you before we're done.* As his senior captain Winstanley must have known Pelham-Martin's weaknesses better than anyone. The commodore surely owed his rank to influence, or perhaps he had just been unfortunate at being available for the appointment when he had not the experience to back up his authority.

A dull bang echoed across the water and Bolitho looked up as a round hole appeared suddenly in the fore topsail. The Frenchman had used a bowchaser for a ranging shot. He turned to watch as a thin feather of spray lifted above the sea far out on the weather beam.

He said, 'Pass the word to the lower gundeck of my intention, Mr Inch.' As a midshipman darted to the ladder he snapped, '*Walk*, Mr Penrose!' The boy turned and blushed. 'There may be a French telescope watching your feet, so take your time!'

There was another bang, and this time the ball slammed hard alongside the larboard bow, throwing spray high above the nettings and making some of the men at the headsail sheet duck down with alarm.

Bolitho called, 'Keep those hands out of sight on the main deck, Mr Stepkyne! We will wear ship in a moment, but I don't want a single man to lay his hand on anything until I give the order!'

He saw Stepkyne nod and turn back to watch the enemy. He wondered what Pascoe was doing at his station on the lower gundeck, and was torn between wanting him within reach and leaving him below behind the additional thickness of the hull.

Strangely, it was usually the older men who took the waiting badly, he thought. The youngsters and the untried were too awed or too frightened to think clearly about anything. Only when it was all over and the sounds and sights were branded into their memories did they start to think about the next action, and the one after that.

The next ball from the Frenchman's bowchaser smashed into the boat tier, lifting the launch bodily from its chocks and filling the air with wood splinters. Three men at the starboard bulwark fell kicking and whimpering, one almost transfixed by a jagged spear of planking.

Bolitho called, 'Send some more hands to the weather forebrace, Mr Stepkyne!' He saw the lieutenant open his mouth as if to shout back at him and then turn away to pass the order, his face angry and resentful.

As yet another shot crashed into the ship's side Bolitho found time to sympathize with Stepkyne's feelings. To keep taking these carefully aimed shots without firing back was almost more than anyone could stand. But if he allowed any sort of reprisal the French commander might immediately guess his true intention while there was still time to alter course.

Gossett murmured, 'The Frogs are sailin' as close to the wind as they can, sir.' He cursed as a ball shrieked over the nettings and ricocheted across the wave crests far abeam. 'If he tries to tack 'e'll be in irons!'

Bolitho saw the wounded seamen being dragged towards the main hatch, their blood marking every foot of the journey, while some of the gunners turned to stare, their faces stiff and unreal.

Closer and closer, until the leading enemy ship was a mere cable's length off the larboard bow.

Bolitho gripped his hands behind him until the pain steadied his racing thoughts. He could wait no longer. At any second now a well-aimed ball, or even a random one might bring down a vital spar or cripple his ship before he could make his turn.

Without looking at Gossett he snapped, 'Starboard your helm!' As the spokes began to squeak over he cupped his hands and yelled, 'Wear ship! Hands to the braces!'

He saw the sails' long shadows sweeping above the crouching gunners, heard the whine of blocks and the frantic stamp of bare feet as the waiting men threw themselves back on the braces, and then, slowly at first, the ship began to swing round towards the Frenchmen.

For a second or two longer he thought he had acted too soon, that both ships would meet head on, but as the yards steadied and the canvas bucked and filled overhead he saw the other two-decker drifting across the larboard bow, her masts almost in line as she drove towards him on the opposite tack.

As Gossett had observed, the enemy could not regain the advantage without turning directly upwind, nor could she swing away unless her captain was prepared to receive *Hyperion*'s broadside through her stern.

Bolitho shouted, 'Full broadside, Mr Stepkyne!'

He saw the gun captains crouching back from their breeches, the trigger lines bar taut as they squinted through the open ports and their crews waited with handspikes to traverse or elevate as required.

A ball smashed through the larboard gangway and a man screamed like a tortured animal. But Bolitho did not even hear it. He was watching the oncoming ship through narrowed eyes, the men around him and the commodore excluded from his thoughts as he saw the *Hyperion*'s topgallants cast a distorted pattern of shadows across the Frenchman's bows.

He raised his hand. 'On the uproll!' He paused, feeling the dryness in his throat like sand. '*Fire!*'

The crash of the *Hyperion*'s broadside was like a hundred thunderstorms, and while the whole ship staggered as if driving ashore, the enemy's hull was completely blotted out in a billowing wall of smoke.

Across some fifty yards of water the effect of the broadside must have been like an avalanche, Bolitho thought wildly. He could see men's mouths opening and yelling, but as yet could hear nothing. The sharper, ear-probing cracks of the quarterdeck nine-pounders had rendered thought and hearing almost too painful to bear. Then above the mounting bank of drifting smoke he saw the Frenchman's yards edging round and then halting as the topsails quivered and shook in the face of the wind.

As his hearing returned he heard his gun captains shouting from every side, and saw Dawson's marines stepping up to the nettings, their muskets lifting to their shoulders as if on parade. Then as Dawson dropped his sword the muskets fired as one, the shots going somewhere beyond the smoke to add to the confusion.

Stepkyne was striding aft along the maindeck guns, his hands chopping the air as if to restrain his men. 'Stop your vents! Sponge out!' He paused to knock down a man's arm. '*Sponge out*, I said, damn you!' He seized the dazed seaman by the wrist. 'Do you want the gun to explode in your bloody face?' Then he strode on. 'Jump to it! Load and run out!'

At each gun the men worked as if in a trance, conscious only of the drill they had learned under their captain's watchful eye and of the towering pyramid of sails which now rose high above the larboard gangway, and the flapping Tricolour which seemed barely yards away.

Bolitho shouted, 'Fire as you bear!' He stepped back choking as the guns roared out again, the smoke and flames darting from the ship's side and making the water between the two vessels as dark as night.

Then the French ship fired, her full broadside rippling down her side from bow to stern in a double line of darting orange tongues.

Bolitho felt the shrieking balls scything through shrouds and sails, and the harder, jarring thuds as some struck deep into the hull itself.

A seaman, apparently unmarked, fell through the smoke from the maintop and bounced twice on the taut nets before rolling lifelessly over the edge and into the sea alongside.

A gun captain behind him was bellowing above the crash of cannon fire and the sporadic bark of muskets, his eyes white in his powder-stained face as he coaxed and pushed his men to the tackle falls.

'Run out, you idle buggers! Us'll give they sods a quiltin'!'

Then he jerked his trigger line and the nine-pounder hurled itself inboard again, the black muzzle streaming smoke even as the men threw themselves forward to the task of sponging and reloading.

Through the drifting curtain of smoke the powder monkeys ran like dazed puppets, dropping their cartridges and scampering back to the hatchways with hardly a glance to left or right.

Pelham-Martin was still by the rail, his heavy coat speckled with powder ash and splintered paintwork. He was staring at the French ship's masts, seemingly mesmerized by the nearness of death as musket balls hammered the deck around him and a seaman was hurled down the poop ladder, blood gushing from his mouth and choking his screams as he fell.

Inch shouted, 'We'll be past her soon, sir!' His eyes were streaming as he peered through the smoke to seek out the next French ship. Then he pointed wildly, his teeth shining in his grimy face. 'Her mizzen's going!' He waved his arms in the air and turned to see if Gossett had heard. 'There it goes!'

The Frenchman's mizzen was indeed falling. A lucky shot must have struck it solidly within some ten feet of the deck, for as Bolitho clung to the nettings to see better he saw stays and shrouds parting like cotton while the whole mast, spars and wildly flapping canvas staggered, swung momentarily enmeshed in the tangle of rigging, before pitching down into the smoke.

But the enemy was still firing, and when Bolitho strained his eyes aloft he saw that the *Hyperion*'s topsails were little more than remnants. Even as he watched, the main royal stay parted with the sound of a pistol shot, and when men swarmed aloft to splice another in its place others were falling, dead or wounded, on to the nets below as the hidden French marksmen kept up a murderous fire across the smoke.

The severed mizzen must have fallen close alongside the enemy's quarter, for as more long orange tongues darted through the smoke and one of the twelve-pounders lifted drunkenly before smashing down across two of its crew, the French ship's blurred outline shortened, and slowly and inexorably she began to turn away.

Gossett was yelling hoarsely, 'The mizzen must be actin' as a sea anchor!' He was pounding the shoulder of one of the helmsmen. 'By God, there's 'ope yet!'

Bolitho knew what he meant. As he ran to the rail seeking out the scarlet shape of Lieutenant Hicks on the forecastle he knew that once the enemy had cut loose the trailing mass of wreckage he would still be ready enough to give battle.

He snatched Inch's speaking trumpet and yelled, 'The larboard carronade! Fire as you bear!'

He imagined that the marine lieutenant was waving his hat, but at that instant the enemy fired another ragged broadside, some of the balls smashing through open ports, others hammering the hull or whipping like shrieking demons overhead.

But through the pall of smoke he heard one resonant explosion, and felt it transmit itself from bow to poop as the fat, crouching carronade hurled its giant sixty-eight pound ball towards the enemy's stern.

As a freak down-eddy pushed the fog aside Bolitho saw the massive ball explode. Hicks had been too eager or too excited, and instead of passing through the enemy's stern windows and along the full length of her lower gundeck it had struck just below her quarterdeck nettings. There was a bright flash, and as the ball exploded and released its closely packed charge of grape he heard screams and terrified cries as a complete section of bulwark collapsed like so much boxwood.

Gossett roared, 'That showed 'em! The old *Smasher*'s taken the wind out o' their guts!'

Bolitho said, 'Her steering seems to be damaged, or else that shot cut down most of her officers.' He felt a musket ball pluck at his shirt with no more insistence than the touch of a child's fingers, and behind him a seaman screamed in agony and rolled away from his gun, his hands clawing into his stomach as the blood spattered across the planking and the men around him.

The whole ship seemed to be in the grip of fighting madness. Men worked at their guns, wild-eyed and so dazed by the din of battle and the awful cries of the wounded that most of them had lost all sense of time or reason. Some gun captains had to use their fists to drive their men through the changeless pattern of loading, running out and firing, otherwise they would have fired at empty sea or hauled a gun back to its port still unloaded.

'Cease firing!' Bolitho gripped the rail and waited as the last few shots roared from the lower battery. The French ship had all but vanished down wind, with only her topgallants showing above the attendant curtain of smoke.

Inch said between his teeth, 'The second one's going about, sir!'

Bolitho nodded, watching the two-decker's yards swinging round as she turned lazily to starboard. The *Hyperion* had already started her second turn, but now instead of passing between the two ships she would—if the Frenchman intended to maintain his new course—be running parallel with the enemy. Above his head the torn sails lifted and cracked in a sudden gust as with tired dignity the *Hyperion* tilted to the wind and then settled on her course away from the land.

Bolitho shouted, 'Starboard battery ready!' He saw Stepkyne signalling sharply to some of the men from the other side and ordering them to the starboard guns.

Pelham-Martin lifted one hand to his face and then stared at his fingers as if surprised he was still alive. To Bolitho he muttered tightly, 'This one'll not be so slow in returning fire!'

Bolitho looked at him steadily. 'We shall see, sir.'

Then he jerked round as more gunfire rolled through the haze of smoke, and he guessed that the *Abdiel* was closing with the enemy frigate.

Inch called, 'We're overhauling him, sir!'

In spite of her torn canvas the old *Hyperion* was doing just that. Maybe the French captain had waited too long to tack or perhaps he had been unable to accept that the solitary two-decker would stand and fight after the first savage encounter. The jib boom was already passing the Frenchman's larboard quarter with less than thirty yards between them. Above the familiar horseshoe shaped stern with its gilded scrollwork and the name *Emeraude* Bolitho could see the flash of sunlight on levelled weapons and the occasional stab of musket fire.

But there was a growing froth beneath her counter, and even as he watched he saw her lean slightly away, gathering wind to her straining sails as she started to pull ahead with increasing power.

Inch muttered, 'We'll not catch her, sir. If she can retake the wind-gage she can come at us again *and* cover her consort until *she* is ready to fight, too!'

Bolitho ignored him. 'Mr Gossett! Helm a'lee!' He held up his hand. '*Easy* now! Steady!'

He saw the *Hyperion*'s bowsprit swing very slightly to windward, so that for a few moments she exposed her full broadside to the French ship's quarter.

'As you bear, Mr Stepkyne!' He sliced downwards with his hand. '*Now!*'

Stepkyne ran down the length of the main deck, pausing by each gun captain just long enough to watch the enemy through the port.

And down the *Hyperion*'s side the guns fired, two by two, the balls smashing into the enemy's quarter and waterline in an unhurried and merciless bombardment.

Someone aboard the *Emeraude* was keeping his head, for she was already turning, pivoting round to keep station on her attacker, so that once more they were drawing parallel.

Then she fired, and along the *Hyperion*'s starboard side the mass of iron smashed and thundered into the stout timbers or screamed through gunports to cause havoc and murder amongst the press of men within.

Through the unending haze Bolitho could see the first ship's topmasts, the bright whip of her masthead pendant as she tacked round and headed back towards the fray, her bow-chasers already barking viciously, although whether the shots were hitting or passing overhead and hitting her own consort it was impossible to determine.

Pelham-Martin shouted, 'If she gets to grips with us they'll smash us from either beam!' He swung round, his eyes wild. 'In the name of God, why did I listen to *you*?'

Bolitho caught a seaman as he slumped back from the nettings, blood already pumping from his chest. To a white-faced midshipman he snapped, 'Here, Mr Penrose! Help this fellow to the main deck!'

Inch was by his side again. 'This one'll stand off until his friend arrives.' He winced as a ball ploughed a deep furrow along the starboard gangway and hurled a corpse aside in two halves.

'If we let him, Mr Inch!' Bolitho pointed at the other ship's bows. 'Larboard your helm! We'll force him to close with us.'

Very slowly, for her sails were almost in shreds, the *Hyperion* responded to the rudder's thrust. Further and further until the bowsprit seemed to be rising high above the enemy's deck as if to drive straight through her foremast shrouds.

Inch watched in silence as again the main deck guns hurled themselves inboard on their tackles, the figures around them darting through the funnelled smoke, their naked bodies black with powder and shining with sweat as they struggled to obey their officers.

But the salvos were more ragged and less well aimed, and the delay between each shot was growing longer. By comparison the enemy seemed to be firing rapidly and with greater accuracy, and the spread nets above the gunners were jumping madly with severed cordage and ripped sailcloth. And there were more than a dozen bodies across the nets, too. Some limp and jerking to the vibrating crash of gunfire, others twisting and crying out like trapped birds in a snare while they struggled and died unheard and unheeded.

Captain Dawson was waving his sword and yelling to his

men in the tops. The marines were shooting as rapidly as before, and here and there a man would drop from the enemy's rigging as proof of their accuracy. Even when a marine fell dead or wounded another would step up to fill his place, while Munro, the huge sergeant, would call out the timing for loading and aiming, beating the air with his half-pike as Bolitho had seen him do at the daily drills since leaving Plymouth.

The French captain was not it seemed prepared to accept the new challenge, but with yards swinging round he steered his ship away yet again, until he had the wind immediately under his stern.

Hicks had fired his other carronade, but again it was a poor shot. It struck the enemy's side and burst below the main deck gunports to leave a ragged gash in the shape of a giant star.

Bolitho looked down at his own men and bit his lip until the skin almost broke. The heart was going out of them. They had acted and fought better than he had dared hope, but it could not go on like this.

A great chorus of voices made him look up, and with sick horror he saw the main topgallant and royal mast stagger and then bow drunkenly to larboard before ripping through sails and men alike on its way to the deck.

He heard Tomlin's voice bellowing above the din, saw axes flashing in the sunlight, and as if in a dream watched a wild-eyed seaman, naked but for a strip of canvas around his loins, run to the main shrouds and swarm up the ratlines like a monkey, Pelham-Martin's pendant trailing behind him as he scampered aloft to replace it.

The commodore murmured thickly, 'My God! Oh, my merciful God!'

Reluctantly the broken spar slithered free from the gangway and bobbed down the ship's side, a dead topman still tangled in the rigging, his mouth wide in a last cry of damnation or protest.

Midshipman Gascoigne was tying a piece of rag around his wrist, his face pale but determined as he watched the blood seeping over his fingers. Amidst the smoke and death, the great patches of blood and whimpering wounded, only

Pelham-Martin seemed unharmed and immovable. In his heavy coat he looked more like a big rock than a mere human, and his face was a mask which betrayed little of the man within. Perhaps he was beyond fear or resignation, Bolitho thought dully. Unable to move, he was just standing there waiting to see the end of his hopes, the destruction of himself and all about him.

Bolitho stood stockstill as a figure emerged from the aft hatchway and stepped over the spread-eagled marine. It was Midshipman Pascoe, his shirt open to the waist, his hair plastered across his forehead as he glanced round, stunned perhaps by the carnage and confusion on every hand. Then he lifted his chin and walked aft to the quarterdeck ladder.

Inch saw him and yelled, 'What is it?'

Pascoe replied, 'Mr Beauclerk's respects, sir, and he wishes you to know that Mr Lang has been wounded.'

Beauclerk was the fifth and junior lieutenant. It was too much of a task to control those thirty twenty-four pounders singlehanded.

Bolitho shouted, 'Mr Roth! Go and take charge below!'

As the lieutenant ran for the ladder he beckoned to the boy. 'Are you all right, lad?'

Pascoe looked at him vaguely and then pushed the hair from his eyes. 'Aye, sir.' He shuddered, as if suddenly ice cold. 'I think so.'

A musket ball, almost spent, struck the deck at his feet, and he would have fallen but for Bolitho's hand.

'Stay with me, lad.' Bolitho held on to his arm, feeling its thinness and the cold clamminess of fear.

The boy looked round, his eyes very bright. 'Is it nearly over, sir?'

Overhead another halyard snapped and a heavy block clanged across a gun breech so that a seaman yelled up at the smoke, cursing and mouthing meaningless words, until the gun fired and he became part of the panorama again.

Bolitho pulled him towards the hammock nettings. 'Not yet, my lad! Not yet!' He showed his teeth to hide his own despair. In a moment they would be at close quarters again with two ships. No matter how much damage they inflicted on them, the end would be certain.

'Captain, sir!' Inch came striding through the smoke. 'The enemy's hauling off!' He pointed wildly. 'Look, sir! They're both making more sail!'

Bolitho climbed into the mizzen shrouds, his limbs feeling like lead. But it was true. Both ships were turning away, and with the wind astern were already drawing steadily clear, the smoke swirling behind them like an attendant sea mist.

And as a shaft of sunlight cut across the water he saw the frigate, too, was under way, her yards braced round, her sails pockmarked and blackened to show *Abdiel*'s efforts to defeat her.

He snatched a glass and trained it across the quarterdeck as the *Abdiel* emerged hesitantly through the billowing curtain of smoke. All her masts were intact, but the hull was scarred in several places as she idled into the pale sunshine.

Bolitho was already peering past the little frigate, and as the glass steadied beyond a curving green headland he thought for a moment he had taken leave of his reason.

There was another ship rounding the spur of land, her sails shining and very white in the morning sun, her tall side throwing back the sea's dancing reflections as she tacked ponderously across the wind before heading towards the *Hyperion*.

Pelham-Martin's voice sounded shaky. '*What is she?*'

Already the *Hyperion*'s seamen were leaving their overheated guns to stand on the gangways and stare at the stately newcomer. Then as the *Abdiel*'s people began to cheer, so too it was carried on by the *Hyperion*, until even the cries of the wounded were lost in the wild chorus of relief and excitement.

Bolitho watched the other ship without lowering his glass. He could see the long tricolour flag at her peak, the ornate gilt-encrusted carving around her poop, and knew that if the *Hyperion* was old, then this one was the most ancient vessel he had yet clapped eyes on.

He replied slowly, 'She's Dutch.' He lowered the glass and added, 'What are your orders, sir?'

Pelham-Martin stared at the Dutch ship as she tacked once more to sail easily under the *Hyperion*'s lee quarter.

'Orders?' He seemed to get a grip on himself. 'Enter harbour.'

Bolitho said slowly, 'Signal *Abdiel* and inform her we will anchor without delay, Mr Gascoigne.' He walked to the opposite side, his head ringing with the cheers, his mind dazed from the closeness of death and defeat.

Inch looked down at Midshipman Pascoe and shook his head. 'Take good heed of this morning. Whatever you do or amount to in later years, you'll never see *his* like again!' Then he strode to the rail and began to rally the remnants of his topmen.

Bolitho did not hear Inch's words, nor did he see the look in the boy's eyes. He was watching the strange, outdated ship of the line turning once more to lead them into the bay. But for her arrival . . . he paused and pulled out his watch. For a moment he thought it had stopped, but after another glance he returned it to his pocket. *One hour.* That was all it had taken. Yet it had seemed ten times that long.

He made himself look down at the main deck as the surgeon and his bloodstained assistants emerged to collect the rest of the wounded. So what must it seem like to his men?

With a sigh he pushed his weary body away from the rail and turned towards the poop. He saw the boy watching him, his dark eyes filled with something like wonder.

'See, Mr Pascoe, you can never be sure, can you?' He smiled and walked aft to consult with the commodore.

As he passed the nine-pounders along the weather side some of the gunners stood back to grin and wave to him. He could feel his own lips fixed in a smile, and listened to his voice as he answered their excited greetings, like someone on the outside of himself. An onlooker.

But when he reached the poop and looked again at the full length of his command he sensed something else. Scarred and bloodied she might be, but she was still unbroken. In spite of everything, the damage and mutilation, the terrible sounds and nerve-searing bombardment, something had happened.

She was no longer a ship which contained a mixed collection of human beings. For good or bad, she was one with the men who served her, as if the short, fierce fight had welded them all together into an entity of purpose and survival.

He saw the surgeon hurrying towards him and steeled himself for what lay ahead. Men had died in the morning sunlight. How many he did not yet know.

As he looked up at the pitted sails and splintered mast he felt strangely grateful to those unknown dead. It was up to him to ensure their sacrifices were not wasted.

8. News for the Commodore

THE MARINE SENTRY snapped to attention as Bolitho entered the stern cabin and closed the door behind him. He noticed that all the windows were wide open and the deckhead and sides shimmered with countless reflections from the ruffled water beneath the counter. The *Hyperion* rolled gently at her anchor, and when he glanced through one of the quarter windows he saw the nearest headland dancing in a heat haze, green and remote from the sights he had just left on the upper deck.

Through the door of the sleeping cabin he heard Pelham-Martin call, 'Well, what have you to report?'

Bolitho rested his hands on the desk and stared emptily at the clear water below the stern. 'Twenty dead, sir. Twenty more badly wounded.' There seemed little point in mentioning all the others. Flesh wounds and burns, or those who had gone deaf, perhaps permanently, from the crash of gunfire.

'I see.' There were sounds of boxes being dragged across the cabin floor, and then Pelham-Martin strode heavily into the reflected sunlight. 'The wounded you mentioned. Will they recover?'

Bolitho could only stare at him for several seconds. The *Hyperion* had anchored less than thirty minutes earlier, and while he had been supervising the lowering of boats and checking the extent of damage to hull and rigging, the commodore had, it appeared, been attending to more personal details. He was wearing his heavy dress coat, and his white shirt and breeches looked as if they had just arrived from the tailor.

He said at length, 'Splinter wounds mostly, sir. But five of them have lost arms or hands.'

Pelham-Martin eyed him severely. 'Well, I shall have to go ashore and meet the governor of this, er, place.' He shook

124

his shirt cuffs free of the gold-laced sleeves. 'Necessary, I suppose but a damned nuisance all the same.' He looked around the cabin. 'You had better stay here and do what you must to put this ship to rights.' He let his glance rest on Bolitho's torn shirt. 'I would suggest that you make some effort on your own behalf, too!'

Bolitho faced him coldly. 'I consider there are other things more important which need my attention, sir.'

The commodore shrugged. 'It is no use your adopting this attitude. You knew the odds, yet you forced an engagement.'

'If we had been here a week earlier, sir, the battle would never have been necessary, unless on our terms.'

The commodore looked at himself in the bulkhead mirror. 'Maybe.' He swung round violently. 'However, we did manage to drive the French away, and I will see that your part in the affair is mentioned in my report at some later date. But now I will have to leave you. If I am needed you may send a boat to the town.' He walked to the stern windows and leaned out across the sill. 'I must say, it is not at all what I expected.'

Bolitho watched him wearily. It was amazing what a change had come over Pelham-Martin since the battle. Of the desperate, pale-faced commodore in a heavy coat there was no sign at all. He looked calm and unruffled, and was even showing some sort of pleasure at what he saw in the distant town.

Bolitho felt the anger stirring his insides like raw spirit. How could Pelham-Martin be so cool and indifferent just now, when any small sign of sympathy and understanding might be of the greatest value to the men who had fought against such odds? Even without the Dutch ship's timely arrival *Hyperion*'s seamen and marines had more than proved their worth.

He said, 'I will call away the barge for you, sir.'

Pelham-Martin nodded. 'Good. It was lucky it survived. I am surprised you retained all the boats inboard during the action.'

Bolitho looked angrily at the fat shoulders. 'There was little enough wind for us to attack twice our number, sir. To tow boats as well would have been too much. And to cast them adrift . . .' He got no further.

Pelham-Martin thrust himself upright and turned to face him. 'I am not very interested in excuses, Bolitho. Now kindly attend to my barge!'

On the quarterdeck the sun was already intense and blinding, but Bolitho hardly noticed it because of his anger.

Inch said, 'All boats alongside, sir. Mr Tomlin is just rigging canvas air ducts above the hatchways, and I've ordered him to open all ports.' He hesitated, aware of Bolitho's grim features. 'Sir?'

Bolitho looked past him. The Dutch ship was already surrounded by small craft from the shore, while others of all shapes and sizes idled closer to the *Hyperion*, their occupants obviously uncertain whether to come alongside or remain at a discreet distance. The *Hyperion* must present a grim spectacle, he thought bitterly. Shot-scarred and blackened by smoke, with most of her sails too rent and pitted even to furl.

He said, 'Get all hands to work repairing damage, Mr Inch. But first they must be fed. Send an officer and two boats ashore as soon as the commodore has left, and tell him to bring off as much fresh fruit as he can lay hands on. I will arrange for meat and water supplies as soon as I can.'

Inch asked, 'May I say something, sir?'

Bolitho looked at him for the first time. 'Well?'

'Just that we're all lucky to be alive, sir. But for you . . .'

Bolitho turned to watch as Perks, the sailmaker, and his mates completed the grisly task of sewing up the last of the dead men in readiness for burial.

'Some were not so fortunate, Mr Inch.'

Inch shifted from one foot to the other. 'But I'd never have thought that new, untrained men could behave as our people did, sir.'

Bolitho felt some of his anger fading. Inch was so serious, so obviously sincere that it was hard to remain untouched by his concern.

'I agree. They did well.' He paused. 'And so did you.' He shaded his eyes to look at the town. 'Now man the side for the commodore.'

As Inch hurried away he crossed to the nettings and stared idly at the distant huddle of white buildings. Stark against the hillside beyond, they looked like part of Holland, he thought. The first Dutch garrison or settlers must have clung to the memory of their homeland, and even through the shimmering heat haze it was possible to see the tall, pointed rooftops of the larger houses and the flat-fronted dwellings along the waterfront which could have been part of Rotterdam or any Dutch port.

Midshipman Gascoigne caught his eye. 'Signal from *Abdiel*, sir. She lost five killed in the action. No serious damage.'

Bolitho nodded. The heavier French frigate had been more concerned with withdrawing the raiding party and recovering her boats once she had realized the uncertainty of the battle. *Abdiel* had done well, but she had had more than her share of luck.

He said, 'Pass my best wishes to Captain Pring, if you please.'

The tired and grimy seamen fell back as the marines clumped to the entry port and fell into line beside the bosun's mates and sideboys. Bolitho looked down at his own rumpled state. The marines were a strange breed, he thought vaguely. Just two hours ago they had been on the quarterdeck and in the tops shooting and yelling, as wild and desperate as all the rest. Now, as Lieutenant Hicks stood at one end of the front rank to check the dressing it was very hard to believe they had been in action at all.

He heard Gossett mutter to someone behind him, 'The bullocks'll always survive so long as they've got their pipe-clay an' their bloody boots with 'em!' But there was genuine admiration in his tone.

Pelham-Martin walked slowly into the sunlight adjusting his cocked hat. Bolitho watched him without emotion. The commodore did not seem to see anyone about him, and when he walked over a wide patch of dried blood where a man had died within feet of him he did not even falter.

Pelham-Martin said, 'When will you have a new topmast swayed up?'

Bolitho replied, 'Mr Tomlin is already dealing with it, sir. We brought plenty of spare spars from Plymouth.'

'Lucky indeed, Bolitho.'

A seaman shouted, 'Boat approaching from the Dutchman, sir!'

Pelham-Martin frowned. 'Damn! I suppose I shall have to stay a while longer now!'

Inch hurried to the entry port, thankful for this unexpected interruption. He had seen the returning hardness in Bolitho's eyes, and had inwardly cursed Pelham-Martin for his stupidity and his ignorance. Did he never stop to consider how hard Bolitho had worked and sweated to get those spars from a dockyard which was more than well trained in withholding everything but the most meagre of ship's stores?

He called. 'The boat has a captain aboard, sir!' He blinked. 'No, sir, *two* captains!'

The commodore grunted. 'Coming to gloat over their part in all this, I shouldn't wonder.'

The boat hooked on to the chains, and as the pipes twittered and the marines' bayoneted muskets were brought to the present the first visitor appeared in the open port.

He removed his hat and looked slowly around the crowded main deck, his eyes pausing on the line of sewn-up corpses, the splintered planking and all the litter of broken rigging and cordage.

He was an elderly man, probably in his sixties, Bolitho thought, and the left sleeve of his coat was empty and pinned beneath a flashing gold order on his breast. His hair was almost white, but his skin was so tanned that it was almost mahogany in colour, and his step was as sure and light as a cat's.

Then he saw Pelham-Martin and stepped briskly to greet him. 'May I welcome you and your ships to St Kruis! I am Piet de Block, Governor in the name of my country, and your ally!' His English was hesitant but extremely good. 'I was visiting another island and returned in time to see your gallant fight.' He paused with obvious emotion. 'I can understand what the decision must have cost, and with my own eyes I have witnessed some of your sacrifice. It was incredible! And now,' he waved his hat around the watching faces, 'now you can still find the strength and the sense of duty to prepare this welcome for *me*!'

Pelham-Martin swallowed hard and flushed. 'I bid you welcome, sir, and greetings from my Gracious Sovereign King George.' He glanced quickly at Bolitho before adding, 'My duty was plain, and I am indeed glad I was able to forestall the enemy's intentions.'

De Block nodded gravely. 'And this is Kapitein Willem Mulder of the *Telamon*. He is as eager for battle as your own men, but now I think it wiser to refit your ships first, is that not so?'

The *Telamon*'s captain was slight and wiry, and as tanned as his governor. He, too, was studying the *Hyperion*'s damage, but his face was more controlled than his superior's.

Pelham-Martin said, 'And this is *my* captain, Richard Bolitho.'

Bolitho stepped forward, conscious of the watching eyes, of Inch's obvious fury at Pelham-Martin's grand acceptance of credit, but above all of the Dutchman's firm handshake.

De Block studied him for several seconds without releasing his hand. He seemed to find an answer in Bolitho's strained features for he said suddenly, 'As I thought, Kapitein.' He paused. 'My *deepest* thanks.'

Pelham-Martin said abruptly, 'You speak very good English.'

'Well, there have been many wars.' De Block shrugged expressively. 'After I lost my arm I had plenty of time to meet with and learn your countrymen's ways and language.'

The commodore eyed him thoughtfully. 'You were a prisoner perhaps?' He shook his head indulgently. 'These things can happen in war.'

The Dutchman smiled. 'After I lost my arm I was put in charge of *our* English prisoners, sir.'

Bolitho coughed quietly. 'Perhaps the Governor would like to go to the cabin, sir?'

Pelham-Martin recovered from his sudden confusion and glared at him. 'Quite so!'

But the island's governor shook his head. 'I would not hear of it. You will come ashore to my house immediately. Kapitein Mulder will remain aboard to give every help at our disposal.'

He looked searchingly at Bolitho, the same expression of understanding in his deepset eyes. 'We are well stocked, and I think able to meet your needs.' He held out his hand again. 'We are in your debt. We will do our best to repay your courage.'

Then as the pipes shrilled once more he followed Pelham-Martin down into his boat alongside.

Bolitho stood by the port watching as the boat headed strongly for the shore. Most of the oarsmen were either coloured or half-castes, but there was no doubting their bearing or discipline.

Mulder said quietly, 'You look tired. It cannot be easy to serve a man so lacking in understanding.'

Bolitho stared at him, but already the other captain was looking aloft to where some seamen were reeving lines in readiness for swaying up the new topmast.

He said shortly, 'Your Governor has been here a long time, I suppose?'

Mulder nodded, his eyes slitting against the glare as he watched with professional interest the sure-footed topmen working high above the deck.

'Thirty years to be exact. Both as a serving officer and then as Governor. St Kruis is his home now, as it is for me.' He seemed unwilling to continue the discussion and added briskly, 'Now tell me, what do you require?'

Bolitho smiled gravely. It was, after all, better to talk as two captains rather than two subordinates. It was safer, and would certainly be more rewarding at this stage.

De Block may not have realized that the ceremonial guard was not, indeed, intended for his benefit, but it was obvious that he more than understood Pelham-Martin's part in the actual battle. He was shrewd and he was wise, and no stranger to local affairs and strategy. Bolitho hoped that Pelham-Martin was not so foolish that he would underestimate the one-armed Governor of St Kruis.

An hour after Mulder had departed with his list of requirements the first boatloads of provisions started to arrive alongside. Like the governor's bargemen, the inhabitants of St Kruis were a mixture of every race in the Caribbean. Laughing and chattering they swarmed aboard, showing sympathy for the wounded as they were carried in boats to more comfortable quarters ashore, and amusement to the seamen who crowded around them, touching them and using their own versions of language and gesticulation to break down the last barriers of strangeness.

Inch said, 'It is like another world, sir.'

Bolitho nodded. He had been thinking the same thing.

The Dutch flag flew above the ancient ship and the town, but the island's inhabitants had seemingly become so interbred over the years, so dependent on their own resources, they would find it hard to bend to another's domination. No matter who it was.

Allday came aft and knuckled his forehead. 'Any orders for me, Captain?'

Bolitho stretched his arms and saw the rent in his sleeve left by the musket ball. Was it possible? Could he have been so near to death?

He said, 'Take the gig, Allday, and go ashore. Keep your ears and eyes open, understand?'

Allday's features stayed expressionless. 'Understood, Captain.' Then he grinned. 'I will be on board again in one hour.'

Bolitho thought suddenly of fresh water and a clean shirt on his back. With a nod to Inch he strode aft to the chartroom.

Commodores and governors could discuss high policy, he thought grimly. But the Alldays of this world often reached the bones of the matter in half the time.

For the *Hyperion*'s company the days which followed their arrival at St Kruis were unlike anything they had ever known. From dawn to dusk the work of repairing damage went on with hardly a pause, but because of the lush surroundings and friendly atmosphere they still found time to lend their attentions to other, more interesting activities. The memory of the battle, even the scars of it, had all but vanished, and as carpenters and seamen worked above the deck or deep in the hull, others, luckier or craftier, dragged out their time ashore collecting fresh water and fruit, and took every advantage to better their relations with the local women.

At the beginning of the third week the *Indomitable* and the *Hermes*, with their two attendant sloops, dropped anchor in the bay, and Bolitho wondered just how long it was going to take Pelham-Martin to decide on a definite course of action. So far the commodore had done little, other than send the two frigates on separate patrols to the south-west, but now he had larger ships at his disposal he might at last be prepared to move.

It had been easy for Bolitho to keep his own men busy. There was ample work to do repairing rigging and decks, and with the battle casualties added to the previous shortages he was now lacking nearly a sixth of the total complement. But even such severe shortages might not be relied on to keep his men out of trouble. He could not, would not, restrict them from going ashore in small parties, but already there had been squabbles, even fights with some of the local menfolk, and the cause was easy to discover.

The dark-skinned women with their ready smiles and bold eyes were enough to set any sailor's heart aflame, and mixed with the blazing sunshine and easily obtained rum it was just a matter of time before something serious happened.

And now, with more ships anchored in the bay, the local people's ready welcome might soon give way to resentment and worse.

When he had told the commodore of his fears he had received no satisfaction. Pelham-Martin was no longer living aboard, but had taken full advantage of de Block's offer to set up temporary headquarters in the governor's own residence by the waterfront.

He had merely said, 'If you cannot trust your people on shore, Bolitho, then you must keep them from going there!'

On another occasion he had implied that he was awaiting news from Caracas which might give some fresh idea as to where Lequiller had gone.

And that was the strangest part of all. Lequiller's squadron had vanished as if it did not even exist.

When the frigate *Spartan* had returned from Caracas, Bolitho had managed to meet her captain before he had been ordered to his new patrol area. Captain Farquhar had been both resentful and impatient.

'The Spanish Captain-General was polite but little else. He gave me ten minutes' audience and no more, and seemed barely interested in our commodore's greeting.' His lips had twisted into a scornful smile. 'He gave me to understand that the English have claimed control of the Caribbean for so long it was *our* duty to prove it.'

Bolitho could well imagine Farquhar's irritation. He had never been noted for his tolerance, and the humiliation of being thus dismissed would not be easy to accept. But if he had been angry, he had not been slow in making full use of his visit. There had been only one ship-of-war at Caracas, and she was obviously being retained as a local escort, probably for one of the Spanish treasure ships. One thing was certain, however. Nobody knew or would say a word about Lequiller's squadron. And yet—Bolitho had considered it countless times —it had to be somewhere, repairing damage as he was, preparing and watching for the next move. But where?

Then, after another week of waiting and fretting, a small armed schooner slipped into the bay and anchored close inshore. She was the *Fauna*, de Block's link with the other Dutch islands, and almost as old as the sixty-gun *Telamon*.

Within an hour Bolitho received a summons to report to Pelham-Martin's headquarters, and as the barge pulled away from the *Hyperion's* side he saw with grim satisfaction that boats were already leaving the other ships and heading for the shore. It must be something urgent for the commodore to call his captains together before lunchtime, he thought. Since taking up residence in de Block's house Pelham-Martin had adopted a grand and remote way of life. If anything, he had grown larger in his new surroundings, and when he entertained some of his officers to dinner, which was not often, his capacity for food and wine was a topic of conversation for days afterwards.

Bolitho found him in the low ceilinged room above the waterfront seated behind a gilt-edged table which was completely covered with charts and loose papers.

He looked up as Bolitho entered and waved one hand towards a chair. Then he said casually, 'News at last, Bolitho.' He seemed to be holding back his excitement with real effort. 'De Block has informed me of Lequiller's whereabouts, so now we can act!'

Winstanley and Fitzmaurice came into the room together followed by Captain Mulder of the *Telamon*.

Pelham-Martin waited for them to arrange themselves in chairs and then said, 'Lequiller's ships have been found, gentlemen.' He watched their sudden interest and added grandly, 'I know that there are some who might have wished to act prematurely,' he let his eyes rest briefly on Bolitho before continuing, 'but as I have always stressed, there is a correct method of bringing an enemy to action, a positive way of showing our strength.' He was warming to his theme, and from the expressions of the other two British officers, Bolitho guessed it was a well-known one. Winstanley looked faintly amused, while Fitzmaurice appeared to be attentively bored.

'We are a safeguard of considerable affairs, gentlemen, and it is the deployment and use of our available resources which is far more valuable than any brief devil-may-care skirmish!'

At that moment de Block entered by a small side door, a chart under his arm. He nodded to the commodore and then unrolled the chart across the others on the table.

Pelham-Martin frowned slightly and dabbed his forehead with a silk handkerchief. 'As I was *saying*, Lequiller has been found, is that not so?'

De Block was filling a long pipe with tobacco, his single hand doing all the functions like a wiry brown animal.

'It *is* so.' He rapped the chart with the pipe stem. 'My schooner spoke with a West Indiaman four days ago. She wished to land one of her officers who was suffering from fever, and made to put into here,' the pipe stem paused and the officers around the table craned forward as one, 'the port of Las Mercedes on the Spanish Main. But they were refused entry.'

Pelham-Martin said, 'Only two hundred miles west of Caracas and yet the Captain-General knew nothing about them!'

De Block eyed him wryly. 'Two hundred miles in distance maybe, but in that country it is like ten times that amount.' He sighed. 'But no matter, the West Indiaman's master reported seeing several ships-of-war at anchor.'

Captain Mulder said, 'This Lequiller has chosen well. It is a . . .' he groped for the word, '. . . a *barren* place.'

Bolitho was on his feet and leaning over the chart. 'I have heard of it. Once the haunt of pirates. A good anchorage, and easy to defend by sea or overland.' He circled the craggy coastline with his finger. 'It has a bay very like we have here, but according to the chart there is a wide river which protects it from any inland assault.'

De Block smiled. 'Not a river. Once maybe, but now it is little more than a swamp. Nobody really knows how far it goes inland, and few have wanted to discover its secrets. It is full of fever and death. No wonder pirates thought themselves safe there.'

Pelham-Martin glared at him. 'When you have all finished, gentlemen!' He eased his heavy body to the edge of the chair. 'I am not interested in what the pirates did or did not do, nor do I care much for the swamp. The fact is that Lequiller has found shelter and sustenance in Las Mercedes, and Spanish Main or not, I intend to seek him out!'

Captain Fitzmaurice shifted uneasily. 'But surely an attack on any Spanish territory would be seen as a hostile act against Spain, sir?'

Winstanley nodded. 'We might be doing what Lequiller wishes. It would drive Spain into the French camp quicker than anything.'

Pelham-Martin dabbed his brow with quick, savage thrusts. 'I was coming to that!'

'Perhaps if I could explain?' De Block stepped forward, his pipe still unlit. 'The captain of my schooner also said it is rumoured there are English sailors in the prison at Las Mercedes.' He shrugged. 'Maybe they are mutineers, or perhaps deserters from some passing ship; it is of no account.' His eyes flashed in the shaded sunlight. 'But their presence at Las Mercedes might be used as an excuse for a closer study, eh?'

The commodore eyed him stonily. 'I was about to say that, de Block.' He sniffed. 'However, as you have put it so well, I think I can state I am in total agreement.'

Bolitho rubbed his chin. In his mind's eye he was seeing the natural harbour, three hundred miles distant from St Kruis. It was an ideal hiding place, and for a man like Lequiller who knew the area well it would have been a careful choice. It was a formidable place, but had Lequiller been able to take St Kruis as well, the situation would have been even worse.

He said slowly, 'You could send a sloop to inform the Captain-General at Caracas, sir. He might wish to withhold any treasure ship until we have found and defeated the French squadron.' He looked up, seeing the sudden hostility in Pelham-Martin's eyes.

'Inform *him*! After his damned insolence!' Pelham-Martin was sweating badly. 'He's probably hand in glove with the governor of Las Mercedes. Inform him indeed!' He controlled his anger with effort. 'I shall be happy to do so when I can produce this traitorous Spaniard to him in person.'

Bolitho looked at the chart. He could hardly blame Pelham-Martin for wanting to keep all the credit as a final return of insults.

He said, 'From my experience, sir, it is not likely that the Captain-General knows about this. The Spanish governors of the various provinces usually keep their own council and are responsible only to the Court in Spain. It takes months to get decisions agreed upon, so many of them act alone and share nothing of their problems in case of recriminations at a later date.'

Winstanley cleared his throat. 'That is true, sir.'

'All the more reason for trusting no one, surely?' Pelham-Martin's good humour was returning. 'I am not waiting for Lequiller to call the tune this time. We will put to sea immediately.'

Bolitho stood back from the table. 'I will have the barge standing by, sir.'

Pelham-Martin looked away. 'Thank you, but it will not be necessary. I am shifting my broad pendant back to *Indomitable*.' He nodded curtly. 'Return to your ships, gentlemen. We will make sail in two hours.'

Later, as Bolitho stood at the *Hyperion*'s quarterdeck rail he wondered what had decided Pelham-Martin to change flagships again. As the broad pendant had broken from the *Indomitable*'s topmast he had seen several of the seamen on the gangways pointing towards it and calling to each other with something like indignation. Rightly or wrongly, they probably considered they had done more than any in the squadron to bring the enemy to close action, and the commodore's change of heart must seem like an unspoken rebuke which they could not understand.

Bolitho did not understand it either, although when he had gathered his officers together in the wardroom to explain briefly what the commodore intended to do, he had made every effort to show neither resentment nor bitterness. At any other time he would have been glad to be rid of Pelham-Martin's presence, but now, with a final and decisive action imminent he would have preferred otherwise. For whereas Pelham-Martin had in the past consulted his captains for even the most trivial despatches, he had added nothing at all to his brief orders prior to sailing.

Inch called, 'Anchor's hove short, sir!'

Bolitho pulled himself from his brooding thoughts and shaded his eyes to peer across at the *Indomitable*. Winstanley was probably cursing Pelham-Martin for returning to his ship. He could see the men along the two-decker's yards, the crouching shapes of others plodding around her capstan. Beyond her, framed against the distant hills, the *Hermes* and the stately *Telamon* were also shortening their cables. Even without a glass he could see most of the island's population crowded along the waterfront and on the headland where Dawson's marines had repaired the battery and had helped to improve the defences in case of any future attack.

In spite of his apprehension at Pelham-Martin's failure to outline any proposed plan of battle, Bolitho could find some comfort at the sight. With the sun beating down across the glittering blue water of the bay, a steady north-easterly ruffling the shrubs and rushes below the headland, the four ships made a splendid picture. As he looked along his own command he could afford to feel satisfied and pleased with the work his men had achieved. As good as his word, de Block had supplied the ship with everything at his disposal, even to the extent of new canvas to replace that lost in battle.

And as Perks, the sailmaker, had remarked, 'It's none o' yer wartime rubbish, sir, 'tis the real stuff.'

Gascoigne yelled, 'General, sir! Up anchor!'

Bolitho nodded. 'Get the ship under way, Mr Inch!' He glanced at Gossett. 'We will take station astern of *Hermes*.'

That was something else. *Hyperion* would be the last in the line in whatever action the commodore intended. With the prevailing wind from the north-east it was a sensible position, for *Hyperion* was the fastest ship in the squadron and could dash down on the van if *Indomitable* got into difficulty and needed support. But to her company, many of whom did not understand these matters, it must seem like a final insult.

He would make it his business to set their minds at rest, he decided.

He heard Inch yelling, 'Get those laggards to the mizzen braces! Mr Tomlin! Wake them up, for God's sake!'

Here and there a rattan swished across a tanned back as the seamen came alive to the business of getting under way. A month of comparative idleness had taken its toll, and it took more than soft words to drive the men to the braces.

'Loose tops'ls!'

Gascoigne ran across the deck as, wheeling ponderously to the wind, the ship went about, her sails cracking and booming overhead and the capstan still turning to the accompaniment of a breathless shanty.

'*Flag* to *Hyperion*, sir!' His eyes were streaming as the sunlight lanced down his telescope. 'Make haste!'

Bolitho smiled. 'Acknowledge.' Pelham-Martin would not wish to see any slackness with a Dutch ship in company. The *Telamon* was a splendid sight, and in the glare her gilded stern shone like some fantastic temple altar, while strung out along her yards the dark skins of her topmen glistened as if they, too, had been stained and polished to perfection.

But she would make little impression on Lequiller's ships, he thought. She was over fifty years old, and her guns were no match for the French artillery. And she had been out here for most of her lifetime, Mulder had said. So her timbers were probably rotten, in spite of the gilded carving and proud flags.

He shifted his eyes to the *Hermes* as she tacked round to take station astern of the Dutchman. She on the other hand looked every inch an experienced warrior. Stained and scarred, with more than one patch in her pale canvas.

Inch said, '*Indomitable*'s setting her t'gallants, sir.'

'Very well. Do likewise, Mr Inch.' Bolitho staggered slightly as the deck lifted slowly beneath him. Like him, the ship seemed pleased to be rid of the land again.

He looked up to watch the canvas spread along the braced yards and the tiny silhouettes of the topmen as they raced each other to obey the orders from the deck far below. He saw Pascoe pause at the maintop, his body tilting to the roll of the ship, his head thrown back to watch the pigtailed seamen swarming past him as still more canvas ballooned and then hardened from the yards. His shirt was open to his waist, and Bolitho could see that his skin was already well tanned, his ribs less prominent than when he had come aboard. He was learning fast and well, but Bolitho knew from what he had seen and heard at St Kruis that the boy still kept apart from the other midshipmen and was nursing his inner hurt like some latent disease.

Gossett intoned, 'Course is west by south, sir!'

'Very well.' Bolitho crossed to the weather side to watch as the headland slipped past, tiny figures running along the lip of crumbling rocks where the French raiding party had stormed up to the battery under cover of darkness.

Far away on the larboard bow he could just make out a tiny white sliver on the sea's edge to mark one of the sloops which had already hurried ahead to contact the frigates and pass Pelham-Martin's instructions with minimum delay.

To Inch he said quietly, 'Set no more sail just yet. With our clean copper I'm afraid we might overreach the *Hermes*!'

Inch showed his teeth in a grin. 'Aye, *aye*, sir.'

It was then, and only then, that Bolitho realized Inch had got the ship under way without a single flaw, while he had been so immersed in his own thoughts he had barely noticed it.

He eyed the lieutenant gravely. 'We'll make a commander of you yet, Mr Inch!'

Leaving Inch with an even wider grin he walked aft to the cabin, where once more he could be alone with his thoughts.

9. Retreat

THE THIRD DAY after leaving St Kruis dawned bright and clear, with the sky empty of cloud and the colour of blue ice. The sea, whipped up by an impatient north-easterly, was broken as far as the horizon in an endless pattern of small wave crests, yellow in the sunlight.

During the night, and in spite of Pelham-Martin's urgent signals, the four ships had scattered, and it took more maddening hours to re-form the line to his satisfaction. Now, close hauled on the larboard tack and leaning heavily to the stiffening wind the ships drove south-east, with the shadowed coast-line stretching away on either bow and only the towering hills further inland bathed in sunlight. The bay of Las Mercedes was still hidden and shrouded in drifting haze which swirled above the sea's face like low cloud.

Bolitho stood on the quarterdeck with one hand resting against the hammock nettings, his body chilled in spite of the early warmth, his eyes aching from studying the land as it grew out of the shadows to take on shape and personality for the new day. Since they had weighed and put to sea with such haste he had thought of little else but this moment. While the ships drove westward, and then under cover of night turned to head more directly towards the land, he had considered what Pelham-Martin might do if the French had already quit the bay and were many miles away, as elusive as before. Or worse, that de Block's schooner had been misinformed, and Lequiller had never been in the vicinity at all.

If either was true it would be hard to know where to pick up the scent again. To draw two forces of ships together in combat was more guess than planning, and Lequiller might have decided to return to France or carry some scheme of his own to the other ends of the earth.

Around and below him he could feel the hull trembling and creaking as, under shortened sail, she followed the other ships towards the bank of pale mist. As soon as it was light enough to read his signals Pelham-Martin had ordered them to prepare for battle, and now, as in the other ships, the *Hyperion*'s company waited in almost complete silence, by their guns or high above the deck, or like Trudgeon, the surgeon, deep in the hull itself, hidden from the sunlight and dependent on others for their own survival.

Several telescopes lifted as if to some silent command, and Bolitho saw a pale rectangle of sail detaching itself from the mist far away on the larboard bow. It was the frigate *Abdiel* which Pelham-Martin had ordered to approach the bay from the opposite side and report any signs of life within its protective headlands.

Lieutenant Roth standing by his quarterdeck nine-pounders said loudly, 'We'll soon know now, eh?' But fell silent again as Bolitho glared at him.

Midshipman Gascoigne was already in the weather shrouds with his telescope, biting his lower lip with fierce concentration, knowing perhaps the vital importance of that first signal.

Steel scraped on steel with the sound of a gunshot, and when Bolitho turned his head he saw Allday striding below the poop carrying the old sword in front of him like a talisman.

In spite of his anxiety Bolitho managed to smile as Allday buckled the sword around his waist. He at least seemed to have no doubts as to what the day would bring.

'*Abdiel*'s signalling, sir!' Gascoigne's voice cracked with excitement. 'To *Indomitable*. Four enemy sail anchored inside bay.' His lips moved soundlessly as he continued reading. Then he shouted, 'Four sail of the line, sir!'

Inch let out a great sigh. 'By God, we've *found* 'em!'

Bolitho pressed his lips together and made himself walk twice from one side of the deck to the other. Four ships. That was only half of Lequiller's force, so where were the rest?

Behind him Gossett muttered, 'This mist'll go shortly. Then maybe *we'll* see the buggers!'

As usual he was right, and when the mist began to roll clear Bolitho raised his glass to study the anchored ships as first one and then the rest hardened into shape. With the sun only just above the hills the four ships looked black and solid, as if they had never, could never break free from their moorings, and as light filtered down above the departing sea mist he saw the reason. They were anchored fore and aft directly across the narrowest part of the bay's entrance, and he could tell from the way in which the water lifted and surged between the nearest ones that there were more hidden cables linking them together into one formidable barrier. Each ship had her ports closed and sails neatly furled, but when more sunlight played across the yards and shrouds he saw tiny figures on every poop and the curling Tricolour at each gaff. There was no longer any doubt. Whether the French had beaten the Spanish garrison into submission, or had merely frightened them to impotent silence, the facts were the same. They were ready to fight, and what was more to the point, must have *known* Pelham-Martin's squadron was on its way. It would have taken a good deal of labour and planning to get the heavy two-deckers moored like that, and the French commander would not have wasted either on pure chance.

Inch said, 'Just as if they've been wanting us to come, sir.'

Bolitho closed the glass with a snap. 'Just so. I wondered why that West Indiaman was allowed to proceed after seeing what she did. Lequiller is no fool, Mr Inch, and I hope the commodore accepts the fact.'

Inch nodded doubtfully. 'I wonder what he intends, sir?'

Bolitho studied the anchored ships for a full minute, aware of the hum of shrouds and rigging, the hissing sluice of water against the hull, yet hearing none of them. It was uncanny to see the ships lying like that, he thought vaguely. They were almost at right-angles to the squadron's line of approach, stretching away on the larboard bow, the furthest vessel still shrouded in mist below the distant headland. If Pelham-Martin maintained this course they would pass astern of the last ship, or he could tack and sail along the anchored line and engage them independently.

Gossett said, 'There's plenty o' water at this side of the entrance, sir.'

'Yes.' Bolitho had already noted that the anchored ships were closer to the other headland, whereas the nearest two-decker was some three cables from the overhanging cliffs which were already bathed in bright sunlight.

Gascoigne yelled, '*Indomitable*'s signalling *Abdiel*, sir!' He climbed frantically up three more ratlines and then said, 'I can't read the hoist, sir! *Hermes* is blocking my view!'

Inch said, '*Abdiel*'s acknowledged, sir, so we shall see.'

Bolitho looked at him gravely. It was strange the way men could discuss the business of tactics and signals, when by nightfall they could all be dead.

The *Abdiel* shortened and then lengthened again, as with sails flapping and billowing from her yards she went about and headed for the rear of the French line.

Some of the seamen below the quarterdeck started to cheer her, although it was more to relieve tension than with any hope of reaching the frail frigate.

Bolitho watched in silence. So Pelham-Martin was sending *Abdiel* in first.

Carried faintly on the wind he heard a trumpet, and as

142

he shaded his eyes against the mounting glare he saw the French ships opening their ports. It was both unhurried and well timed, so that as the double lines of gun muzzles trundled into view it seemed as if one man's hand was in control. A puff of smoke drifted above the *Abdiel*'s bows, followed seconds later by the jarring crash of the shot. A ranging ball, or just sheer high spirits, it was hard to tell. Maybe *Abdiel*'s captain was just loosing off a shot to break the tension. It was a pity that for the second time the lot of closing the enemy was going to Captain Pring and not Farquhar. The *Spartan* had not been found by the searching sloops, or at least had not yet arrived. Maybe Farquhar had troubles of his own, but just now Bolitho would have wished him in the van rather than Pring. The latter was keen enough, but seemed to lack Farquhar's cold self-control.

More smoke, and this time a ragged broadside, the balls throwing up thin waterspouts abeam of the last French ship, which Bolitho could now recognize as the one he had crippled at St Kruis. Without a glass he could clearly see the gaping holes in her bulwark and the crude jury rig replacing her severed mizzen.

Gascoigne called, 'General signal, sir! The commodore intends to pass astern the enemy's line to obtain the weather-gage!'

'You may load and run out, Mr Inch.' Bolitho stepped clear of the sudden activity around the quarterdeck guns as the order was passed, and strode to the poop ladder. By standing a few steps above the deck he could see the *Indomitable*'s larboard tumblehome cutting across the rearmost Frenchman. In another two cables Pelham-Martin would cross her stern and then lead the line round and parallel with the anchored ships. The French gunners would not only have the sun in their eyes, but also be deluged with smoke once the firing began.

Overhead the topsails flapped loudly and then refilled to the wind. So close to land it was difficult to keep them drawing well, and Bolitho watched with satisfaction as Tomlin's men manned the braces in readiness for the next order.

Inch touched his hat. 'Larboard battery loaded and run out, sir!' In spite of the distant bangs from *Abdiel*'s guns he seemed relaxed and vaguely cheerful. 'They knocked a few minutes off their time, too!'

Bolitho saw the *Hermes* lifting uneasily to some offshore current, and noted that she, too, had run out her larboard battery ready to engage.

He said slowly, 'Now the *starboard* guns, Mr Inch.' He gripped the teak rail as through the criss-cross of rigging he saw the *Abdiel*'s shape shorten until she was stern on, yards braced round to seize the wind, her scarlet ensign streaming from the gaff like a sheet of painted metal.

Inch had been with Bolitho long enough not to question his orders, and as his men faltered, off guard, he cupped his hands and yelled, 'Load and run out, you idlers! Petty Officer, take that man's name!'

It had the desired effect, and with squeaking trucks the guns lumbered towards the ports, the seamen skidding on the damp planking as the heavy cannon took charge and rolled down the canting deck. Below on the lower gundeck the ports might be nearly awash as the ship leaned dutifully to the wind, but Bolitho breathed more easily. It was going well, but perhaps too well.

He looked at Inch and shrugged. 'It is always prudent to be prepared.'

Someone aboard the *Hermes* had apparently found time to drag his eyes from the enemy ships, for seconds later her starboard port lids opened and here and there a gun muzzle poked out, like hastily awakened beasts sniffing the air.

Inch grinned. 'That caught 'em, sir!'

One of *Indomitable*'s bow-chasers fired, the flash masked by the ships astern of her, and Bolitho swung round to watch as the ball ricocheted across the cruising ranks of white horses before ploughing close to the sternmost Frenchman. There was more cheering, and from one of the ships—Bolitho thought it was the *Telamon*—came the sounds of drums and fifes.

'Deck there! *Abdiel*'s under fire!'

The masthead lookout's cry was drowned by the ragged crash of cannon fire, and as Bolitho ran to the rail snatching a glass from a startled midshipman, he saw the frigate's hull surrounded by leaping waterspouts.

Inch yelled, 'The French must have some stern-chasers out!'

But Bolitho dragged him from the nettings. '*Look*, man! Those balls are coming from the land to starboard!' He winced as the *Abdiel*'s foremast toppled sideways and plunged towards the deck, and even as he watched he saw her sails quiver as more balls slammed through shrouds and canvas alike, so that the sea around her seemed alive with splintered woodwork and whirling pieces of debris.

Bolitho gritted his teeth. It was a trap, just as he had half feared, half expected. *Abdiel* was being pounded by several guns at once, the hidden marksmen unhampered by movement or range as they fired again and again at the ship which must be lying below and right across their sights.

'Pring's trying to go about!' Inch was almost weeping with anguish as the *Abdiel*'s mizzen lurched and hung suspended in the tangle of rigging before falling across her quarterdeck, the sound carrying even above the gunfire.

Gascoigne shouted wildly, 'General signal! Tack in succession!'

The *Indomitable* was already turning very slowly to larboard, her jib boom pointing towards the poop of the sternmost French ship as she wallowed round into the face of the wind. For an instant she appeared to be all aback, but as more men ran to the braces she staggered across the short steep waves, her topsails flapping and lifting madly as if to tear themselves from the yards.

Bolitho yelled, 'Stand by, Mr Gossett!' He watched sickened as the moored Frenchman fired a controlled broadside, the paired line of orange tongues licking from her hull as she slammed her double-shotted salvo into the *Indomitable*'s side where the ports still showed shut and useless.

Bolitho raised his hand, his eyes moving swiftly above the crouched gunners, shutting the sounds of splintering timber from his ears, concentrating his full being on the ships ahead of him. No wonder the enemy had waited so patiently and confidently. Instead of receiving a controlled line of ships across their rear they were now faced with something approaching chaos. *Indomitable* was swinging ponderously across the wind, her jib blowing in ribbons, her foretopmast and main topgallant dangling amidst her littered rigging like savaged trees. She had still not run out her other guns, and Bolitho could imagine the slaughter of that first broadside. Now the next ship was firing, and the sea around Pelham-Martin's flagship was boiling with white spray and falling wreckage.

A voice cried, 'Oh, God, *Abdiel*'s ablaze!'

Bolitho tore his eyes from the *Hermes*'s high counter and turned in time to see the frigate broaching to, her sails and forward rigging burning like tinder, the blaze leaping from spar to spar, while small, pitiful figures dropped from the rigging like dead fruit to fall alongside or on to the deck itself.

'General signal!' Gascoigne sounded shrill with despair. 'Close around the commodore!'

Bolitho snapped, 'Do *not* acknowledge!' Then to Gossett, 'Now! Helm a'lee!'

Something like a great groan floated over the water, and he guessed that the *Telamon* had collided with the *Indomitable*'s quarter. With so much smoke it was hard to see what was happening.

Forward his men were already loosing the headsail sheets, and as the rudder went over, the bowsprit began to swing slowly and then more rapidly across the *Hermes*'s stern.

'Off tacks and sheets!' It was amazing that men could think, let alone act, and they moved more from rigid training than with any sense of understanding.

Bolitho looked up, holding his breath as the yards came round, the sails in confusion and disarray as the bows swung across the wind.

'Let go and haul!' Inch was screaming through his trumpet. '*Haul!*'

'Get the t'gallants on her, Mr Inch!'

A ball whimpered above the quarterdeck but hardly a man looked up. It was probably a misfire from the embattled *Indomitable*, but all eyes were on the *Hermes* as with extra canvas drawing loudly and the deck canting to the opposite thrust the *Hyperion* surged past her, the seamen coughing as the smoke drifted above them.

The *Hermes* was firing past her two consorts, which were locked together in helpless confusion, the Dutchman's jib boom rammed through the *Indomitable*'s shrouds like a lance. And while men ran with axes to hack away rigging and entangled nets, the French maintained a devastating fire at a range of some fifty yards. Bolitho could see men falling from aloft and others being pared away like so many rags by both grape and canister from the nearest enemy vessels.

As the *Hyperion* sailed on past her three consorts Bolitho thought he saw Pelham-Martin on his quarterdeck, his gold-laced hat glittering in the sunlight as he strode this way and that, arms flailing, his voice lost in the roar of cannon fire.

The smoke was dense and rising as high as the topsail yards, and Bolitho tried to count the minutes while his ship moved steadily along the hidden enemy line, her yards braced round so far that they were almost fore and aft.

It must be time. It *had* to be. Desperately he glanced astern and saw *Indomitable*'s ragged outline surrounded by smoke and flickering gun flashes. Smoke hid the *Hermes* and the snared Dutchman, and the drumming of the enemy's bombardment went on and on without a single break or hesitation.

He yelled, 'Stand by to go about!' He saw Inch gripping the rail, his teeth bared as he peered into the smoke.

'Ready ho!'

Bolitho ran to the starboard side. If he had misjudged the distance, or the wind failed him, he would probably drive into the nearest enemy ship and be as helpless as the *Telamon*.

'*Now!*'

As the ship started to swing back again across the wind he cupped his hands and shouted at the main deck gunners. 'Starboard battery fire!'

It was like a double roll of thunder, the lower gundeck being caught unprepared for the order. He felt the ship stagger as gun after gun hurled itself back on its tackles, the flashes masked instantly by the choking smoke which came funnelling inboard through the ports to turn day into night.

He heard the smashing impact of some of the balls striking home, but shouted to the larboard gunners, '*Ready*, lads!' He was grinning wildly, and was only half aware of the ship swinging beneath him, the rigging jerking as if to tear from blocks and yards alike.

While the starboard gunners reloaded with feverish haste the *Hyperion* continued to turn, until with the suddenness of magic Bolitho saw the topmasts and yards of an anchored ship swinging across the bows barely fifty yards clear.

Then as the wind cleaved the smoke aside he saw the French two-decker clear and stark, some of her guns already firing as the *Hyperion* pushed out of the drifting smoke and started to sail back along the line of ships. It was the leading Frenchman, and when Bolitho leaned across the nettings he saw with cold satisfaction that the next astern was smoking from a dozen holes in her bulwark and gangway where his blind broadside had scored several hits.

'Fire as you bear!' The larboard guns were ready and eager, and as captain after captain jerked his lanyard the smoke came back above the gangway in an unbroken wall.

'Deck there! Her mainmast's goin'!' A cheer rippled along the shrouded deck, voices breaking in coughs and curses as the lower battery fired once more.

A seaman came running aft, whirled round in his tracks and fell dead at Stepkyne's feet. The lieutenant strode on, pausing merely to step over the corpse as he controlled his gunners in their fighting madness.

Bolitho felt someone grip his sleeve and saw it was Gascoigne. He must have been signalling to him, his voice lost in the din.

'Sir! Signal from *Indomitable*!' He gasped as a ball shrieked close overhead and parted a handrail like a cotton thread.

'Well, boy?' Bolitho felt the deck quiver and knew that some of the enemy's shots were hitting home.

'Signal says "*Discontinue the action*", sir!'

Inch came aft wiping his face. 'What's that? Discontinue action?' He seemed dazed.

'Acknowledge,' Bolitho met his despairing stare. 'It means *retreat*, Mr Inch.' He turned on his heel and walked to the opposite side to watch as the *Hermes*'s bows pushed downwind from the tangle of battle, her stern-chasers still firing and all masts intact.

The gunfire suddenly ceased as if every man had been rendered deaf. And when the wind pushed the smoke aside Bolitho saw that already they had moved well clear of the anchored ships, and while the *Telamon* wallowed round to follow the battered *Indomitable*, the *Hermes* was already clawing about to take station astern of her once more.

The *Indomitable* was a pitiable sight. She had now lost

all her topmasts, and her upper deck and starboard side were splintered and gouged from stem to stern.

Then across the water came the exultant cheering mixed with derisive cries and jeers that seemed to beat on the ears of the *Hyperion*'s seamen and marines like some final damnation.

'General signal, sir.' Gascoigne sounded crushed. 'Steer south-west.' And that was all.

Bolitho climbed the poop ladder and stared across the larboard quarter. Beyond the jubilant French ships he could see a few smouldering remains of the *Abdiel* and some thrashing survivors, like so many dying fish in a poisoned stream. Then as the headland crept out to hide their misery he found that he was shivering uncontrollably as if from fever.

Allday climbed up beside him. 'Are you sick, Captain?'

Bolitho shook his head, almost afraid to speak. 'Not sick, just *angry*!'

He stared unseeingly at the endless panorama of hills and lush green undergrowth above the distant surf. Retreat. It stuck in his mind like a barbed hook. *Retreat*.

Inch clattered up the ladder and touched his hat. 'Two men killed, sir. None wounded.'

Bolitho looked at him, not seeing Inch's pain as he recoiled from his captain's cold eyes.

'Two men, eh?' He turned away, the words choking in his throat. They had been outwitted and outgunned, but not beaten. They had not even started to be beaten. He looked forward along the silent men restoring the lashings to their guns. They had been made to slink away because of Pelham-Martin's blind, arrogant stupidity!

Inch asked quietly, 'What will we do now, sir?'

'*Do?*' Bolitho faced him savagely. 'Write a bloody report, I shouldn't wonder! Let us hope the *Abdiel*'s people will be satisfied with it!'

With a sudden impulse he unbuckled his sword and handed it to Allday. 'Next time we sight the enemy you had best bring me a white flag instead!'

Then he swung on his heel and strode to the ladder.

Inch looked at Allday. 'I have never seen him so angry.'

The coxswain turned the sword over and caught the sunlight on its worn hilt. 'Begging your pardon, sir, but it's time someone got angry, if you ask *me*!' Then holding the sword against his chest he followed his captain.

As the *Hyperion*'s barge pulled swiftly across the choppy wavelets Bolitho sat motionless in the sternsheets, his eyes fixed on the anchored *Indomitable*. For four hours after the collapse of Pelham-Martin's attack the ships had continued south-west, following the curving shoulder of coastline, their speed reduced to a painful crawl as the crippled *Indomitable* endeavoured to maintain her lead.

At a point where the land curved more steeply inshore again and the sea's bottom afforded a temporary anchorage the commodore had halted his retreat, and now, tugging above their own reflections the ships lay in an extended and uneven line, their bows pointing towards the land which was less than two miles distant.

Bolitho lifted his gaze to explore the full extent of the *Indomitable*'s damage, and knew that his bargemen were watching his face as if to search out their own fate from his tight expression.

Against the two-decker's battered side the *Hyperion*'s barge crew seemed clean and untouched, as from a sharp command they tossed oars and the bowman hooked on to the chains.

Bolitho said, 'Stand off and await my call.' He did not look at Allday's concerned face as he reached for the chains. There was enough bitterness aboard his ship without letting the barge crew converse with the *Indomitable*'s people and carry back further gossip to demoralize them to an even greater extent.

He was met at the entry port by a lieutenant with one arm in a crude sling. He said, 'Could you make your own way aft, sir?' He jerked his head towards the other ships. 'Captain Fitzmaurice and Captain Mulder will be coming aboard at any moment.'

Bolitho nodded but did not speak. As he strode towards the quarterdeck ladder he was conscious of the smells of burned wood and charred paintwork, of blistered guns and the sweet, sickly scent of blood.

Since leaving Las Mercedes the *Indomitable*'s hands had

been busy, but all around was evidence enough of their plight and their near destruction. Several guns had been up-ended, and there was blood everywhere, as if some madman had been at work with bucket and brush, while beneath the foremast's trunk the corpses were piled like meat in a slaughterhouse, and as he paused at the top of the ladder more were carried from below to add to the grisly array.

He walked beneath the poop and thrust open the cabin door. Pelham-Martin was leaning with both hands on his table amidst a litter of charts, watched in silence by a captain of marines and a ship's lieutenant who could not have been much more than nineteen years old.

The commodore glanced up from the charts, his eyes shining in the reflected glare thrown through the shattered stern windows.

Bolitho said flatly, 'You sent for me, sir?'

'A conference.' Pelham-Martin looked round the littered cabin. 'This is a bad business.'

Somewhere below decks a man screamed, the sound suddenly terminated as if a great door had been slammed shut.

Bolitho asked, 'What do you intend to do?'

The commodore stared at him. 'When the others arrive I will make my . . .'

He swung round as the door opened and a master's mate said, 'Beg pardon, sir, but the cap'n is askin' for you.'

Pelham-Martin seemed to realize Bolitho was watching him and said heavily, 'Winstanley fell as we came clear. He is down on the orlop.' He shrugged, the movement painful and despairing. 'I am afraid he is done for.' Then he gestured to the others. 'Apart from the lieutenant on watch, these are the only officers not killed or wounded.'

Bolitho replied, 'I would like to see Winstanley.' He walked to the door and then paused, realizing that Pelham-Martin had not moved. 'Will you come, sir?'

The commodore looked at the charts and ran his fingers over them vaguely.

'Later, perhaps.'

Bolitho gestured to the two officers. 'Wait outside.'

The marine captain made as if to protest and then saw Bolitho's eyes.

When the door was closed behind them Bolitho said quietly, 'I think you *should* come, sir.' He could feel the bitter anger welling inside him like fire. 'It is the least you can do now.'

Pelham-Martin stepped back from the table as if he had been struck. 'How dare you speak to me in that tone?'

'I dare, sir, because of what you have done!' Bolitho heard his words and could not control them. Nor did he want to any more. 'Yours is the honour of commanding these ships and these men. It is also your responsibility. Yet you threw both away, with no more thought than a blind fool!'

'I am warning you, Bolitho!' Pelham-Martin's hands were opening and closing like two crabs. 'I will have you court martialled! I will not rest until your name shares the ignominy of your brother!' He paled as Bolitho took a step towards him and added thickly, 'It was a trap, I did not expect . . .'

Bolitho gripped his hands behind him, feeling the commodore's words in his mind, knowing they were the man's last, desperate defence.

He said, 'There may be a court martial, sir. We both know *whose* it will be.' He saw it strike home and added slowly, 'I do not care one way or the other. But I will not stand by and see our people shamed and our cause dishonoured. Not by you, or anyone else who thinks more of his own personal advancement than his duty!'

Without another word he threw open the door and hurried along the sundrenched quarterdeck. At any moment he expected Pelham-Martin to call for the captain of marines and place him under arrest, and if it had happened he did not know how his own fury and contempt would use him.

He did not remember finding his way down to the orlop, and his mind only recorded vague scenes of men working at repairs, faces and bodies still blackened with powder smoke, eyes staring and wild from fatigue and worse.

The orlop was in darkness but for the swinging deckhead lanterns, all of which were clustered above the central spectacle of agony and horror. Around the curved sides of the hull the waiting wounded twisted and sobbed, their faces or broken limbs catching a brief pattern of lamplight before the ship swung again and plunged them into merciful darkness once more.

Captain Winstanley lay propped against one of the stout timbers, one eye covered with a thick dressing, the centre of which gleamed bright red like an additional unwinking stare. He was naked to the waist and his lower body was covered with a square of canvas.

Beside it lay his curved hanger which he had been carrying during the action.

Bolitho dropped on one knee, seeing the sweat pouring from Winstanley's broad chest, the slow, heavy breathing which told its own story.

Gently he took the other captain's hand. The fingers were like ice. 'I am here, Winstanley.' He saw the remaining eye turn towards him, and then the recognition, as slow as the man's breathing.

The fingers moved slightly. 'It was you I wanted.' He closed his eye and screwed up his face in sudden agony. Then he added faintly, 'I—I was going to tell Pelham-Martin . . . was going to tell him . . .' The eye swivelled away and towards a thin man in a long bloodied apron. The *Indomitable*'s surgeon nodded briefly and walked back towards the lanterns, where his assistants were dragging a limp body from his butcher's table.

Winstanley's mouth tried to smile. 'Mr Tree is impatient, Bolitho. He is wasting time on me.' He lolled his head to stare around the orlop. 'Let him see to these poor fellows. I am done for.' Then his fingers tightened over Bolitho's hand like a steel trap. 'Don't let him leave my ship to carry his disgrace! In the name of Christ, don't let it happen!' The eye was fixed on Bolitho's face, willing him to answer.

Nearby a young midshipman shrunk back against the ship's side, his eyes wide with terror as the assistant surgeon said curtly, 'This one next. His arm will have to come off.' The boy rolled on to his side, weeping and struggling as the surgeon's mates loomed from the shadows.

Winstanley gasped, 'Be brave, lad! Be brave!' But his words went unheard.

Bolitho turned away, sickened. He was thinking of Pascoe, of what might have happened if he had obeyed Pelham-Martin's signal to close around this ship and await complete destruction.

He said, 'I have a plan, Winstanley.' He shut his ears to the sudden shrill scream at his back. It was like a tortured woman. 'I will do what I can for your ship.' He tried to smile. 'For all of us.'

Bolitho felt someone brush his shoulder and looked up to see the surgeon and his assistants standing beside him.

Winstanley said quietly, 'It seems I cannot be moved, Bolitho.'

The surgeon muttered impatiently, 'I am sorry, Captain Bolitho, you will have to leave now.'

Bolitho recoiled as the canvas was dragged aside. Even the attempt at bandaging could not hide the horror of Winstanley's leg and thigh.

He said tightly, 'I'll not wait, Winstanley. I will visit you later to explain my plan, eh?'

The other man nodded and let his hand drop beside him. He knew as well as Bolitho there would be no other meeting on earth. And something in the single eye seemed to pass a message of thanks as Bolitho stepped back into the shadows. Thanks for a promise of a plan that even he did not truly understand. Thanks for not staying to watch his final misery and degradation under the knife, which even now gleamed beneath the low-hung lanterns.

On the quarterdeck the sun was hotter and brighter than ever, but the sickness in Bolitho's stomach remained, leaving him cold, like Winstanley's hand.

Some of the seamen watched him pass, their expressions guarded but in some ways defenceless. They had been fond of their captain, and he had served them well, whereas Bolitho was a stranger.

In the stern cabin he found Fitzmaurice and Mulder waiting with the commodore, their faces towards the door, as if they had all been watching it for some time.

Bolitho said quietly, 'I am ready, sir.'

Pelham-Martin looked around their faces. 'Then I think we shall discuss . . .'

He glanced up as Fitzmaurice said harshly, 'Lequiller's other ships are on the high seas somewhere while we stand here talking! We cannot leave Las Mercedes without destroying those we have just fought.' He watched the commodore without emotion. 'Yet if we attack again we face the same treatment now that the balance has shifted against us.'

The commodore dabbed his forehead automatically. 'We *tried*, gentlemen. No one can say we did not do our best.'

Bolitho tugged at his neckcloth. The words, the heat of the cabin were making his head swim.

He said, 'There is still a way in which we might surprise the enemy.' He watched narrowly as Pelham-Martin's features endeavoured to cover his inner confusion. 'Time is not on our side and this plan, *any* plan may prove better than total failure.'

The others were watching him, but he did not drop his eyes from the commodore's face. It was like a line stretched between them, and one sign of faltering or uncertainty could finish everything.

As if from far away he heard Pelham-Martin say, 'Very well. Then be so good as to explain it.' As he lowered himself into a chair his hands were shaking badly, but there was no hiding the hatred in his eyes.

Bolitho saw the expression and rejected it. He was thinking of Winstanley down there on the orlop. Amongst his men, and suffering the agonizing torment of the surgeon's saw.

10. Code of Conduct

THE *Hyperion*'s lieutenants and senior warrant officers stood shoulder to shoulder around Bolitho's desk, their faces set in various attitudes of concentration as they watched their captain's chart and listened to the quiet insistence of his voice.

Beyond the stern windows the sea was in total darkness, and while the ship still tugged at her anchor the deck and gangways were alive with busy feet and the creak of tackles as a boat was hoisted outboard to the accompaniment of orders and muffled curses.

Bolitho sat down on the bench seat so that he could see the faces below the lanterns, to try to estimate how much or how little they understood and accepted his plan.

When he had described it earlier, before Pelham-Martin and the other captains, he had been surprised just how clearly the words had come to him. His anger and contempt, as well as his sorrow for Winstanley, had perhaps made his mind extra clear, so that the plan, vague and hazy when he had climbed from the misery of the *Indomitable*'s orlop, had unfolded in time with his words, had hardened into possibility with each passing second.

He said, 'We will take four cutters. Two will be ours and the others will come from *Hermes*. Captain Fitzmaurice will be supplying the bulk of the landing party, as his ship is best supplied with men at present. The importance of timing and discipline are paramount, gentlemen. Also I shall expect every man and each boat to be checked before we leave. Just enough beef and biscuit and no more. Fresh water barricoes for the same period of time, but no extra allowance for accident or mis-timing.' He looked at each face in turn. 'It is going to be a very hard task, and to complete it with any hope of success we must travel light, no matter what the discomfort.'

Captain Dawson said gruffly, 'I'd be happier if you were taking my marines, sir.'

Bolitho smiled. 'You will have your chance later.' He cocked his head to listen as more thuds and shouts announced the arrival of boats alongside. The rest of his landing party must be here already.

He said quickly, 'The *Hermes*'s first lieutenant will be my second in command. That is only fair as his ship is supplying the major part of the force.' He saw Inch nod, accepting the sense of the argument, but no doubt realizing at the same time that his own prospect of advancement or sudden death had retreated accordingly. Bolitho added, 'Mr Lang will go with us as the other officer.'

Lang was the third lieutenant, and had been slightly wounded during the battle at St Kruis. His wound had healed well enough, but he had seemingly been left with badly stretched nerves, so that his round, open face was now almost permanently set in a puzzled frown.

He bobbed his head. 'Thank you, sir.' He was still frowning.

Stepkyne said abruptly, 'As second lieutenant I think it is *my* right to take part, sir.'

Bolitho had been expecting the protest, and could hardly blame him for making it. Promotion was hard to win at any time, and for a man like him it was doubly difficult.

He said, 'This ship is under strength, Mr. Stepkyne. You are very experienced and cannot be spared.'

'It is my *right*, sir!' Stepkyne seemed oblivious to those around him.

Bolitho pushed Stepkyne's problems to the back of his mind. 'There is more at stake here than your promotion or my funeral! And I would remind you that what you tend to regard as a right is in fact a privilege. So let that be an end to it!'

The cabin door opened and Captain Fitzmaurice walked into the lamplight, his first lieutenant at his heels.

He held up his hand. 'Forgive the intrusion, Bolitho. I thought I would speak with you before you leave.' He nodded curtly to the others. 'This is Mr Quince, my senior.'

Quince was a tall, lean lieutenant with a hard mouth and extremely bright eyes. Bolitho had already learned from Fitzmaurice that Quince was ripe for advancement and more than capable should the chance come his way.

Bolitho said, 'For the benefit of our guests, gentlemen, I will go over it briefly once again.' He straightened the chart across his desk. 'The landing party will consist of four cutters and eighty officers and seamen. They will be tightly packed, but to use more boats would deprive the squadron of the ability to provide a diversion elsewhere.'

It was not merely for Fitzmaurice's entertainment that he was repeating his instructions. It took time for words to set in men's minds, to translate into probability or solid fact. As he glanced quickly at the men around him he knew he had been right. They were looking at the chart, but the eyes were more relaxed, more thoughtful, as each saw the scene from his own point of view.

'As you have seen, the mouth of the river which protects the rear of Las Mercedes is about a mile wide. You may also have observed it is little more than a swamp, filled with rushes and sandbars, and for that reason is not suitable for large craft. Deeper inland it gets much worse, which is why our four boats must be as light as possible.' He let his words sink in. 'The landing party has to cover thirty miles in three days. Little enough when walking across Bodmin Moor to visit your mistress.' Several smiled, in spite of his words. 'But the swamp is uncharted and dangerous. Some might say it is impassable. *But* we will do it.'

Fitzmaurice cleared his throat. 'Three days. Not much time.'

Bolitho smiled gravely. 'Tomorrow the squadron is making a mock attack on Las Mercedes. The French will be expecting us to do something, and unless some sort of action is mounted they will guess what we are about. The sloop *Dasher* is patrolling the entrance of the bay at this moment, so Lequiller's men will see we mean to try again.'

He looked at Captain Dawson. 'The rest of the squadron's boats will be used to mount a mock landing below the headland. Every ship will send her marines, and you will take charge overall.' Some of Dawson's earlier resentment melted as he added, 'Make a good display, but do not risk losing men to no purpose. They will earn their keep later.'

He faced the others again. 'This diversion will of course be terminated, but by that time the landing party will be well inside the swamp. But in three days from dawn tomorrow the squadron will attack in earnest, gentlemen, so you can see the vital importance of the thirty miles we must travel before we can pave the way to success.'

Inch asked, 'If you cannot reach there in time, sir, what will happen?'

Bolitho looked at him thoughtfully. 'You will have to decide, Mr Inch. For if that happens, *Hyperion* will have a new captain, eh?'

Inch stared at him, his jaw hanging open. Now, maybe for the first time, he understood why Bolitho was leaving him behind.

Bolitho added sharply, 'Carry on, gentlemen. From our own people I will want a good gunner's mate and a bosun's mate. Also two midshipmen, but *not* Gascoigne.'

Inch asked vaguely, 'May I ask why, sir?'

'You may. Mr Gascoigne is the senior midshipman and well versed in signals. You will have more need of him here when you close the enemy.'

He watched them file from the cabin and then said, 'Well, Mr Quince, I hope you have chosen your people carefully?'

Quince showed his teeth in a slow grin. 'Aye, sir. All trained men. I picked them myself.' The grin widened. 'I told them it would take a very brave man to be a coward under *your* command, sir.'

Fitzmaurice coughed politely. He was obviously unused to his subordinate's sudden flash of humour. 'Wait on deck, Mr Quince.'

Alone with Bolitho, Captain Fitzmaurice got down to his true reason for coming aboard. 'You have heard, I suppose, that Winstanley died of his wounds?' He shrugged. 'The surgeon no doubt speeded his end, but his loss is hard to accept nevertheless.'

'He was a good captain.' Bolitho watched Fitzmaurice's weary features, conscious of the sounds beyond the sealed door, the urgency and need for final appraisal of his sketchy plan. But something in Fitzmaurice's tone told him there was more to come.

'Our commodore has written his orders for the landing, Bolitho. I expect you have read them as carefully as I?'

He nodded. 'They are much as I would expect.'

'Winstanley is dead. *You* are now the senior captain. Whatever you do ashore is your responsibility.' He seemed suddenly tired of trying to phrase his words diplomatically. 'In his orders Pelham-Martin has stated that he will make an attack in three days' time in support of your action ashore.' He spread his hands angrily. 'That one word *support* alters the whole meaning of the written orders! I know it is wrong for me to speak my mind like this, but I cannot stand by and allow you to take the weight of all responsibility. You are supporting the commodore, and not the other way round.'

Bolitho studied him gravely. Fitzmaurice had never struck him as a man of much imagination beyond the limits of duty. He was moved by this sudden concern and understanding, and knew what it must have cost him to make his feelings known. He did not after all know Bolitho, and there were many who might have used Fitzmaurice's display of concern to further their own standing with the commodore. By even hinting at Pelham-Martin's deceit he was leaving himself open to grave charges of conspiracy and insubordination.

He replied, 'Thank you for speaking so openly. I will not forget it. But I believe we must think only of the task ahead. Of what it means, and the disastrous consequences of failure.'

Fitzmaurice eyed him admiringly. 'So you realized what was implied without my saying it?' He smiled. 'It is a strange service which we follow. If we fail we stand the blame alone. If we succeed there are always those elsewhere who take the credit.'

Bolitho thrust out his hand. 'I hope we remember that if ever *we* reach flag rank.'

Fitzmaurice followed him on to the darkened quarterdeck. 'I doubt it in my own case. I have often found that the attraction of arriving at some prized destination has overshadowed the effort of reaching it.'

Allday spoke from the darkness. 'Your sword, Captain.'

Bolitho tightened the belt at his waist, letting his eyes become accustomed to the gloom and sensing the watching faces all around him.

Allday said quietly, 'I didn't bring the white flag this time, Captain.' His teeth gleamed in his face. 'I hope I've done right?'

Bolitho looked away. 'If anything should happen to me, what would become of you? No captain in sound mind would tolerate your insolence as I do!'

Inch strode aft, his head thrust out as he searched for Bolitho amongst the silent figures.

'Boats ready alongside!' He faltered. 'Good luck, sir, and God speed.'

Bolitho nodded. Suddenly he realized the weight of his mission. He was not merely leaving the ship, but heading for a place which was little more than a vague sketch on his chart. Another world, a different continent, with heaven knows what at the end of it all.

He said, 'Take good care, Inch.'

Inch looked up at the black tracery of rigging swaying gently against the bright stars. 'I'll keep good care of her, sir.'

Bolitho walked slowly to the ladder. 'I know that. But I meant of *yourself*.'

Then he ran down the ladder to the entry port, brushing past anonymous shapes and watching faces, and very aware of the great silence over the whole ship.

Stepkyne touched his hat, his voice flat and expressionless. 'All in the boats, sir. I have detailed Midshipmen Carlyon and Pascoe for the duties required. They being the most junior and least needed to work the ship.'

Bolitho kept his voice low. 'You were most considerate, Mr Stepkyne.'

Without another word he followed Allday's broad shoulders down into the nearest cutter. He should have been more careful and less concerned with his own part in all this. Stepkyne had chosen the only way he knew to show his resentment at being left behind. The one way in which Bolitho was unable to override his choice without showing favouritism.

He settled himself in the sternsheets. 'Cast off. Allday, we will lead.' He raised his voice as the lines were freed from the other boats. 'Mr Quince, you will follow at the rear and ensure the rest maintain regular distances apart.'

The oars dropped into their rowlocks, and at Allday's command dipped and pulled steeply into the choppy wavelets.

In the bows Bolitho could just make out the shape of Shambler, an experienced bosun's mate, crouching with a hand lead and line in readiness to feel the way into the first part of the choked river. The cutter felt heavy and sluggish in the current and between the men's legs he could see the gleam of piled weapons and the sparse rations for the journey.

When he looked astern the next boat was already pulling into line, but when he strained his eyes further he found that the ship had seemingly disappeared into shadow, with not even a single light showing from her hull to betray her activity.

Not that it was likely for anyone to be watching from the shore, he thought grimly. This was a forsaken stretch of coast. A waste-ground which had long defied nature and man alike.

He touched the hilt of his sword and thought suddenly of

Cheney; further and further away. It seemed as if the separation would never be eased. That she had become part of the dream which home and country always represented to the sailor.

He shivered suddenly as if in a cold wind. Next month would bring spring to the hedgerows and fields of Cornwall. And to the house below Pendennis Castle it would bring him a child.

Shambler called hoarsely, 'Surf ahead, sir! 'Bout a cable's distance away!'

Bolitho came back from his brief dream. 'That'll be the tide across the river mouth. You may begin sounding directly.'

A seaman moved his foot, perhaps from cramp, and a musket clattered loudly on the bottom boards.

'Keep those men silent!' Bolitho lifted slightly to peer above the crowded figures as the river mouth opened up on either bow.

'Aye, aye, sir!'

He stiffened. It was Pascoe's voice, and he had not even known he was in this boat.

Allday moved the tiller very slightly and then muttered, 'Thought it best to have the young gentleman aboard, Captain. Just to keep an eye on him, so to speak.'

Bolitho glanced at him. 'No wonder you never married, Allday. You would leave little for a woman to worry about!'

Allday grinned in the darkness. The rasp in Bolitho's tone was as familiar to him as the wind in the shrouds. It was just his way. But in a moment or so the captain would make amends.

Bolitho dropped back into the sternsheets. 'But thank you, Allday, for your concern.'

Without looking at his watch Bolitho knew it was close on noon. The sun which had been in his face since early dawn now blazed down from directly overhead with the fierce heat of an open furnace.

He touched Allday's arm. 'We will rest here.' His lips felt cracked and dry, so that even few words were an effort.

'Easy all! Boat your oars!'

The seamen hauled the long oars inboard, while from forward came a splash as the bowman hurled a grapnel into the nearest clump of reeds.

Bolitho watched his men lolling across the thwarts and gunwales like corpses, their eyes closed and faces turned away from the sun which pinned them down in its relentless glare.

Dawn had found the four boats pulling strongly and well in spite of the salt-stained rushes and occasional sandbars. Zigzagging between the various obstacles had not been too difficult at first, and at most times the boats were all in sight of each other. Then as the blue sky faded in the mounting glare the stroke became slower, and time after time one boat and then another would lose valuable effort in backing from some hidden wedge of sand, or be thrown into confusion as its oarsmen caught their blades in the encroaching clumps of reeds.

But now, as the next boat pushed slowly through the motionless fronds to drop a grapnel nearby, Bolitho had forcibly to control his despair. It was like wandering in some insane maze, with only the sun and his small compass to show him the key to the puzzle. The reeds, which had broken and parted so easily near the river mouth, now stood all around the boats, thick and dark green, and in most places higher than the tallest man. If wind there was, the sweating and gasping men gained no relief from it, for the tall reeds and interlaced creepers acted as a cruelly effective barrier, so that the sun blazed down on the boats without pause, making movement unbearable.

Lieutenant Lang leaned across the gunwale of his cutter and rested one hand on the smooth wood for just a few seconds before jerking it away with a curse.

'My God, it's as hot as a musket barrel!' He tugged his shirt open across his chest and added, 'How far have we come, sir?'

Bolitho said, 'About five miles. We must push forward if we are to make up the time. We will rest at night, otherwise the boats could get scattered and lost.'

He looked down over the side. There was a current of sorts, twisting and turning amidst the reeds in countless tiny rivers. It was a dark, secret world, and the choked water seemed alive with tiny bubbles, released gases from drowned vegetation and rotten roots, but giving the impression of unseen life, or creatures waiting for the intruders to pass.

'After this the men will have to work shorter watches. Six men to a side, half an hour at the most.' He wiped his face with the back of his hand and stared at a bright winged insect on his skin. 'They will face forrard and paddle. There is no room for rowing now.' He waited until more splashes told him the other boats were drawing close. 'Tell the bowmen to use boathooks and *feel* the way through. At the deepest part there seems little more than eight feet or so of water. And it will become shallower, I have no doubt.'

Lieutenant Quince's cutter idled broadside amongst the clinging rushes, the men drooping on the oar looms, the hull scarred in many places by the slow tortuous passage.

Quince looked alert enough, and had a strip of canvas across the back of his neck. 'I make it five miles, sir.' He stood up in the boat and tried to peer above the nearest clump. 'I can't even see a hill. It seems to go on and on forever.'

Bolitho snapped, 'Don't let the men sleep!' He shook the oarsman nearest to him. 'Wake up, man! Keep those insects from eating you alive or you'll be dead in a matter of days!'

The sailor in question dragged himself upright and half-heartedly slapped aside some of the countless flies and buzzing insects which had been constant companions since daybreak.

Quince said suddenly, 'May I suggest you lash an oar upright in your boat, sir? If we get separated it would give us an aiming mark.'

Bolitho nodded. 'See to it, Allday.' It was good to know that Quince at least was thinking as well as suffering.

One of the seamen craned over the gunwale and cupped his hands in the sluggish stream. Allday barked, 'Avast there!' Then as the man withdrew his hands he dipped his neckcloth in the water and tasted it on his tongue.

He spat savagely across the gunwale. 'Muck!' In a calmer tone he added, 'Tastes of salt and something else, Captain.' He screwed up his mouth with revulsion. 'As if a thousand corpses were buried here.'

Bolitho raised his voice. 'D'you hear that? So hang on

and wait for the proper issue of fresh water. The stink here is bad enough, so just think what the water would do to your entrails!'

Here and there a man nodded soberly, but Bolitho knew they would all have to be watched. He had seen men drink salt water and go raving mad in a matter of hours. In spite of any amount of training and experience thirst could always be relied on to drive men to taking that first drink, even though they might have just witnessed the horrible death of one so tempted.

Wearily he said, 'We will proceed. Raise the grapnel!'

Groaning, the selected seamen rose to their feet and poised the oars along the sides like paddles. It was an uncomfortable way to move, but less wasteful than having the boat halted every few minutes while oars were jerked free from rushes and mud.

And what mud it was. When one of the men withdrew his blade Bolitho saw it was dripping with reeking black filth which shone in the sunlight like boiling pitch. Anxiously he watched as the man dipped his oar again and then breathed more easily. It moved without hindrance this time, and he knew the boat had edged once more into deeper water.

He saw Pascoe squatting on one of the barricoes, his head in his hands as he stared outboard at the passing wall of green fronds. His shirt was torn across one shoulder, and already the bared skin gleamed dull red through his tan, as if he had been struck by a hot ember.

He called, 'Come aft, Mr Pascoe.' He had to repeat the invitation before the boy lifted his head and then climbed slowly above the lolling seamen as if walking in his sleep.

Bolitho said quietly, 'Cover your shoulder, lad. You'll be as raw as beef directly if you give the sun its opportunity.'

He watched him pulling the torn shirt into place, seeing the fresh sweat breaking across his forehead with the effort. He thought suddenly of Stepkyne and cursed him beneath his breath.

He continued, 'I may want you to shin up that oar in the bows tomorrow and take a look around us. You are the lightest soul aboard, so you had better save your strength.'

Pascoe turned his head and looked up at him, his eyes

half hidden by his unruly hair. 'I can do it, sir.' He nodded vaguely. 'I will do it.'

Bolitho turned away, unable to watch the boy's feverish determination which seemed to dog him every hour of the day. He would never shirk any task, even if it was normally allotted to a hardened seaman, and Bolitho knew he would kill himself rather than admit defeat. It was just as if he nursed his father's shame like a permanent spur. As if he considered that he must prove himself, if only to wipe away Hugh's disgrace.

As the boy peered astern to look for the following cutter Bolitho stole another glance at him. What would he say if he knew the real truth? That his father was still alive, serving as a convict in New Holland under another man's name? He dismissed the thought immediately. Distance healed nothing, he knew that now. It would only drag out the boy's agony, fill him with new doubts or impossible hopes.

Allday licked his lips. 'Change round! Next men on the oars there!'

Bolitho shaded his eyes to look at the bare sky. Only the occasional gurgle of water around the stem made any sense of movement. This jerking, wretched progress seemed endless, as if they would go on and on into green oblivion and die of thirst, their graves the boats in which he had committed all of them to this hopeless gesture.

He groped for the compass and stared at it for a full minute. An insect crawled across the glass cover and he brushed it aside with something like anger. At best they might manage a full ten miles before nightfall. And this was the easiest part of the journey. Tomorrow, and the day after that would bring more hazards as the boats pushed further and further into the swamp. He glanced quickly at the seamen nearest to him. Their unfamiliar faces were strained and apprehensive, and they dropped their eyes when they saw him watching them.

Fighting and if necessary dying they could understand. Surrounded by men and objects aboard their own ship which shared their everyday life the demands of battle were as familiar as the harsh discipline and unquestionable authority which had made them the breed they were. But such standards were born as much from trust as from any code of conduct. The trust of each other, the measure of skill of their officers who ruled their very existence.

But now, under the command of a man they did not even know, and committed to an operation which must appear as treacherous as their surroundings, they must be feeling their first doubts. And from such uncertainty could grow the beginnings of failure.

He said, 'Pass the word to anchor again. We will break out rations and rest for half an hour.' He waited for Allday to call to the boat astern before adding, 'One cup of water per man, and see that it is taken slowly.'

Pascoe asked suddenly, 'When we reach the other end of the swamp might we be able to find some more water, sir?' His dark eyes were studying Bolitho with grave contemplation. 'Although I expect we will fight first.'

Bolitho watched the first seaman at the barricoe, the pannikin to his lips while he held back his head to make certain of the last drop. But he was still hearing Pascoe's words, his quiet confidence which at this particular moment did more to steady his thoughts than he would have believed possible.

He replied, 'I have no doubt we shall discover both water *and* fighting.' Then he smiled in spite of his parched lips. 'So take your drink now, lad, and let the rest come in its own good time.'

It was in the evening that progress ground to a sudden halt. No amount of thrusting or levering would budge the boat from its bed of sludge and rotting weed, and in spite of Shambler's threats and Allday's stubborn efforts the seamen leaned on their oars and stared at the setting sun with something like defiance. They were worn out and ready to collapse, and as Lang's boat lurched close astern Bolitho knew he must act at once if the last hour of daylight was to be used.

'Over the side! Lively there!' He strode along the tilting boat, ignoring the resentful faces and stinging insects. 'Get those lines up forrard, Mr Shambler! We will warp her through to the next stretch of deep water!'

As the bosun's mates hauled the coils of rope from the bottom boards Bolitho stood in the bows and stripped off his shirt and swordbelt, and then gritting his teeth lowered himself into the pungent water and reached up to take one of the lines.

Allday shouted, 'Move yourselves!' And vaulting over the gunwale he took another line and looped it round his shoulders like a halter, before wading after Bolitho without even a glance to see who was following.

Bolitho strode slowly through the clinging filth, feeling it around his thighs and then his waist as he struggled forward, the line biting his shoulder as it took the full weight of the boat. Then there were other splashes, followed by curses and groans as the men left the boat and one after the other took their places along the two towing lines behind him.

'Heave, lads!' Bolitho strained harder, trying to hold back the nausea as the stinking gases rose about him, making his mind swim as if in a fever. 'Together, *heave!*'

Reluctantly and very slowly the boat slid forward and down into another trough of deeper water. But there was another barrier waiting for their hesitant steps, and more than one man slipped spluttering and choking as the sludge clawed his feet from under him.

Then they were through, and shivering and coughing they dragged themselves back into the boat, where yet another horror awaited them.

Most of the men had great leeches fixed to their bodies, and as several tried to drag the slimy creatures free Bolitho shouted, 'Mr Shambler, pass the slow-match down the boat! Burn each off in turn, you'll not free yourselves otherwise!'

Allday held the slow-match to his leg and cursed as the fat leech dropped to the bottom of the boat. 'Drink my blood, would you? Damn your eyes, I'll see you fry first!'

Bolitho stood to watch the dying sun as it painted the tops of the rushes with red gold, so that for an instant the menace and despair were shaded with strange beauty.

The other boats were still following, the crews plunging through the shallows, their bodies pale in the fading light.

He said, 'We will moor for the night.' He saw Lang nodding to his words from the other boat. 'But we will get under way before dawn and try to make up lost time.'

He looked down at his own boat, where the seamen lolled

together unable to do little more than sit as they had done throughout the day. 'Detail one man for the watch, Allday. We are all so weary that otherwise I fear we would sleep through dawn and beyond.'

He lowered himself slowly into the sternsheets again and saw that Pascoe was already asleep, his head on the gunwale and one hand hanging almost to the water. Gently he lifted the boy's arm inboard and then seated himself against the tiller bar.

High overhead the first stars were pale in the sky and the tall rushes around the boat hissed quietly to a sudden breeze. For a few moments it was almost refreshing after the heat and filth of the day, but the impression was merely a passing one.

Bolitho leaned back and watched the stars, trying not to think of the hours and days which still lay ahead.

Near the bows a man groaned in his sleep, and another whispered fervently, 'Martha, Martha!' before falling silent once again.

Bolitho drew his knees up to his chin, feeling the caked mud hard against his skin. Who was Martha? he wondered. And was she still remembering the young man who had been snatched from her side to serve in a King's ship? Or maybe she was a daughter. A mere child who perhaps could no longer remember her father's face.

He looked down at Pascoe's limp body. Was he dreaming, too? Of his father whom he had never seen? Of a memory which had turned his mind to hate and shame?

Then he rested his forehead on his folded arms and was instantly asleep.

11. Dawn Attack

THROUGHOUT the following day the nightmare passage across the swamp continued with the sun always there to add to the slow torture. Poling from the boats, or wading through shallows to pull them bodily from the clinging mud, it now made little difference to anyone. They had lost count of time, or the number of occasions they had left or re-entered the boats, and their bodies and torn clothes were thick with filth, their faces cracked from fatigue and strain.

They had now found a more open stretch of swamp where there was no apparent current at all to break the surface. It was covered in a thick layer of green slime, while the rushes were in separate, isolated clumps, like strange creatures from another planet.

In the late afternoon, when it had become necessary to tow the boats across a half-submerged island of soft sand, one of the men had let go the line and had fallen thrashing and screaming, and because of the mud and slime on his body it was difficult at first to see what had happened. While the others had clustered apprehensively around the boat Bolitho and Allday had hoisted the writhing man aboard, and using a shirt dipped in fresh water Bolitho had cleaned away some of the mud from around a small droplet of blood deep in the man's groin. He must have trodden on some sort of snake, for the bright punctures were easy to see. While Allday had stayed with the seaman Bolitho had ordered the rest back to the towing lines, knowing that the snake's poison was already beyond cure, and to let his men stand by and watch their companion's wretched end would do nothing but harm.

As they had struggled on through the swamp they had been followed by the man's awful cries, and once when Bolitho had glanced across his shoulder he had seen the other seamen watching him, their eyes red-rimmed through the filth on their stubbled faces, their expressions filled with more hatred than pity. Mercifully the poison took little more than an hour to complete its work, and the lifeless body had been pushed clear of the boat, a grim warning to the others who were following close behind.

Most of the men could no longer face their rations of beef and hard biscuit, and lived rather than waited for the meagre issue of water from the barricoes. Bolitho had watched them during the brief rests, conscious of their jerky movements and dull-eyed faces. Of the way they watched each pannikin of water, with expressions more of animals than men.

Yet in spite of everything they had managed to keep moving. Bolitho knew their forbearance had changed to hatred towards him, that it only needed some small spark to turn the mission into a bloody mutiny.

During the night he let all the men sleep, taking turns to keep watch with Allday and Shambler alone. But in the second boat the vigilance was not enough. Or perhaps Lieutenant Lang had misjudged his own ability to control his men.

As Bolitho awoke from a restless doze he felt Allday tugging his shoulder and the touch of cold metal in his hand as the coxswain thrust a pistol towards him.

'What is it?' For a second longer he thought he had overslept, but when he peered over the gunwale he saw that there was only a hint of light in the eastern sky, and along the boat the men still lay entwined like crude statuary.

'Mr Lang's sent word that the water's been broached in his boat, Captain! The news'll be badly received when his people awake.'

Bolitho lurched to his feet. 'Here, keep the pistol.' He climbed over the gunwale and felt the slime pressing against his legs in a cool embrace, his feet sinking with each step that he took towards the other boat.

Lang was waiting for him, his face screwed into a frown.

'How bad is it?'

Lang shrugged. 'Hardly a drop left, sir. I've only one barricoe for the rest of the journey *and* the return passage.'

A voice echoed across the swamp from another boat. 'Time to call the hands, sir!'

Bolitho hauled himself into the boat. 'Go to Mr Quince and warn him at once, and then pass the word to Mr Carlyon.' He gripped the lieutenant's wrist. 'And *no pistols*, d'you understand?'

When the men of the second cutter dragged themselves from their sleep they stared blearily at Bolitho and then at each other as he said, 'During the night someone aboard this boat broached the barricoe. He took a goodly helping, and in his guilty haste allowed the rest of its contents to run through the bottom boards.' He gestured towards their feet, to the glint of water amidst the caked mud and slime brought inboard during the previous day. He added slowly, 'I think you know what this will mean!'

Someone near the bows yelled, 'Mr Lang must'a done it, lads. 'E 'ad the watch hisself!' There was an answering growl as he persisted, 'The officers 'ave bin 'elping theirselves!'

Bolitho stood quite still in the sternsheets, his hands on his hips. He was aware of the sudden desperate anger, of the fact he was alone and unarmed. But more than this he was conscious of something akin to shame, as if he was indeed responsible.

He said quietly, 'You are wrong, but I did not come to plead with you or to make my case for your understanding. You have done well so far, better than anyone could expect. You have attained already what some thought impossible, and if necessary you will do better, even if there is no water at all and I have to drive you with my bare hands!'

A probing shaft of early sunlight played down on the piled weapons, and he saw more than one man glance meaningly towards them.

He snapped, 'If you think that by killing me your thirst will be relieved, then you had better make a move! But otherwise I intend to raise the grapnels and get under way again.'

The voice yelled, 'Don't listen, lads! 'E's tryin' to protect 'is lieutenant!'

Bolitho stepped down and walked slowly towards the nearest men. Across the swamp he could see the others watching in silence, and Allday poised with one foot on the gunwale as if to hurl himself bodily to his captain's aid. He would be too late. Before he could even reach the boat's side any man could snatch a cutlass and cut him down.

He said evenly, 'I have sometimes found that the louder the voice, the greater the guilt.' He stopped on one thwart, his back to more than six of the men as he stared down at a heavily built sailor by his feet.

'Yesterday I had to use fresh water to clean a man's wound. To try and find where the snake had bitten him.'

There was not a sound in the boat, and those near him were staring at his face as if he had gone quietly mad.

He continued in the same even tone, 'I did not even know that man, as I do not know any of you. But he did his duty, and he did his best.' He was conscious of the sun's frail warmth against his cheek, of his heart's savage pounding as he stared fixedly at the man by his feet. If he had made a mistake he was done for. More to the point, there would be a senseless and bloody slaughter, with no victors at the end of it, just some lost and thirst-maddened wretches left to wander in the swamp until they too died, or killed each other.

He said, 'When I cleaned the mud from that seaman his skin seemed white against the filth he had gathered in his efforts to help me, and you, to achieve our objective.' His hand shot out and gripped the man's hair before he could move clear. '*Look at his chest!* See where the water, your water, spilled down it as he drank his fill and let the rest run to waste!'

The man shouted hoarsely, 'It's a lie, lads! Don't listen to 'im!'

Bolitho released the man's hair and said, 'Stand up and open your shirt.'

'I'll see you damned first!' The seaman crouched back against the gunwale, his teeth bared.

'I think not.' Bolitho walked aft to the sternsheets adding, 'You have one minute!'

The man looked round at the others. 'What d'you say, eh? Shall we do for the buggers now?'

A thin seaman with a cruel scar down one side of his face said tersely, 'Do like he says, 'Arry! You've nothin' to fear if yewm in the right!'

'You bastard!' The accused man glared round the boat. 'You snivellin' buggers!' Then he tore open his shirt. 'So I stole some water!' The flask swung into view across his chest, its neck still moist in the sunlight.

Something like a great sigh came from the watching seamen, but still nobody moved. Every eye was on the flask, as if it was a symbol of some awful disclosure which no one could yet understand.

Bolitho said quietly, 'Fetch Mr Lang. This man will be taken to the ship and tried for his crime.'

From one corner of his eye he saw a seaman clamber over the gunwale and begin wading towards the other boats. The tension was breaking, and in its place came a wave of fury.

"'Ang the bugger!' Some of the seamen peered round as if searching for a tree. 'Cut 'is gizzard, the thievin' scum!'

Bolitho lowered himself over the side and beckoned to Lang. But as he stared towards him he heard a shout of warning and the sudden rasp of steel. When he turned he saw the accused seaman right above him on the gunwale, a cutlass poised over his head.

'*Now*, Cap'n! You done for me, so it's my turn . . .' He got no further.

There was a soft thud, and with hatred changing to astonishment in his eyes he fell forward face down in the slime beside the boat. Between his shoulder blades was a bone-handled knife.

The scar-faced seaman stood by the gunwale watching the corpse as the blood made thin scarlet tendrils between the patches of slime.

'*No*, 'Arry. You already 'ad your turn!'

Lang stared at the stricken faces and muttered, 'I'm sorry, sir, it was my fault. I must have fallen asleep.' He hung his head. 'It'll not happen again, sir.'

Bolitho looked towards the leading boat and saw Allday sliding a pistol beneath his shirt. He had been ready, but at that range it was unlikely he would have been able to save his life.

He said shortly, 'I know it will not happen again. For if it does, I will personally see that you are court martialled!' He waded past him adding, 'Retrieve the cutlass from that corpse and get under way!'

Allday reached down to help him into the boat, his face lined with concern. 'By God, Captain, that was a fierce risk you took!'

Bolitho sat down and tried to wipe some of the slime from his legs. 'I had to be sure. It is not necessary for these men to like me. But trust me they *must*.' He looked across at Pascoe's worried face. 'And I must trust them. I think we have all learned a lesson this morning. Let us hope there is still time to gain profit from it.'

He stood up and looked calmly along the boat. 'Rig the towing lines again. Mr. Shambler. There's still some way to go.'

174

He watched them leave the boat, bodies caked and plastered almost beyond recognition, their eyes fixed on some point beyond the next layer of reeds and swamp.

Wearily he followed them and took his place at the head of the towline. Allday was right. It had been madness to make such a gesture. Most captains would have had the man seized and flogged to ribbons in spite of their situation. More as an example for open defiance than with any sense of judgement for stealing water from his messmates.

The line went slack and he almost pitched on his face, and when he turned he saw that the men were pulling so strongly the boat was riding above the swamp with the reeds and scum parting across its stem as if being controlled by invisible hands.

The man nearest him panted between tugs, 'We'll get there, sir! Have no fear o' that!'

Bolitho nodded and turned back to peer at the swaying reeds ahead of him. Or were they swaying? He brushed his hand roughly across his eyes to clear the mist, but when he looked again it was still there.

Allday, leading the other line, glanced at him and sighed. He had seen the surprise in Bolitho's eyes, the sudden emotion as he had realized the men were trying harder than ever, not for any cause, but for him alone.

Allday had known for a long time that most seamen would do anything for an officer who treated them fairly and humanely. It was strange that Bolitho did not know this fact, especially as he of all people should have done.

In the early afternoon Bolitho signalled a halt, and gasping from exertion the men clambered back into the boats, too weary even to watch as the barricoes were placed in readiness for their water issue.

Bolitho examined each boat in turn, his mind rebelling against what he saw. They were almost finished, and hardly a man was looking beyond his own boat. Most just sat on the thwarts, heads hanging, oblivious even to the buzzing flies which explored their eyes and cracked lips while they waited like dumb beasts for the next order.

He beckoned to Pascoe. 'Well, my lad, this is the moment.' He kept his voice calm but saw the boy's face light up with sudden eagerness. He continued, 'Climb up the oar and have a look round. Take your time, and don't show disappointment if you sight nothing.' He rested his hand on the boy's shoulder. 'They'll all be watching you, remember that!'

He sank back against the tiller bar as Pascoe walked forward between the listless figures, his head tilted to stare at the oar lashed upright in the bows. He shinned up the oar, his body silhouetted against the washed-out blue sky as he twisted slowly to peer above the reeds and far beyond them.

Allday whispered, 'By God, I hope there's something to see.'

Bolitho did not move, as if by distracting the boy he might destroy their last chance of survival.

'Nothing ahead, sir!'

Some of the men were on their feet looking up at the slim figure above them, arms limp at their sides like prisoners under sentence of death.

'Larboard, sir!' Pascoe slipped and then wrapped his legs more firmly around the smooth oar. 'A hill! About two miles away!'

Bolitho lowered his eyes to the compass, hardly daring to look. Larboard bow. About north-west from where they were lying.

He called, 'Is it pointed with a ridge down one side?'

'Yes, sir.' The boy's voice became suddenly assured. 'Yes, I can just see it.'

Bolitho looked at Allday and closed the compass with a snap. 'Then we have arrived.'

Pascoe slithered down the oar and walked unsteadily amongst the cheering, croaking seamen who banged his thin shoulders and called his name as he passed, as if he alone had saved them from disaster. When he reached the stern he asked dazedly, 'Is it all right, sir?'

Bolitho studied him gravely. 'It is, Mr Pascoe.' He watched the pleasure spreading across the boy's grimy features. '*It is, indeed!*'

Feeling his way like a blind man Bolitho pulled himself slowly to the top of a flat boulder and stood upright, waiting to regain his breath while his ears explored the surrounding darkness. Overhead the sky with its limitless ceiling of stars was already much paler, and as he turned slightly towards the light breeze he imagined he could smell the dawn. It was very cold, and through his open shirt his skin felt chilled and clammy.

He studied the undulating humps of land beneath the sky's edge and found time to wonder that any of his small force had lived to see them. It was just as if he had arrived here alone and without support, that he was the only man alive in this forsaken place. Yet behind him at the foot of the steep slope the others were already awake and preparing to move, groping for their weapons and waiting to do what they must, no matter how impossible the odds or how futile the gesture.

Bolitho stretched out his arms and felt his muscles protesting at the sudden movement. Without effort he could picture those same men when they had blundered out of the swamp on the previous evening. Filthy and near collapse, their eyes glazed with something like gratitude just to feel the land beneath their feet. Many had not set foot ashore for months, and after the agonizing passage through the swamp they had been almost incapable of standing, so that they had reeled about like drunken men or clung to each other for support. He bit his lip, wishing there was more time. Perhaps these men were already too weary, too dulled by their experiences to complete the work they had come so far to do. Or maybe Pelham-Martin had changed his mind and would not even launch another attack as he had promised.

Almost savagely he shook himself free of the nagging doubts and climbed back down the slope where Lieutenant Lang was waiting for him.

'All the men have been fed, sir. I gave them a double water ration as you ordered.'

Bolitho nodded. 'Good. No one could expect them to make that journey back across the swamp, so it is well for them to fight on a full stomach.'

Lang said nothing, and Bolitho imagined he was probably thinking of the other alternative. That without any rations left to sustain them the men would have to fight and win. Or surrender.

Bolitho shifted restlessly. 'Mr Quince should be back by

now. We will have to move off directly if we are to get into position.'

Lang shrugged. 'It is strange to realize the sea is just over those hills, sir. This place feels like a wilderness.'

A voice called hoarsely, 'Here comes Mr Quince, sir!'

The lieutenant's tall figure emerged from the gloom like a spectre, his ragged shirt blowing in the breeze as he strode quickly down the slope with the three seamen he had taken as scouts to spy out the land.

'Well?' Bolitho could hardly keep the anxiety from his voice.

Quince lifted a flask to his lips and drank deeply, the water running unheeded down his chest.

He said, 'Just as you thought, sir. The headland yonder is where the guns are sited.' He belched noisily. 'It's like a deep saddle between those two humpy hills, so no wonder the battery was hidden from seaward.'

Bolitho shivered slightly. 'How many?'

Quince rubbed his chin. 'Seven or eight field-pieces, sir. There are sentries on the headland itself, and more to our right. There's a kind of track which leads around the bay to the town, and we saw a lantern at its narrowest part.'

'I see.' Bolitho felt the excitement running through him. 'And no sentries between those two posts?'

'None.' Quince was emphatic. 'And why should there be? With the swamp at their backs and the bay before 'em, they must feel very safe indeed.'

'Then we will move off.'

Bolitho turned to walk down the slope but stopped as Quince added, 'The Frogs feel so safe that they're not even bothering to hide themselves, sir. There are a few tents near the guns, but my guess is that the bulk of the artillerymen are quartered in the town. After all, it will take hours for our ships to get into position for another attack. The French have all the time in the world.'

He fell in step beside Bolitho, adding, 'It proves too that Las Mercedes is in enemy hands.'

'Fortunately that is not our concern. The ships *are*!'

Quince chuckled. 'We'll give them something to chew on right enough. One good rush should do it. Then over the

178

cliff with the guns, and we can withdraw to the swamp and wait for the squadron to pick us up.'

Bolitho did not answer, and he had to forcibly drag his mind to the immediate problem of sorting out his men in the gloom. Quince's words had started another train of ideas moving. The French were confident, and even without the supporting cliff battery could still do much damage to the attacking squadron. And this attack was not the answer to the puzzle. None of the French ships wore Lequiller's command flag. He was still out there somewhere, free and unhampered, while Pelham-Martin's small force was being pared away.

He reached the shadowy figures at the foot of the slope and marvelled at the change which had come over them. Even in the poor light he could see the assured way they waited patiently by their muskets, their faces pale against the scrub and thick foliage which masked the limits of the swamp.

Fox, the gunner's mate, knuckled his forehead. 'All loaded, sir. I checked each musket meself.'

Bolitho said, 'Listen to me. In a moment we are going to climb the hillside in three separate parties. Do not bunch together, and be sure not to slip. If any man looses off his musket by accident we are all done for. We must reach the high ground before dawn without being seen.'

He added evenly, 'Just over yonder lies the bay. And below the cliffs are the remains of the *Abdiel* and all her company. Remember her fate when the time comes, and do your best.'

He drew the lieutenants to one side. 'Mr Quince, you will occupy the headland while I seize the guns. Mr Lang will cover the track to the town and prevent any one leaving or entering the area.'

Lang asked, 'And the midshipmen, sir?'

'They will keep contact between us.' He looked at each in turn. 'If I fall, it will be Mr Quince's duty to complete our task. And if we are both killed, then you will do so, Mr Lang.'

Allday padded from the shadows. 'Ready, Captain.'

'Right, gentlemen. I think we have wasted enough time with words.'

Quince checked the pistols in his belt and muttered, 'What will become of the boats, sir?'

'We will leave them hidden. If we take the battery we may

retrieve them later.' He looked away. 'If not, they will lie rotting as our memorial!'

Without another word he started up the slope, and while Quince's scouts vanished ahead into the shadows the lines of seamen began to follow.

Bolitho wondered what the first thought would be of the enemy sentries when they saw the sailors charging down on them. Wild, ragged and caked with mud, they would strike terror into the strongest hearts.

It had needed almost forcible restraint to prevent the men from trying to wash themselves once they had recovered from their passage through the swamp. Unlike land creatures, sailors always tried to stay clean, no matter how meagre their rations of water, or how primitive the conditions.

He glanced to his left and saw Quince's thin column of men pushing up the slope, and already he could make out individual figures, the slung muskets and lethal gleam of fixed bayonets. As Quince looked across he waved his arm, showing that he too understood the importance of haste with the dawn so close upon them.

One of the scouts came scurrying back down the hillside, his musket above his head as he jumped from rock to rock as if he had been doing it all his life.

'All clear, sir.' He pointed towards the curved edge of the hill where already the first weak sunlight was easing away the shadows and painting the coarse stubble and loose stones with colour.

Bolitho saw that the scout was the scar-faced seaman who had saved his life with a well-aimed dirk. 'You've done well.'

He signalled to Lang and saw him lead his party away to the right of the hill. To Allday he said, 'Tell the men to wait here. I'm going up to take a look.'

With the lean seaman at his side he hurried up the last of the slope and then lowered himself to the ground, groping for his small telescope, as with breathtaking beauty the bay opened up before him. Far to the right was the tall, pointed hill which Pascoe had sighted from the swamp, its crest and sides gleaming in the pale sunlight like a polished arrowhead. The town at its foot was still in black shadow, but Bolitho was already moving his glass towards the open sea and the ships, which as before were anchored across the bay's entrance.

The seaman lifted his arm. 'There's the guns, sir!'

Bolitho dipped the glass and steadied it on a piece of rock. The heavy guns, seven in all, were standing very near to the edge of the cliff, their muzzles clearly etched against the cruising whitecaps far below. It was indeed like a great natural saddle, and where the next hump-backed hill lifted towards the end of the headland he could see a line of pale tents and a solitary sentry pacing slowly back and forth. The track which followed the hillside towards the distant town was invisible from here, but Bolitho guessed that the sentry was well in sight of his opposite number at that end.

Stones rattled noisily and Midshipman Carlyon clambered up beside him. 'Mr Lang's compliments, sir, and his men are in position above the roadway.' He peered down at the guns and shivered. 'There's only one guard at his end, sir.'

Bolitho levelled his glass on the sentry beyond the line of tents. Soon now. What in heaven's name was keeping Quince?

He blinked rapidly and readjusted his glass. For a moment longer he imagined his eye had played a trick on him. One second the sentry was strolling along the edge of the cliff, hands deep in pockets and his chin on his chest as no doubt he considered what the day might bring. Then nothing, as if he had been spirited bodily over the side of the headland. Bolitho waited a few more seconds and then saw something white lift above a low-lying bank of gorse. It was the signal, and the luckless sentry would never have to think about this day, or any other.

Bolitho snapped, 'Tell Mr Lang we are about to attack!'

As the startled midshipman fled down the hillside he turned and waved to Allday. 'Follow me, lads! No noise, and no shooting until I give the word!'

Then as the sun showed itself for the first time above the distant hills he sprinted down the slope towards the battery, his sword in his hand and his eyes fixed on the silent tents.

The sheltered side of the hill was steeper than he had imagined, and as he gathered speed he felt as if he was falling headlong. Behind him the noise grew louder as anticipation and tension gave way to wild excitement which not even threats could control, and from one corner of his eye he saw a seaman already passing him, his levelled bayonet held out like a pike while he charged full tilt at the head of his companions.

Somewhere in the far distance a pistol cracked, the sound puny against the pounding feet and fierce breathing, and even as Bolitho vaulted over some splintered boulders a man emerged from one of the tents and stood stockstill, as if turned to stone.

Then he whirled round, tearing at the tent flap and yelling, '*Aux armes! Aux armes!*'

Figures tumbled wildly from the other tents, some with weapons, but mostly without as they ran this way and that, probably still unaware what was happening.

More shots rattled in the crisp air, and several of the Frenchmen fell untidily beside the tents. As Quince's ragged line of seamen appeared around the hill someone, probably an officer, fired his pistol and drove his startled men towards the guns. It was then, and only then that the awakened artillerymen saw Bolitho's party charging towards them.

Here and there a musket banged, and once Bolitho felt a ball pass within inches of him. But the resistance was over before it could begin, and as soldier after soldier threw down his weapon Bolitho heard Quince bellowing above the shouts and cried, 'Hold your fire, damn you! Give quarter!'

Bolitho saw a seaman drop on one knee to aim his musket at a French soldier who not only held up his hands in surrender, but was within five feet of the muzzle, staring at it like a terrified rabbit. Bolitho struck the man's arm with the flat of his sword and saw him drop the musket with dazed disbelief. He snapped, 'Save your energy!' And as the seaman stumbled after the others he gestured towards the French officer who alone and defiant stood with his back to the sea, a sword gripped firmly in his hand.

'Drop your sword!' Bolitho saw the hesitation on the man's face change to sudden fury as with a cry he hurled himself forward, his blade stabbing in the sunlight like burnished gold.

The sudden rasp of steel on steel seemed to bring the attack to a halt. Even the victorious seamen lowered their weapons, as if stunned by the desperate bravery of one against so many.

Bolitho could feel the man's breath on his face, as hilt to hilt they locked swords and reeled against one of the heavy cannon, their feet stirring the dust while they fought to hold and exploit a first advantage. He twisted his shoulder behind the sword and pushed with all his strength, seeing his opponent stagger away, his blade already reaching up to protect his neck.

Between his teeth Bolitho rasped, 'Strike, damn you! *Strike!*'

But the Frenchman only seemed more inflamed, and with another bound sprang forward to a fresh attack. Bolitho parried the blade aside, paused, and as the other man lurched against the cannon's massive wheel he drove forward and down, feeling the grating impact of steel against ribs, and then the final thrust which forced the other man's breath from his lungs in one awful cry.

Bolitho stood for several moments staring down at the lifeless figure draped against the wheel. "Fool!" He looked at the sword in his hand, red in the sunlight. 'Brave fool!'

Allday came across to him, his heavy cutlass swinging in his fist like a toy. 'Well *done*, Captain!' He jerked the corpse from the gun and pushed it towards the cliff edge. 'That's one less to worry about.'

Bolitho held up the sword and stared at it, amazed his hand was so steady when every fibre in his body seemed to be shaking uncontrollably.

He said heavily, 'I hope I die as bravely when the time comes.'

Quince panted past the prisoners and grinned at him. 'Not lost a man, sir! There are only twenty prisoners, so we'll not be hard put to watch over 'em.' He studied Bolitho worriedly. 'Are you feeling well, sir?'

Bolitho stared at him. 'Thank you, yes.' He slid the sword back into its scabbard. 'But now that we have seized the guns I have second thoughts about them.'

Quince licked his lips as a trumpet blared from the moored ships. 'We've not long, sir. The Frogs will be sending boats ashore with more men than *we* can manage.'

Bolitho did not hear him. 'Something you said earlier, Mr Quince.'

'*I* said, sir?'

'You remarked that the squadron will have a hard fight, even without the battery to oppose them.'

Quince shrugged. 'Well, sir, if I *did* say that, I am sorry to have given you cause to doubt.' He shook his head admiringly. 'After the way you got us here and took these damned guns, I'll be thankful *and* grateful to leave it at that.'

Bolitho walked to the edge of the cliff. 'It is not enough. The *Abdiel* was hit and ablaze within minutes of the first attack.' He gestured to a rough earthworks beside the tents. 'They used heated shot from that crude oven to do it so quickly.'

Quince nodded grimly. 'I know, sir. 'Tis a pity the embers are cold. We could have set one, maybe two of 'em ablaze for good measure before we quit this place.'

Bolitho watched the ships, his face masked in concentration. 'But if you were a French captain down there you might expect such an attack.' He nodded firmly. 'Fetch Mr Fox and tell him to prepare the guns for firing!' As Allday hurried away he added, 'Set light to one of those tents and then douse the flames with water, Mr Quince. With luck the French will believe we are heating shot, eh? That will have to suffice for the present.'

Shambler called, 'Boats shovin' off from two of the Frenchmen, sir!'

Bolitho nodded. The ships would have men to spare while they were at anchor and still have sufficient to work their guns when Pelham-Martin arrived. He gripped his hands behind him. *If* Pelham-Martin arrived.

'Send a man to the hilltop to watch for our ships!'

Shambler looked at him. 'Aye, aye, sir.'

At that moment the gunner's mate arrived at his side. He was a wiry little man and not unlike his namesake.

'*Now*, Mr Fox.' Bolitho watched narrowly as the first boats gathered way and started to pull towards the shore. 'Get to work on these guns and lay for the second ship in the line.'

Fox touched his forehead and then said gruffly, 'I kin get the furnace goin' too, sir. Given 'alf an hour.' He chuckled and showed his teeth. 'My father were a blacksmith, sir, an' taught me well enough 'ow to raise the embers in a 'urry.'

Bolitho felt the excitement running through him. Pelham-Martin or no, it would not all be wasted if he could help it.

He shouted, 'Tell Mr Lang to hold the road! With the

cliff edge on one side and his men on the other, it should not be too difficult!'

He made himself walk slowly along the edge, watching the oared boats far below him, puny and impersonal.

Fox exclaimed. 'Ready, sir!' He was crouching behind the nearest gun, his face screwed up with professional concentration.

Bolitho replied, 'Fire a ranging ball!'

Fox jumped aside and held his slow-match above the breech. The roar of the gun crashed between the twin hills, and from the cliffs below came hundreds of screaming birds, wheeling and circling above the watching seamen in an enraged chorus.

'Short!' Fox was grinning gleefully. After the swaying platform of a ship's gundeck this was child's play to him. He was already bawling at his men again. ''Andspikes there! Muzzle to th' right!' He was prancing behind the breech even as the others were sponging out and reloading. 'Steady! That should do it!' He waited with obvious impatience for the massive ball to be rammed home, then, 'Right now, elevate th' old lady!' He shook his fist in a seaman's sweating face. 'Easy, lad, *easy*!'

The slow-match came down again and with a roar the gun jerked back against the hard rock, the smoke rising above the cliff in a solid brown cloud.

'Over!' Fox rubbed his hands. 'Now the next un'll do it!'

Quince walked to Bolitho's side to watch as first one boat then another faltered and then started back towards their respective ships. 'They must have spotted my smoke.' He chuckled, 'What now, sir?'

Bolitho could well imagine the consternation aboard the anchored ships. To be bombarded like this was bad enough, but with the prospect of heated shot for good measure, each captain would have to act soon if he was to withdraw out of range.

Fox stood back. '*Fire!*' He ran to the cliff edge, shading his eyes to see the fall of shot.

A tall waterspout rose alongside the second ship's quarter, and Bolitho guessed it must have hit her close on the waterline.

Fox seemed to have hidden stores of energy. 'All guns

elevate!' He scuttled from gun to gun, peering back at the first one to make quite sure of an exact salvo. '*Fire!*' The line of guns jerked back in unison, and around the target ship the waterspouts arose like enraged ghosts.

'Captain, sir!'

Bolitho turned and saw Pascoe staring up at him. He was breathing hard and had obviously run all the way from Lang's outpost by the road.

'What is it, lad?'

'Mr Lang said to tell you there are soldiers coming down the road from the town, sir. They are about two miles away but marching very fast.' He peered at the ships as if seeing them for the first time.

Quince muttered, 'How many of them, Mr Pascoe?'

The boy shrugged. 'Several hundred, sir.'

Bolitho looked at Quince. 'French or Spanish, it matters little to us. They will be out for our blood, and Mr Lang can't do much more than delay the attack by minutes.' He dragged out his watch. 'Where the *hell* are our ships?'

Pascoe was still watching him. 'Is there a message for Mr Lang, sir?'

He turned to look at Fox as the little gunner's mate jumped in the air and yelled wildly, 'Two hits, lads! That'll teach 'em manners!'

Bolitho said calmly, 'Tell him to keep me informed.' He watched Pascoe run back towards the hillside and then added, 'Unless the commodore makes his attack very soon, Mr Quince, I fear he will be too late.' He pointed at the nearest ship where men were already climbing aloft and along the yards. 'That one has lost his nerve. Our commodore will arrive to find us dead and the ships gone within an hour or two.'

Quince nodded glumly. 'Maybe he has been delayed, sir.'

Bolitho watched the smoke being sucked across the cliff edge. The wind was still brisk and steady. There was no excuse for the ships not being here as promised.

He said curtly, 'Continue firing. And tell Mr Fox to hurry up with his damned furnace!' Then he walked quickly to the line of tents, his face deep in thought.

12. Mr Selby

TRUE TO HIS WORD, Fox, the gunner's mate, was working wonders with the crude furnace. Using liberal helpings of sprinkled gunpowder and hastily-gathered gorse he crawled around its iron door, peering and nodding with satisfaction before running back again to supervise his men.

Bolitho looked at the sun, now clear and vivid above the pointed hill, and then walked to the cliff edge to watch the anchored ships far below. The first signs of panic had been replaced by orderly preparations for getting under way, but he guessed that all the vessels had been so carefully and strongly moored together it would still take as much as half an hour to complete the operation.

He snapped, 'I am going to see Mr Lang. Inform me when you are ready with the heated shot.' With Allday striding at his side he turned and hurried towards the rough track, dazzled by the sea beneath him and conscious of his own mounting desperation.

He found Lang and his men scattered above the narrow track, sheltering as best they could behind fallen rocks, their muskets pointing towards the wide bend which vanished around the side of the hill from which the attack had started.

Lang saw Bolitho and stood up hastily. 'We've lost sight of the soldiers, sir. But they'll be coming around that curve at any time now.'

Bolitho beckoned to Carlyon. 'Tell Mr Quince to send twenty more men at the double!'

To Lang he continued, 'We can hold this road for a while provided the soldiers don't infiltrate behind us.' He was thinking aloud, trying to see the hillside and the country beyond as it would appear to seasoned troops. It seemed incredible for so many soldiers to be gathered in such a place, and if Lequiller had transported them in strength it was even harder to understand his purpose.

As more armed seamen panted along the track he shouted, 'Spread out on the hillside! Do not fire until I give the order!'

Lang shifted his feet uneasily. 'Any sign of the squadron, sir?'

Bolitho shook his head. 'Not as yet.'

He watched the ragged seamen climbing above the track, noting the strain on their faces, the apprehensive glances thrown towards the sea. They would know the impossibility of their position without having to be told. No more rations, and soon the sun would be high overhead to quell their last resistance and will to fight.

Then he heard the new sound, the steady tramp of booted feet beating on the rough track like an army of drums.

The first soldiers swung around the curve in the road, and at a shouted command halted less than a hundred yards from the nearest seaman.

A foot skidded on the stones and Pascoe arrived gasping at Bolitho's elbow. 'Mr Quince says the first ball is heated and ready, sir!' He peered at the motionless array of soldiers across the track and added thickly, 'The French!'

Bolitho lifted his glass and studied the silent soldiers for several seconds. 'Only the uniforms are French, Mr Pascoe.' In the small lens he could see the soldiers swaying with fatigue from their forced march, their dark skins and the careless way with which they held their bayoneted muskets. 'No French infantryman would slouch like that.' He added sharply, 'Tell Mr Quince to open fire on the second ship at once. He will know what to do.'

The boy hesitated, his eyes still on the soldiers. 'Will you stay here, sir?'

Bolitho thrust the glass into his pocket. 'Away with you! There is no time for gossip!' As the boy turned to go he added, 'All will be well with us, provided you can hit that ship!'

Lang muttered, 'Some of the troops from the rear are making for the hill, sir!'

Bolitho nodded. 'Prepare to fire!' He withdrew his sword and rested the blade across his shoulder. 'They will try to rush us, Mr Lang, so keep your wits about you!'

A whistle shrilled from around the bend of the road and the first files of troops began to trot purposefully towards the narrowest part where a small avalanche had cut a deep cleft, the sides of which fell straight down to the sea below.

'Take aim!' Bolitho held the sword over his head, feeling the sweat running down his chest and the parched dryness on his lips. 'Fire!'

Forty muskets shattered the silence in a ragged fusilade which came from every piece of cover afforded to the seamen. As smoke swirled out over the bay Bolitho saw the soldiers falling and reeling, some pitching out of sight over the side of the cliff itself.

'Reload!' He tried to keep his voice calm, knowing that any sort of panic would turn his slender defences into a rout. Some of the troops were still coming on, but as they reached the bodies of their fallen comrades, hesitated and then paused to kneel and fire blindly towards the hillside. Musket balls whined and ricocheted in all directions at once and, as more troops trotted around the curve, Bolitho shouted, 'Take aim! Fire!'

The response was more uneven, for some had not yet had time to reload in their cramped positions, but as the balls swept savagely into the packed soldiers it was more than enough. Firing as they went the soldiers fell back, leaving some dozen dead and wounded on the track, while others had vanished completely into the waiting sea beneath the cliff.

A heavy crash echoed around the hillside and Bolitho said, 'I hope Fox still has the range, Mr Lang.'

A musket ball whimpered past his face and he jumped down behind the rocks as more shots hammered almost directly from the hillside above the track.

'Skirmishers!' He shaded his eyes to the glare and saw several small shapes darting across the summit, some falling motionless as the seamen returned fire as fast as they could reload.

He gripped the lieutenant's shoulder. 'Hold on here. I am going to see what is happening at the guns.' He saw Lang nod vaguely. 'And keep your men in cover no matter what the enemy tries!' Then he turned and ran down the slope, the musket fire and shouts ringing in his ears until the hillside reached out to deaden the sound like a curtain.

He found Quince standing on the cliff edge, just as he had left him. He pointed excitedly towards the ships where the nearest two-decker was fighting to free herself from what appeared to be a fouled hawse, so that she swung helplessly to the wind, her stern held fast by the extra cables. The second ship seemed unchanged, but as he lifted his glass Bolitho saw a telltale plume of smoke rising from her poop and the sudden rush of figures with buckets and axes as the smoke blossomed into a full-scale cloud.

Fox was almost beside himself. 'A *hit*!' He swung on the cheering gunners. 'Another ball, you buggers!' He ran to the furnace as his men staggered sweating with the unwieldy iron cradle upon which a fat, thirty-two pound shot gleamed with fierce heat.

Bolitho said, 'Mr Lang will not be able to hold out much longer.' He felt Quince stiffen. 'There must be at least two hundred soldiers on the move, and probably more in the town.'

Quince stared at him. 'But why, sir? What could Las Mercedes need such a force for?'

Bolitho saw the smoke fading above the French ship as the buckets of water quenched the embedded shot before it could take hold.

Fox seemed oblivious to the closeness of danger as he checked the wad to make sure it was well soaked before he allowed the glowing ball to be cradled into the muzzle.

Bolitho replied, 'I am not sure, Mr Quince. Not yet.'

The gun lurched back again, and for a split second Bolitho saw the ball reach the apex of its flight before pitching down towards the anchored ship. Like a black spot on the sun, he thought.

It struck the ship just forward of the quarterdeck on the starboard side, although for a few moments several of the watching gunners imagined it had missed completely. Then as the smoke fanned out and upwards, Bolitho knew it was a fatal shot. He saw the first licking flames beneath her upper gun-ports, the sudden rush of smoke, as if forced from the tinder-dry timbers by some giant bellows.

'The furthest ships are aweigh at last, sir.' Quince banged his fists together as a great tongue of flame shot up the stricken vessel's main shrouds so that the whole centre part of the hull changed in an instant to one terrible torch.

'Shift your target, Mr Fox!' Bolitho swung round as

Carlyon appeared at Quince's side. He was cut on both knees and had a gash across his forehead.

'I—I fell, sir!' He winced as the gun banged out behind him. 'I ran as fast as I could . . .' he broke off, his face crumbling with shock and despair.

Bolitho seized his arm and shook him. 'What is it?'

'Mr Lang has been hit, sir! Our people are falling back!' He reeled and would have fallen but for Bolitho's grip. 'The troops are all around the hill, sir! We can't hold them any more!'

Bolitho looked at Quince and shouted, 'Train that gun towards the road!' As the men faltered he added harshly, 'Lively there!' He gestured to the watching seamen. 'Put those prisoners to work and push the other guns over the cliff!' He glared at Quince's grim features. 'They'll not fire *those* again!'

As the first cannon lumbered over the edge he added, I must go back to our people on the road. Make sure the remaining gun is loaded and aimed.' Then he ran off before Quince could question him further.

When he reached the barrier of fallen boulders, where only hours earlier he had led his men to the attack, he saw the seamen falling back towards him, some shooting their muskets towards the hillside, others dragging themselves on shattered limbs, or holding on to each other in an effort to reach some sort of safety.

'Over here!' Bolitho waved his sword towards the stone barrier. 'Take cover and reload!' One man tried to run past him and he shouted, 'Stand to, or by God I'll kill you myself!'

Allday muttered harshly, 'Where is Mr Pascoe?'

At that moment Bolitho saw him. He was coming down the track with Lang staggering against him, one arm wrapped tightly around the boy's shoulders. Lang was smeared with blood and his eyes were covered by a rough bandage.

More shots shrieked from the hillside where the enemy had paused to take more careful aim from their advantageous positions. A seaman rolled away from the barrier, and another dropped out of sight without even a cry as a ball found its mark.

Pascoe stumbled gasping into Allday's arms, and while others dragged the wounded lieutenant behind the rocks

Bolitho asked, 'Are you all right, boy?' He pulled him down against the sunwarmed stones and added. 'That was a very brave thing you did.'

Lang whimpered, 'My eyes! Oh Christ, I can't see!'

Pascoe stared at him fixedly. 'A musket ball struck the stones by his face, sir.' He shuddered but did not blink. 'The splinters hit both eyes . . .' He turned away suddenly and vomited into the dust.

Bolitho dragged his eyes from the boy's trembling shoulders and looked up as one of the seamen leapt to his feet and ran crazily towards the cliff edge. For an instant he thought the man had gone mad or was making one last futile attempt to escape. But then as the man's frantic cries made others turn to stare he saw a pale shape rising through the smoke from the burning ship, and imagined he could feel a hot wind as the sound of a full broadside thundered across the water and against the cliff face like an avalanche.

The seaman was rocking from side to side, his hands locked together across his chest like someone at prayer. He shouted wildly, '*Look*, lads! 'Tis the old *Hermes*!'

Then he fell headlong over the edge, his death cry lost in the rumble of cannon fire as yet another set of topsails loomed through the smoke. The sight of his own ship coming at last to his aid must have been the last thing he saw.

Bolitho stood up and yelled, 'Back, lads! Fall back to the headland!' Shots whimpered around him, and still more men fell as they ran crouching across the long stretch of open ground.

Allday had Lang bodily across his shoulders, and Bolitho saw Pascoe trying not to falter as a seaman by his side whirled round, his scream choking on blood as a ball smashed the back of his skull to pulp and splintered bone.

As the first of the soldiers reached the undefended barrier Fox held the slow-match carefully in place and then jumped aside to watch as the ball cleaved through the packed men like a giant axe.

That last shot and the sight of the ships pushing slowly into the bay were enough. The attack dropped away, and then, in spite of the shrill whistle and bellowed commands, the troops turned and ran headlong towards the hillside. It was likely they would keep running until they reached the town, for fear of being cut off by a fresh landing from the avenging ships.

Quince reached Bolitho and said between deep breaths, 'A *close* call, sir.'

Bolitho did not reply for a moment. He was watching his own ship, the old *Hyperion*, as she tacked slowly around the nearest Frenchman, her gunsmoke masking the destruction and chaos as two by two the muzzles poured their broadside into the helpless enemy. She was too far away to pick out the details, but he could see Inch in his mind's eye, watching and gauging the moment to tack, with Gossett nearby like an immovable English oak. He looked round, suddenly sick of the land, the staring corpses and the huddled cluster of frightened prisoners.

They had come thirty miles to do this. Thirty miles of swamp and impossible hardship, yet only once had the morale nearly broken. He watched the hobbling wounded and the ones still left who could stand and fight. There were very few of the latter.

Quince added quietly, 'Mr Fox reports that the sloop *Dasher* is anchored below the headland, sir. She's lowering boats to take us off.'

'Very well.' Even speech was too much. 'Have the wounded carried down to the foreshore as soon as the last gun is over the edge.' He turned to watch as the heavy cannon rolled over the cliff and plunged into the deep water amidst several bobbing corpses.

When Quince returned he found Bolitho standing alone, his eyes on the ships in the bay.

The lieutenant said, '*Hermes* has lowered boats, sir. I think she is putting a raiding party ashore to add to the Frogs' discomfort.'

Resistance had ceased aboard the nearest French ship, and she was already listing badly with her lower ports awash. The second one was burning so fiercely that for one brief moment Bolitho imagined Inch had taken his ship too close to the savage flames and would perish with her. But as *Hyperion*'s topsails filled and hardened on the new tack he saw the sparks and drifting ashes passing well abeam, while some of the French survivors paused in their frantic swimming to tread water and stare up at the slow-moving two-decker with her fierce-eyed figurehead and cheering seamen.

Of the other two French ships there was no sign at all, and he guessed they had weighed and clawed around the far headland even as the attacking squadron entered the bay at the opposite end.

He saw Pascoe standing by the abandoned furnace, his dirk still in his hand.

'Come with me, boy. You have seen and done enough for ten men today.'

Pascoe looked at him gravely. 'Thank you, sir,' was all he said.

The lieutenant in charge of the sloop's boats watched the ragged and bleeding survivors with something like horror. 'Where are the rest?' He could not even recognize an officer amidst the exhausted figures which waded or were carried into the boats.

Bolitho waited until the last man was aboard and then followed. He said coldly, 'We are the *rest*!' Then he sat in silence watching his party which could hardly fill two boats let alone the four which had been left far behind.

He saw the *Telamon* going about, her yards bedecked with signal flags, as she heeled to the fresh breeze from the shore. There was no sign at all of the *Indomitable*, but Bolitho was too weary to care.

Quince said, 'That's the signal to withdraw, sir. The commodore must be aboard the Dutchman.'

Bolitho glanced up, unable to hide the bitterness any longer. 'Then for his own safety I hope he stays there!'

Then he looked at his men again. Lang, sobbing quietly, his hands across his bandaged eyes, and the others too spent and drained even to respond to the men who cheered them from the anchored sloop. They had done what had been asked of them, and more beside, but the spark had gone with the last shot, the inner strength quenched as survival and help had driven away the madness and desperate bravery of battle. Now they just sat or lay like mindless beings, their eyes turned inward, examining perhaps the last stricken images, which given time they might recall with pride or terror, with sadness for those left behind, or with thanksgiving for being spared at their expense.

The sloop's young commander met Bolitho and said excitedly, 'Welcome aboard, sir! Is there anything I can do for you before I weigh?'

Bolitho stared past him towards the blazing ship. She was almost gone now, just a few blackened timbers which still defied the fire, and some last buoyancy to keep her afloat and bare her misery to watching eyes.

He replied, 'Get me to my ship.' He tried to force his mind to obey him, to hold back the dragging weariness which made his limbs feel like lead. 'And see that these men are cared for. They have come a long way and must not suffer to no good purpose.'

The commander frowned, uncertain what Bolitho meant. Then he hurried away to pass his orders, his mind busy with what he had witnessed and how he would retell it one day.

Later, as the ships sailed from the bay and re-formed into line, the smoke was still following them on the wind, the air heavy with ashes and a smell of death.

Lieutenant Inch stepped hesitantly into the stern cabin and blinked at the glare from the sea below the counter.

'You sent for me, sir?'

Bolitho was stripped to the waist and shaving hurriedly, a mirror propped on the top of his desk.

'Yes. Have there been any signals from the *Telamon*?'

Inch watched round-eyed as Bolitho towelled his face vigorously and then pulled a clean shirt over his head. Bolitho had been back aboard his own ship less than five hours but had hardly paused to take a meal, let alone rest after his return from the swamp and the destruction of the enemy battery.

He answered, 'Nothing, sir.'

Bolitho walked to the quarter windows and stared at the haze-shrouded shoreline far away on the starboard beam. On a slow larboard tack the ships were making little progress, and when he peered astern at the *Hermes* he saw that her sails were almost flat and unmoving, her hull shimmering above the haze of her own reflection.

He had expected Pelham-Martin to call his captains aboard the *Telamon* for a conference, or to send some sort of congratulations to the exhausted raiding party. Instead, the signal to heave to had been hoisted, and after another frustrating delay boats had shoved off from the *Hermes* loaded to the gunwales with men and headed immediately for the *Hyperion*'s side.

Lieutenant Quince had come with the boats to announce that the *Hermes*'s brief raid on the waterfront at Las Mercedes had found and breached the prison and had released some sixty seamen held prisoner there, fifty of whom Captain Fitzmaurice had sent across to supplement Bolitho's own company. Also, Quince had come aboard to say goodbye. Pelham-Martin had appointed him as acting commander of the disabled *Indomitable*, with orders to make sail forthwith for Antigua, some six hundred miles to the north-east, where English Harbour could afford the necessary facilities for repairs, enough at least for her return to England and the refit she so sorely needed.

Bolitho had been on deck to watch the listing seventy-four as she had edged slowly away from her consorts, showing her scars and battered hull, the clanking pumps telling only too well of her struggle to stay afloat. No wonder she had played no part in the final attack on Las Mercedes. One more broadside and she would likely have keeled over and sunk.

It was good to know Quince had received a reward for his unfailing efforts, and as Bolitho had watched the *Indomitable*'s shape melting into the sea haze, her torn sails and shattered topmasts somehow symbolic of the pain and death within her hull, he had thought of Winstanley, and how pleased he would have been to know his ship was in such good hands.

But now they were sailing eastward again, with no apparent thought for chasing the two French ships which had escaped the attack, and no intimation at all of what Pelham-Martin intended to do next.

During his brief visit Quince had said, 'It seems that our commodore is well pleased with the results, sir. Two French sail of the line destroyed and the others put to flight.'

Bolitho had replied coldly, 'We could have destroyed them all!'

Quince had been watching him soberly. 'You did all that

you could, sir. I think the whole squadron knows that, and rightly.'

Bolitho had merely shrugged. 'I cannot be content with half measures.'

He laid the razor on the desk and sighed, 'Have you sworn in the new men, Mr Inch?'

'Aye, sir. I have questioned some of them too, just as you instructed.'

Bolitho walked restlessly to the opposite side and shaded his eyes to stare at the empty horizon. It was like a bright gold line in the late afternoon sunlight. He had wanted to meet and question these released men himself, but had been unable to face anyone as yet. Like the moment he had returned aboard, the cheers and yells of welcome ringing in his ears as he and the others had climbed from the sloop's jolly boat, the noise and force of the greeting making him more aware of his own complete fatigue.

And Inch most of all. Bobbing and grinning, his anxiety giving way to an almost incoherent flood of pleasure which even Bolitho's false harshness could not dispel.

Inch said suddenly, 'All of them are prime seamen, sir. They were survivors of a merchantman, *Bristol Queen*, which was wrecked a while ago in a storm while bound for Caracas. Some of the crew managed to get away in the boats, and eventually reached Las Mercedes where they were thrown into prison.' He grimaced angrily. 'The damned Dons have no feeling for shipwrecked seamen, it seems.'

Bolitho rested his hands on the desk and stared absently at the uppermost chart. 'There were no officers saved, I take it?'

'None, sir.' Inch slapped one hand against his thigh. 'But there was one strange piece of good fortune, sir. There is a master's mate amongst them.' He nodded cheerfully in response to Bolitho's unspoken question. 'Aye, sir, a Navy man!'

'Well, do not keep me in suspense, Mr Inch.'

'It seems he and another were picked up a few months back. They had been washed overboard from the *Cornelia*, seventy-four, and were clinging to an upturned quarter boat, at least the master's mate was. The second man had already died, sir.'

Bolitho nodded thoughtfully. 'Saved from death to be

imprisoned, eh? Well, he will be both welcome and useful aboard, Mr Inch. I trust you made sure they were all able to send messages to their homes by way of the *Indomitable* before she left the squadron?'

'Lieutenant Quince assured me that was so, sir. But the master's mate sent neither letter nor message. Unlike the others, I suspect he has no life other than shipboard.'

Bolitho listened to the shrill of pipes and the patter of feet overhead as the watch went about its business.

'What is his name?'

'Selby, sir.'

'Well, send Mr Selby to me now. He might have seen or heard something at Las Mercedes. And I am not satisfied we know half enough that is happening there.' He frowned, unaware of Inch's puzzled expression. 'All those Spanish soldiers in French uniforms, the readiness of the ships and careful siting of a field battery.' He shook his head firmly. 'No, Mr Inch, I am not at all pleased with our lack of knowledge.'

As Inch departed, he returned once more to examining the chart. Where was Lequiller now?

He thought suddenly of Lieutenant Lang, now aboard the *Indomitable* with all the other maimed and wounded, en route for Antigua, and thence to England. What would become of him? The surgeon had been brief and without hope. Lang was completely blind. Having neither private means nor influence he was being sent home to certain oblivion. To join the wretched flotsam which you saw in every port, in every place where the sea was a constant reminder of their uselessness and rejection.

This master's mate was very welcome now. Bolitho would have to promote Gascoigne to acting lieutenant, experienced or not, and one more professional in the afterguard would be worth his weight in gold.

There was a rap on the door and Inch stepped into the reflected sunlight. 'Mr Selby, sir.' He stood aside as the other figure moved into view. 'There is a signal from the *Telamon*, sir. To reduce sail and retain close station in readiness for the night.'

Bolitho leaned back against the desk, his fingers locked around its edge in an effort to control his limbs. 'Thank you,

Mr Inch.' His voice seemed to come from a great distance. 'Carry on, if you please.'

Inch opened his mouth and then shut it again. With a brief glance at the master's mate he left the cabin and closed the door quietly behind him.

Bolitho could hear his own breathing, yet could feel nothing of his limbs at all but for the pressure of his fingers on the edge of the desk.

The figure across the cabin was badly stooped, and the hair which was pulled back to the nape of his neck was almost completely grey. But there was no mistaking the firm chin, the steady eyes which watched him now with something like resignation.

Bolitho's reeling mind seemed to register incredulity and despair, just as he understood the forces of luck and circumstance, of coincidence and fate which had at last drawn them together once again. As if in a dream he could recall exactly his father's tired face when he had told him of Hugh's disgrace, of his desertion from the Navy, and of his final disappearance in the Americas.

He could remember, too, that meeting when he had been Hugh's prisoner aboard the American privateer, *Andiron*, and later, nearly two years ago now, when he had been within yards of him during the collapse of the campaign in St Clar and Cozar, yet had not seen him.

He said tonelessly, 'I suppose our meeting again is inevitable.' He gestured to a chair. 'Sit down if you will.'

His brother lowered himself into the chair, his eyes still on Bolitho's face.

He replied, 'I did not *want* to come, Dick. I thought I was being kept aboard the *Hermes*. I did not even know your ship was in the Caribbean.'

Bolitho reached out and poured a glass of red wine. 'Drink this. Then tell me why you were here.' He gestured to his clothes. 'How you came to be in the King's service.'

Hugh Bolitho drank deeply and ran his fingers through his hair.

'Two years back, when I was bound for New Holland as a convict, you gave me, albeit unknowingly, another chance. They took most of the convicts back to Gibraltar to await deportation after we left St Clar.' The deep lines around his mouth softened slightly. 'I was put aboard a man-o'-war bound for Botany Bay, and during a storm I decided to try and escape. I managed to reach the quarter boat, but was seen and chased by the master's mate of the watch. He climbed down after me.' He shrugged, his eyes dreamy as he relived the moment. 'There was a fight and the boat came adrift. We both realized the ship had sailed on without knowing we were missing, so we made the best of it. The storm got worse and the boat capsized. We had no water, nothing. When we were picked up, Selby, that was his name, had died. I was almost ready to follow.'

Bolitho passed his hand across his forehead. The fatigue and strain of the past days were taking their toll, and he had to think carefully before each word.

'But why did you take the other man's identity?' He felt the sweat running down his chest. 'You must have known you would be collected by a King's ship in due course?'

Hugh nodded, the gesture both familiar and yet strange.

'I was, and am tired of running, Dick. Changing names, and always looking over my shoulder. So I thought, where better to hide than in a King's ship?' He smiled wearily. 'But it seems I was wrong even about that.'

On deck a bell chimed and feet shuffled around the poop skylight. At any second someone might enter.

Bolitho said harshly, 'You of all people ought to have known you might meet someone from the past.'

'I wanted to find something familiar where I could hide and wait until that ship reached England.' He nodded heavily. 'I just wanted to reach home once more. Nothing else seemed important.' He stood up suddenly and laid the glass on the desk. 'I am sorry about this. More so than I can say. I know you have your duty to do. I've had my luck. I'll not blame you now for putting me in irons until my trial.'

He fell back a pace as someone tapped the door.

Bolitho could feel his brother's eyes fixed on his face as he called, 'Enter!'

Midshipman Pascoe came into the cabin, a telescope beneath his arm. 'Mr Roth's respects, sir. He wishes permission to take in a second reef. The wind is freshening from the nor'-east, sir.'

Bolitho looked away, the boy's voice ringing in his brain like one more part of the dream.

'Very well, Mr Pascoe. I will come up directly.' He stopped him as he made for the door. 'This is Mr Selby, master's mate.'

He faced his brother impassively. 'Mr Pascoe distinguished himself greatly during the recent raid.'

As the door closed again he added, 'That boy has had more to bear from life than you know. His father disgraced him, and he now looks to me for trust and guidance, both of which I am proud to offer.'

'I do not understand.'

'I will not destroy that boy completely by arresting the man he now believes dead! Whose name is in Falmouth church beside my father's!' He saw his brother stagger but could not control his words. 'He walked right across Cornwall, alone and without help, just to see that name. *Your* name!'

Hugh's voice was hoarse. 'I did not know.' He looked up, his eyes suddenly desperate, 'His mother?'

'Dead. Even she had to give her body to some damned landlord to keep her son in clothes and food!'

'I really did not know.' There was no more strength in his voice. 'You *must* believe that!'

Bolitho swung round, his eyes blazing. 'I don't care what you knew or believed, d'you hear? I am captain of this ship, and *you* are Mr Selby, master's mate in the larboard watch!'

He saw his brother's face pale beneath the tan. 'If you imagined you could run away from the past, you were mistaken. The man who commands the frigate *Spartan* was also your prisoner. My second lieutenant and several of the hands are Cornishmen.' He shook his head. 'You are surrounded by the past, as *I* am!'

'Thank you for giving me the chance to . . .' His voice trailed away.

Bolitho walked to the stern windows and stared hard at the slow-moving *Hermes*.

'There was never any choice. If we reach England together I will see what can be done, but I make no promises, so remember that!' He gestured curtly to the door. 'Carry on, and report to the master.' In the glass of the nearest window he saw his brother's stooped shadow reach the bulkhead. He added quietly, 'And if you so much as whisper the truth to that boy I will personally have you hanged!'

The door closed and Bolitho threw himself heavily into the chair. How *could* this be happening? The commission might last for many more months, even years. It was unbearable, as it was unfair.

The door opened again and Inch asked anxiously, 'Did Mr Pascoe pass the request to take in another reef, sir?'

Bolitho stood up, feeling his arms and hands trembling in spite of his efforts to control them.

'Yes, thank you. I will come up.'

Inch walked beside him to the quarterdeck. 'Did Mr Selby give you any useful news, sir?'

Bolitho stared hard at him, caught off guard. 'News? What news?'

'I'm sorry, sir, I thought . . .' He quailed under Bolitho's fierce stare.

'Yes, I see.' Bolitho walked to the weather side and looked at the tautening rigging. 'Very little.'

As the pipes shrilled and the duty watch swarmed up the ratlines Bolitho stood unseeingly by the weather nettings, his fingers playing with the small locket inside his shirt.

When darkness reached the ships and the small stern lanterns showed their reflections like fireflies on the ruffled water he was still standing in the same place, his eyes clouded while he stared out into the darkness, and far beyond it.

Only when Gossett, heavy footed and smelling strongly of rum, came on deck to inspect the traverse board and speak with the helmsmen did the spell seem to break. Bolitho walked past them all without a word and entered his cabin.

Gossett watched him pass and rubbed his heavy jowl with sudden apprehension. Then he looked aloft at the reefed top-sails and tapped the hour-glass with one massive finger.

A new day would wipe away the memories of the battle, he decided. There was not much that a change of wind and weather could not alter for any man.

13. Return of the *Spartan*

NOON THE FOLLOWING DAY found the depleted squadron one hundred and twenty miles east of Las Mercedes, out of sight of land, and leaning steeply to a brisk north-easterly. The sky was cloudless, and in spite of the wind the heat was almost unbearable, so that men not employed in working ship sought what comfort they could between decks, or in any patch of shadow they could find.

Bolitho walked to the poop ladder and watched the *Hermes* as she wallowed some two cables astern. With the wind sweeping almost directly across the larboard bow her yards were braced round at maximum angle, so that every sail showed its hard belly as if to push the ship right on to her beam ends.

He had just been addressing the newly acquired seamen, and had come aft feeling tired and strangely dispirited. As he had spoken to them he had tried to discover their reactions to his words, to find some spark of enthusiasm or resentment. There was probably more of the latter than anything, he had decided. The first flush of wild excitement at their unexpected rescue from unjust imprisonment had changed to doubtful acceptance, if not actual dismay. They were now faced with the prospect of serving in a King's ship, perhaps for years, and some would never live to know any other life at all.

Gone were the privileges of comfortable quarters and tolerant routine, of good pay with the chance to return to their homes at the end of each profitable voyage. Their resentment would find little sympathy amongst the *Hyperion*'s company, for as was the way in the Navy, the attitude of the average seaman was that if it had happened to him, then why not to others?

But in Bolitho's mind any resentment was bad, and he had done his best to ease, if not dispel, their apprehension. That he had failed left him feeling both weary and ill at ease, although he knew in his heart that but for his personal problems he might have found some last reserve to draw upon.

He turned his head to watch the midshipmen assembled on the lee side of the quarterdeck, their faces squinting with concentration as Gossett rumbled through the daily routine of instruction and explained still further the mysteries and rewards of using a sextant.

'Step lively, Mr Pascoe!' The master sounded hoarse and a little irritable, and was no doubt thinking of the midday meal within the cool shadow of his own mess, and a richly deserved glass to wash it down. 'Show us 'ow you can 'andle it!'

Pascoe took the glittering sextant and stared at it thoughtfully.

Gossett groaned. 'Time's awastin'!' He beckoned with one huge fist. 'Mr Selby, lay aft and show the young gennleman. I'm all but wore out!'

Bolitho found he was gripping the ladder's teak rail with all his strength as he watched his brother cross the deck and take the sextant from the boy's hands. He was too far away to hear what was said, but he could tell from the boy's intent expression, the occasional nods, that Hugh's quiet words were reaching their mark.

Lieutenant Stepkyne was officer of the watch and had been studying the instruction with obvious impatience. 'Don't take so much time over it, Mr Selby!' His harsh voice made the boy glance at him with something like hatred. 'A lesson is a lesson aboard this ship. We don't expect individual tuition!'

'Aye, aye, sir.' Hugh kept his eyes down. 'I'm sorry, sir.'

Bolitho looked for the master but Gossett had already vanished to his quarters.

Stepkyne walked casually towards the watching midshipmen. 'Just so long as you understand.' He rocked back on his heels, his eyes examining the master's mate like a farmer looking over a beast at market.

Pascoe said quickly, 'He was explaining it to me, sir. How an officer should always show . . .'

Stepkyne turned and glared at him. 'Was he indeed?' He swung back again. 'An *officer*? What in God's name would you know about that, *Mr* Selby?'

Bolitho saw the midshipmen exchanging quick glances. They were too young to understand Stepkyne's malice. They were ashamed of him, which was worse.

But Bolitho was concerned only for his brother. For just one brief moment he saw a flash of anger in his eyes, a defiant lift to his chin. Then he replied quietly, 'You're quite right, sir. I know nothing of such things.'

Stepkyne still stood by the rail, his anger giving way to heavy sarcasm. 'Then I am relieved to know it. We cannot have our people getting ideas above their station, can we?'

Bolitho strode out of the shadow, his limbs carrying him forward before he knew what he was doing.

'Mr Stepkyne, I would be equally relieved if you would attend to *your* duties! The hour for instruction is over!'

Stepkyne swallowed hard. 'I was making sure they were not wasting their time, sir.'

Bolitho eyed him coldly. 'It seemed to me you were using their time to amuse yourself. In future, if you have nothing better to do, I will be pleased to know. I am quite sure I shall be able to supply your talent with more worthwhile and rewarding tasks.'

He turned and walked back to the poop ladder, his heart throbbing painfully with each step. In all his years at sea he could not recall ever having reprimanded an officer in front of his subordinates. He despised those who did it as a matter of course, just as he mistrusted them.

But Stepkyne was a bully, and like others of his type only seemed to understand similar treatment. And yet Bolitho could find no comfort in what he had done, and like the midshipmen was more shamed than satisfied.

He began to pace back and forth along the weather side, ignoring the sun's heat across his shoulders and the eyes of the watchkeepers. In trying to help with his brother's deception he might have achieved just the opposite. When Stepkyne recovered from his surprise and discomfort he might pause to consider the captain's behaviour, and when that occurred . . .

Bolitho stopped dead and looked up as a lookout yelled, 'Deck there! Sail on th' weather bow!'

Snatching a telescope from its rack he climbed into the mizzen shrouds, feeling the salt wind across his lips like blown sand. For a moment he thought the lookout had mistaken the little sloop *Dasher* for a newcomer, but a quick glance told him otherwise. Far out on the larboard beam, her topgallants barely visible on the haze-shrouded horizon, he could see the sloop on her correct station as before.

He waited until the *Hyperion* had completed another steep plunge and then trained the glass towards the bow, seeing the crisscross of rigging, the colourful splendour of the *Telamon* at the head of the line with Pelham-Martin's broad pendant at her masthead, and then, a mere shadow beneath the clear sky, he saw what must be the approaching ship.

She was running before the wind, carrying every stitch of canvas, and seemed to be rising bodily from the haze as she headed straight for the squadron.

'Deck there! She's a frigate, an' English by th' looks of 'er!'

Bolitho climbed down to the quarterdeck and handed the telescope to the midshipman of the watch.

Inch had arrived from the wardroom, his jaws still chewing on the remains of his meal.

Bolitho said shortly, 'Call all hands, Mr Inch, and prepare to shorten sail. That frigate'll be up to us directly and she's in a great hurry to tell us something.'

He heard the shrill of pipes and the immediate rush of feet as the order was relayed along both decks, and blinking in the bright sunlight the seamen poured through the open hatchways and dashed to their stations.

Midshipman Carlyon, very conscious of his new appointment in charge of signals, stood with his men by the halyards, while an experienced petty officer crouched in the mizzen shrouds with a telescope, his legs curled around the ratlines, balanced perfectly against the ship's heavy roll.

Bolitho took the glass once more and studied the fast approaching frigate, as with the spray bursting over her forecastle and her rakish hull tilting to the wind she started to go about, flags already breaking from her yards.

He said quietly, 'So Captain Farquhar has returned to the squadron.'

Inch was about to speak when Carlyon yelled, '*Spartan* to *Telamon*. Have urgent despatch for commodore.'

He jumped as Inch barked, 'Watch the flagship, damn you!'

'S—Sorry, sir!' Carlyon swung his glass round towards the *Telamon* as flags broke stiffly in the glare. He stuttered, 'General signal. Heave to.'

Bolitho nodded curtly. 'Carry on, Mr Inch, or the *Hermes* will beat us to it.'

He walked between the scurrying seamen and marines to watch the *Spartan* completing her manœuvre. Farquhar was wearing ship even before *Telamon*'s acknowledgement had been lowered.

As the *Hyperion* wallowed heavily into the wind, her sails vanishing from her topgallant yards to the accompaniment of threats and curses from the deck, Bolitho wondered what news Farquhar was bringing with him. It would certainly take more than a display of excellent seamanship to appease the commodore.

The deck canted heavily in the wind, and every shroud and halyard cracked and vibrated as the topmen fought to secure the rebellious canvas while they clung to the dizzily swaying yards.

Inch said breathlessly, 'The *Spartan*'ll get no thanks for missing the attack on Las Mercedes, sir.'

Bolitho wiped his watering eyes as more flags appeared above the *Telamon*'s pitching hull. But for the sloop's inability to find him, Farquhar might now be lying with his ship beside the charred bones of the *Abdiel*.

The signals petty officer called, 'Boat shovin' off from *Spartan*, sir!'

Bolitho clung to the nettings to watch the little jolly boat as it rose and dipped across the lively crests, the oars rising and falling like gulls' wings. He could see Farquhar's straight-backed figure in the sternsheets and his gold-laced cocked hat gleaming above the straining oarsmen as an additional encouragement to their efforts.

He heard Lieutenant Roth say, 'It'll be bad news no doubt.'

Inch retorted, 'Keep your opinions to yourself!'

Bolitho saw the boat hooking on to the Dutchman's main chains, the small hull pitching and crashing against the steep tumblehome as the men fought to keep it from capsizing. He had noted the bitterness in Inch's voice. The same tone he had used to explain Pelham-Martin's delay in attacking Las Mercedes. It seemed that the commodore had been unwilling to trust Bolitho's landing party to destroy the hidden battery, even to accept that they would finally cross the swamp.

Bolitho could find some understanding for Pelham-Martin's qualms, but could equally well imagine the frustration and anger throughout the ships while they waited for the sloop *Dasher* to report the sounds of gunfire.

But Bolitho was sure of one thing. If he had merely destroyed those guns without using them to fire on the anchored French ships, Pelham-Martin would never have made that last, vital assault, and he and his remaining men would have perished. And as Fitzmaurice had remarked before the raid, the responsibility would have rested on Bolitho's shoulders in any report which eventually reached England.

He gritted his teeth with mounting impatience until Carlyon shouted, 'General signal. All captains repair on board forthwith.'

Bolitho jerked his hand. 'Call away the barge.' He looked round for Allday, but he was already carrying the goldlaced coat and hat.

As he threw off his faded coat he saw some of the seamen staring at the activity aboard the *Telamon*, and wondered briefly what they were thinking. Only very few of those aboard really understood where the ship lay or the name of the nearest land. They had no say in affairs at all. They obeyed and did their duty, and some people said that was enough. Bolitho believed otherwise, and one day . . .

He looked up as Inch reported, 'Barge alongside, sir.' He had not even noticed it being swung outboard. He was too tired, too strained, and it was beginning to tell.

He nodded and ran down the ladder to the entry port. Below his legs he could see the lower gunports awash, and the next instant as the hull heeled violently away from the barge the copper on the ship's fat bilge rolled shining into the sunlight.

A quick breath. Count the seconds and then jump. Hands seized his arms and thigh, and as he staggered into the sternsheets he saw the *Hyperion* already sliding clear, the barge's oars hacking at the crested water while Allday brought the bows towards the *Telamon*.

He had hardly regained his breath when it was time to ascend the Dutchman's side and into her ornate entry port.

As he followed a swarthy lieutenant towards the poop he

noticed more flags being hoisted under the supervision of an English petty officer, and guessed the ships were being ordered to resume course and station. So it was to be another conference.

He heard a chorus of shouts and saw a bosun's chair being swayed out above the gangway. Captain Fitzmaurice of the *Hermes* was not taking any chances it seemed, and preferred the indignity of being hoisted inboard like a piece of cargo to the real risk of drowning or being crushed against the ship's hull.

In the stern cabin it was very dark after the sea's blinding reflections, and it took several seconds for him to distinguish Pelham-Martin's massive bulk squeezed into a chair, the legs of which were lashed firmly to two ringbolts to prevent it and its occupant from sliding to the opposite side of the ship. Farquhar was standing by the table, his slim figure relaxed to take the uncomfortable motion, while Mulder, the *Telamon*'s captain, was framed against the stern windows, head cocked as if to listen to his men's efforts on the deck above.

'Ah, Bolitho.' Pelham-Martin nodded curtly. 'We will wait for Fitzmaurice before we begin.'

Bolitho had wondered how he would feel when he met him again. Disgust or anger? He was surprised to find he could feel nothing which he could easily recognize. He had expected the commodore to display some sort of pleasure after the destruction of two enemy ships. Quince had hinted that he was to carry more than wounded men in the crippled *Indomitable* to Antigua. A glowing report which would tell the admiral and the whole of England of his victory, and not of the ships which had escaped or the puzzle which was as unsolved as ever.

Instead Pelham-Martin sat in the shadows, quite still, and in complete silence. As his eyes grew accustomed to the gloom Bolitho saw Farquhar's face, strained and tired, his lips set in a thin hard line. Seeing Bolitho's glance he gave a small shrug.

Then Fitzmaurice entered, and before he could apologize for his lateness Pelham-Martin said harshly, 'Captain Farquhar has just brought grave news.' He looked at the young captain and added heavily. 'You had best repeat it in your own words.'

Farquhar was swaying with fatigue, but his voice was as crisp and as impersonal as ever. 'Four nights ago I was patrolling to the nor'-west of Tortuga when gunfire was reported to the east'rd. At first light we sighted two frigates at each other's throats. One Spanish, and the other the *Thetis*, a French of forty guns.' He knew they were hanging on his words, but showed neither emotion nor pride. 'I soon recognized the Spanish frigate as the one I saw in Caracas, an escort being retained for the annual treasure ship. She was in a poor way, and all but dismasted.' He sighed suddenly, the sound strangely human from such a controlled throat. 'I set my people to quarters and engaged the *Thetis* without delay. We fought for close on an hour, and although I lost ten killed, we must have slaughtered five times that number.' His tone hardened slightly. 'Then the Frenchman broke off the action and I set about trying to rescue the remnants of the other ship.'

Fitzmaurice asked, 'You let him escape?'

Farquhar eyed him bleakly. 'I thought the Spaniard's intelligence more valuable than a prize.' He added, 'Or the prize *money*!' He swung round as Bolitho spoke for the first time, as if expecting someone else to question his actions.

Bolitho said, 'That was good work.' It was also very fortunate for Farquhar that he had found and engaged the enemy, no matter what the end result. For it was obvious he was well clear of his proper station, and no wonder that neither of the searching sloops had discovered his whereabouts.

He added slowly. 'Did you find out anything worthwhile?'

Farquhar relaxed again. 'Only one officer was still alive. He told me that his frigate was escorting the treasure ship, *San Leandro*, which left Caracas six days ago bound for Tenerife. Off Tortuga they were pounced upon by four sail of the line and the frigate *Thetis*. To all accounts the Dons put up quite a fight but stood no chance at all. The *San Leandro* struck her colours and a prize crew went on board. The Spanish frigate was too far damaged to prevent it, or even to pursue, and while the squadron sailed off with their prize the *Thetis* hove to, to await daylight and award the *coup de grâce*. The rest you know, gentlemen.'

The following silence in the great cabin was oppressive and strained, as each of those present considered this piece of news for himself.

Then Farquhar said simply, 'I could not save the Spaniard even when I took her in tow. A wind got up and she rolled under with most of those who survived the battle.'

Mulder crossed the cabin and leaned heavily on the table. 'What more did you find from the Spanish *luitenant*?'

Farquhar shrugged. 'My surgeon had to take off his right foot and he is in bad health at present. I think he feels the loss of the *San Leandro* far more than that of his foot. But he did say something more, though I know nothing of the value. Immediately after the treasure ship was seized he saw a flag being hoisted at her main. A yellow flag with a black eagle emblazoned upon it.'

Captain Fitzmaurice who had been staring glumly at the deck jerked upright. 'But that was the flag which flew above the town at Las Mercedes! My landing party saw it as they freed the prisoners from the jail.' He stared at Bolitho's grave features. 'It is the standard of the governor there!'

Pelham-Martin's small hands lifted slightly from the arms of the chair and then dropped again as if rendered lifeless. He said heavily, 'What is the point of all this? Another deception, one more ruse to throw us off the scent. It could mean anything, or nothing.'

Fitzmaurice looked past him, his eyes screwed tight with concentration. 'If Lequiller captured the treasure ship, surely that must do harm to his cause? The Dons will feel less inclined to change sides as they have done in the past.'

Pelham-Martin's voice sounded strangled. 'If it *was* Lequiller!'

'There is no doubt of it, sir.' Farquhar watched him without expression. 'The Spanish lieutenant saw the leading ship very clearly. A three-decker with a vice-admiral's command flag at the fore.'

The commodore sank further into the chair. 'Everything we have tried to do, each phase of our movements has been foreseen by this Lequiller.'

Farquhar looked surprised. 'But at least we have now halved his squadron, sir.'

Fitzmaurice interrupted bluntly, 'Two escaped at Las Mercedes.'

'If only I had more ships.' Pelham-Martin did not appear

to be listening. 'Sir Manley Cavendish knew what I was against, yet gave me no more than a pitiful force to deal with it.'

Farquhar turned towards Bolitho. 'What do *you* think, sir?'

Bolitho did not reply directly. While the others had been speaking and Pelham-Martin had been searching his mind for reasons and excuses, he had been trying to find some link, any small indication which might at least solve what he had always thought of as a puzzle.

He asked, 'What do we know of the governor of Las Mercedes?'

Mulder spread his hands vaguely. 'Don Jose Perez. It is said he was sent to the Caribbean more as a punishment than reward. He is highborn and of wealthy family, but we are told he outraged the Court of Spain by misusing the taxes of his lands. Las Mercedes must be as a prison to such a man, and after twenty years I would think . . .'

Bolitho cut him short. '*Twenty years?*' He began to pace the cabin, the others watching him with amazement. 'I am beginning to understand! Lequiller served here during the American Revolution and often used Las Mercedes as a temporary base, as well as many other places. He would have known all about Perez's background, might even have shared his confidences and discussed his hopes for the future.' He halted in his stride and looked at each man in turn. 'I believe I know what Lequiller intends, and what his orders were when he broke through our blockade!'

Fitzmaurice said, 'An attack on the Spanish Main?'

'Far more daring and rewarding than that!' Bolitho walked to the stern windows and stared at his own ship. 'Any attack on Spanish territories out here would most certainly inflame opinion against him. But should he return to *Spain itself*, imagine the impact it would have!'

Pelham-Martin gasped, 'But that is absurd! The Spanish Court would hang this Perez, aristocrat or not!'

'Alone and unaided, perhaps.' Bolitho eyed him coolly. 'But backed by Lequiller's squadron, and a ship with more than a king's ransom in her holds, just consider the effect!' He hardened his voice, seeing the uncertainty giving way to panic on the commodore's round face. 'Lequiller has made all the moves. Divide and conquer has been his method, and he has achieved almost everything he has attempted. We were warned that he is dedicated and ruthless. The fact that he hanged helpless prisoners of war should have told us just how determined he is to achieve his ends!'

Farquhar nodded firmly. 'You are right, by God! What confidence the Spanish government might have had in our ability will go at the first sight of Lequiller's squadron. Any anger retained by the Court for this Perez will soon fade when their treasure is safely delivered.'

'The Church will see to that!' Fitzmaurice sat down wearily. 'Much of the gold plate will no doubt find its way to *their* coffers!' He added less vehemently, 'Then all our efforts have been to no purpose? Even now Lequiller's ships may be homeward bound.' He glanced tightly at the commodore's motionless figure. 'We can do nothing!'

Bolitho said, 'All along I have tried to see things through Lequiller's eyes. His tactics, his complete disregard for everything but his ultimate objective. When I saw those Spanish soldiers in French uniform I should have guessed just how great were his intentions. They must have been training those men for months, maybe longer, and the uniforms were merely to disguise the governor's real purpose. At worst he could have pleaded that his town and defences had been overrun by the enemy.' He paused before adding, 'At best he will have a trained force at his back when he returns to his own country, where no doubt there will be many eager to rise to his standard.'

He saw Fitzmaurice nodding and continued relentlessly, 'Just think of the impact this will have on England. Spain is our only foothold in Europe, the one country still strong enough to show arms to the enemy. With a sudden uprising it would all be over in weeks, maybe days, and there would be *nothing* between England and a united Europe. Nothing but a strip of water and a thin line of ships!'

Bolitho looked quickly at Mulder, seeing the anxiety his words had caused. Perhaps for the first time Mulder was thinking as a Dutchman and not as the guardian of St Kruis. No amount of ocean or distance could ease the pain he must be feeling for his own homeland, now crushed under the enemy's heel. Perhaps even now his country had been forced to declare war on England. It would merely be a formal signature on a treaty, but it would make this ancient ship an enemy and leave him with only one last decision.

Just thinking about it filled Bolitho with unreasoning anger and dismay. All these weary and frustrating weeks while they had sailed and searched for the elusive enemy, Lequiller had been playing the game by his own set of rules. Rules which they had only just begun to learn when it was almost too late. It took a very determined and ruthless admiral to leave half his squadron to face whatever the hunters tried to do, yet he had been prepared to lose four ships while he went after the big prize, the laden treasure ship and all that her wealth entailed for his cause. He must have known that even if Pelham-Martin had succeeded in destroying all four vessels his own force would have suffered so severely in battle and under the bombardment of the hidden battery they would be in no fit state to hinder him for some time to come.

He said, 'I can see no other possible explanation, sir. Nor can I see any choice for us but to act on the facts at our disposal.'

Pelham-Martin tugged a handkerchief from his pocket and stared at it blankly. 'We do not *know*, Bolitho. Yours is just supposition. Think what it would mean if I ordered the squadron in pursuit to somewhere—the exact location of which is a mystery—when all the time Lequiller is *here*, attacking and raiding, destroying the vital links which were so hard to forge!'

'It would be prudent to consider the alternatives, sir. Our orders were to seek out and to destroy Lequiller's squadron. We have failed.' He watched the words reaching the commodore's confused mind, and added, 'Now the *San Leandro* is taken, in seas which we were ordered to control and make secure. Even if we desired it, we cannot waste more time in seeking Lequiller's ships. We have only the *Spartan* for patrolling away from the squadron. The sloops are too frail, and easy prey for the enemy.'

'What are you suggesting now?' Pelham-Martin again tried to restore his own composure. 'A return to Las Mercedes?'

'No, sir. It would take more valuable time, and that we do not have. I believe Lequiller attacked St Kruis when he first entered the Caribbean knowing he might need an alternative base for his ships. Due to our unexpected arrival and the show of courage by the Dutch defenders it was denied to him. That is why I am sure Lequiller did not come here just to raid and plunder. Privateers and frigates would have been more useful for such tasks. But you cannot hide a squadron of the line forever.' He shot a quick glance at Farquhar. 'How much did you damage the frigate *Thetis*?'

'Foremast and rigging were well hit, as well as considerable damage to her main deck.'

Bolitho nodded. 'And one of the ships which escaped from Las Mercedes was also badly crippled aloft. If it was essential for Lequiller to reach here with his squadron intact, it will be equally important for any future operations now that he has lost some of his force to us.'

Again it was Farquhar's quick mind which took up the train of Bolitho's spoken thoughts.

'Then there must be some other base?' He tugged his chin doubtfully. 'But we are surrounded by countless islands, it would take a fleet and a century in time to search amongst them.' Then he nodded sharply. 'But you are right. An anchorage where the damage can be put right and the last plans prepared.'

Fitzmaurice asked, 'Do you know of such a place?'

'Not yet.' Bolitho glanced at Mulder. 'But I will give it some thought.'

Pelham-Martin levered himself to his feet and leaned against the back of his chair. 'If only my reinforcements would come!' Then he gave a great sigh. 'But alas, I should have been warned by my past experiences.' He looked at Bolitho, his face suddenly despairing. 'You are my senior captain and I must consider your advice, knowing as I do that it is born of knowledge gained in the King's service. But *I* am in command, and mine is the final decision. We will return to St Kruis with all haste, and then I will send a sloop with my despatches direct to England.'

Bolitho watched him impassively. It never failed to surprise him how quickly Pelham-Martin could rally and emerge from almost complete despondency. The idea that there was still some possible chance of redeeming his honour before

Admiral Cavendish learned of his failure to destroy the enemy seemed to have given him fresh hope and authority. Even now he was looking at Farquhar with something approaching his old severity.

'I had intended to reprimand you for straying from your patrol area. However, since your initiative has given us the only piece of information, I must treat you with leniency and place your action on record.'

Farquhar regarded him coldly, his arrogant features set in a faint smile. 'When I served under Captain Bolitho as a midshipman I had an excellent teacher, sir. I learned then that to try and fight without information is like sending a blind man to war with a musket.'

Bolitho cleared his throat. 'Will you return to my ship now, sir?'

Pelham-Martin shook his head. 'Later. I must have time to think. Rejoin your commands, gentlemen.'

Outside the cabin the three captains stood in silence while Mulder hurried away to summon their respective boats.

Fitzmaurice spoke first. 'When I heard young Farquhar's report I was without hope. I felt as if I had been made foolish, that all I have tried to do with my life had been wasted.' He studied Bolitho searchingly. 'But listening to you as you outlined your ideas I felt new strength.' He searched for the right way to express himself. 'My first lieutenant, Quince, put it into words when he returned from the swamp. He said that had you been in command of the squadron, Lequiller would never have lost sight of the French coast.'

Farquhar smiled. 'Let us hope it not too late to make amends.'

Bolitho watched his barge pulling round from the *Telamon*'s quarter. It was typical of Farquhar to be outspoken when speaking with Pelham-Martin, yet refuse to give way to sentiment amongst his fellow captains.

Farquhar need have no fear of Pelham-Martin's influence outside the Navy. His own father owned half of Hampshire, and he came of a long line of famous sea officers, several of whom had been admirals. But to display any sort of confidence which might later be construed as conspiracy or a failure to support his commodore to the letter of his orders was as alien

216

to his nature as it was to treat an ordinary seaman as an equal.

Later, as he stood on the *Hyperion*'s quarterdeck and watched the *Spartan* clawing ahead of her slower consorts, Bolitho found a touch of envy in his heart. There was always something special about a frigate. Fast, independent, and entirely personal, where the face and behaviour of every man aboard became as familiar as the set of her sails. In a ship of the line it was like living over a tightly compressed world where several hundred souls were crammed together at every moment of the day, yet so completely separated by the standards of discipline and station. And now even this remote link with the way of life he loved so dearly seemed to be drawing further away. While he had been outlining his sketchy plan to the others he had been made conscious of the fact, and it troubled him. From obeying other captains to commanding a small ship of his own. From the harsh necessity of seeking an enemy and laying his ship alongside her until victory or destruction, to the need of understanding tactics and how they could affect other ships and outflung squadrons. And as he had spoken his mind aloud he had been very aware of what he was doing. By revealing his innermost ideas, which might later be translated into actual deeds, he had taken one more irrevocable step in his career.

But strategy, as Pelham-Martin and others before him had been made to understand, could determine far more than the death of its planner. It might decide the fate of a cause, the very existence of a nation.

Inch came to his side and touched his hat. 'Any orders, sir?'

Bolitho was still staring after the *Spartan* as she lifted and ploughed into the uneven ranks of whitecaps.

'I am going to the chartroom.' He hesitated, knowing he was going to take one more step, more personal, but no less vital. 'Pass the word for the new master's mate, Selby, and send him down to me.'

Inch shuffled his feet, his face filled with obvious curiosity.

Bolitho looked at him. 'See that I am not disturbed.'

In the dark panelled chartroom he leaned his shoulders against the bulkhead in an effort to control the sudden flood of misgivings. The normal shipboard sounds were muffled here, and the distant clank of the pump seemed to keep time with his heartbeats.

There was a tap at the door and he said, 'Enter!'

His brother stood on the opposite side of the chart table, his eyes guarded and watchful. 'You sent for me, sir?'

Bolitho plucked one corner of the uppermost chart, conscious of the enclosed silence, as if the ship was holding her breath.

He said slowly, 'I have need of information.' He kept his tone formal, as if the man opposite was indeed a mere master's mate. 'When you served in the Caribbean before.' His tongue lingered on the word. Before. What grief and uncertainty it had caused their father. He added sharply, 'When you commanded the privateer *Andiron* you must have made good use of the islands.' He circled the rambling shapes on the chart with his finger. 'You had only your own resources. You must then have known of inlets and bays where you could rest your men and carry out repairs.'

His brother moved closer, his features suddenly lined and tired beneath the spiralling lantern.

'That was a long while ago.' He nodded. 'Yes, I knew of many such anchorages.'

Bolitho walked round the table touching the lockers and the swinging cot, yet noticing none of them.

'You know of Lequiller of course, and what we are doing here. I believe that he will repair his ships which were damaged in battle before he . . .' He broke off, aware that his brother was watching him, his eyes pensive.

'I have heard many things. That Lequiller has seized the treasure ship and you intend to try and catch him again.' He shrugged. 'News has fast legs on the lower deck, as you know.'

'When you were in Las Mercedes, did you see or hear what was going on there?'

'Not much. We saw the troops drilling, and when the French ships put into the bay there was a great deal of excitement. I knew then that it would mean trouble for us.'

Bolitho could not contain his bitterness. 'For *us*? That is a change of heart, surely?'

His brother eyed him with tired gravity. 'Perhaps. But even in my short stay aboard your ship I have learned to know you again. Like that time in St Clar when the convicts stood

218

and cheered you.' He grimaced. 'There is little difference between a convict and a seaman in a King's ship, and I have heard what they think of you.' He looked down at the chart. 'They'd follow you anywhere. Don't ask me why, and do not expect anyone to tell you. It is something which you have, which you give to them.' He gave another shrug. 'But no matter. I am saying that I do not think you should throw all away just to save your commodore's good name.'

Bolitho said harshly, 'I did not call you here for an opinion on my motives!' He tapped the chart. 'Well?'

'There is a suitable place here.' His finger paused. 'The Isles of Pascua. Maybe fifty miles nor'-west of St Kruis.' His eyes shone with professional interest as he stooped over the chart. 'Two small islands linked together by several tiny islets and a whole pattern of reefs. A dangerous anchorage, a last resort usually.' He nodded slowly. 'The main advantage is that it has a dozen exits between the reefs. With your small squadron you could never control them all.' His lined face twisted in a private smile. 'I gave Rodney's frigates the slip many a time there!'

Bolitho studied his lowered head with sudden understanding and near compassion. Hugh was only four years his senior, yet looked old and grey, like his father had been at their last meeting. Now he was here, reliving that one period in his life when, right or wrong, he had achieved something.

He asked quietly, 'What would *you* do?'

His brother looked up at him, the expression changing from surprise to disbelief. Then he replied, 'A frigate could enter through the reefs. A surprise attack would probably make any ships inside the anchorage put to sea by the main channel, where you could be waiting.'

Bolitho studied him gravely. 'It needs a man of great experience to take a ship through the reefs, does it not? Someone who knows the exact bearings from every obstacle?'

The other man watched him, his eyes shrewd with understanding. 'It does. It would be madness otherwise. When I used it for the first time I had an old mulatto fisherman as bosun. He knew it well enough and taught me what he had learned the hard way.'

Bolitho straightened his back. 'Will you do it?' He saw the

guard drop in his brother's eyes and added, 'I know it is a great risk. The captain of our only frigate is Charles Farquhar. He might remember you as his captor.'

'I remember *him*. Insolent young puppy!'

'But if all goes well, it could go a long way towards a free pardon, a last chance for you.'

His brother smiled sadly. 'It is just as many of your people say. You *never* think of yourself first.' He slapped his hand on the table. 'I was not thinking of my own skin for once. Don't you realize that if Farquhar or anyone else knows about me, it would be *your* loss? Hiding a fugitive, compounding an act of treason, why, they would crucify you!'

When Bolitho did not reply he added hotly, 'Think of yourself! Stop worrying about your damn commodore, me, and all the rest of them! Just this time, take care of your own self!'

Bolitho looked away. 'It's settled then. When we reach St Kruis I will inform the commodore. We may find nothing at this anchorage of yours. But we shall see.'

His brother stepped back to the door. 'There was only one man who ever got the better of *me* in the Caribbean. So perhaps your luck will stand you in good stead a *second* time.'

'Thank you.' But when Bolitho turned his head the chart-room was empty.

14. Aft, the Most Honour . . .

AS HIS BARGE came to rest alongside the crude wooden piles of the jetty, Bolitho climbed from the sternsheets and then paused to stare back at the bay. Pelham-Martin's squadron had anchored just two hours earlier, but even in that short time a change in the weather was apparent. The sky was hidden by a film of pale cloud which distorted the afternoon sunlight into an angry glare and painted the irregular wave-crests with a harsh bronze hue. When he shaded his eyes to study the ships he noted the way they strained at their cables, as if fearful of the land's nearness.

Boats plied busily back and forth to the ships, while along

the coast road and jetty, parties of seamen waited to lower freshly filled water casks and hastily gathered fruit, before tramping inland again to collect another load.

Inch and Gossett clambered up beside him and stood in the swirling dust clouds which covered their faces and clothing in a matter of seconds.

The master said hoarsely, 'Wind's still steady from the nor'-east, sir.' He shook his head. 'I'll be 'appier when we puts to sea again.'

Bolitho followed his gaze and saw the waves leaping and breaking across the protective necklace of reefs to the eastern side of the bay. 'I agree.'

He turned and strode along the dusty road towards the blurred outline of the governor's residence. He walked fast, aware of the others hurrying behind him, of the needling urgency in his mind. For twenty-four hours the ships had driven back to St Kruis under all available sail, and while he had waited fretting and uncertain of the commodore's final decision, Pelham-Martin had gone ashore to see de Block, accompanied only by Mulder of the *Telamon*.

When the *Hyperion* had dropped anchor, Bolitho had seen that the missing sloop was already moored below the headland. Her commander having failed to locate the *Spartan*, to return to St Kruis was the obvious course to take. But it was time gone. Time which might have been used to send her speeding with all haste to alert other, stronger forces of Lequiller's possible intentions.

Small groups of islanders stood in the doorways of their houses and shacks as they hurried past. There were few smiles or greetings this time, and most of them seemed to be watching the sea beyond the reef.

In another month the first hurricane would come, and these same people would have more to contend with than the affairs of war. And a war of others' making, for a cause they did not understand or share, could only add to their worries and anxieties.

They reached the welcome shelter of the wide stone entrance and Inch asked breathlessly, 'Will Mr Selby stay down here, sir?'

Bolitho stopped to face them. When the message had at

last arrived on board to say that the commodore required all captains, first lieutenants and sailing masters to report to him at once, he had known a decision had been reached. He should have anticipated that Pelham-Martin would want to meet the one man whom Bolitho had suggested as a pilot to guide the frigate between the reefs, but the summons came as a shock nevertheless.

He was there now, three steps below Inch and Gossett, his face calm and immobile as he waited for Bolitho to reply.

'Yes. He can wait here.' Bolitho added, 'He might not be required just yet.'

He saw Fitzmaurice and his two officers hurrying up the road towards him.

'Well, let us not delay any longer.'

As he entered the long room above the waterfront he could feel his palms sweating badly, yet the place was cool after the hot, dusty road. Every moment his brother was confronted by others, the odds of being discovered mounted accordingly.

He nodded vaguely to those already present, only half aware of their greetings or remarks. The commanders of the two sloops were conversing in low tones by the window, and he saw Farquhar with his first lieutenant studying a chart on the table.

A native girl with a loaded tray moved to Bolitho's side. He took a glass and sipped slowly. It was some sort of wine, and as cold as ice.

Inch also took one and smiled shyly at the servant girl who was watching him with unblinking admiration.

Fitzmaurice came into the room banging dust from his coat, his voice suddenly loud in the stillness. He coughed awkwardly and beckoned to the servant who, still smiling at Inch, crossed reluctantly with her tray.

The other door opened and Pelham-Martin walked slowly and heavily to the table. He was accompanied by de Block and Mulder, and the latter looked strained and on edge as he waited for Pelham-Martin to speak.

Bolitho watched him carefully. The commodore's movements were slow and ponderous, but his eyes which fastened now on the commander of the second sloop seemed nervous and agitated.

'Very well, Appleby.' He lifted a fat envelope from his coat pocket. 'Here are my despatches. You will take the *Nisus* to sea immediately and hand them to the first senior officer you can.' As he held out the envelope to the sloop's captain Bolitho saw that it was shaking badly. 'A squadron of the Channel Fleet if possible, but if not, then on to Plymouth with all the speed you can muster!'

The officer thrust the envelope inside his coat and turned on his heel. Just for a few brief moments he allowed his eyes to stray across the others around him, as if he was seeing them all for the last time.

Pelham-Martin watched him until he had vanished through the doorway, and Bolitho wondered if even now he was thinking of recalling him, of withdrawing those despatches which might so easily spell his ruin.

'I have called you together, gentlemen.' Pelham-Martin cleared his throat and took a quick swallow of wine. 'For a last conference before we sail.'

There was a quick murmur of speculation and he added, 'With the little information that we have, I can see no alternative but to accept the plan put forward by Captain Bolitho.' He lowered his eyes and two small droplets of sweat ran down beneath his hair. 'It now appears that this plan has more value than first showed itself.' He looked slowly at de Block. 'The governor of St Kruis has informed me of the disappearance of his schooner, *Fauna*. She sailed with supplies to some neighbouring islands and has not returned.' He looked at Bolitho before adding, 'One of her calls was at the Isles of Pascua.'

Bolitho said quietly, 'I thought they were uninhabited?'

De Block nodded. 'There is only a mission and a few fishermen. They are due to return here before the storms come again.'

Pelham-Martin said, 'Quite so. Now let us continue. There is much to do, and very little time left.'

Bolitho was surprised by the sharpness in his tone. It was as if Pelham-Martin could not act fast enough now that he was committed.

'As soon as this meeting is concluded Captain Farquher will weigh and proceed to the nor'-west. If he is to make this passage through the reefs it is essential for *Spartan* to be in position by first light tomorrow.' Pelham-Martin looked at Bolitho again. 'I will hoist my broad pendant in *Hyperion*, and together with *Hermes* we will beat to the north-east of the islands. That will give us the wind-gage if and when the enemy breaks out.' He glanced at the *Dasher*'s captain. 'Your sloop will patrol to the south'rd. If the enemy succeeds in escaping, you will have to maintain contact as best you can.'

He paused and sipped at his glass. 'Questions?'

De Block asked, 'You have made no mention of the *Telamon*?'

'That is true.' Pelham-Martin studied the chart as he spoke. 'I cannot further order you to take station under my command. With the schooner lost, the *Telamon* is your one link with the outside world. Your only protection against privateers or pirates. With all respect, she is an old ship, and her days in the line of battle are long past.'

Bolitho watched the two men, feeling the tension around him like a wall.

It was difficult to measure Pelham-Martin's true concern. He could still be looking for an excuse, some reason to give in a future defence. Without the *Telamon*'s support, outdated and undergunned though she was, he might be able to justify any further retreat in the face of heavy odds.

De Block replied softly, 'There is no doubt in my mind, or in that of her captain. When you saved St Kruis from Lequiller all of us here knew we had a debt to repay. And should Lequiller escape and return to his own country, then I think our future is doomed anyway. His country was reborn under a reign of terror. If he escapes to tell how we defied him, who can say what will become of us?'

Then he looked at Bolitho, his eyes suddenly sad. 'Kapitein Mulder told me what you said. It seems our two countries will soon be at war again. If it comes it comes, but I should like one small piece of honour to remember when all this is over.'

Farquhar said, 'Then if everything is settled, sir, perhaps I could meet this master's mate?'

His interruption seemed like a splash of cold water, but Bolitho felt it was welcome nevertheless. The sooner it was finished then the quicker they could get back to sea, if only to prolong the deception.

As his brother entered the room Bolitho pressed his spine against the chairback and tried not to watch him as he approached the table.

The commodore said, 'I am told you can pilot the *Spartan* through the reefs on the western side of the islands?'

'Aye, sir.'

Farquhar leaned over the chart. 'There are few marks, Mr Selby.' For once he was displaying his inner feelings, those of a captain about to entrust his ship, and possibly his career to a man entirely unknown to him.

They all watched as the master's mate traced a course with his finger.

'There's a good channel here, sir. Deep water, but with two difficult ridges of reef. I suggest that you have the boats swung out in case the wind drops. We could warp her through under such circumstances.' He rubbed his chin. 'And we shall need two good leadsmen in the chains.' He broke off, aware of Farquhar's searching stare. 'Sir?'

Farquhar asked, 'Are you sure you have never sailed under me before?'

'Quite certain, sir.'

'I see.' Farquhar still watched him thoughtfully. 'Where did you serve to gather such knowledge?'

Bolitho gripped the arms of his chair, feeling the sweat gathering on his brow as he waited for Farquhar's expression to change to sudden recognition.

But the reply was calm and assured. 'In the old *Pegasus*, sir. We were doing a survey out here some years back.'

Farquhar's frown faded. 'Then you did not waste your time, Mr Selby. Have you never considered seeking a commission?'

'I am content, sir.' He bent over the chart again. 'You know what they say, sir. Aft the most honour. But forrard the better men!'

For an instant Bolitho thought he had gone too far. Farquhar stepped back as if suddenly conscious of close contact with an inferior, his mouth tightened into a thin line.

Then he shrugged and gave a curt nod. 'Do they indeed?'

Pelham-Martin stood up. 'Then we are done here, gentlemen.' He paused as if seeking some phrase which they might all remember. 'If we find Lequiller, see that your people fight bravely and with no thought of defeat.' He lowered his glass to the table and stared at it without recognition. 'Return to your ships and recall all boats immediately. If we are to clear the reef and claw to windward of Pascua then we must suffer no further delays.'

Bolitho crossed to the table as the other officers began to file from the room. 'That was a wise decision, sir. And if I may say so, a brave one.'

Pelham-Martin looked past him, his eyes opaque. 'Damn you, Bolitho!' He did not raise his voice. 'If you are mistaken about this place and what we might discover there, no amount of good intentions will save me.' His eyes swivelled round and fixed on Bolitho's face. 'Or you either. If, as I very much doubt, you live long enough, you will discover that bravery is not always sufficient. I hope, if that time ever comes, you will be equal to it!'

Bolitho picked up his hat. 'Yes, sir.'

As he made his way down the stairway he still retained a picture of Pelham-Martin in his mind, so that his words seemed to follow him like an epitaph.

Perhaps after all Pelham-Martin was more entitled to pity than respect for his authority. Unlike so many others he was desperately afraid. Not just of dying or making a mistake. But fear of failure and of showing his own uncertainty, and things which Bolitho could only try to imagine. Yet in all his career he must have realized his own weakness, but had seemingly allowed himself to be carried on and upward by a system he had failed to master and understand.

Earlier or later in his life it might not have mattered so much. But now, at this very moment in time, while the little *Nisus* spread her sails and gathered way from the bay, he could see nothing but complete disgrace, and worse, the scorn of those he had tried for so long to emulate.

Inch asked, 'Are you ready, sir?'

Bolitho glanced along the jetty and saw Farquhar speaking with his first lieutenant while they waited for their boat to arrive. His brother was standing a little apart, arms folded, his eyes on the distant frigate as she rolled uneasily at her cable. Then he saw Bolitho watching him and walked slowly to meet him.

Bolitho waited until Inch and Gossett were out of earshot and then said fiercely, 'You fool! You nearly gave yourself away back there!'

'He made me angry. If he did know who I was he'd let his ship founder rather than have *me* at the helm!' He smiled sadly. 'You'll take care of the boy if anything happens to me, won't you?'

Bolitho studied him for several moments. 'You know that.' He heard Farquhar yelling, 'Bring that boat alongside, damn your eyes!' It made a sudden urgency, and he had to check himself from touching his brother's arm. 'Take care of *yourself*.'

Then he turned and walked back to the others.

Inch said cheerfully, 'Poor old Selby! Out of one ship into another!'

'Kindly lend your thoughts to receiving the commodore on board, Mr Inch!' Bolitho turned his back to watch the barge drawing nearer and did not see Inch's confusion or Gossett's unsympathetic grin. He knew the brief anger was only to cover his own uncertainty. To hide the fact that he did after all care about his brother, even though he suspected Hugh was really laughing at him in spite of his constant danger. It had always been so between them, and it seemed now that even the threat of arrest and a traitor's rope could change nothing.

Allday stood and removed his hat as the officers scrambled into the barge.

'I shall want you to return and collect the commodore as soon as I'm aboard.'

Allday nodded. 'Aye, aye, Captain.' He gestured to the bowman. 'Cast off! Out oars there!' He watched the back of Bolitho's head, sensing his mood. 'Give way all! *Together!*'

Bolitho sat rigidly in the sternsheets, his eyes fixed on the black silhouette of the *Hyperion*'s upper yards. He had seen the quick exchange of glances between the bargemen, like privileged persons hearing some secret information. How did men such as these really see their commanders? he wondered. A stern face at a flogging or pronouncing punishment, or a man who strode his quarterdeck, aloof and untroubled by the crowded world beneath his feet? And during battle, did they seek out that same, shadowy figure with any sort of real understanding or warmth?

He recalled how these same men had reacted when Pelham-Martin had hauled down his broad pendant, their resentment and hurt, as if their ship, and therefore they themselves, had been slighted. Now they knew the pendant was returning and seemed genuinely pleased by it. He wondered what they would think of the man beneath the command flag. One so beset with inner worries and personal doubts that, faced with another reverse, he might well break under the strain.

He looked up and saw the hull high above him, the scarlet-coated marines at the entry port, the gleam of harsh sunlight across upraised bosun's pipes.

As Allday guided the barge beneath the ship's lee he thought suddenly of what Hugh had said. *They'd follow you anywhere.* But men who followed must have the right leadership. It was no use feeling sorry for Pelham-Martin merely because he was out of his depth. These men needed leadership. He frowned. No, they should have it as a *right*.

He climbed up the side, still thinking of Pelham-Martin even as he returned the salutes and made his way aft to the poop.

'Captain, sir?'

Bolitho opened his eyes and stared dully at the chart beneath his forearm. In the enclosed cabin the deckhead lantern was gyrating wildly, throwing shadows back and forth like spirits in torment, and he was immediately conscious of the increased motion around him.

Allday stood beside the table, a giant pot of coffee tightly grasped against his body.

'What time is it?'

'Seven bells, Captain.' Allday took a cup from the rack and poured some black coffee, between the ship's uneven plunges.

Seven bells. Bolitho leaned back in the chair and rubbed his eyes. He had been on deck almost continuously since the ships had quit the bay and butted out into a rising wind. Then for perhaps two hours he had tried to rest. To restore his tired mind before first light. He groaned. The middle watch still had half an hour to run.

Allday stood back to watch him drink. Then he said, 'Mr Inch's respects, and the wind's freshening.'

'From the nor'-east?'

'Aye.' He slopped more coffee into the cup.

'Well, that's something to give thanks for.' If it veered now they would have to beat further away from the hidden islands. Without searoom they might still be caught off guard when the enemy made a dash for it. But if the wind got up or shifted they would be seen the moment the sun rose, and the way would be open either for Lequiller to escape or give battle on his own, overwhelming terms.

He slammed down the cup. *If . . . when . . .* He was beginning to think like the commodore.

Allday helped him into his coat. 'Will I call the commodore, Captain?'

'No.' He walked out of the chartroom and almost stumbled over the cabin servant who was curled up and asleep in the passageway.

He said, 'Leave the rest of the coffee with him.' He glanced at the sealed door of the stern cabin, the marine sentry swaying in the lantern light like a toy soldier. 'He can give it to the commodore in a moment.' He's not even asleep, he thought. Probably lying there staring at the deckhead, listening to every sound.

The quarterdeck was in total darkness, and the sudden noise of wind and sea told him instantly of the increasing force behind them.

Inch groped towards him. 'We'll have to shorten sail again, sir.'

Bolitho walked up the tilting deck and cupped his hand over the compass bowl. South by west. He could picture the desperate, struggling course they had taken since leaving St Kruis. Up and round in a great circle, mostly into the teeth of the wind, with all hands on deck for much of the time. Now they were sailing south again, on what was to have been the easiest part. The islands were somewhere across the starboard bow, and with the wind pushing down on the opposite quarter they would have all the advantage if an enemy came out of shelter. It would spoil everything now if they overreached their proper station.

'Very well, Mr Inch. Take in another reef.'

He wondered if the *Spartan* was near those treacherous approaches yet. Whether his brother could remember so long back . . . he broke off as Inch said, '*Hermes* is still on station, sir. We saw her close astern at six bells.' He was yelling above the wind, his face shining with spray in the dim compass light.

'And the *Telamon*?'

'No sign, sir.' Inch broke off to yell at some men nearby who had not heeded or heard the demanding call of the bosun's pipe.

Overhead the sails cracked and thundered remorselessly as the hands fought to contain them in pitch darkness. Bolitho could well imagine the terror of being up there. Yet it was excellent sailing weather. If only they could free themselves from these wretched islands. Sail and fight as had been intended, instead of taking the power out of the old ship's sails when she had such strength to offer.

Inch shouted, 'How do you think Mr Selby is managing, sir?'

It was an innocent question and he was obviously trying to make amends for what he still imagined was his own lapse whilst waiting for the barge.

'Well enough.'

Inch nodded vaguely. 'He has a way with him. Like Captain Farquhar, I thought him familiar at first.'

Bolitho stiffened. Inch couldn't possibly have remembered him also. In St Clar his brother had passed Inch in the darkness before the final evacuation, had handed him a ring, his mother's ring, to give to him as an only sign of recognition, and to say that he was not dead after all.

Inch said, 'It must be something about the man, sir.' He showed his teeth in an uncertain grin. 'Young Mr Pascoe's quite taken with him and seemed quite worried when he left the ship. Strange how these things happen.'

Stranger than you know. Aloud he replied, 'Now, if you have quite finished, Mr Inch, perhaps you would be good enough to rouse the commodore and inform him of the weather. If the wind mounts further we will wear ship and gain more searoom.'

Inch paused as Bolitho added coldly, 'Just tell the commodore the barest details, if you please. I am sure he will be in no mood for light conversation at this time of morning.'

He saw a shadow move by the lee rail and called, 'Mr Gascoigne! How do you enjoy your first watch as acting lieutenant?'

Gascoigne staggered up the slanting deck, paused and then almost fell as the ship wallowed sickeningly into a steep trough.

'Quite well, sir.' He swallowed hard and added lamely, 'Although only when Mr Inch is on deck too, sir. Once when I was left alone I had a great dread that the ship was carrying me and every soul aboard into something solid yet invisible.' He shuddered. 'All this fabric and spars, the men below and the great weight of guns, yet I could find no word, even had there *been* danger.'

'That is natural.' Bolitho gripped the rail, feeling it wet and cold under his hand. 'Once you are over that sensation you start to learn how to master the ship yourself, without waiting for others to say and do things for you. You get the *feel* of her. You discover her moods, good or bad, and learn to give her her head when the moment offers itself.'

Gascoigne grinned. 'I never thought of it like that.' He walked away as Inch reappeared.

'Well?'

Inch replied, 'I told him, sir.'

There was something else. He asked more gently, 'Was he asleep?'

'No, sir.' He sounded puzzled. 'He is just sitting there on the bench seat, the most uncomfortable place in a quarter sea in my opinion. He is fully dressed, sir. Just sitting there.' His voice trailed away.

Bolitho clapped him on the shoulder. 'The privilege of rank, my lad!' Then he strode to the weather side before Inch could see his expression.

So it was worse than he had thought. Pelham-Martin was unable to lie down let alone sleep. Figures ran across the main deck and once he heard a man laugh, the sound strangely sad in the chorus of wind and straining rigging. He wanted to pace to quieten his troubled mind, but knew the motion was too savage for that. Here, on this very quarterdeck, two admirals had died within feet of him. One had been brave but stupid, while the other had died uncomplaining of his wound. He had been as courageous as he had been misguided, but never at any time had he faltered from what he thought to be his set duty. And before them perhaps other flag officers had fallen here. The lucky ones to be buried at sea or carried home to weeping relatives in casks of spirits to be laid to rest in some family vault. The unlucky had lingered on to die at a surgeon's hands.

He banged his fist on the rail, his eyes staring into the leaping patterns of spray. But none so far had died of fear, yet that was the greatest threat in any battle.

He was still by the rail when two hours later the first grey tentacles of light showed above the horizon far abeam and played across the faces of the men around him.

Allday appeared with a fresh jug. 'Coffee, Captain?' He held out the cup, his stocky body swaying at an angle with the deck.

Bolitho sipped it slowly, feeling its rich heat burning into his stomach.

To Gascoigne he said, 'See that all our people get a hot drink before they douse the galley fires.' To Inch he added, 'We shall go to quarters in half an hour. It will help wake them up and drive the weariness from their bones.'

'Deck there! Land on th' lee bow!'

He threw the cup to Allday. 'Aloft with you, Mr Carlyon! Report what you see, and lively with it!'

Gossett ambled across the deck, his hands deep in the pockets of his misshapen watchcoat. 'A fair landfall, sir.' He sounded vaguely satisfied. ''Bout five mile distant, I would think.'

Carlyon slithered down a backstay and blurted, 'Islands, sir. Sou'-west of us!'

He realized that Bolitho had remained silent and added, 'All overlapping, but there's a great hill on the nearest one.' He rubbed his nose and added doubtfully, 'Like a slab of cheese, sir.'

Gossett whispered, 'Gawd Almighty!'

Bolitho smiled grimly. 'Never mind, Mr Gossett. That was as close a description as fits the chart. A slab of cheese suits it exactly.'

He saw Inch stiffen, and turned to see the commodore's bulky figure emerging beneath the poop ladder.

He touched his hat. 'We have sighted the islands, sir. I am about to send the hands to quarters.'

He paused, seeing the deep shadows around Pelham-Martin's eyes. 'Have you had some coffee, sir?'

Pelham-Martin walked unsteadily to the rail and gripped it firmly. 'I do not want any.' He turned his head, squinting at the low clouds. 'Where is the *Hermes*?'

'On station, sir.' Bolitho stepped beside him to shield his face from the others. 'She will be able to see your signals directly.'

'And the Dutchman?'

'Not sighted her yet, sir.'

The small head seemed to twist in either direction quite independently of the massive frame beneath it.

'*What?*' Pelham-Martin peered across the tilting main deck below him. 'Where is she?' He was shouting. 'She *must* be here!'

Bolitho said, 'We had to change tack twice during the middle watch, sir. *Telamon*'s spars may be too old for such violent treatment in this wind. She probably retained her original course at a more favourable pace.' He was speaking quietly, aware of the watching eyes nearby. 'But Captain Farquhar will be safe enough. He will have had the lee of the land to protect *his* approach.'

Pelham-Martin did not seem to hear. He was staring at the sea as the growing light opened it up and displayed the hardening line of the horizon and the dark untidy cluster of land which seemed to trail from the plunging jib boom like weed.

'Empty!' He groped inside his heavy coat as if to produce his silk handkerchief. 'Nothing!'

There was a click as a boy turned over the half-hour glass beside the compass.

Bolitho nodded to Inch. 'Send the hands to quarters and clear for action.'

The commodore stared at him, his eyes bare and desperate. 'Just two ships!' He fell silent as the drums started to rattle and the seamen and marines poured on deck and scampered to their stations.

Bolitho said, 'They will suffice, sir.'

He could almost feel the man's anxiety. It was just as if the sight of this vast expanse of tossing sea and the huddle of islands had finally brought home the reality of his responsibility. In a moment he might lose his last shred of control. Just as young Gascoigne had described his own fear of his first watch on deck unaided, when everything appeared to be running away with him, beyond human control.

He said harshly, 'It is a fine day for it, sir. And if the French *are* here they'll be asleep most likely when *Spartan* pays them a call.'

Bolitho realized the thumps and bangs below decks had stopped, and when he looked down over the rail he saw the men at their stations, the only movement being made by the ship's boys as they scurried from gun to gun, sanding the decks as they ran. The gunners would need plenty of grip for their feet if the wind rose further.

Pelham-Martin said tonelessly, 'Would you send someone for my sword?' He fumbled awkwardly with the heavy coat and then removed it.

Bolitho saw he was wearing the same gleaming dress coat in which he had come aboard. In which he had sat out the night.

One of the seamen on the larboard battery had been about to tie his neckerchief around his ears. Seeing the commodore he waved it over his head and yelled, 'A cheer, lads! *Hurrah!*'

Bolitho said quietly, 'You see, sir? They look to you today!'

Then he turned away, unable to watch as Allday buckled the sword around the commodore's huge waist. His face seemed to have crumpled at the sound of that solitary cheer, and his expression was that of a man within the shadow of a gibbet.

15. The Message

BOLITHO straddled his legs and waited until the deck had completed another steep roll and then raised the telescope to his eye. In the fast-growing light he could see the nearest island, its ragged crest grey against the low clouds, and beyond it, overlapping like the prow of some ancient galley, a smaller islet, below which the sea lifted and boiled in continuous movement. Reefs most likely, he thought. Or parts of the cliff worn away by the years to fall as one more natural barrier against would-be intruders.

He lowered the glass, wiping his eye with the back of his sleeve. Around and below him the seamen waited by their guns, watching his face, or merely staring at the sealed ports in readiness for the next order.

Pelham-Martin said suddenly, 'Surely to God something will happen! Maybe the *Spartan* is aground!' He turned his small head and peered at Bolitho with something like shock.

'We'll know soon, sir.' He walked a few paces clear, unwilling to listen in case his own reserve of confidence should fade also.

'Sir!' Carlyon had his hands cupped over his ears. 'Gunfire, sir!'

Bolitho looked at him doubtfully. But there was no mistaking the expression on the boy's face. He was young and untroubled beyond his own duties, and his ears must have caught the far-off sounds before anyone else, in spite of the wind.

'Mr Inch! Pass the order to load! But do not run out 'til I give the word!'

To Gossett he called, 'Mark our course well. The reefs sweep right out from that far headland.'

The master nodded. 'I've noted 'em, sir. We've a good four mile as yet.'

'Deck there!' The masthead lookout's voice seemed puny in the din of wind and thrashing canvas. 'There's a ship breakin' from the channel!'

Bolitho gripped his hands behind him to control the rising excitement. 'Mr Inch! Alter course two points to lee'rd! Pipe the hands to the braces!'

Then he snatched a telescope from Carlyon's hands and peered at the clump of islands. They seemed to be pitching like flotsam across the spray-dappled glass, but even as his eye began to water from strain he saw the edge of the slab-sided island harden and darken, and where there had been a sliver of broken sea something was moving. A ship.

He heard Gossett call, 'Course sou'-west by south!'

Inch stared at him. 'It's a frigate!' A muscle jumped in his cheek as a sullen rumble of cannon fire echoed across the water. 'By God, the Frogs *are* there!'

Bolitho pushed past him. 'Shake out those reefs! And set the forecourse and t'gallants!'

He walked to Pelham-Martin's side as Inch dashed to the rail with his speaking trumpet. 'Well, sir, there are *some* in the bag today.'

He watched the men dashing out along the yards, the immediate response from every stay and shroud as first one then another of the topgallant sails filled to the wind, the thrust making itself felt to the very keel. With the wind almost dead astern the ship seemed to be leaning forward and down, and when the great spread of canvas bellied out from the forecourse Bolitho thought he could hear the sea parting across the bows like water in a millrace.

'You may run out, Mr Inch!' He watched narrowly as Pelham-Martin craned over the rail to watch the long twelve-pounders squeaking towards the open ports, their crews yelling to each other as if it was another contest.

Inch shouted, 'The frigate's cleared the channel, sir!'

Bolitho watched the distant ship, her shape shortening as she turned slowly from the nearest spur of land. With the wind driving down from the north-east she had little room to tack, and being so close inshore she might be in irons and driven back into the channel if she mis-timed it. He saw her yards swinging wildly, the spray leaping above her raked stem as she settled once more, this time on a converging course with *Hyperion*.

A hasty glance astern told him that Fitzmaurice needed no

instruction as to what was needed. The *Hermes* was already spreading her topgallants, and he could see her leaning sickeningly to the press of canvas as she swung purposefully across the *Hyperion*'s wake. Like the jaws in a trap. When the other French ships broke from the channel they would have to pass between two prepared and eager captains.

He snapped, 'Alter course another point! Steer southwest!'

He saw Stepkyne glance up at him from the main deck and then turn his head to speak with a gunner's mate. And there was Tomlin, already pushing his men to the braces again, his voice carrying like a trumpet above the bedlam of sea and canvas.

Now there was more gunfire, louder than before, and Bolitho twisted his head to watch as several columns of water burst close to the frigate's counter.

'Deck there! 'Nother ship comin' out!'

Pelham-Martin was clinging to the rail, his eyes half closed with concentration.

Bolitho said, 'Now we shall see!' He ran to the lee side to study the first ship while she clawed away from the treacherous line of reefs and then tilted steeply on the larboard tack. It was a dangerous manœuvre. At any second she could be all aback and at the mercy of the reefs, but her captain had no choice but to fight clear and give himself searoom.

Bolitho lifted his hand. 'Steady as you go!' His eyes watered in the spray and wind but he kept them fixed on the other ship. Two miles only separated them. He heard the grate of handspikes as the gun captains increased their elevation, and wondered momentarily if Fox was remembering the hill battery as he managed his own section on the lower deck.

Inch shouted wildly, 'Sir, sir! The second ship is the *Spartan*!' He sounded stunned. 'She's signalling!'

Bolitho turned away and looked at Pelham-Martin. If *Spartan* was close astern of the enemy it meant one thing only. There were no other ships to attack.

Carlyon yelled, 'From *Spartan*, sir! One enemy ship to the south-west!'

He swung round, his mind grappling with the signal as a lookout shouted, ''Nother ship on th' larboard bow, sir!'

Inch squinted up at the masthead. 'What the *hell* is he talking about?'

But Bolitho pointed with the telescope, his voice bitter. 'She must have found her way through another channel! Look, man, you can see her topmasts!'

He felt fingers locked into his sleeve and swung round to stare into the commodore's wind-reddened face.

'Do you see what you've done? She's escaping, and you cannot catch her now!' He was almost screaming. 'I'll see you hung for this, damn you! *Damn you!*'

Bolitho tore his arm free. 'Alter course three points to larboard! Steer south by west!'

The men threw themselves on the braces again, as with her sails booming and wrenching at the yards the *Hyperion* swung heavily towards the second islet, against which the Frenchman's topsails seemed to shine as if in one final mockery.

The enemy frigate seeing the *Hyperion* swing back on her original course, turned towards the open sea. Her attempted escape could have been a ruse to allow her consort to gain the other channel, or her captain might still have believed he had a chance for his own ship. But as the *Spartan* tacked dangerously around the reefs the *Hermes* began to wear ship. For those with time to watch she was an impressive sight, her sails very white against the dull clouds and her tall side shining with spray as she presented her double line of guns to the French frigate. Then she fired. It was at an extreme range, and when Bolitho turned his eyes from the other ship to look, he guessed that Fitzmaurice had fired across more than a mile of tossing water. But it was enough. The frigate's foremast and bowsprit crumpled in the barrage, and as the wind took charge he saw the ripped canvas and broken rigging whipping about like things gone mad, while the ship, moments before a picture of grace and beauty, ploughed drunkenly into a deep trough between the waves and began to broach to.

He turned back to look for the other vessel, and felt the anger and despair tugging at his throat as he saw her grow into sharp silhouette beyond the jutting prow of land.

She was a two-decker, probably one of those damaged by *Hyperion*'s blind broadside during the first fruitless attack on Las Mercedes. Now she was clearing the land, and if she got away, as well she might. Lequiller would soon know the failure of this attack and the weakness of Pelham-Martin's squadron.

Gossett said harshly, 'We can still catch 'im, sir!' But he sounded wretched.

'Deck there!' Every eye went aloft. Surely nothing worse could happen? 'Sail weatherin' the 'eadland!' A brief pause. 'It's the Dutchman, sir!'

Bolitho ran to the nettings and jammed his telescope tightly against his eye.

The French ship was well away from the reefs now, but beyond her, her sails yellow in the strange light, he saw the other vessel. It *was* the *Telamon*. There was no mistaking that high poop and the shining splendour of her figurehead. She was close hauled and standing almost into the teeth of the wind, and in the jerking glass appeared to be touching the land itself.

Inch muttered fiercely, 'For God's sake, Mulder'll be aground if he's not careful!'

Pelham-Martin seized Inch's glass. 'What's happening? Is the *Telamon* going to engage?'

Bolitho closed his telescope with a snap. He could feel the ship straining every spar and timber, and when he looked up he saw the hard-bellied sails gleaming like steel as the ship threw herself in pursuit.

Mulder's ancient command stood no chance at all against the powerful two-decker, and he must know it. Just as he must have seen that if the French ship maintained her present course she could slip around the headland and make for one of a hundred hiding places until further help arrived.

There were more dull explosions from astern and he heard the marines on the poop yelling to the men at the quarterdeck guns. 'The frigate's hauled down her colours, lads! She's struck to the *Spartan*.' The responding cheers only added to Bolitho's growing anxiety. To the ship's company any victory was an event, but viewed against the overall pattern it was almost nothing.

Inch said thickly, 'God, look at the Dutchman!'

The *Telamon* had changed her tack, and when Bolitho lifted his glass again he saw her swinging wildly across the wind, her sails in confusion and her masthead pendant streaming out abeam like a strip of metal.

'Frenchman's wearing ship, sir!' Inch was hoarse with excitement.

It was true. The enemy captain had little alternative now. With the reefs to starboard and the careering *Telamon* swinging across his bows, he had to act quickly to avoid collision or grounding his own ship in a last attempt to slip past.

But as the French ship's shape lengthened to overlap that of the *Telamon* everyone on the quarterdeck heard the ragged crash of a full broadside, and watched with dismay as the Dutchman's sails disappeared in a towering pall of dense smoke.

Bolitho pounded the rail, willing Mulder to tack again and break from the deadly embrace. He could hear the *Telamon*'s ancient cannon firing now, disjointed but defiant, the smoke billowing inboard to blind the gunners as Mulder continued to hold a course parallel with his adversary.

Gossett said, 'Gawd, the *Telamon*'s given us time to get to grips with the bugger!'

'Stand by on deck!' Bolitho saw Stepkyne touch his hat. 'Starboard battery, *ready*!'

He heard Pelham-Martin whisper fervently, 'Catch him, Bolitho! In the name of God, *catch him*!'

The French two-decker was still firing with hardly a pause between salvos, and as the wind drove some of the smoke clear Bolitho saw the *Telamon*'s mizzen vanish in a welter of broken rigging, and imagined he could hear the enemy's weight of iron smashing into her hull.

Lieutenant Roth muttered tightly, 'There goes her foremast!'

At the mercy of wind and sea the *Telamon* was already dropping past the Frenchman's starboard quarter, and although a gun still fired here and there along her side, she was crippled almost beyond recognition.

Bolitho needed no glass to see the enemy's yards swinging, and while she ploughed past the *Telamon*'s shattered bows men were already aloft as in final desperation her courses broke out to the wind so that she tilted still further, showing her copper in the dull sunlight. It had to be now or never.

Bolitho yelled, 'Starboard your helm!'

Drunkenly the *Hyperion* started to edge round, every spar and shroud slamming and creaking in protest. Muffled cries came from below, and he guessed that the impetus of the turn was sweeping the sea through the lower ports.

Round and still further round, until the two ships lay almost level with some two cables between them. It was a difficult range, but with every sail holding the ship over as rigidly as a fortress there would never be another chance.

'Fire as you bear!'

He seized the rail and watched as the ship shook violently to the controlled broadside. The French two-decker was already swinging away, but as the sea came alive with leaping spray the bulk of the *Hyperion*'s metal raked her poop and quarterdeck with the sound of thunder.

Her yards were coming round again, and Bolitho knew that her captain had at last realized his predicament. He should have stayed to fight the pursuing *Hyperion* in the first place. Then there was always a chance of crippling, even destroying her. But now as she wallowed back, Bolitho could almost feel the torment within her hull as the sea explored the rents left by that one smashing broadside. Leaning to the press of canvas she had exposed a whole expanse of bilge, into which many of the lower battery's twenty-four-pound balls must have carved a path of devastation which the pumps could never contain under such conditions.

He heard Stepkyne barking, 'Run out! Fire as you bear!'

The gunners were whooping with wild excitement as they poured another double salvo at the struggling ship which lay right across their sights. The Frenchman was trying to shoot back, but so great was the confusion and so dense the smoke from the *Hyperion*'s guns that only a few balls came close. Most of them whimpered overhead, and on the poop the marines were cheering and yelling, unable to use their long muskets at such a distance.

The range was closing, nevertheless, until both ships were less than two hundred yards apart. The enemy's sails were pockmarked with shot holes, and above her littered decks the rigging hung like torn creeper as she wilted to one more savage broadside.

Inch shouted, 'Look, sir! She's breaking off the action!'

Bolitho shook his head. 'We must have smashed her steering.' He watched coldly as the enemy ship began to idle downwind, her motion becoming more sluggish and haphazard with every nerve-wrenching minute.

Gossett said, 'She's done for!' Several turned to stare at him and he added flatly, 'The reef! She'll never claw off in time!'

Bolitho nodded. The long line of white breakers which reached out from the headland was overlapping the stricken ship, and nothing but a miracle could save her.

The quarterdeck gunners began to cheer with the jubilant marines, although they had not been able to fire either.

Bolitho crossed to the opposite side and stared for several moments at the *Telamon*. Alone and disabled, she, too, was in great danger of driving ashore. Yet for those few moments he was unable to move as he watched her plight and the complete destruction she had suffered. Dismasted, but for a stump of her main, with her side broken in countless places, she was almost a total wreck. Other ships of her size might have taken the punishment and lived to fight again. But her old timbers were welded together by time and weather, so that instead of individual planks and beams being broken, whole areas of her hull gaped open to the sea, while from her scuppers the blood ran down into the flotsam alongside as a testament of her sacrifice.

He said, 'Tell Mr Tomlin to lay out the towing cable. Secure guns and get every available man aft.'

Some of the gunners on the main deck climbed on to the gangways, realizing for the first time what their own victory had cost the Dutch ship and her company.

Then he turned as Pelham-Martin rasped, 'The Frenchman has not hauled down his colours!' His eyes were gleaming strangely. 'He might still repair the damage!'

Bolitho stared at him. 'And the *Telamon*?'

Pelham-Martin gestured fiercely with one hand. 'Signal *Hermes* to take her in tow!' His eyes were still fixed on the drifting two-decker. '*I want that ship sunk!*'

Bolitho looked at Gossett. 'Lay a course to weather the reef.' To Inch he continued in the same impassive tone, 'One broadside as we pass. There will be no second chance once we clear the reef.'

He crossed to the commodore's side again. 'They'll be hard aground in a moment, sir.' He knew it was pointless even as he spoke. There was something wild about Pelham-Martin's expression, a kind of inhuman eagerness which filled him with disgust.

'Do as I order!' Pelham-Martin clung to the nettings as the ship heeled slightly and Gossett said, 'Course sou'-west, sir!'

Far astern Bolitho could hear cheering aboard the *Hermes*, and as he looked over the nettings he saw figures standing on the *Telamon's* gangways waving and cheering with them. Someone had nailed a new flag to the broken mast, and amidst all the destruction and horror it seemed remote and strangely sad.

But aboard *Hyperion* not a single man called out now. Even the marines watched in silence as the ship bore down towards the dancing breakers along the reef. Here and there Bolitho saw the black tooth of a jagged rock, and found himself praying that the French would strike their colours before it was too late. There was a stiff sea running across the reef, and the survivors would be hard put to get ashore in safety even without this last battering.

But the flag was still there above the poop, and although the hull was low in the water he could see the men at their guns and a few figures standing on her quarterdeck as before.

'Stand by!' Stepkyne's harsh voice cut through the stillness.

Bolitho clenched his fists. Strike, damn you! *Strike!* Even as he willed the other captain to make the final gesture of surrender he knew that in a similar position he would have acted the same way.

The enemy was drifting almost on end now, so that he could see the great scars in her poop, the trailing rigging above her gilded name, *Le Fortune*. He thought he saw an officer wave his sword towards the *Hyperion* as she bore past, and then with a double roar the enemy fired his last shots from the two sternchasers below the shattered cabin windows.

Bolitho felt the shuddering crash of a ball slamming against the quarterdeck bulwark and heard the hiss of wood splinters ripping past him, but all this was lost as the *Hyperion* rolled back ponderously to the weight of her own broadside.

As the smoke swirled high overhead he saw the enemy's main-mast come crashing down. But it did not vanish in the sea alongside for at that very moment the ship quivered and then struck hard on the reefs. Above the cry of the wind they could all hear the grinding smash of timbers and the immediate inrush of water through her bottom. That last broadside must have killed or wounded most of the seamen on her main deck, for with her torn sails still driving her abeam she lifted again and then lurched once more across the reefs, her foremast toppling amongst the stampeding figures which swarmed helplessly across the forecastle.

Bolitho turned away, sickened. He could hear the other vessel tearing herself apart, and imagined the panic and disaster below decks as the great guns broke loose from their tackles and smashed from side to side, while the trapped seamen struggled amidst the rushing water in a vain effort to escape.

But the Tricolour had gone at last. Not struck, but blasted away in the fury of the *Hyperion*'s gunfire.

He turned slowly. 'Orders, sir?'

Then he stared as Pelham-Martin swayed and began to slip to the deck. His coat had blown open in the wind, and from beneath his armpit and spreading quickly across his white waistcoat was a bright patch of blood.

Bolitho shouted, 'A hand here! Mr Carlyon, pass the word for the surgeon!' Then he dropped on one knee and slipped his arm around the commodore's shoulders. 'Easy sir!'

Pelham-Martin seemed unable to speak and his expression was more one of amazement than any sort of pain.

'Carry the commodore to his cabin.' Bolitho stood aside as Trudgeon, the surgeon, accompanied by his mates hurried on to the quarterdeck.

Pelham-Martin gasped, 'Oh, God! Take care, blast you!'

Inch asked, 'Is it bad, sir?'

Bolitho walked to the bulwark and looked at the ragged scar above the nearest gunport. The ball, probably a nine-pounder, had carved away the timbers like the blow from an axe.

The gunners beside that port had been standing to watch

244

the other ship. Otherwise they would have acted as a shield for Pelham-Martin.

He replied at length, 'Wood splinters make the worst wounds, as you know. I am surprised he did not feel it more.'

Then he crossed to the rail and peered over the starboard quarter to watch the enemy two-decker foundering heavily across the reef. From the angle of her poop deck he guessed she had already broken her back. It was strange to realize that but for Pelham-Martin's insistence on that final attack he would still be unharmed.

Inch said, 'The *Hermes* has *Telamon* in tow, sir.'

Gossett walked across the deck and touched the scarred woodwork with astonishment. 'What made the Frogs fire that last lot, I wonder?'

Bolitho felt the tiredness sweeping over him. 'Wouldn't *you* have done so?' He turned to Inch again. 'Does *Spartan* have her prize secure?'

'Aye, sir.' Inch watched him worriedly. 'She is passing a tow across to her boarding party now.'

'Very well. Get the hands aloft and shorten sail. Then have a signal made to *Hermes* and *Spartan*.' He frowned, trying not to remember the sounds of the ship dying on the reef, the pointlessness of the last gestures. 'We will return to St Kruis. Make all sail conformable with weather and report when ready to proceed.'

He looked round as Trudgeon came beneath the poop wiping his hands. 'Well?'

The surgeon was a frim-faced, taciturn man who never wasted words, 'A splinter, true enough, sir. Pierced his side under the right armpit. In very deep, I'd say.'

'Can you remove it?'

'If he were a common seaman I'd not hesitate, sir.' He shrugged. 'But the commodore seems unwilling to let me touch him.'

'Stay with him until I am free to come aft.' As Trudgeon made to leave he added coldly, 'And if I catch you treating a *common* seaman with less care than one of my officers, I can assure you it will be the last time for you!'

Inch hesitated until the surgeon had departed. 'Must we return to St Kruis, sir?'

'The *Telamon* will never survive unaided.' He thought of the cheers, the destruction and the unquestioning courage of the Dutch sailors. 'De Ruyter would have been proud of them,' he added quietly. 'And I'll not leave them now!'

He walked to the quarterdeck rail and rested against it, feeling the ship trembling through his body as if they were linked together. Below him the seamen were relashing their guns and swabbing the decks free of powder stains, chattering and calling to each other, probably quite unaware their commodore had been wounded. The irony of it was made harder to understand, as he had been their only casualty.

Inch watched the topmen shinning down the backstays and said, 'This means that you will command the squadron now, sir.'

Bolitho smiled. 'Not while that pendant flies, Mr Inch.'

He thought suddenly of all those who had died or been maimed for life since the ship had sailed from Plymouth Sound.

'I doubt that the commodore will be laid low for long. Once we are in more sheltered waters Mr Trudgeon will be better placed to remove the splinter.'

Carlyon said, 'Signal from *Hermes*, sir. Both tows secured and ready to proceed.'

'Acknowledge.' Bolitho looked at Inch. 'You may wear ship now. Take station to windward of the others. We will be able to keep an eye on them to better advantage.' He glanced up at the set of the sails. 'I shall inform the commodore.'

He found Pelham-Martin lying in his cot, his body well cushioned and protected against the ship's uneasy movements, and a great wad of dressing wound around his chest and shoulder. His eyes were closed, and in the faint sunshine from the skylight his skin looked like wax.

Trudgeon crossed the cabin and said dourly, 'I have examined the wound again, sir.' He shifted beneath Bolitho's gaze. 'The fact is, there's so much fat it's hard to tell the depth or extent of the splinter.'

Bolitho glanced down at the commodore's face. 'I see. Very well, wait outside.' When the door had closed he bent over the cot and was immediately aware of the overpowering smell of brandy. A half empty decanter was propped by one of the pillows.

'Sir?' He heard the distant shouts and the rumbling creak of steering gear, and knew that Inch was already turning the ship as he had instructed. It would be a slow haul back to St Kruis, and even if it was unlikely they would meet an enemy, they had to be prepared to defend their battered charges at a moment's notice. He said more urgently, 'We are on course for St Kruis, sir. Do you have any further orders?'

Pelham-Martin opened his eyes and looked at him glassily for several seconds. Then he said faintly, 'Lequiller was not there! He has slipped from our hands again!' His head lolled and he peered down at the decanter. 'I must rest. I do not wish to talk any further.'

Bolitho stood up. 'I would suggest that we hand over the prize to de Block when we reach St Kruis, sir. The *Telamon* will be useless except for what they can salvage. With the frigate they will at least be able to defend themselves.'

'Do what you like.' Pelham-Martin closed his eyes and sighed. 'I am far from well.'

'When we enter the bay I have told Trudgeon what he must do, sir.'

The effect of his words was staggering. Pelham-Martin struggled on to his elbow, the sweat pouring down his face and neck in a small flood.

'I'll not have him touch me, *do you hear*? You'd like that, wouldn't you? To see me cut about by that blundering fool while you take over my command?' He sank back breathing hard. 'We will return to St Kruis. I have yet to decide what to do.'

Bolitho studied him gravely. 'We still do not know of Lequiller's whereabouts. He has the *San Leandro* and most of his squadron intact. I would think it likely he is ready to proceed with his plan.' He hardened his voice. 'We cannot wait any longer, sir.'

But Pelham-Martin turned his face away and remained silent.

Bolitho walked to the door. 'I will keep you informed, sir.' As he stepped into the passageway he heard the clink of glass behind him.

On the quarterdeck Inch was waiting, his horseface anxious as Bolitho looked at the compass and then the set of the sails.

He said, 'South by west, sir.'

Bolitho nodded absently, his mind still grappling with Pelham-Martin's strange manner. He had expected him to show dismay at being wounded, at the very unfairness which had singled him out from all the rest of the ship's company. It was almost as if he had found his excuse at last. One which nobody could dispute or question. He had been wounded. In his own view, not badly enough to be relieved of his command, but sufficient to deprive him of any active part in the vital decisions which now confronted him.

Inch said, 'I was wondering what we might be asked to do next, sir?'

Bolitho walked past him. 'We tread warily, Mr Inch.'

'Sir?'

'Before, we had very little to use for information.' He glanced towards the captured frigate as she yawned astern of the *Spartan*, a bright red ensign flying above her Tricolour. 'Now we have some prisoners. We may yet learn something of Lequiller's intentions.' He shifted his gaze upwards towards Pelham-Martin's broad pendant. 'And when we do, Mr Inch, we will have an edge on *him* for a change.'

He walked to the lee side and peered across the starboard quarter. The sunlight was forcing steadily through the layers of cloud and he could feel the warmth returning to his tired body as he studied the small islands fading into a growing haze. There was much to do, and Farquhar would have more information which might be useful. But it was essential to get the crippled ships and their wounded back to St Kruis first.

There would be many grieving hearts there when the *Telamon* returned, he thought sadly. It was to be hoped that their great sacrifice was not to be in vain.

By noon the following day there was little sign of the threatening sky and wind which had hastened their departure. As the slow procession of ships entered the bay and dropped anchor the sun blazed down on the clear water as if eager that nothing should be left hidden from the silent watchers on the shore.

Bolitho stood on the poop shading his eyes from the glare as the *Telamon* was warped, listing and with her lower ports under water, to rest on a strip of sand at the foot of the headland. Every available boat had been lowered to take off her wounded, and Bolitho could see tiny figures, mostly women, wading through the shallows to peer into each incoming craft, their grief made no less terrible by distance,

Anchored below the hilltop battery the captured frigate was already seething with activity as Farquhar prepared to land the prisoners and make good the damage with whatever facilities were still available. Hugh would be returning soon. Bolitho bit his lip. It was strange how his own personal troubles had deserted him in the anxiety of the chase. And there was still the commodore to be roused from his unreachable torpor.

He swung round as a gun boomed dully from the hillside.

Inch clattered up the poop ladder. 'They have sighted a ship, sir!'

Bolitho stared towards the open sea beyond the headland. She must be around the point and heading for the bay. A single ship could not be an enemy. He looked at Inch with sudden understanding. 'One of our reinforcements.' He walked quickly to the rail. 'At *last*!'

It took another half hour for the incoming vessel to show herself, and as she tacked slowly towards the bay Bolitho could hardly contain the sensation of relief and hope which her flapping topsails seemed to offer. She was a two-decker, but smaller than *Hyperion*, and in the bright sunlight he could see the sheen of new paintwork on her spray-dashed side and her figurehead agleam with fresh gilt.

Flags appeared as if by magic on her yards, and he heard Carlyon shouting to the officer of the watch, 'She's the *Impulsive*, sixty-four, sir! With despatches for the commodore!'

Inch said, 'From England!' It sounded like a cry from the heart.

Bolitho did not speak. The *Impulsive* was here, and with her his friend Thomas Herrick. He could feel his limbs trembling, like the return of his old fever, but he did not care. At last he would have someone to confide in. The one and only man with whom he had ever really shared his hopes and fears.

Once his first lieutenant, now as captain of a ship of the line he was *here*, and nothing could ever be so grim as it had seemed before the sound of the signal gun.

He hurried down the ladder, seeing his men crowding the gangways to stare at the new arrival, and like himself accepting her as more than a mere reinforcement. She had come from England. She represented something different to each man, a memory, a village, a green field, or the face of one particular and dear to him.

Lieutenant Roth was already at the entry port mustering the side party.

Bolitho watched as the anchor splashed down beneath the *Impulsive*'s bows and noted the smartness with which the sails vanished along her yards. Herrick had always been worried by the prospect of command. Bolitho had told him often enough that he had no need to doubt his ability, and the excellent seamanship he had just displayed was surely proof enough.

He heard Inch telling Roth that the captain who was about to be received on board had been *Hyperion*'s first lieutenant before him, and he wondered if Herrick would notice the change which authority and hard work had wrought upon Inch. It would probably seem like a small miracle. He found himself smiling at the prospect of the confrontation.

From the corner of his eye he saw Captain Dawson raise his sword and the paraded marines stiffen to attention as the *Impulsive*'s barge hooked on to the chains.

As a cocked hat appeared in the entry port and the pipes shrilled their salute Bolitho stepped forward, his hands outstretched in welcome.

Captain Thomas Herrick climbed through the port and removed his hat. Then he seized Bolitho's hands and held them for several seconds, his eyes, as clear and bright blue as the first day they had met, studying him with obvious emotion.

Bolitho said warmly, 'It is *good* to have you here, Thomas.' He took his arm and led him towards the quarterdeck ladder. 'The commodore is suffering from a wound, but I will take you to him directly.' He paused and looked at him again. 'How are things in England? Did you manage to visit Cheney before you sailed to join us?'

'I put into Plymouth for stores, then I went overland to

visit her.' Herrick swung round and seized his hands, his tone tight with sudden anguish. 'In God's name, how can I *tell* you?'

Bolitho stared at him, chilled by Herrick's distress. 'What *is* it? Has something happened?'

Herrick looked past him, his eyes blurred as he relived his own part of the nightmare.

'She had been visiting your sister. It was to have been her last journey before the child was born. Close by St Budock something must have startled the horses, for the Berlin went off the road and overturned.' He paused, but when Bolitho said nothing continued, 'The coachman was killed, and your steward, Ferguson, who was with her, knocked almost senseless. When he recovered he carried her two miles.' He swallowed hard. 'For a one-armed man it must have been like a hundred!' He gripped Bolitho's hands tightly. 'But she was dead. I saw the doctor and a surgeon from the garrison who rode from Truro. There was nothing they could do for her.' He dropped his eyes. 'Or for the child.'

'*Dead?*' Bolitho pulled his hands free and walked to the rail. Around him the dismissed marines walked chatting to their mess, and high above the deck a seaman was whistling while he worked on the mainyard. Through a mist he saw Allday watching him from the top of the quarterdeck ladder, his shape shortened against the clear sky and his face in shadow. It was not happening. In a moment he would awake, and it would be all as before.

Herrick called, 'Allday, see to your captain!'

And as Inch came aft, his face startled and curious, he rapped, 'I must have audience with the commodore, wounded or not!' He held up his arm as Inch tried to reach Bolitho's side. 'At *once*, Mr Inch!'

Allday walked slowly beside Bolitho until they reached the chartroom, then as Bolitho sank into a chair by the bulkhead he asked quietly, 'What is it, Captain?'

'My wife, Allday! *Cheney* . . .'

But the mention of her name was too much. He fell forward across the chart table and buried his face in his arms, unable to control the agony of his despair.

Allday stood stock still, stunned by his grief and by his own inability to deal with it.

'Just you rest here, Captain.' The words seemed to flood from him. 'I'll fetch a drink.' He moved to the door, his eyes on Bolitho's shoulders. 'We'll be all right, Captain, just you see . . .' Then he ran from the chartroom, his mind empty of everything but the need to help.

Alone once more Bolitho prised himself from the table and leaned back against the bulkhead. Then, very carefully, he opened the front of his shirt and took out the locket, and held it in the palm of his hand.

16. A Personal Thing

ALLDAY walked slowly into the stern cabin and stood the big coffee pot carefully on the table. The early morning sunlight threw a bright pattern of shimmering reflections across the beamed deckhead, and for a moment longer he was unable to see Bolitho.

'What do you want?'

He turned and saw Bolitho lying on the bench seat below one of the open windows, his back propped against the heavy frame so that his face was thrown into silhouette by the glittering water beyond. His shirt was crumpled and open to the waist, and his black hair was plastered across his forehead as he stared listlessly towards the distant hills.

Allday bit his lip. It was obvious that he had not slept, and in the clear light he could see the shadows around his eyes, the absolute despair on his tanned features.

He replied, 'Brought you some coffee, Captain. I've told Petch to arrange your breakfast just as soon as you're ready for it.' He moved carefully around the table. 'You should have turned in. You've not slept since . . .'

'Just leave me alone.' There was neither anger nor impatience in his tone. 'If you *must* do something, then fetch some brandy.'

Allday darted a quick glance at the desk. Beside a crumpled letter was one empty glass. Of the decanter there was no sign at all. 'It's not wise, Captain.' He faltered as Bolitho turned his head towards him. 'Let me get some food now.'

Bolitho did not appear to hear him.

'Do you remember what she said when we left Plymouth, Allday? She told us to take care.' He pressed his shoulders against the frame. 'Yet while we were out here, *she* died.' He brushed vaguely at the rebellious lock of hair above his eye and Allday saw the savage scar white against his skin like the mark of a branding iron. The gesture was so familiar, as was everything about him, that Allday felt strangely moved.

'She wouldn't have wanted you taking on, Captain.' He took a few more steps. 'When she was aboard the old *Hyperion* in the Mediterranean she had more courage than many of the men, and never once did I hear her complain when times got bad for us. She'd be distressed to see you all-aback now.

'Then there were those times at Plymouth when we were fitting out, Captain. They were good days.' Allday rested his hands on the desk, his voice suddenly pleading. 'You must try and think of those times, Captain. For her sake, as well as yours.'

A marine rapped on the cabin door and Allday whirled round with a muffled oath. 'Get out, damn you! I gave word that the captain was to be left alone!'

The marine's face was wooden. 'Beg pardon, but I'm to inform the captain that there's a barge shovin' off from *Impulsive*.'

Allday strode across the cabin and slammed the door. 'I'll tell him!' Then he rubbed his hands on his thighs, his mind busy with what he must do.

A quick glance at the sealed door and the sleeping cabin told him that the commodore was still asleep. His lip curled angrily. Or drunk, more likely. Captain Herrick was coming aboard, and he was a friend. And as far as Allday could see it seemed as if Herrick was the only one who could help Bolitho now.

He set his jaw in a tight line. But not even Herrick would see Bolitho like this. Crumpled and unshaven, with his stomach more full of brandy than he was used to.

He said firmly, 'I am going to shave you, Captain. While I'm getting the water from the galley you can be starting on this coffee.' He hesitated before adding, 'It was packed by her when we left Plymouth.'

253

Then he hurried from the cabin before Bolitho could answer.

Bolitho lowered his feet to the deck and then thrust out a hand to steady himself as the nausea flooded through him. He felt dirty, and tired enough to collapse, but something in Allday's last words made him move across to the table.

He gritted his teeth as he poured some coffee into the cup. His hand was shaking so badly that it took two attempts, and he could feel the sweat running down his spine as if he had just emerged from a nightmare. But it was no nightmare, and it could not be broken, now or ever.

He thought of Allday's desperate attempts to rouse him from his anguish, of the glances thrown his way whenever he had shown himself on deck during the night. Some had been pitying and full of compassion, as if, like Allday, they shared his grief in some private fashion of their own. Others had watched him with curiosity and unveiled surprise. Did they imagine that because he was their captain he was beyond suffering and personal despair? That he was above such human feelings, just as he was beyond their world of common submission?

During the night he had moved restlessly about the upper deck, only half aware of what he was doing or the direction his feet had taken him. He had felt some small security from the night sky and the ship's high web of rigging above him, and while he had wandered aimlessly on her deserted decks he had sensed the ship all about him, as if she, too, was hushed by his torment and loss. It had been then he had returned to his empty cabin and had sat by the open window, drinking the neat brandy without tasting it, knowing of the letter on the desk, yet unable to find the courage to read it. Her last written word. So full of hope and confidence, not just for them, but for the future and for the men who shared his everyday life.

Allday padded into the cabin and laid his razor on the desk. 'Ready, Captain?' He watched as Bolitho moved wearily to his chair. '*Impulsive*'s captain'll be aboard shortly.'

Bolitho nodded and leaned back in the chair, the absolute tiredness rendering him helpless as Allday rubbed his face with soap.

Feet moved overhead and he heard the steady sluice of water as the daily routine of swabbing down commenced.

Normally he would have listened, finding strange content in the familiar noises, and would have pictured the men who called to each other, even though they were hidden from view. He felt the razor moving swiftly across his cheek and knew Allday was watching him. Now it was all changed. It was just as if the closed cabin door was not only cutting him off from the ship, but from the world and everything in it.

The razor halted in mid-air and he heard Inch call from the doorway, 'Captain Herrick is come aboard, sir. The other captains will be arriving at eight bells.'

Bolitho swallowed and tasted the brandy like fire on his tongue. The other captains? It took physical effort to remember. Hazy faces swept across his blurred mind. Herrick returning from his brief audience with the commodore. Inch, torn between sorrow and concern, and many others which seemed lost in the overall confusion of his thoughts.

Inch added, 'There is to be another conference, sir.'

'Yes. Thank you. Please tell Captain Herrick to take some coffee while he is waiting.'

The door closed again and he heard Allday mutter savagely, 'And a fat lot of good a conference will do!'

He asked, 'Has the commodore been roused yet?'

Allday nodded. 'Aye, Captain. Petch is dealing with him now.' He could not keep the bitterness from his tone. 'Shall I ask Captain Herrick to explain things to him?' He wiped Bolitho's face with a damp towel. 'If you'll pardon the liberty, I think it's wrong that you should have to deal with this meeting.'

Bolitho stood up and allowed Allday to strip the crumpled shirt from his back.

'You are right. That *is* a liberty. Now kindly finish what you are about and leave me in peace.'

Petch came out of the sleeping-cabin, Pelham-Martin's dress coat across one arm.

Allday took the coat and held it up to the reflected sunlight. The dried bloodstain looked black in the bright glare, and as he poked a finger through the small splinter hole he said, 'Not much bigger'n the point of a rapier.' He threw the coat to Petch with obvious disgust.

Bolitho tightened his neckcloth and felt the clean shirt cool

255

against his skin. His mind recorded all these facts, yet he felt no part of them. The tiny splinter hole, Pelham-Martin's clear intention of remaining an invalid, even the need for some sort of strategy, all seemed beyond his reach and as remote as the horizon.

The sudden prospect of meeting with the other captains only succeeded in unnerving him again. The watching eyes, the condolences and sympathy.

He snapped, 'Tell Captain Herrick to come aft.' As Allday made for the door he added sharply, 'And I will have another decanter at once.'

He dropped his eyes, unable to watch Allday's anxiety. The man's concern and deep desire to help were almost more painful than contempt. Allday might have cared less for him had he seen him sobbing against the open window; had he known of his sudden impulse to hurl himself after the empty decanter and scatter the reflected stars beneath the ship's dark counter.

Herrick stepped into the cabin, his hat beneath his arm, his round face set in a grave smile.

'This is an intrusion, but I thought it best to see you before the others.'

Bolitho pushed a chair towards him. 'Thank you, Thomas. Yours is never an intrusion.'

Petch entered the cabin and placed a full decanter on the desk.

Bolitho looked at his friend. 'A glass before we begin, eh?' He tried to smile but his mouth felt frozen.

'Aye, I could relish one.' Herrick watched Bolitho's hand as the decanter shook against the glasses.

Then he said quietly, 'Before we meet the commodore again there are things which I should tell you.' He sipped at the glass. 'The news I brought from England is not good. Our blockade is stretched almost beyond safety limits. Several times in recent months the French have broken out of their harbours, even from Toulon where they were met and repulsed by Vice-Admiral Hotham's squadron.' He sighed. 'The war is gaining in pace, and some of our superiors seem left astern by the speed of the enemy's thinking.' His eyes followed the decanter as Bolitho poured another full glass. 'Lord Howe has given up the Channel Fleet to Viscount Bridport, so we may be assured of some improvement there.'

Bolitho held the glass up to the light. 'And what of us, Thomas? When do all our reinforcements arrive? In time to hear of Lequiller's final victory, no doubt?'

Herrick watched him gravely. 'There *are* no more ships. Mine is the only one to be spared for the squadron.'

Bolitho stared at him and then shook his head. 'I imagine that our commodore was *interested* in this piece of news?'

He drank some more brandy and leaned back in the chair as it explored his stomach like a hot iron.

Herrick replied, 'I got no impression from him at all.' He placed his glass on the desk but held his hand above as Bolitho made to refill it. 'He must be made to act. I have spoken with Fitzmaurice and young Farquhar, and I have heard what you believe of Lequiller's intentions. They make good sense, but time is against us. Unless we can call the French to action we are useless here and would be better employed with the fleet.'

'So you have been discussing it with them, eh?'

Herrick looked at the desk. 'I have.'

'And what else did you discover?'

'That any success this squadron has achieved has been at your doing.' Herrick rose to his feet, his features suddenly stern. 'I have been with you in action many times and have sailed by your side in worse conditions than many think exist. You know well enough what our friendship means to me, and that I would die for you here and now if I believed it would help. Because of this, and what we have seen and done together, I feel I have earned the right . . .'

He hesitated as Bolitho asked flatly, 'What right is that?'

'The right to speak my mind, even at the risk of destroying that friendship!'

Bolitho looked away. 'Well?'

'In all the years I have never seen you like this.' He gestured to the decanter. 'Always you have been the one to help and understand others, no matter at what cost to your own feelings. Your loss has been a terrible one. She meant much to me also, as I think you know. There is not a man aboard this ship who knew her who does not share your pain at this moment.' He added harshly, 'But viewed against what you believe and have taught others to accept in the past, it is a *personal* thing. And one which cannot, *must* not influence your deeds when you are most needed by all of us.'

Bolitho looked at him coldly. 'Have you finished?'

'Not quite. Often you told me that responsibility and authority are privileges, not the rights of every man for the taking. When we served in frigates there was a world of difference, with little at risk but our own lives. Here, our few ships might decide greater events which we cannot even begin to understand.' He looked hard at the sleeping-cabin door. 'And when we require an example, what do we have? A man so filled with self-deception and ignorance that he can see no further than his own skin.' He turned and faced Bolitho again, his eyes troubled but stubborn. 'So we will be looking to *you*. As the captain of the *Hyperion*, and a man who has never put self-advancement before honour and duty.' He took a deep breath. 'As the man chosen by Cheney Seton for her husband!'

In the muffled distance Bolitho heard the squeal of pipes, the sounds of boats alongside. The whole cabin seemed to be swimming in mist, and the words of anger and scathing retort would not come.

As he stood beside the desk Herrick stepped forward and seized his hands. 'Believe me, Richard, I know what you are suffering.' He studied his features with sudden determination. '*I know!*'

Bolitho looked at him and gave a small shudder. 'Thank you, Thomas. I do not know of anything which could ever break our friendship. And speaking your mind to me is not one of them, I am sure of that.'

Herrick nodded but did not release his grip. He said, 'I have been a sea officer long enough to learn that it is not the Pelham-Martins of our life who really matter. You, and those like you, who have found the time to think and plan for others will finally decide the rights and wrongs of our cause. And one day, perhaps in our lifetime, we will see a better Service because of that example. One which men will take as a calling, and not an enforced and heartless existence which can be determined by the whim of mere individuals.' He smiled briefly. 'Tyrants and influential nincompoops have a way of fading in the smoke of real danger.'

Bolitho swallowed hard. 'Sometimes I believe that I set you a wrong example, Thomas. You always were an idealist, but now that you have a command you must be sparing with those ideals and be content with the improvements of your own making.' Then he smiled. 'Now we will greet the others.' He looked down at the decanter for a long moment then added softly, 'There is little solace there either!'

But later as he stood with the other captains around Pelham-Martin's cot he knew it was going to be far worse than he had thought possible.

The small cabin was oppressively hot, with the skylight tightly shut and only one small port partly open to allow the sea air to penetrate. The commodore had apparently enjoyed a large breakfast for there were several empty plates beside the cot, and the atmosphere was sickly with the aromas of brandy and sweat.

Pelham-Martin looked much as before, his round face shining and pink with heat, and his body covered by a sheet right up to his throat, so that it was more like standing around a bloated corpse than awaiting the word of their senior officer.

Bolitho said, 'We are all present, sir.' He glanced at the others, noting their mixed expressions and feeling his own complete sense of detachment, as if he was a mere spectator.

Fitzmaurice looked grimfaced and worried, while Farquhar seemed more irritated than concerned for the commodore's appearance. Beside Herrick's sturdy figure, Lambe, the sloop *Dasher*'s young commander, was perhaps the most obviously affected. He appeared quite unable to tear his eyes from Pelham-Martin's face, and was peering into the cot like a man witnessing something entirely beyond his understanding.

Pelham-Martin's tongue moved across his lower lip and then he said thickly, 'You have all heard Captain Herrick's news. You will no doubt have realized the impossibility of our present position.' He gave a hollow sigh. 'It was fortunate I despatched the *Nisus* when I did. Others will have to decide on a course of action if Lequiller ever returns to France, or whatever country his orders take him.'

Fitzmaurice asked, 'What do you intend for us, sir?'

'Without the rest of my ships, what *can* I do?' His lips tightened in a frown, so that for an instant he looked like a fat, petulant child. 'I was given an impossible task. I do not intend to further the chances of my enemies by sailing on a wild-goose chase!'

Herrick spoke slowly and carefully. 'It is my belief that Captain Bolitho is right, sir. This Perez from Las Mercedes would be an obvious pawn for the French to use to arouse a rebellion, to drive another wedge between us and the Dons.'

The commodore's eyes swivelled towards him. 'Are you suggesting I should sail this squadron *five thousand miles* on some stupid, unsubstantiated rumour?' He winced and allowed his head to fall back on the sweat-stained pillow. 'If you think that, Herrick, you are more stupid than I would have given credit.'

Fitzmaurice glanced at Bolitho as if expecting some lead or example. Then he said shortly, 'I think you should take heed of your wound, sir. It is unsafe to leave it untended.'

Pelham-Martin scowled. 'Your concern fits you well. It is a pity that others have been so sparing in their attention.'

Bolitho clenched his fists and stared at the bulkhead beyond the cot. The heat in the cabin, the brandy and the overwhelming sense of defeat left him almost indifferent to the tension around him. As he fixed his eyes on the bulkhead yet another memory flitted through his mind, so that he could almost hear his own despair. It was here, in this very cabin that Cheney had slept during the voyage from Gibraltar to Cozar. In this cabin and in this same cot, while he had stayed at a distance from her, yet had felt drawn closer with every passing hour.

The others looked at him as he said sharply, 'There is no alternative. You must give chase.' He kept his eyes above the cot. 'Captain Farquhar has some prisoners from the prize, including her captain. We should be able to discover something.'

Pelham-Martin's sudden anger at Bolitho's interruption gave way immediately to something like triumph.

'Did you not know? Farquhar found no documents or sealed orders aboard!'

Farquhar turned as Bolitho looked at him questioningly.

'That is true. Every sort of evidence had been thrown overboard when we closed to give battle. The first lieutenant was killed, and now only the captain knows anything of use, and he will not betray his trust.' He shrugged. 'I am sorry, but there was nothing I could do.'

Pelham-Martin wriggled beneath the sheet. 'I shall want a new dressing. Send for my servant immediately.' He raised his head to peer above the cot. 'That is *all*, gentlemen. I have nothing further to add at present.'

They filed out into the stern cabin and stood by the open windows in silence.

Then Farquhar said bitterly, 'That seems to be an end to it!'

But still none of them moved away from the windows, and Bolitho could almost feel their uncertainty, the unwillingness of each man to take a first irrevocable step.

He said quietly, 'To go in the face of the commodore's orders is to overrule him.' He looked at each of them in turn. 'The only way to force a change of tactics is to relieve him of his command!' His voice remained quiet, yet each of the other officers seemed stricken by it. 'I will not implicate you further by asking what you think or consider our chances of success. The commodore is wounded, how badly we cannot know without a proper examination, and that he will not allow. To relieve him I, as senior captain, must confront him and haul down his broad pendant.' He walked to the desk and touched the lip of the decanter with his fingers. 'After that, I am committed, and rightly or wrongly, so are those who would follow my example.'

Herrick said firmly, '*I'm* with you, and here's my hand on it!'

Bolitho smiled. '*Think* before you plunge beyond your depth. If the commodore recovers his health and denounces our action, there will be only one verdict. Even if he does not, it will be seen as disloyalty amounting to mutiny, especially as there is an excellent chance of failure at the end of this effort.'

Fitzmaurice studied him grimly. 'It is a serious and disturbing supposition. I would rather face one hundred broadsides than your decision.'

Bolitho walked away from the desk and paused by the cabin bulkhead below his sword.

'Consider your alternatives carefully. If you remain here at anchor until the commodore recovers sufficiently to change his plans, you might be criticized, but you cannot be harmed for obeying his last order. Whereas,' the word hung in the air, '. . . if you join with me now, you could suffer disgrace and worse within the next few weeks.'

Farquhar said calmly, 'Then you have already decided?' He crossed to his side and looked up at the old sword. 'That brings back a memory or two!' Then he said, 'There is no doubt in my mind.' He looked at the others. 'I am for going on with the hunt!'

Bolitho turned and studied him gravely. Farquhar, out of all those present had perhaps the most to lose. It was strange to consider that he had been a midshipman while Herrick had been his first lieutenant. Now he was a post-captain, with enough youth and ambition to gain whatever heights and honours which might lie before him. Herrick's reaction to his words had been instant and predictable. He saw nothing but immediate loyalty, and had never paused to consider the dreadful consequences of his ready conspiracy. Fitzmaurice would fall in with the rest, while young Lambe was too junior to be seriously implicated, no matter what happened later.

He gripped his hands behind his back and tried to clear the dragging mists from his mind. Was he merely recording their reactions, or had he in fact planned this from the very beginning? He heard himself ask, 'The French captain, is he ashore under guard?'

Farquhar shook his head, his eyes still on Bolitho's face. 'No. I have him and the rest of his officers aboard *Spartan*. His name is Poulain and he is, I suspect, a very hard man.'

Bolitho took down the sword and turned it over in his hands. So many voyages, so many battles against his country's enemies. It appeared in nearly every portrait in the old house in Falmouth. Captains and admirals, gone now like their ships and their conflicts. There might have been a son to wear it one day. But perhaps it was better as it was. If this sword was to be smeared by disgrace, it was best forgotten, as he would eventually be.

He said, 'Bring Captain Poulain aboard *Hyperion* with his remaining officers.'

He paused, seeing the concern on Herrick's face. 'I will also want ten of his seamen.'

Herrick said hoarsely, 'Then we are agreed?'

'It seems so.' Bolitho nodded slowly. 'I hope you will not live to regret your agreement.'

Farquhar picked up his hat and studied it calmly. 'At least we know one thing. Lequiller has no frigates now that we have seized the *Thetis*. So what we lack in strength we might make up with agility.' Then he smiled, a brief, humourless movement of his lips. 'Poulain will be as curious as I am when he hears of this summons. He seems concerned more for his son, who is a lieutenant under his command, than for the loss of his ship. Lequiller must have instilled a great confidence in victory in his subordinates!' He clapped the hat on his head, adding, '*I* would not take so kindly at losing my ship, no matter what the intention!'

Fitzmaurice watched him leave and then asked, 'When will you see the commodore?' He was almost whispering, and Bolitho could find something like compassion for him. Fitzmaurice had no influence outside his rank and personal achievements. It would be little comfort to him to know he was not alone at the moment of decision.

'Presently. Now, if you care to remain here I will go on deck. I must have a word with Allday about a small matter which will not wait.' He returned the sword to its rack and walked towards the door.

As it closed behind him Lambe said fiercely, 'My God, how can he be so calm when his own head is at stake?'

Herrick said, 'Many is the time I have asked that question.' He thought of Bolitho's eyes and the pain held behind them as he had spoken his thoughts aloud. 'I still do not know the answer.'

Less than an hour later, as two bells chimed out from the forecastle, Bolitho walked slowly on to the quarterdeck and rested momentarily against the rail. The sun was shining brightly and throwing dark shadows from the shrouds and yards, and across the bay he could see the little wavelets cruising towards the anchored ships with the promise of a fresh wind in spite of the growing heat.

The ship seemed strangely quiet, but he was conscious of the watching seamen on the gangways and others working aloft who were staring down, their hands stilled as they waited for the drama to commence.

In the centre of the main deck the selected French prisoners stood surrounded by a scarlet rectangle of marines, their faces curious and apprehensive as they, too, watched the solitary figure by the quarterdeck rail.

Captain Dawson crossed the deck and touched his hat, his florid features grim and vaguely anxious.

'Ready, sir.'

'Very well.'

Bolitho faced the mounting breeze and took a deep breath. He heard boots clumping behind him and turned to see Farquhar and a marine escort, and with them the French captain. He was old for his rank, but gave an immediate impression of competence and assured self-control. He seemed, above all, a hard man, as Farquhar had described.

'Do you speak English, Captain?' Bolitho faced him, his voice calm, but very conscious of the dryness in his throat and the countless watching eyes.

'When I choose.' Captain Poulain watched him with equal gravity. 'But I 'ave nothing to add to what I told your young officer 'ere.'

Bolitho nodded. 'Ah, yes. The young officer who took your ship from you. Yes, I understand.'

Poulain's eyes flashed angrily. 'I will say nothing more! I know my rights and the code of honour which you 'old so dear to your decadent souls!'

Bolitho saw Dawson biting his lip, but continued calmly, 'I would prefer not to discuss matters of honour, m'sieu. I understand that when the *Spartan* made passage between the reefs at Pascua they discovered the remains of the Dutch schooner *Fauna*? Destroyed, I believe, by your guns while she tried to escape.'

Poulain regarded him coldly. 'It is war. There was no time for sentiment.'

'But she was unarmed and contained some helpless fishermen and their families.' Bolitho clenched his fingers behind him, willing himself to continue without any sign of emotion. 'I repeat, there is little point in discussing matters of honour.'

'Then I would wish to be taken ashore.' Poulain's mouth lifted slightly in a smile. 'No doubt I will be exchanged for some of the many prisoners my country 'as taken, yes?'

Bolitho nodded. 'No doubt, Captain. But first there is one small detail which I require explained.' He fixed his eyes on the other man. 'I wish to know your destination after you had completed your repairs, and by this I mean, where does your Vice-Admiral Lequiller intend to make his attack?'

For one brief instant he saw the Frenchman's eyes light up with surprise. Then the shutter closed and his expression became controlled as before.

'I know nothing. If I did, I would not tell you.'

'We both realize that you are lying of course.' Bolitho could feel the sweat pouring down his back and chest, his shirt clinging to his skin as he added, 'Lequiller sailed from the Gironde with orders. He executed the first part of those orders at Las Mercedes and when he seized the *San Leandro*. Now all I wish to know is the final part. Nothing more.'

'Then you are a fool!'

Bolitho heard Inch's quick intake of breath and saw one of the marines plucking angrily at his bayonet.

He moved to the opposite side of the quarterdeck. The sun was burning his shoulders so that he felt faint and sickened from the brandy in his empty stomach, but he made himself walk slowly, conscious of the silence and the men gathered along the deck of the *Spartan* nearby.

'Mr Tomlin, clear the larboard gangway!'

He did not need to raise his voice, and even the men in question fell back towards the forecastle as if fearful of breaking the silence.

Without turning his head he continued, '*Now*, Captain Poulain, I am going to shoot one of your men. *Execute* him, if you would prefer the term?' He hardened his voice. 'Perhaps you will recall those prisoners who were hanged aboard your admiral's flagship? It may help you to arrive at a decision.'

Two red-coated marines marched slowly along the larboard gangway, their tunics gleaming like blood in the bright sunlight. Between them, blindfolded and with his arms bound was a man in the uniform of a French master's mate.

The marine lieutenant came aft and said formally, 'Prisoner and escort ready, sir!'

'Very well, Mr Hicks.' Bolitho held out his hand. 'A pistol, if you please.'

Then he walked along the gangway, above the twelve-pounders and past the tiered boats, his step unhurried and the pistol hanging loosely at his side. Halfway along the gangway he turned and looked aft towards the group on the quarter-deck, his vision blurred by strain and the unbearable tension.

'*Well*, Captain Poulain?'

'I will see you *damned* for this!' Poulain took a pace forward but was restrained by the marines. 'You call yourself a captain! You are not fit to live!'

Bolitho swung round, and as the marines stepped aside, lifted the pistol and fired, the crash of the shot making more than one seaman call out in alarm and horror. The blindfolded figure jerked back against the nettings and then fell heavily on the gangway. His legs kicked only once and then he lay still.

Bolitho turned again towards the quarterdeck, the pistol smoke drifting past him as he watched the French captain for several seconds.

Poulain's voice sounded as if he was being throttled. 'France will not forget this! You are a butcher! But you can shoot me and all of my men, and it will do you no good!' He struggled forward against the marines' grip. 'I spit on you and your ship!' Then he twisted round as two more marines appeared at the head of the gangway.

Bolitho watched his sudden anguish as he said, 'Not the *rest* of your men, Captain, but your son!'

He gestured towards Lieutenant Hicks as the young French officer was led, blindfolded, to halt above the other man's still figure.

'Another pistol, Mr Hicks!' As he received it he had to grip it with all his strength to stop it from shaking.

'You have one minute.' He raised the pistol, seeing the French lieutenant's chest across the barrel, while the rest of the ship and the motionless marines blurred in haze. Very deliberately he thumbed back the hammer, the sound making one of the marines flinch as if he had been struck.

'*Stop!*' The cry was torn from Poulain's throat. 'Do not shoot! In the name of mercy, do not kill my son!'

Bolitho remained by the nettings but lowered the pistol slightly. 'I am still waiting, Captain!'

Poulain shouted, 'I 'ave my written orders with me. They are sewn in my coat!'

Bolitho swayed and pressed his arm against his forehead. Then he heard Farquhar's voice, as if from a great distance. 'I have them!'

Bolitho handed the pistol to Hicks and walked slowly towards the quarterdeck.

'Thank you, Captain. I have no pride in what I have done. But as you were quick to tell me, it *is* war. Now you will be taken ashore and placed in the care of the Dutch governor.'

He watched the French lieutenant being led below again and added coldly, 'When next you are tempted to kill helpless people, maybe you can find some worth in this lesson today.'

Poulain eyed him with undisguised hatred. 'You are a murderer no less than I!'

Bolitho replied emptily, 'Not *quite*, Captain.' He gestured towards the gangway. 'You may get up now, Allday, it is finished.'

A great gasp of astonishment rose from the watching seamen as the corpse struggled to its feet between the two grinning marines.

'As you see, Captain, he is little the worse for his perform-ance!' Then he turned away, sickened at the dismay and shame on Poulain's face.

Herrick stepped from beneath the poop and reached his side in three strides. 'That was a *close* call.' He took Bolitho's arm and guided him past the grinning and relieved seamen. 'I had no idea, nor did any of us.'

Bolitho listened to the laughing and shouting behind him and thought of the other captain's stricken features. 'It was not a task I enjoyed, Thomas.'

He paused by the ladder and studied his hands, expecting to see them shaking violently.

Herrick asked, '*Would* you have shot the lieutenant if

Poulain had resisted further?' He watched the prisoners being led to the waiting boats. 'Could you have done it?'

Bolitho looked past him. 'I do not know, Thomas.' He shook his head. 'In God's name, I do not know!'

17. Of One Company

COMMODORE MATHIAS PELHAM-MARTIN lay quite still in his cot, his eyes fixed on some part of the deckhead as Bolitho outlined what he had discovered from Poulain's orders. If anything, the cabin was hotter than it had been some four hours earlier, and Bolitho found time to wonder how the commodore could endure such added discomfort.

But as he spoke he was thinking more of the other captains and of his own disappointment when together they had read and re-read the Frenchman's curtly worded instructions. No wonder Lequiller had been chosen for this task. He was indeed as wily as a fox. There was no mention at all of the final destination, nor was any port named or described. Poulain and the captain of the other damaged ship were to complete minimum repairs and sail with all haste to rendezvous with Vice-Admiral Lequiller's squadron at a position one hundred miles to the north-west of Cape Ortegal, the very corner of the Spanish mainland. As he had studied the written instructions Bolitho had found little consolation in his own early assessment and solution of Lequiller's secret plan.

If the French admiral intended to enter a Spanish port and uphold Perez in an immediate rebellion, then he must be very sure of which harbour was the most suitable, both for himself and to produce the necessary sympathetic reaction from the local population. But this rendezvous was far out in the Bay of Biscay, and there was a choice of many such ports, from La Coruña in the north-west to Santander which lay a mere hundred miles from the French frontier.

Pelham-Martin said suddenly, 'So you were wrong after all, Bolitho. You still do not know where Lequiller is bound.'

Bolitho studied him impassively. 'There is a chance we can bring him to action if we can reach the rendezvous in time, sir. We know his intention, if not the final destination. I believe the former more important. By catching him prior to any contact with the land we will have destroyed his chances completely.'

The commodore closed his eyes. 'We do not *have* that time, but even supposing there was a chance of reaching the rendezvous as you suggest, Lequiller may have sailed on without waiting for the damaged ships to meet with him. I see no point in discussing it further.'

'I think it is a chance we have to take, sir.'

'I will not discuss it any more, Bolitho!' Pelham-Martin's eyes flicked open as pipes shrilled along the main deck and feet padded across the poop overhead.

'What is that?'

Bolitho felt strangely relaxed and devoid of tension. 'I have ordered all hands aft, sir. In view of what we have learned, and the need for haste, I must use my authority as senior captain.'

Pelham-Martin stared at him in disbelief. 'You *what*?'

'You have been wounded, sir, and as I have stated before, you should have the injury attended to without further delay.' He watched the other man calmly. 'Under the present circumstances, however, I see no alternative but to relieve you until such time as you are able to reassume overall command.'

'Do you realize what you have said?' Pelham-Martin's breathing grew faster and faster. 'If you take this step, you will place yourself open to arrest and trial.' His eyes were watering with concentration. 'And I will see to it that you suffer the exact penalty which you so richly deserve!'

Bolitho waited in silence. But Pelham-Martin seemed to have exhausted himself in the brief outburst and lay quite still but for the quick breathing beneath the sheet.

He turned on his heel and left the cabin. Framed against the stern windows the other captains were still waiting for him, their faces hidden in shadow.

Then Herrick asked quickly, 'Is it done?'

'I have told the commodore of my intention.' Bolitho picked up his hat and walked over to the bulkhead. 'It is fair to tell you that he was entirely opposed to my plan.' He saw Fitzmaurice turn away, his shoulders sagging with anxiety.

Then he reached up and removed his sword from the rack and moved with it to the door. He paused and looked back at them.

'When you accepted my proposals this morning you were not then aware of the real difficulties which lay ahead. I intend to make sail within two hours. I would not blame any of you should you decide to remain at anchor.' Then he left the cabin and walked out into the sunlight.

Inch touched his hat, his face set in a worried frown. 'All hands laid aft, sir!'

Bolitho nodded and crossed slowly to the quarterdeck rail. So many times he had made this short walk. To watch the seamen at drills or to supervise the making or furling of sails. To witness punishment or merely be alone with his thoughts.

He saw his officers lined against the opposite side, the paraded marines, the minute drummer boys, and Captain Dawson with Hicks beside him.

He removed his hat and placed it beneath his arm, and then looked along the length of his command. The gangways and main deck were covered with men and upturned faces, while others clung to the shrouds or stood on hatch covers so that they should see him.

In the silence, and as his eyes passed over the waiting men below him, individual faces stood out for the merest seconds before they merged once more into the mass. Some of those who had been pressed and had come aboard lost and terrified, and now stood shoulder to shoulder with the seasoned men, and were as tanned and confident as any. The grizzled tin miner who with nearly forty other Cornishmen had walked half across the country to volunteer for service in the *Hyperion*. Not because they had ever met Bolitho, but because of his name, one which was known and trusted, and as familiar to many of them as the port of Falmouth itself.

He saw his brother standing beside Tomlin, his greying hair moving slightly in the breeze, and wondered what he must be thinking and feeling at this moment of their lives. Of his own future when once the ship returned to England and the constant threat of the gibbet becoming stark reality? Or of his son, who now stood so grave-faced beside the other midshipmen, the living reminder of what might have been?

Perhaps after all he was merely watching Bolitho with nothing but pity or indifference? Seeing him as the younger brother and reawakening the old contest between them?

Gosset cleared his throat uncomfortably and Bolitho realized he must have been standing in silence for over a minute.

He said, 'When we came out here to seek the enemy and destroy him we had little but uncertainty, and more than enough to discourage any man. But not all the time has been wasted. Now you all know me, and I many of you.' He paused, feeling the hopelessness crowding across his thoughts. 'We are leaving this island today and giving chase once again.' He saw several men exchanging glances. 'Not westward this time, but to the east'rd, and to Spain! We will bring Lequiller to grips, fight him on open water in the manner which English seamen understand!' Someone raised a cheer but fell silent again as he added harshly, 'It took six weeks to reach here from the Bay of Biscay. Six weeks, because we were groping and searching along the way. But we will drive east'rd and reach Spain in thirty days!' He heard some of the seamen gasp with astonishment. '*Thirty days*, if we have to tear the sticks out of her to do it!'

He gripped his hands behind him, feeling the sweat across his wrists.

'Our commodore is still too ill to manage our affairs. So, by the authority invested in me, I am assuming command.' He ignored the flurry of excitement which ran across the main deck like wind over a cornfield. 'Carry on, Mr Tomlin!'

As the bosun loosened the halyards and the marines stamped to attention Bolitho heard feet moving across the deck at his back. When he turned he saw Herrick and the other captains forming into line and removing their hats as very slowly the big broad pendant was hauled down once more.

In the quick glance it was impossible to tell which captain had made the first move to join him on deck. But they were here, and in front of the ship's company as well as those of the nearest vessels. And by doing so had openly allied themselves to him, and had deprived themselves also of any defence should he be proved guilty for his actions.

Tomlin came aft, the pendant rolled beneath one massive

arm. He handed it to Carlyon, who received it with equal gravity.

Bolitho leaned on the rail and added slowly, 'When we run Lequiller to earth it will be a hard fight, but that you know. I cannot ask you to give of your best, for you will know I am *depending* on it.' He straightened his back and said, 'You must not falter. England will be waiting to reward you...'

He broke off, unable to find any more words. To see them watching him, listening to his empty hopes and promises, visualizing honour and glory when they should be thinking of the odds against such reward, pared away his determination like the blade of a knife.

A voice shattered the silence and made him turn, startled and off guard.

'A cheer for the cap'n, lads! An' another for the old *Hyperion*!'

Bolitho could not hear what else the unknown man said, for at that moment the air seemed to quake from the force of the wild cheering which echoed across the dancing whitecaps to be held and taken up from the other ships close by.

He swung away from the rail and saw Herrick grinning at him, and even Fitzmaurice looked confident and strangely excited. It was all the madness of a moment, but as the cheers swept over him from every side and Herrick stepped from the assembled officers to pump his hand, he could not control his own emotion, even gratitude, to all of them. For their simple trust, and so many other things which he could feel but not explain.

Farquhar shouted above the noise, 'Whatever the end to all this, it has been a fair beginning!'

But Herrick was more definite. 'We'll show 'em, by God!' He was grinning so widely his eyes had almost disappeared. 'With you in the van we'll give 'em a lesson to remember!'

Bolitho looked at each of them in turn. 'Thank you, gentlemen.' He tried again. 'It will be a hard chase and little rest for any of us. I doubt that we will have time to meet again before we close with the enemy.' He paused, very conscious of his last words. Some of them would never meet again if by achieving his demands they eventually met with Lequiller's powerful squadron. 'But we know each other's ways now,

272

and there is little else needed in a sea fight but to drive alongside an enemy and keep him there. Our people will do the rest.
I only hope we are not too late.'

Fitzmaurice said quietly, 'I'd rather face the French than a
court martial.' He shrugged. 'But slow or not, the *Hermes* will
give you every support when the time comes.'

Bolitho shook hands with each one in turn. 'Go back to
your people and tell them what we are about. We will weigh
at four bells.' He followed them down the ladder to the entry
port and raised his hat as one by one they climbed into their
waiting boats.

As Herrick made to leave he said quietly, 'I cannot thank
you enough, Thomas. This morning I was near to madness.
Tomorrow, who can tell?' He smiled and then stood aside
to allow Herrick to leave. 'But at this moment I am grateful
to you.'

Herrick nodded slowly. 'Take care. You obtained me my
first command.' He grinned. 'Now I'll be content only with
a knighthood!'

The pipes twittered again and he was gone.

Inch said, 'I've not had a chance to say how I feel about
your loss, sir.'

Bolitho looked at him gravely. 'Then say nothing, Mr Inch.
For both our sakes.'

Inch watched him walk aft to the poop and wondered.

'Thirty days, eh?' Gossett ambled across to him. 'There'll
be precious little sleep for you, I'm thinkin'.'

Inch shook himself from his thoughts. 'And I'll not stir
on deck without calling the master. *Mr* Gossett!'

Halfway through the afternoon watch Bolitho returned to
the quarterdeck and stood watching the land, his mind explor-
ing the past weeks, the hopes and frustrations which had been
constant companions. Around him he could feel the ship
coming alive again, and from forward the steady clank of the
capstan with an accompaniment from the shantyman's fiddle.
And Tomlin's powerful voice raised above the tune as he
mustered his men at their stations. It was a very old shanty
which had found its beginning in the West Country, where
most of the *Hyperion*'s company had originally started life.
As they moved busily about the decks and along the yards

273

high overhead some of them were probably thinking of it now, Bolitho thought. Spain was a long, long way from Devon or Cornwall, but it was still better than the other side of the Atlantic.

He turned as Inch crossed the quarterdeck and touched his hat. 'Anchor's hove short, sir.'

'Very well.' Bolitho glanced over towards the *Impulsive* and at the activity on her yards. Beyond her the hulk of the *Telamon* lay as a reminder of what had gone before, and a grim warning to all of them. Along the waterfront he could see the silent watchers, and wondered if de Block was there also. He had come aboard an hour earlier to pay his respects and to offer his thanks for the captured frigate. Neither had mentioned the fact that if Holland was drawn into the war as an enemy again the ship might be called to action against the donors. That, too, was part of what had gone before and had no place between them.

De Block had handed him a small and finely carved model of a Dutch man-of-war. 'To *remind* you, Captain. To give your son, perhaps?'

Bolitho had seen him over the side and had watched him rowed back to his lonely existence where he would end his days. It was to be hoped he, at least, would live the rest of that life in peace.

He straightened his shoulders and said curtly, 'Carry on, Mr Inch! Get the ship under way, if you please.'

With the signal to up anchor streaming at her yards the *Hyperion* broke free of her moorings and swung heavily from the thrust of the steady wind. Bolitho gripped the nettings as the ship canted over and lifted his head to watch the topmen strung out above the deck, their arms working in fierce unison as more and more canvas bellied out from the yards. The men at the braces needed no urging, and with her anchor swinging clear of the water the ship went about and gathered way towards the last headland and the dark blue lines of the horizon beyond.

As she pushed steadily abeam of the hill battery, Bolitho saw the Dutch flag dipping in salute, and then turned to watch the other ships spreading their topsails and edging clear of the anchorage in obedience to his signal.

Hermes, Impulsive and the lithe *Spartan*. The last to clear the headland was the little sloop, her hull almost awash as she fought clear of the reefs before tacking busily to windward of the depleted squadron.

It was not much of a squadron, he thought. But at that particular moment he knew he would not have changed it for a fleet.

The second morning at sea dawned as fine and clear as those which had preceded it, but when Bolitho came on deck after a hasty breakfast he could feel the difference around him like a physical thing. Close-hauled on the larboard tack the ship was leaning steeply from the wind, but the short whitecaps had overnight been replaced by longer, serried ranks of crested rollers which made the motion awkward and more violent.

For during the night they had slipped past Trinidad and were now standing out into the Atlantic itself, with no sight of land to break the horizon in any direction. He glanced at the swinging compass and then at the trim of the sails. They were still heading due east, and when he leaned across the rail he saw the *Impulsive* plunging over and down through a lively roller, her hull shining in spray as she followed some three cables in *Hyperion's* wake. The *Hermes* was almost hidden by the little two-decker's topsails, but he could judge her to be more than two miles astern and already lagging badly.

Inch was waiting for him to complete his morning inspection.

'*Dasher's* on station to wind'rd, sir.'

Bolitho grunted and walked slowly up the slanting deck. The *Spartan* was already out of sight, probing far ahead of the other ships. As usual, he felt slightly envious of Farquhar and his complete freedom from the heavier and slower vessels.

'We will alter course in fifteen minutes, Mr Inch. Call all hands!'

He did not feel like talking just now, and his mind was still busy with calculations and the mental picture of his chart.

Gossett touched his battered hat. 'Three 'undred an' fifty mile logged already, sir. That's a fair showin'.'

Bolitho looked at him. 'We shall see what she can do next.'

'Where do you think the French are now, sir?' Inch was

back at his side, his eyes screwed up against the wind as he watched the men hurrying to their stations.

'It is my guess that Lequiller sailed back to Las Mercedes to collect Perez and his mercenaries. I expect the latter will be embarked in the treasure ship as a double security.' He looked up at the masthead pendant. 'He will be on his way now, but at slower pace because of the *San Leandro*, I imagine.'

He turned impatiently and gestured to Gossett. 'We will alter course seven points and lay her on the opposite tack.' He felt the spray dash across his face and tasted the salt on his tongue.

The master nodded, 'Aye, aye, sir.'

To Inch, Bolitho added, 'When we are on our new course I want the royals on her.' He paused, seeing his words working on Inch's long face. 'And *then* you can set the stuns'ls for good measure!'

Inch swallowed. 'With all that canvas, sir, the *Hermes*'ll never be able to keep up with us.'

'Just do as I say, Mr Inch.' Bolitho eyed him impassively. 'We do not have the trade winds blowing beneath our coat tails this time, so we must drive to the north'rd before we can run for Spain with the westerlies.' He relented slightly. 'But the trade winds are still friendly to us, Mr Inch. So be patient.'

He turned away and snapped, 'Put the helm down!'

As the two seamen at the double wheel threw their bodies against the spokes Bolitho watched the rush of figures by the forecastle letting go the headsail sheets, while others tensed at the braces in readiness to haul round the straining yards on to the new tack.

'Helm a-lee, sir!'

Labouring and plunging, the ship began to swing clumsily across the wind, the sails flapping and cracking with the sounds of gunshots.

Bolitho gripped the rail, letting his body ride with his ship as she continued to turn across and then past the eye of the wind.

'Mainsail *haul*!'

Men scampered in orderly confusion, their tanned bodies shining with blown spray as the sea broke above the starboard bulwark and cascaded over the deck.

Bolitho slapped his palm on the rail, '*Now*, Mr Inch!'

'Let go and haul!' Inch's hat had been knocked awry, but he was managing to make himself heard above the thunder of canvas and whining rigging.

Bolitho watched with grim satisfaction as the yards began to creak round, the men at the braces hauling like madmen, digging their toes into the slanting deck, their bodies almost parallel with it.

Overhead the sails boomed angrily and then filled taut and bulging as the ship heeled to the opposite tack, blocks screaming and shrouds vibrating like demons until she had settled on her new course.

Bolitho nodded. 'Now get the royals on her!' A quick glance astern told him that Herrick had been ready and waiting. His ship was already plunging round in pursuit, her figurehead and bowsprit concealed in a great mass of bursting spray and spume.

Gossett shouted, 'Nor' by east, sir! Full an' bye!'

'Very well.' Bolitho felt the deck shiver as more canvas bellied out from the yards. Far above the deck the tiny figures seemed beyond reach and invulnerable, but he knew it was another illusion. One slip and it would mean instant death, if the man who fell was lucky. If not he would drop into the creaming sea alongside, to be left astern to drown in sight of his ship. For to try and stop the *Hyperion* under such a press of canvas would be to invite disaster. It was possible that such a manœuvre might even dismast her completely.

On the main deck he saw the sailmaker and his mates hauling out the studding sails, extra canvas to lash on to the mainyards like great wings, which with luck, might give the ship another knot if the wind held.

The rigging and shrouds seemed black with figures scrambling back and forth, up and down as they hurried to obey the urgent calls from the warrant officers of their divisions.

Suddenly he saw Pascoe climbing up the futtock shrouds, his slim body lying back above the sea, and held his breath as his foot slipped and a shoe fell lazily down and into the leaping spray. Then the boy regained his hold and continued after the others, his black hair whipping out in the demanding wind.

When he dropped his gaze Bolitho noticed his brother by the foremast, shading his eyes as he, too, peered up at the midshipman. Then he saw Bolitho watching him and gave what might have been a small shrug. Or it could have been a sigh of relief.

Lieutenant Roth called, '*Hermes* has tacked!' He chuckled. 'She's not keeping up at all well!'

Bolitho turned on him hotly. 'Don't be so damned smug about it! If the *Hermes* cannot stay with us, *you* will be seventy-four guns short when you most need them!'

Roth flushed. 'Sorry, sir.'

Bolitho walked to the weather side and steadied his body against the nettings. He must get hold of himself. To show resentment at such an innocent remark was pointless and stupid. Roth was more intent on showing pride in his own ship than deriding the weed-encrusted *Hermes*. He thought suddenly of his own fretting impatience in the Mediterranean when, like *Hermes*, this ship had been dragging with sea-growth and barnacles, left behind the fleet and with little sympathy from his admiral. But it was useless to think along those lines.

He said, 'Make a signal to *Hermes*, Mr Carlyon!' He frowned, remembering too Fitzmaurice's brave gesture to support him. '*Make more sail.*' He hesitated. 'That is all.' Fitzmaurice would not appreciate any sympathetic addition to the signal, any more than he would have done. He was as committed as any of them now, and must do more than his best to keep up with the squadron, if it meant knocking the wedges from the masts.

'She's acknowledged, sir.' Carlyon sounded surprised.

Shouts and curses came from the main deck as the larboard studding sail flapped and billowed like a snared sea monster. It was not filling too well, but was better than nothing. In any case it kept the men busy, and they had a long way to go yet.

Inch said, 'I have never seen her sail like this, sir.'

'We may find less favourable winds to the north'rd.' Bolitho was thinking aloud. 'We must push her all we can and take every advantage of the trades.'

The topmen were already sliding back to the deck, their voices loud, even jubilant at the great display of power which they had released and mastered.

Bolitho said shortly. 'I will be in the chartroom, Mr Inch. You may dismiss the watch below.'

In the small cabin he sat at the table and stared fixedly at the chart. Everything was ready, but there seemed nothing to add to his careful calculations. He flicked the pages of his worn log book, each one a small record of miles sailed, ships sighted. Men killed or injured. He closed it with a snap and stood up. He must stop thinking back. Stop remembering, when there was nothing left to hold on to.

There was a rap at the door. 'Enter.'

He looked round and saw his brother standing inside the chartroom, watching him with expressionless formality.

Bolitho said, 'Shut the door.' Then quietly, 'You may speak your mind. There is no one to hear you.'

'I wanted to talk with you about . . .' He faltered and then added flatly, 'I heard about your wife. I am sorry. What more can I say?'

Bolitho sighed. 'Yes. Thank you.'

'When I was at Cozar with the other convicts I used to see her walking by the old fortress. I think I fell in love with her also.' He smiled sadly. 'Do you think you will find the French this time?'

Bolitho looked at him. 'Yes.'

'If you do, and the fates are kind, what will you do about me?'

'I have not decided.' Bolitho sat down wearily and massaged his eyes. 'If we succeed in finding and beating Lequiller . . .'

His brother lifted an eyebrow. '*Beating* him?'

'To cripple him will be sufficient.' It was strange how Hugh could see what others had not even suspected. A sea fight, perhaps one hundred miles out in the Bay, could mean as much destruction for victor as for vanquished.

He continued abruptly, 'I can hand you to the authorities with a plea for pardon. In view of your work in the *Spartan* I do not see how it could be refused.' He held up his hand. 'Hear me and *then* speak. But if you wish, I will have you sent ashore on some duty.' He looked away. 'Then you can desert and make your own way.'

'Either course leaves you open to criticism and real danger, Dick. The latter more so, because you will have to live with the knowledge that you have at last been influenced from your plain duty by personal bias.'

Bolitho stared at him. 'For God's sake, do you think I care about that any more?'

'I do. You are offering me the chance to desert, not only because in your heart you mistrust the leniency of any court martial, but also because you fear the effect on my son if he sees me tried and hanged for treason.' He smiled gently. 'I know *you*, Dick!'

'Well?' Bolitho stood up and walked to the chart rack.

'I will take your offer and run.' Hugh sounded suddenly tired. 'Not to Cornwall where I might be recognized.' He paused. 'But it will be England and not some poxy jail at the other end of the earth.'

Bolitho faced him. 'Perhaps we will speak again later.'

'I think not.' His brother eyed him calmly. 'By the way, I think you are foolish to act as you are now. You should have let Pelham-Martin take the blame and stay at anchor in St Kruis. Now, whichever way it goes, he may be the victor.'

'Maybe.'

Hugh nodded. 'And perhaps I'd have done the same. All Cornishmen are said to be slightly mad, and it seems we are no exception.'

Feet clattered in the passageway and Midshipman Pascoe thrust his head around the door.

'Mr Roth's respects, sir, and may he take in a reef? The wind has freshened slightly.' His eyes moved from Bolitho to Hugh. 'Sir?'

Bolitho said, 'No, he may not take in a reef, Mr Pascoe. Not now, not at any time, unless we are faced with a hurricane.'

Pascoe nodded. 'Aye, aye, sir, I'll tell him at once.'

Then he asked, 'Would it be all right for Mr Selby to continue with the sextant instruction, sir? I seem to be slower than the others.'

Bolitho studied him gravely. 'Not slower, Mr Pascoe. Just younger.'

Then he looked at his brother. 'If you find that convenient with your other duties, Mr Selby, you have my permission.' He added quietly, 'In view of our recent conversation, I imagine you can be trusted to make *good use* of the time?'

Hugh nodded, his eyes suddenly bright. 'The time'll be well spent, sir. You have my word on it.'

When they had gone, Bolitho rested his head in his hands and stared blindly at the chart. Once he had felt sorry for his brother, and the pointlessness of his future. Now he felt only envy. For even though the boy remained ignorant of his instructor's identity, Hugh would have him to himself, and could cherish the memory and the knowledge that his son would be safe from shame and live to be the extension of the life he had thrown away.

While *he* had nothing. He found his fingers touching the locket again. Only memories, and over the years they, too, would be as elusive as the wind and offer no comfort.

With a jerk he stood up and reached for his hat. Here was a bad place to be alone. On deck he at least had the ship, and for this mission he would try and make that suffice.

18. At last, the Signal

AS BOLITHO HAD ANTICIPATED, the first infectious excitement of heading out into the Atlantic soon gave way to strain and long days of backbreaking work for every man aboard. Once clear of the friendly trade winds and into the Horse Latitudes they were beset by maddening and frustrating delays, for in that vast, empty expanse of ocean the winds backed and veered, sometimes twice in a single watch, with all hands fighting to trim and then re-trim the yards so that not even a cupful of power should be lost.

Once the wind fell away altogether and the *Hyperion* idled uncomfortably in a steep swell, her sails flapping and limp for the first time since leaving St Kruis. Most of the ship's company had been grateful, when at any other time they might have cursed the wind's perversity and the helplessness they felt under such conditions. But any hope for a rest was soon dispelled when Bolitho had ordered Inch to turn them to again and use the lull to bend on heavy weather canvas for the change he knew would soon be upon them.

Sixteen days after weighing anchor they picked up a stiff

south-westerly and beneath leaden skies tacked and headed eastward for the final leg of the voyage.

Bolitho knew that many of the seamen cursed his name whenever the cry, 'All hands! All hands aloft and reef tops'ls!' drove their weary bodies to the shrouds and up to the vibrating yards once more. Theirs had become a world of shrieking wind and drenching spray, where they fisted and grappled sodden canvas high above the decks, fingernails torn and bleeding while they struggled to keep from falling to certain death. But he could find little time to spare for their inner feelings, any more than he allowed himself a moment's rest.

At any other period he might have felt elation, even pride for the manner in which the old ship and her company were behaving. As the miles rolled away beneath the keel and the sea's face changed to dull grey he knew that such a fast passage would be envied by many captains. As always, whenever he came on deck the *Impulsive* was never far astern, her heavy weather sails giving an appearance of purpose and grim determination. Of the *Hermes* there was no sign at all, and Bolitho had once found himself wondering if Fitzmaurice had, after all, decided to fall back deliberately and leave him to his own devices. It had been unfair and pointless even to think like that, but he knew it had been because of his own uncertainty, his overpowering need to drive the ship as never before, if only to keep his despair at bay.

Every day he had visited the commodore in his sleeping-cabin, but even that seemed of little value now. Pelham-Martin rarely spoke to him, and merely stared up from his cot without even bothering to disguise his satisfaction at Bolitho's empty reports. In spite of Pelham-Martin's silent hostility, however, Bolitho was worried at his appearance. He was eating less and consuming a good deal of brandy as compensation. He seemed to trust no one near him, and had even driven Petch away with a string of threats when the wretched man tried to bathe his perspiring face.

Strangely, he had sent for Sergeant Munro, a seasoned marine who had once been an inn servant before enlisting and knew something of the way of his betters. But Bolitho suspected the commodore looked on Munro more as a bodyguard against some imaginary enemy than any sort of lackey.

Pelham-Martin's voice was certainly stronger, but he had refused to allow Trudgeon to inspect, let alone change his dressings for over a week, and Bolitho had told himself repeatedly that he was merely shamming and biding his time until he admitted failure.

He had not spoken to his brother again, but during one night when the wind had risen unexpectedly to a full gale he had seen him dashing aloft with some seamen to restrain the mizzen staysail which had split from luff to leach with the sound of tearing silk, audible even above the howl of sea and rigging. Pascoe had been with him, and when they had at last returned to the deck Bolitho had seen their quick exchange of grins, like conspirators who shared something private and special.

As day followed day, Bolitho remained aloof from his officers and restricted his contact to the requirements of duty. The south-westerly wind showed no sign of lessening, and while the ship plunged and staggered across the endless expanse of creaming rollers, Bolitho paced the quarterdeck, heedless or unaware of his soaked clothing until Allday finally persuaded him to go aft for some warm soup and a brief rest. Everything was damp, and below decks behind shuttered ports the men off watch crouched together in their crowded messes, willing the voyage to end, sleeping, or waiting for the next frugal meal. The cooks had little to offer, and in their crazily swaying world, amidst a litter of pots and broached casks of salt pork or beef, it was hard to see what else they could provide without some sort of miracle.

At noon of the twenty-seventh day Bolitho stood by the quarterdeck rail and watched Inch and Gossett working busily with their sextants. Overhead the sky had cleared a little and the clouds were broken into long, ragged banners, between which the watery sunlight gave an illusion of warmth.

Gossett said slowly, 'I'd never 'ave believed it, sir!'

Bolitho handed his own sextant to Carlyon and touched the worn rail with his hand. Twenty-seven days. Three less than the impossible target he had imposed at St Kruis.

Inch moved to his side and asked quietly, 'What now, sir?'

'*Spartan* will have been patrolling for several days, Mr Inch.' Bolitho looked at the blurred horizon. It seemed to shine like gunmetal, yet there was no true division between sky and sea. 'We will continue on this tack until dusk. Perhaps by then we might have some news from Captain Farquhar.'

But no news came, nor any sight of a sail to break the unending monotony of broken rollers. At nightfall they went about and under reefed topsails butted almost into the teeth of the wind. There was nothing the next day, or the one after that, and as the masthead lookouts changed and the daily routine dragged out its minutes and hours Bolitho knew that like himself there were few aboard who still retained any hope.

Tempers became frayed, and here and there within the ship's confined world old conflicts flared into open violence. Three men were flogged, and a trusted and well-disciplined bosun's mate was placed in irons for refusing to turn out of his hammock during the night watches. There was no sane reason for his behaviour, it just seemed part of the whole pattern of bitter disappointment and frustration.

Five days after reaching the supposed rendezvous the lookouts sighted the *Spartan* clawing out from the south-east. For a few more moments something of the old excitement returned as men clambered into shrouds and rigging to watch her as she went about and ran down under the *Hyperion*'s lee.

Midshipman Carlyon lowered his glass and looked at Bolitho. 'Nothing to report, sir.' He dropped his gaze as if he felt partly to blame. '*Spartan* requests instructions, sir.'

Bolitho knew Inch and the others were watching him, although when he turned his head they immediately appeared engrossed in anything but in his direction.

He replied slowly, 'Signal *Spartan* to take station to wind'rd with *Dasher*.'

He saw the frigate falling away, her yards swinging round as Farquhar let the wind carry him clear. The *Spartan* was streaked with salt and there were several figures aloft in her rigging, splicing and repairing damage caused by the buffeting she had endured. What it must be like aboard the sloop, Bolitho could not imagine. But *Dasher* had kept up with them, had smashed through heavy weather and suffered calms, her topsails always visible to greet each morning watch.

Bolitho said, 'I am going aft, Mr Inch.'

The lieutenant crossed to the weather side and asked hesitantly, 'Will you see the commodore, sir?' He saw Bolitho's eyes and added, 'There is *still* time, sir. We can all ride it out if you give the word.'

Bolitho smiled. 'There is no point in enforcing this misery now.' He studied him gravely. 'But thank you just the same. You have been given a hard time lately.'

As he strode away he heard Inch say, '*God damn* those Frogs!'

He paused outside the sleeping-cabin and then thrust open the door. Pelham-Martin watched him in silence for several seconds. Then he asked, 'Well? Do you submit now?'

Bolitho gripped his hat tightly beneath his arm. 'There is nothing in sight, sir. The rendezvous is overdue.'

Pelham-Martin's eyes gleamed faintly. 'Fetch me my writing pad.' He watched Bolitho at the bulkhead bureau. 'As of this moment I am going to relieve you of your command. You disobeyed my orders, you took advantage of my wound, and I shall write a report to that effect.'

Bolitho placed the pad on the cot and watched him without emotion. His limbs felt light, as if he was drugged, and he could find no involvement in what was happening to him.

The commodore snapped, 'Fetch a witness!'

At that moment Inch appeared in the doorway and stared at them curiously.

He said, 'The masthead has just sighted the *Hermes*, sir.'

Pelham-Martin struggled beneath the sheet. 'Good. Now the whole squadron will be able to return to England.' His eyes moved to Inch. '*You* will be the witness to this document. If you behave yourself I will try to spare your commission at the court martial.'

Inch said thickly, 'Sir, there is nothing which has happened that I did not agree . . .'

Bolitho interrupted harshly, 'Just witness the document, Mr Inch and do not be a fool!'

'Quite so!' Pelham-Martin seemed entangled in the sheet. He shouted, 'Munro! Come here *at once*!'

The marine sergeant entered the cabin and stood beside the cot.

'Lift me up, damn you!'

As the marine took his shoulder Pelham-Martin gave one terrible cry, so that he let him fall back again to the pillow.

Bolitho snapped, 'Stand away!' He pulled down the sheet and then stared at the man's shoulder beneath the bandage. 'Fetch the surgeon immediately.' He felt sick and appalled. The commodore's upper arm and the visible part of his shoulder glowed hard yellow, like a ripe melon, and when he touched the skin with his hand it felt as if it was on fire.

Pelham-Martin peered up at him. 'What is it? For God's sake, *what are you staring at?*'

Inch muttered, 'My God!'

'The wound has become poisoned, sir.'

'You're lying!' The commodore tried to struggle up but fell back with a gasp of pain. 'You are just saying that to save yourself.'

Trudgeon pushed past Inch and stared at the discoloured skin in silence. Then he said tonelessly, 'It must come off, sir.' He looked at Bolitho, his eyes doubtful. 'Even then I'm not sure . . .'

Pelham-Martin shouted wildly, 'You'll not touch me! I am *ordering* you to keep away!'

'It's no use, sir.' Bolitho studied him sadly. 'You may have thought such a small splinter could do you no real harm. It was probably some infection from the wood,' his eye rested on the empty decanter. 'Or your blood may have become affected.' He looked away, unable to watch the man's growing terror.

You fool. You poor, frightened fool. To avoid a decision, just one decision, he had allowed this terrible thing to happen to himself.

He thought suddenly of the ships and all the men who had been depending on him and added flatly, 'There is no other course, sir.' He nodded to Trudgeon. 'You have my consent.'

Pelham-Martin screamed, 'I am ordering you!' He writhed in the cot, the sweat pouring across his chest as he peered at Inch. 'I was dismissing Captain Bolitho from his command!'

There was a clatter of feet on the poop above and then a muffled wave of cheering. They looked at each other and then turned to the door as Midshipman Carlyon burst into the cabin.

'*Sir!*' He controlled his voice as he saw the stricken commodore. '*Hermes* is signalling!' He fumbled with his tattered book. '*Strange sail to the nor'-west!*'

Bolitho stared at him. 'Thank you, Mr Carlyon. Now back to your flags at the double!' To Inch he snapped, 'I will be on deck directly.' Then he smiled. 'And thank you for your loyalty.'

He turned and looked down at the commodore. 'It must be Lequiller's squadron, sir. I will keep you informed whenever I am able.' He moved to the door as Trudgeon beckoned his mates to enter.

On deck the air was bracing and clean with light drizzle, and the sun was again covered by cloud. But the wind was still steady from the south-west, and the masthead pendant almost rigid against the dull sky.

Gossett reported, 'Course west by north, sir. Full an' bye!'

Bolitho nodded and lifted a telescope to his eye. Far away across the larboard bow he could see the *Hermes*'s topsails etched on the horizon, the balls soaring to her yards and breaking to the wind in stiff, bright patches of colour.

Carlyon yelled, 'From *Hermes*, sir! *Estimate five sail of the line!*'

Bolitho lowered his glass and looked at Inch. All the weeks and days, the waiting and the planning had brought them to this point on the sea, this moment in time.

He said, 'Alter course a point to starboard. Steer west-nor'-west!'

As Inch groped for his speaking-trumpet Bolitho beckoned to Midshipman Carlyon and saw Inch pausing to listen.

'Mr Carlyon, make this general signal to the squadron.' He hesitated, sensing the eyes around him, the men on the main deck and the ship around all of them.

'*Enemy in sight!*'

As the flags soared aloft and broke to the wind Bolitho wondered briefly what the other captains would be thinking as they read the signal. At St Kruis, while they had listened and mulled over his ideas and suggestions they must have had doubts, many doubts. Now, the sight of his signal would clear their minds of everything other than the need to fight. To fight for their very survival.

Astern, aboard *Impulsive*, the acknowledgement was already hoisted, and he could imagine Herrick looking around his ship, his first command, which might be lost to him in a matter of hours.

He pulled his watch from his breeches pocket and flicked open the cover. It was exactly two o'clock, and even as he returned it to his pocket four bells chimed out from the forecastle belfry.

When he raised the telescope again he saw the *Hermes* growing larger and more distinct, and found time to thank God for the keen eyes of her masthead lookout. Later or earlier, and the two squadrons might have slipped past each other, or been lost in a rain squall in the vital moment of contact.

Lequiller would most likely have sighted the *Hermes*, but he had no choice but to engage. There were many hours of daylight yet, and with the open sea behind him he must fight and destroy the flimsy force across his bows, unless he was to become the hunted and not the hunter.

Bolitho said, 'Make to *Hermes*. *Take station astern of me*.' He thought of Herrick again. The signal would disappoint him certainly, but if his sixty-four was to survive the first clash then he must allow the heavier two-deckers the opening broadsides. He added, 'Then make a general signal, Mr Carlyon, *Prepare for battle!*'

'Deck there!' The masthead's call made every eye look up. 'Sail fine on the lee bow!' The merest pause. 'More'n one ship, sir!'

Bolitho nodded to Inch. 'Beat to quarters and clear for action.'

The two marine drummers hurried to the quarterdeck ladder and started their insistent tattoo. The rapid drumming seemed to act like the final confirmation, and as more men swarmed up from below and ran to their stations those already on watch cheered and waved their neckerchiefs towards the *Hermes* as she started to tack steeply towards the centre of the line. Bolitho saw Fitzmaurice with his officers, and lifted his arm in response to the other captain's greeting.

Between decks he could hear the thuds and clatter of screens being torn down, the rush of feet as other men hurried aloft to rig the chain-slings to the yards and assist Tomlin's deck party with the protective net above the gunners.

He said to Inch, 'Pass the order to sway out the boats for towing astern.' He thought of the distance they were from land, the very hopelessness of survival should the worst happen.

Inch came back seconds later, his face pale with excitement. 'Cleared for action, sir!' He managed to grin. 'Six minutes exactly!'

'Very good.' Bolitho found himself smiling. '*Very* good!'

He walked back to the rail and looked searchingly over the crowded main deck. Every gun was manned and ready, the captains facing aft, their bodies hung about with the tools of their trade. The decks were well sanded, and in the stiff breeze the men would need all the grip they could afford.

He said, 'Signal the squadron to shorten sail.' He looked up at the pendant and shivered. Soon now. Very soon. It was to be hoped the first sight of the enemy at full strength would not destroy this first determination.

'Deck there! Five sail o' the line an' one other, sir!'

Gossett rumbled, 'That'll be the Dons' treasure ship.'

Bolitho made himself walk slowly aft, his hands behind him. As he passed the quarterdeck nine-pounders some of the gunners twisted round to watch him. As if by meeting his eye they could share his apparent calm and hold it like a talisman.

Captain Dawson clattered down from the poop. Above him and ranged around the nettings his marines were already swaying in neat lines, their muskets at their sides, their dressing faultless as usual.

Bolitho nodded to him. 'Go for'ard and speak with your lieutenant. The carronades will have plenty of work directly, and I want your sharpshooters to give them all the cover they can.'

Dawson tugged at his collar. 'Yes, sir.' He glanced bleakly at the grey water. 'I'll not fancy a swim today.'

More seamen thudded down from the shrouds as the big mainsail was finally furled and the ship settled into a state of watchful tension. Apart from the hiss of spray and a steady thrumming tune from the rigging, all was silent once more.

Inch said, 'Will we take the weather-gage, sir?'

'It is too soon to say.' Bolitho reached out and snatched a glass from Carlyon. As he steadied it against the nettings he saw the enemy ships for the first time. It was difficult to fix their formation at such a distance, and the overlapping top-sails and streaming flags gave the impression of one huge nightmare creation, climbing up and over the horizon, intent on destruction and death.

He returned the glass. There had been no mistaking the ship at the van of the squadron. The big three-decker. Lequiller's own flagship, *Tornade*. She was a bare two years old, and mounted a hundred guns. It would be better to remember her at anchor with the wretched prisoners hanging from her main-yard than to contemplate the devastation of her massive artillery, he decided grimly.

But for her, the odds might have been acceptable, if unfair. Five to three. But the *Tornade*'s overwhelming superiority in firepower made all the difference in the world.

He compressed his mouth into a firm line.

'Wind's droppin' a bit, sir.' Gossett regarded him glumly. 'There's the spite of the Bay an' no mistake.'

Bolitho nodded. If it fell away altogether it would make the first embrace all the more devastating and reduce their chances of crippling Lequiller's ships enough to delay if not deter him.

He heard a ripple of voices below the rail and as he looked down he saw some of the seamen clinging to the gangways to watch the approaching ships, realizing perhaps the magnitude of their foe.

That was bad. Waiting to close an enemy was always the worst part. It seemed to take an eternity, and all the while there was little to do but watch and consider, to lose confidence and find despair.

He beckoned to one of the drummers. 'Here, boy!' He saw the lad staring up at him from beneath his shako, his tanned face pinched with growing fright. 'Can you play that fife of yours, eh?' He forced a grin, feeling the skin cracking at the corners of his mouth with the effort.

'Yessir!' The boy blinked rapidly and removed the fife from his white crossbelt.

At that moment, as Bolitho tried to recall some tune or shanty which might attract the men's attention from the other ships, a terrible cry floated up from the poop. It seemed to go on and on, at one level, while the men at the guns around him stared past the wheel towards the dark passageway which led to the stern cabin. Even one of the helmsmen released his grip on the spokes to swing round in horror.

The dreadful cry stopped, but the sound still seemed to hang there as before.

Bolitho gritted his teeth and tried not to picture the gross, naked body being held across the table, that first frightful incision of Trudgeon's knife.

He said sharply, 'Well?'

The drummer lifted the fife, his small, rough hands shaking badly as he placed it to his lips.

Then Gossett said gruffly, 'How about *Portsmouth Lass*?' He glared at the gunners and the motionless marines. '*Sing*, you lily-livered swabs, or I'll be amongst you this minute!'

And as another horrifying scream rent the air the fife's feeble notes were picked up by the seamen on the quarterdeck, and then, slowly at first, by those at the twelve-pounders, and even by some high in the fighting-tops.

Bolitho walked to the weather side and turned his face to the sea. The men's voices, strengthening and lifting above the wind, the mental picture of Pelham-Martin's agony, all were part of the unreality around him.

But almost worst of all were the words of the song which Gossett had suggested with such haste, and in order to drown the sounds from the stern cabin.

'*I knew a lass in Portsmouth Town . . .*'

The same shanty they had sung when *Hyperion* had worked clear of Plymouth Sound on that bitter winter's morning.

He turned his head as one of Trudgeon's mates walked from beneath the poop with a canvas bundle in his hands. The man paused to listen to the singing before hurling the bloodstained parcel over the lee rail.

Bolitho asked, 'How was it?'

The surgeon's mate grimaced. 'A small splinter, sir. No bigger than me fingertip.' He shrugged heavily. 'But there was enough pus and muck around it fer ten men.'

'I see.' It was pointless to question him further. He was merely an extension of Trudgeon's arms, the strength to hold still a victim, and one so hardened by the horrors of his trade that he was beyond compassion of any kind.

Bolitho walked past him and raised the telescope once more. How quickly the French ships had tacked into line and how utterly indestructible they looked. Under reduced sails, with their hulls gleaming dully in the strange light, they seemed to be moving along an invisible thread, on a converging tack with the three English ships. Much further astern, her high poop just visible beyond the formidable line, he could see the *San Leandro*, where no doubt Perez and his advisers were waiting to see the way opened for his return to power and wealth.

De Block had told him that the governor of Las Mercedes was over seventy years old. It was unlikely he would live long enough to enjoy his return, even if the French allowed him to.

He slammed the telescope on its rack. He was already thinking in terms of defeat. Lequiller would *not* succeed and Perez would only live to see his new ally's destruction!

Barely three miles separated the two squadrons now, but it was still impossible to tell which ships would keep to windward. It was better to retain the present controlled approach than to lose station in some last-minute manœuvre.

The singing had stopped, and as he looked along the ship's length he saw the men standing beside their guns, staring aft towards him.

He nodded. 'You may load and run out, Mr Inch. It is time we showed our teeth!'

Inch grinned and hurried away. Minutes later the port lids swung upwards, and to the accompaniment of squealing trucks the guns trundled against the bulwarks, the captains gripping the trigger lines and speaking quietly to their own men.

Midshipman Pascoe dashed through the main hatch and ran aft to the foot of the quarterdeck ladder.

'Lower battery loaded and ready, sir!' He turned to hurry back but paused as Bolitho called, 'Come here, Mr Pascoe!'

The boy ran on to the quarterdeck and touched his hat. He looked bright-eyed and there were patches of colour on his cheeks.

Bolitho said quietly, 'Look yonder.' He waited as the boy climbed on to a bollard to peer above the hammock nettings.

Pascoe stared for a full minute at the great array of sails stretching towards the starboard bow. Then he climbed down and said, 'There are a lot of them, sir.' He lifted his chin, and without effort Bolitho could see his face pictured with all those others hanging in the empty house at Falmouth.

Impulsively he reached out and gripped his arm. 'Take *care* Mr Pascoe. No heroics today, eh?' He thrust his hand into his pocket and took out the small carved ship which de Block had given him. 'Here, take this. A souvenir of your first voyage.'

The boy turned it over in his hands and said, 'It's beautiful!' Then he placed it inside his coat and touched his hat again.

Bolitho watched him go, his heart suddenly heavy with concern.

'He'll be safe down there, Captain.'

He turned to find Allday standing behind him, the sword and his best dress coat draped across his arm.

Several men watched him as he slipped out of his faded seagoing coat and thrust his arms into the one with the white lapels and bright gold lace. The coat which Cheney had admired so much.

Allday adjusted the swordbelt around his waist and stood back with a critical glance.

Then he said quietly, 'It is going to be fierce work before we're done today, Captain. There's many a man who'll be looking aft when things get bad.' He nodded, apparently satisfied. 'They'll want to see you. To know you're here with them.'

Bolitho lifted the old sword a few inches from its scabbard and touched the blade with his finger. Old, maybe, but the man who had forged it had known a thing or two. It was lighter than most of the modern ones, but the blade was like a razor. He let it drop into the scabbard and thrust his hands beneath his coat.

He said, 'If I fall today, see that the boy is safe.'

Allday stood at his back, a heavy cutlass naked in his belt.

If you fall it will be because I am already pulped, he thought. Aloud he replied. 'Never fear, Captain.' He showed his teeth in a grin. 'I'll be an *admiral's* cox'n yet!'

There was a dull bang, and seconds later a thin waterspout rose lazily across the larboard bow. Bolitho watched the brown smoke being whipped away from the three-decker's forecastle by the wind.

He imagined Lequiller and his captain watching their slow approach and felt his breathing becoming more controlled, even relaxed. The last calm before madness began. The moment when there was no more room for conjecture or regret.

Another ball ploughed through the white-tipped rollers and ricocheted towards the horizon.

He found that he was smiling, his skin tight like a mask. You will have to get closer than that, my friend. Much closer.

Then he drew his sword and laid it flat along the quarter-deck rail.

The waiting was done. The time was now.

19. Final Embrace

BOLITHO turned his back on the approaching ships and raised his glass to study the *Spartan*. With the little sloop close astern of her she was plunging through steep swells about a mile to windward. He caught a brief glimpse of Farquhar's elegant figure, his face turned towards him, and then lowered the glass again.

'Make a signal to *Spartan* and *Dasher*.' He saw Carlyon's hands shaking as he picked up his slate and pencil. '*Attack and harass the enemy's rear.*'

The suddenness of Farquhar's acknowledgement and the instant activity on the frigate's deck and yards told him of the relief his signal had unleashed. Unlike the two-deckers, Farquhar had no need to wait to be pounded blow for blow. As his sails filled to the wind and more canvas billowed from his topgallant yards Bolitho knew he would give of his best. At any other time it would have been sheer lunacy to despatch such frail vessels headlong into the fray, but as Farquhar had observed, the enemy had no frigates left, and feint attacks around the French rear might help to cause some momentary diversion.

Inch whispered, 'The *Dasher* too, sir?'

Bolitho glanced at him. 'There can be no spectators today.'

There was a sporadic rumble of cannon fire, and he saw the *Tornade*'s upper battery light up in a long ripple of orange tongues. But the *Spartan* was already thrusting past and ahead of *Hyperion*'s larboard bow, her ensign streaming from the gaff as she spread more sail and headed towards the opposite end of the French line. Some of the balls ripped through the water and raised more spray beyond her, but she was a difficult target, and it was obvious that the sudden move was quite unexpected.

Flags soared up the *Tornade*'s yards, and the two rearmost two-deckers began to idle clear of the line, their topsails flapping as they tacked slowly and ponderously towards the oncoming frigate.

Bolitho smiled tightly. The treasure ship meant more to Lequiller than anything. Without her and her cargo of men and wealth this would be a battle of no value, either to him or his country.

Some of the other ships were firing now, the sounds intermingled and jarring as their gunners tried to wing the two spray-shrouded vessels before they could sail past.

Bolitho held his breath as the sloop rocked violently, her low hull completely bracketed with leaping columns of water. But she sailed on, her driver and maintopsail punctured in a dozen places. One of those balls from the French line would smash her delicate timbers to boxwood, and her commander needed no encouragement to spread more sail and clap on speed.

Bolitho turned away and stared fixedly at the leading enemy ship. They were almost bow to bow now, with the three-decker less than half a cable away and slightly to starboard.

Inch murmured, '*We* have the wind-gage it seems.'

'And the wind is still fresh, Mr Inch.' Bolitho looked up as one more gun fired from the *Tornade*'s lofty forecastle and a ball slapped through the mizzen topsail directly overhead. 'But the smoke from our broadsides will be better protection than agility.'

He pressed his palm on the sword's flat blade. 'Stand by on the main deck!' He saw the gunners crouching down, their faces tight with concentration as they peered through the open ports, hands like claws on tackles and rammers, as if they would never move again. He heard the word being passed below decks, and tried not to think of the lower battery, the hell it would be soon, and his nephew down there enduring the living nightmare.

The three-decker's yards moved very slightly and he saw her swing away. Lequiller's captain intended to pass exactly parallel with the English line and not waste a single ball.

Bolitho watched the oncoming giant, her triple row of guns shining dully in the light, the lower battery comprised of massive thirty-two-pounders.

He lifted his left hand very slowly and could almost feel Gossett tensing behind him. He made himself wait until the *Tornade*'s yards had settled again and then shouted, 'Larboard your helm!' He heard the spokes creaking frantically and saw the bowsprit beginning to swing slowly until it was pointing straight for the enemy's figurehead. 'Steady!' He slapped the rail, his voice harsh but controlled. '*Now*, Mr Gossett! Bring her back on course!' The wheel started squealing again, and along the main deck he saw vague impressions of men hurling themselves at the braces, while overhead the yards creaked and grated in protest. He ran to the nettings and peered at the French flagship. She was turning away, her captain momentarily unnerved by what must have looked like a head-on collision.

He yelled, '*Broadside!*'

Stepkyne dropped his sword, his voice cracked with strain. '*Fire!*'

Every gun hurled itself inboard, the crashing roar of explosions seeming to drive into Bolitho's brain with the force of a musket ball. He watched as the dense smoke billowed away and heard the splintering thunder of his broadside striking home.

The smoke lifted violently as if touched by some other wind, and lit up scarlet and orange, while around and above the *Hyperion*'s quarterdeck the air came alive with screaming metal as the *Tornade*'s gunners recovered their wits and fired back.

Bolitho staggered and seized the rail to stop himself falling as a ball sliced through the bulwark and smashed into a nine-pounder on the opposite side. He heard screams and yells, and more cries as another burst of cannon fire raked the hull from stem to poop.

Above the writhing fog he saw the Frenchman's masts, the speckled flashes from unseen marksmen in her tops, and waited counting seconds as the *Hyperion's* second broadside blasted the smoke aside and shook the deck beneath him as if striking a reef.

He yelled, 'Lively, Mr Roth!' The rest of his words were drowned as the quarterdeck nine-pounders jerked inboard on their tackles, their earsplitting barks adding to the din and confusion about him.

Musket balls thudded into the deck planking, and he saw a marine staggering and reeling like a drunken man, hands pressed to his stomach, his eyes closed as he reached the rail and pitched headlong into the net below.

But the *Tornade's* topmasts were already passing the starboard quarter, and as the *Hyperion's* lower battery fired again he saw the balls smashing into the three-decker's tall side, the splinters and lacerated shrouds lifting above the smoking gunports in crazy torment.

And here came the second one, a two-decker with a figurehead in the form of a Roman warrior, her bowchaser firing blindly through the gunsmoke as she endeavoured to keep station on her flagship.

Bolitho cupped his hands, 'Fire as you bear, Mr Stepkyne!' He saw the lieutenant crouching inboard of the leading gun, his hand on the captain's shoulder.

More heavy firing came from astern, and Bolitho knew the *Hermes* was engaging the flagship, but when he peered over the nettings he could see nothing but topmasts, all else hidden in the great pall of smoke.

'*Fire!*'

Gun by gun the main deck battery engaged the second ship, the men cheering and cursing as they threw themselves on the tackles, their naked bodies shining with sweat and blackened from powder smoke, while they sponged out the muzzles and rammed home the next charges.

Bolitho felt the hull quake below his feet, and winced as more balls smashed along the ship's side, hurling splinters into the smoke or ripping through ports to plough into the men beyond. He saw a complete gun hurled bodily on to its side, with one of its crew pinned screaming and writhing beneath it. But his cries were lost in the roar and crash of the next broadside, and Bolitho forgot his agony as he turned to watch the two-decker's foremast begin to slide down into the smoke.

He grabbed Inch's arm so that the lieutenant jumped as if receiving a musket ball. 'The carronades!' He did not have to add anything and saw Inch waving his speaking trumpet towards the hunched figures on the forecastle. The throaty roar of a carronade fanned the smoke downwards into the main deck, and he saw the massive ball explode just below the Frenchman's poop. When the wind laid bare the damage he saw that the wheel and helmsmen had vanished, and the poop looked as if it had been struck by a landslide.

Crippled, and momentarily not under command, the ship started to swing downwind, her high stern and flapping Tricolour rising above the smoke like an ornate cliff.

The second carronade lurched back on its slide, and Bolitho heard someone cheering as the ball burst inside the stern cabin above her name, *Cato*, and the handful of marksmen who were still trying to shoot at the *Hyperion*'s forecastle as she edged past. He could picture the murderous devastation as the ball sent its contents scything through the crowded gundeck to add to the confusion already apparent on her shattered poop.

Vaguely he could see a marine waving and gesturing from the forecastle, and when he ran to the weather side he saw something dark and covered with green weed sliding past the larboard bow like a grotesque sea monster.

Inch cried hoarsely, 'Christ Almighty! The *Dasher*!'

Bolitho pushed past him as the third ship's topmasts and braced yards loomed above the fog of battle. The sloop must have taken a full broadside, or sailed too close to the Spanish treasure ship. Her upturned keel surrounded by bursting air bubbles and flotsam was all that remained.

He snapped, 'Ready, lads!' He could feel himself grinning, yet was conscious only of numb, pitiless concentration.

A voice yelled, 'Ship on th' weather bow!'

As the smoke swirled abeam he saw the other two-decker across the larboard bow, her sails almost aback as she drifted towards him. She was one of the ships detached to protect the *San Leandro*, and as her upper guns blasted their orange tongues from the ports he knew it would be a double engagement.

He felt the salvo ripping overhead and saw the net bouncing with fallen blocks and full lengths of rigging. A man dropped from the mizzen top and fell hard across the breech of a nine-pounder. Bolitho heard his ribs cracking like a wicker basket trodden underfoot, saw the terrible agony on the man's face as the seamen pulled him clear and rolled his body free of their gun.

'Stand by the larboard battery!' He was hoarse with shouting and his throat felt like raw flesh. 'Get ready to show them, my lads!' He waved his sword at the waiting gunners and saw more than one of them grinning up at him, their teeth very white through the grime.

'Fire!'

The larboard guns crashed out for the first time, the double-shotted charges blasting into the newcomer's bow and side with the sound of thunder. Bolitho watched coldly as the enemy's foremast and main topgallant buckled and curtsied into the drifting smoke, and then shouted, 'Mr Stepkyne! All spare hands to the larboard gangway!' He saw Stepkyne, hatless and dazed, staring up at him. 'Repel boarders!' He gestured with his sword as the French ship began to sidle slowly towards the larboard bow.

The third ship in the enemy line was abeam now, but had tacked further away than her predecessors. She seemed to lift from the *Hyperion*'s smoke, and then as the grey light touched her figurehead and catted anchor she fired a full broadside, the shockwave of the double line of guns blasting the air apart with the power of a searing wind.

Bolitho fell choking and spitting as the deck bucked and staggered beneath him. Men were crying and yelling all around him, and he stared up as Captain Dawson rolled across the splintered planking, blood gushing from his mouth and one eye bouncing grotesquely on his cheek.

When his hearing came back he heard the marines calling to each other, firing and loading, and vying with their comrades in the tops as they tried to pick off the French marksmen with their muskets.

Inch yelled, 'The bastards are boarding us!'

Bolitho dragged himself to the rail and felt the ship lurch as the other two-decker came to rest across the forecastle bulwark.

The larboard guns were firing with hardly a break, their balls smashing into the enemy's hull at a few yards range. But across the bows he could see the glint of steel, an occasional flash of a pistol as the boarders and his own men came to grips.

'Get the marines up forrard!' He was almost knocked from his feet as the scarlet-coated figures charged past him, their bayonets shining in the gunflashes as the passing ship fired once more through the smoke.

Inch shouted wildly. 'The mizzen topmast! It's coming down!'

Bolitho looked up and then pushed Inch against the nettings as with a splintering crack the topmast, complete with top-gallant and yards came pitching through the smoke to smash across the larboard side. Men were falling and dying, their blood running in great patterns across the deck, while some were still trapped in the severed rigging, their cries lost in the thunder of *Hyperion*'s guns.

Tomlin was here with his men, faces grim and intent, axes flashing while they cut the dragging wreckage clear, their ears deaf to the pitiful screams and pleas from those still enmeshed in the broken topmast. As it pitched into the water alongside Tomlin gestured with his axe and stood aside while his men began to throw the mangled corpses overboard and others dragged the protesting wounded down the ladder towards the main hatch and the horror of the orlop.

Bolitho stared up, his eyes smarting from the gunfire. It seemed bare and vulnerable without the great mast overhead and all its complex rigging and spars. He shook himself angrily and ran to the lee gangway to try and see the ship which was still locked around the bows.

There were scarlet coats there now, and the arrowhead of choppy water between the two hulls was covered with bodies, dead or wounded, it was impossible to say. Blades hacked and flashed above the nettings, and here and there a man would fall kicking into the mêlée, or be thrown bodily into the sea by the press behind him.

But Stepkyne was holding the boarders off, although the French captain appeared to have stripped his guns of men to overwhelm his enemy by sheer numbers. He was paying for it now. For as the *Hyperion*'s big twenty-four-pounders smashed ball after ball into the lower hull, the French guns remained silent. But the musket fire was fierce and accurate, and Bolitho saw more than one gun on the main deck with the dead heaped around it like so much meat.

He seized Roth's sleeve. 'Get the marksmen, for God's sake!'

Roth nodded grimly and strode along the larboard gangway to yell up at the swivel gunners in the maintop. He had moved only a few paces when he received a charge of canister full in the chest. His body rose like a tattered, bloody rag and then bounced across the nets to lie gaping at the sails above.

Bolitho snapped, 'Mr Gascoigne! Lively there!' He watched the young acting-lieutenant scramble along the nettings and begin to climb up the shrouds. Just a boy, he thought dazedly.

Inch clapped his hand to his head and then beamed foolishly as his hat was plucked over the rail.

Bolitho grinned. 'Walk about, Mr Inch! You make a promising target it seems!'

'*Blast!*' Allday pounced forward, his cutlass raised as some handful of figures started along the gangway towards the poop. They were French seamen, a young lieutenant running ahead with drawn sword and a pistol pointing at the quarterdeck.

The sharp crack of the maintop's swivel gun made some of the men falter, but as the canister swept away many of the others who were pressing forward in readiness to board, the lieutenant waved his sword and charged headlong for the poop. He saw Bolitho and slithered to a halt, his pistol surprisingly steady as he aimed it directly at him.

Allday started towards the gangway but fell back as Tomlin muttered an oath and hurled his axe with all the strength of his hairy arm. The keen blade struck the lieutenant in the chest, and as he toppled amongst his men his eyes were popping with astonishment as they stared at the axe, firmly embedded as if in a tree.

The others broke and ran back towards their comrades, only to be met by some crazed and jubilant marines.

Bolitho tore his eyes from the flashing bayonets and the blood which splashed down on the gunners below the gangway like scarlet rain.

'Another ensign, Mr Carlyon!' He nodded as the boy ran past. '*Walk*, Mr Carlyon!' He saw the midshipman staring at him, his features like chalk. He added gently, 'As befits a King's officer.'

More cries came from forward, and as axes flashed he saw the battered two-decker begin to nudge slowly along the *Hyperion*'s side, her hull hammered every yard of the way by the lower battery.

Bolitho ran on to the gangway and waved his sword at the main deck gunners. 'Come on, lads! Speed his passing!'

The seamen scrambled back to their guns, pausing only to drag the corpses and moaning wounded aside before hurling themselves on the tackles with renewed effort.

Bolitho stood quite still as captain after captain raised his hand in the air. More than half the larboard battery had been knocked useless, or so denuded of men as to be silent. So it had to be a careful broadside. He saw the stricken ship drifting past while the *Hyperion*'s pockmarked sails carried her slowly and painfully towards the remaining French two-decker which had been sent to protect Perez's *San Leandro*. On her quarterdeck he could see the dead and wounded heaped around the guns, the great rents in her poop and engaged side. By the carved quarterdeck ladder an officer clung to the rail for support, one leg twisted like that of a broken doll. It must be her captain, he thought absently. He dropped his sword.

'*Fire!*'

By coincidence both decks fired together, and as the smoke came billowing inboard through the ports and the men groped choking and cursing for the water and sponges, Bolitho saw the enemy's main and foremasts come down as one into the sea between them.

Inch yelled, 'Two crippled at least, sir! And *that* bugger'll never see another dawn if the sea gets up!'

Bolitho wiped his smarting eyes with his sleeve and watched the last guardship's outline hardening through the smoke, her guns already firing while she tacked awkwardly across the *Hyperion*'s bows. He swore savagely. There was not a gun which would bear yet, and if the enemy's broadside was ill aimed, it was still lethal. He jerked round as a great ball smashed through the bulwark and ploughed into the men at the larboard nine-pounders.

The crouching figures, naked to the waist, pigtailed and determined, were like a little group of statuary or part of a great painting of some forgotten battle. As the smoke whipped away Bolitho had to bite on his nausea, to look away from the bloody tangle of limbs and flesh, the bones shining like pale teeth through the carnage.

Trudgeon's men were busy dragging and cursing the screaming wounded into silence, and he saw Carlyon stooped double and vomiting into the scuppers.

Allday said calmly, 'That was a poor bit o' shooting, Captain.'

But at that instant the French ship fired a second time. Her captain had no intention of grappling with a ship which had already crippled two of his consorts with little outward damage to herself but the loss of a topmast. He was intending to sail downwind, to fire one more broadside into the English seventy-four's bows and then get clear.

The air seemed thick with screaming metal, the deck alive with flying splinters, and men torn and ripped as if from a beast gone mad. Bolitho watched tight-lipped as the foretopmast quivered, like a sapling feeling the first blow of an axe, and then almost wearily pitched down with smashing impact across the crowded forecastle. The ship yawed heavily as the wind groped blindly through the remaining canvas, and from forward he heard the shrill cries of men trapped beneath the great weight of spars and rigging. Seamen and marines, who seconds earlier had been training the carronades towards the enemy, were pulped into the splintered deck planking or swept bodily over the rail and into the sea.

Tomlin and his men were clambering towards the wreckage and confusion, but they were moving more slowly now, and their numbers were fewer.

Inch called, 'Here comes the *Hermes*!'

Bolitho walked to the starboard side, feeling his shoes slipping in blood and flesh as he clambered up to peer above the hammock nettings. The *Hermes* was without her mizzen, too, but her guns were still firing at a French two-decker, and he could see the balls slamming into the enemy's side and along her waterline.

Further astern the smoke was so tall and dense it was impossible to tell friend from foe, but there was plenty of gunfire, and he knew that Herrick was still there. Still fighting.

He felt Inch dragging at his coat, and as he jumped back to the deck he saw him pointing wildly, his eyes bright with anxiety.

'Sir! The *Tornade*'s gone about!' He followed Bolitho to the side. 'She's outsailed *Hermes* and is coming for us!'

Bolitho watched while the smoke darkened and parted to reveal the out-thrust bowsprit and then the figurehead of the great hundred-gun flagship. In spite of the noise and confusion on every side he could still feel a cold admiration for the French captain's superb seamanship as he edged almost into the eye of the wind, his massive armament bursting into life as with methodical savagery he poured a slow broadside into the *Hermes*'s unprotected stern.

Even at the distance of two cables Bolitho could hear the great bombardment raking the ship from stern to bow, the balls smashing the full length of her hull and turning it into a slaughterhouse.

The great thirty-two-pound balls must have sliced away the mainmast at its foot, for it was falling complete with top and yards, with struggling men, and the masthead pendant still whipping defiantly to the wind.

Black smoke belched from her main deck, as if forced upwards by some great bellows, and as the men at the *Hyperion*'s guns stared astern in shocked horror, the air was rent by one deafening explosion. The *Tornade* had sailed clear and was already clawing round towards the *Hyperion*'s larboard quarter, but for her it was a close thing.

The explosion, probably her magazine, had blasted the *Hermes* almost into two halves, in the centre of which a giant fire reached towards the sky, consuming the foremast and remaining sails in one lick, like an obscene dragon plucking down a lance.

Another explosion and another rocked the shattered hull, and within minutes of the broadside she started to roll over.

As she tilted steeply into the waves Bolitho saw the sea pouring through her lower ports, while on her blazing decks the few remaining survivors ran haphazardly in all directions, some ablaze like human torches, others already driven beyond reason. Her ports glowed like lines of red eyes, until finally as the sea surged into her hull and she began to slide under the littered water, she was completely hidden in a seething wall of steam.

One of the helmsmen had run from the wheel to watch. He dropped on his knees, crossing himself and whimpering, 'Jesus! Oh, sweet Lord Jesus!'

Gossett, one hand hidden in a bloody bandage, pulled him to his feet and snarled, 'This ain't no floatin' Bethel! Get back to your station or I'll gut you like a bloody herrin'!'

Bolitho swung away and snapped, 'Clear that hamper from the bows!' He saw Inch still staring at the dying ship. '*Get for'ard* and see to it! That ship'll be up to us directly!'

He turned back to watch the *Tornade* as she steadied on her new course, her fore topsail pitted with holes from the previous encounter. *She* had the wind-gage this time, and was preparing to overhaul the crippled *Hyperion* and smash her to submission as she passed.

He found that he could watch her confident approach almost dispassionately. It was nearly done. They had caused so much damage to Lequiller's force it was unlikely he could continue fully with his plan. Far away he could hear the sharp detonations of the *Spartan's* guns, and guessed Farquhar was playing cat and mouse with the *San Leandro*. It had been a brave gesture. He looked down at his own ship and felt the pain in his heart like a knife. There were dead and dying on every hand, and with men working to clear away the wreckage from the bows there was hardly a gun still fully manned.

Then he looked up at the mainmast where a new ensign flapped briskly above the drifting smoke. Lequiller was probably watching it, too. Recalling this same ship which had anchored in the Gironde Estuary alone and outnumbered to block his escape to sea. Now they were meeting again. For the final embrace.

He walked slowly across the broken planking, his chin on his chest. But this time the *Hyperion* was here to block his return to land. He looked up startled, as if someone had spoken the thoughts aloud.

He shouted hoarsely, 'Get a move on, Mr Inch!' Then to Gossett he added, 'Will she answer the helm like this?'

The master rubbed his chin. 'Mebbee, sir.'

Bolitho stared at him, his eyes cold. 'No maybes, Mr Gossett! I just want steerage way, nothing more!'

Gossett nodded, his heavy face crumpled with strain and worry.

Then Bolitho ran to the ladder and down to the main deck. At the top of the hatch he yelled, '*Mr Beauclerk!*' He stared as a grubby-faced midshipman peered up at him.

'Mr Beauclerk's dead, sir.' He shivered but added firmly, 'Mr Pascoe and I are in charge.'

Bolitho looked up at the maintop, seeking out Gascoigne. But there was no time now. He tried to clear his mind. To think. Just two boys. Two boys in command of an enclosed, deafening hell.

He said calmly, 'Very well, Mr Penrose. Send all the starboard side gunners on deck at the double!' He checked the midshipman and added, 'Then load and double-shot your guns to larboard.' He waited. 'Do you think you can do that?'

The boy nodded, his eyes suddenly determined. 'Aye, aye, sir!'

Inch strode aft. 'It will take another quarter hour, sir.'

'I see.' Bolitho looked above the tattered hammock nettings and saw the French ship's fore topgallant high above the larboard quarter, moving slowly but surely towards the final contact.

'We have no more time, Mr Inch.' It was strange how quiet it appeared to be. 'Muster all the available men but keep them down below the bulwark. I want fifty of them aft in the wardroom and stern cabin.'

Inch's eyes were on the other ship's topgallant and the vice-admiral's command flag which flew above it.

Bolitho continued in the same expressionless tone, 'I am going to board her.' He saw Inch staring at him but said, 'It is the only hope.' Then he clapped his shoulder and grinned. 'So let us have some enthusiasm, eh?'

He turned and ran back to the littered quarterdeck where

Allday stood beside the guns, his cutlass dangling from one hand.

A ball shrieked overhead and slapped through the main topsail, throwing a seaman from his perch on the yard and hurling him down on to the net, where he lay with his arms outstretched, as if crucified.

Bolitho said shortly, 'Stand by, Mr Gossett!' He did not turn as the detailed seamen and marines dashed past him into the gloom beneath the poop, while others hurried to the wardroom on the deck below.

Gossett could not see the enemy because of the poop, but was watching Bolitho's face with something like awe.

Inch clung to the ladder and said, 'Here she comes!'

The *Tornade*'s jib boom was already passing the quarter windows, and as she began to overhaul, Bolitho saw the men high in her tops, the sudden stab of musket fire as they tried to mark down the *Hyperion*'s officers. The swivel gun banged again and he heard Gascoigne yelling and cheering as the canister ripped away the wooden barricade around the enemy's foretop and blasted the marksmen down like birds from a branch.

The first three guns on the *Tornade*'s side belched tongues of flame, and Bolitho felt the balls smashing into his ship and gritted his teeth against her pain and his own as shot after shot crashed into the old timbers or cleaved through ports to cause carnage and terror inside the lower battery.

Gossett said between his teeth, 'She can't take much more, sir!'

Bolitho replied harshly, 'She *must*!' He flinched as a ball smashed through a group of men who were carrying a wounded comrade towards the main hatch. Arms and legs flew in grisly profusion, and he saw an old seaman gaping at the deck where his hands lay like torn gloves amidst the great spreading bloodstains. Then he was lost from view as the *Tornade* fired again, the rolling thunder of her broadside matched only by the terrible din as the massive weight of iron drove into the *Hyperion*'s side and upper decks.

Bolitho said, 'Now, Mr Gossett! Larboard helm!' He saw a quartermaster fall kicking and screaming, and threw his own weight to the wheel. He felt the spokes jerking under his hands, as if the ship was trying to hit back at those who were letting her be destroyed. He yelled, 'Heave! Over, lads!'

He could see the French ship right alongside now, barely thirty feet clear, her guns firing and then running out to shoot again almost before the smoke had been driven away. The lower battery was shooting in reply, but the sporadic salvos were lost in the enemy's deeper roar.

Men were waving weapons and yelling from the *Tornade*'s poop, and he saw others gesturing towards him and pointing him out to the marksmen in the tops.

Inch muttered tightly, 'Oh God, she's feeling it . . .' He broke off and threw one hand to his shoulder, his face twisted in agony.

Bolitho held him against the wheel. 'Where are you hit?' He tore open his coat and saw the bright blood pouring down his chest.

Inch said weakly, 'Dear God!'

Bolitho shouted, 'Mr Carlyon!' When the boy ran to him he snapped, 'Tend to the first lieutenant!' He added quietly, 'Rest easy, Inch.'

Then he tore himself away and shouted, 'Keep the helm over!' He ran past the helmsman, his ears deaf to the screams and the awful crash of splintering wood which seemed all about him.

On through the stern cabin, half filled with vague figures, and unfamiliar with burned panelling and gaping shot holes.

The ship was sluggish with a dozen rents beneath her water-line, but she was answering. Slowly and painfully she was swinging away from her attacker, the impetus of her turn bringing her battered stern towards that of the three-decker.

Bolitho kicked open the nearest window, the sword in his hand, his eyes wild and suddenly angry.

Then he saw his brother and Pascoe with the others, and felt the despair crowding through his reeling mind like a final torment.

He heard himself shout, 'Now, lads! Let's get to grips with the bastards!'

He almost fell into the sea as the two ships ground together with a jarring crash, but after a moment's pause he leapt out-wards for the ornate sternwalk and clung to it with all his strength, while yelling and screaming like madmen the others surged across with him. Below his legs he saw Stepkyne leading his party from the wardroom windows, and a man falling, seemingly very slowly, into the water below the two interlocked sterns.

Guns crashed and men cried in agony, while the ships continued to grind together, but Bolitho threw himself through the stern windows and plunged wildly across a deserted cabin, his sword ready, his mind empty of everything but the fury of battle.

Then there was a door, kicked open by a bosun's mate, who dropped dead from a pistol shot before he could jump aside. A midshipman holding the pistol screamed as a cutlass hacked him down. And then they were through and out on to the *Tornade*'s great quarterdeck. Startled faces and flashing steel seemed to pin Bolitho against a ladder, but as more of his small party surged beneath the poop and fighting became general he forgot everything but the need to reach the forepart of the deck, where he could see a gold-laced hat surrounded by a group of officers and several armed seamen.

When the smoke swirled clear he saw his own ship close alongside, held fast by grapnels which might have been cast by either side. She looked small and strangely unreal, and as he turned away to parry a cutlass he saw her mainmast going over the side, leaving her bare, like a listing hulk in some forgotten shipyard.

He did not even hear the mast fall, but saw only faces and wild eyes, his ears deafened by cries and savage curses, the clash of steel and the fierce determination which gripped his men like insanity.

But it was no use. Step by step they were being forced back to the poop again as more men ran from the guns in support and others fired down from the mizzen top, heedless of friend or foe in the desperation to clear their ship of boarders.

A figure darted beneath his arm and he saw it was Pascoe. As he reached out to stop him a French lieutenant struck the sword from his hand then brought the hilt savagely against the side of his head, knocking him to his knees. Bodies and swords swerved and slashed all around him, and he saw

Pascoe reaching to help him to his feet, while framed against the sky a French petty officer stood quite still, a pistol aimed straight at the boy's shoulder.

Another figure blotted out the light, momentarily silhouetted by the pistol's bright flash. Then as a body rolled against him Bolitho saw it was his brother.

Sobbing for breath he snatched up his sword from between the stamping feet and lunged upwards at the petty officer, seeing his face open from mouth to ear in a great scarlet gash. As the man reeled back shrieking he hacked down the French lieutenant and kicked his body aside even as he fell.

He gasped, 'See to him, Pascoe! Take him aft!'

Allday was striding at his side, the cutlass swinging back and forth, up and down with merciless precision. Men were screaming and dying, but so many were crammed on the quarterdeck it was impossible to measure the rising cost. There was no quarter asked or given, and Bolitho threw himself to the forepart of the deck realizing only vaguely that his men were advancing once more. He cut down a distorted face and drove his sword between the shoulders of an officer who was trying to fight his way through the press behind him.

He had lost his hat, and his body felt bruised and broken, as if he had been struck a hundred times.

But above and through it all he saw only his brother. His last gesture as he had thrown himself as a shield for his son, and perhaps for him.

A man in captain's uniform, his forehead laid open in a deep gash, was shouting at him through the struggling seamen, and Bolitho stared at him, trying to understand what he was saying.

The French captain yelled, 'Strike! You are beaten!' Then he went down as a marine impaled him on his bayonet.

'*Beaten!*' Bolitho shouted, 'Strike their colours!' He saw a man running to slash away the halyards and drop from a musket ball even as the great Tricolour fell and covered him like a shroud.

Stepkyne was pushing up beside Allday, his curved hanger crossing with a French lieutenant's sword. He raised his arm and then screamed as a man darted beneath his guard and drove a dirk up and into his stomach. The man ran on, too dazed to know what he had done or where he was going. A pigtailed seaman watched him dash past and then hacked him across the neck with his cutlass with no more expression on his face than a keeper killing a rabbit.

Bolitho reeled against the bulwark, his eyes blinded with sweat. He was cracking, he had to be. For above the harsh grate of steel and the awful screams he thought he could hear cheering.

Allday was yelling into his face. 'It's *Cap'n Herrick*, sir!'

Bolitho looked at him. Allday had never called him *sir* in living memory.

He dragged himself past the interlocked, swaying figures and peered across his ship at the braced yards and tan coloured sails of another vessel driving alongside. Then as grapnels thudded into the splintered bulwark he saw seamen and marines pouring across the *Hyperion* like a bridge, cheered on by the wounded and the surviving gunners still left to work the dismasted ship, their voices mingling with those of the enraged attackers.

No guns were firing now, and as more men surged hacking their way through boarding nets and defenders alike, Bolitho saw the French admiral's flag fluttering down to the deck, and heard the hoarse cries of Herrick's lieutenants for the French to submit and lay down their arms.

Herrick himself came aft to the poop, his sword in his hand. Bolitho stared at him. All fighting had ceased, and as the wind moved the limp sails overhead he saw the *Spartan* driving close by, her men cheering in spite of the damage and death around them.

Herrick seized his hand. 'Two others have struck to us! And the *San Leandro* is ours!'

Bolitho nodded. 'The rest?'

'Two made off to the north'rd!' He wrung his hand wildly. 'My God, what a *victory*!'

Bolitho released his hand and turned towards the poop. He saw Pascoe kneeling beside Hugh's body, and with Herrick beside him pushed between the exhausted but jubilant seamen.

Bolitho knelt down, but it was over. Hugh's face seemed younger, and the deep lines of strain were gone. He closed his brother's eyes and said quietly, 'A brave man.'

Pascoe stared at him, his eyes very bright. 'He saved my life, sir.'

'He did.' Bolitho stood up slowly, feeling the pain and exhaustion clawing at his nerves. 'I hope you'll always remember him.' He paused. 'As I will.'

Pascoe looked at him searchingly and some small tears ran down his stained cheeks. But when he spoke his voice was steady enough. 'I shall never forget. *Never.*'

Allday said, 'They've caught the French admiral, Captain.'

Bolitho swung round, the despair and the sense of loss flooding through him like fire. The chase and the disappointments, and all the dead still to be counted. And Lequiller had lived through it.

He stared at the little man standing between Lieutenant Hicks and Tomlin. He was bent and bearded, a small, wizened man whose stained uniform seemed too large for him.

Bolitho looked away, unable to watch the expression of stunned disbelief on Lequiller's face. He felt suddenly cheated and ashamed.

In war it was better for the enemy to be faceless.

'Take him under guard to *Impulsive.*' He walked towards the ladder, his men cheering him, their hands, some covered in blood, reaching out to touch his shoulders as he passed without a word.

On the *Hyperion*'s quarterdeck he found Inch waiting for him, one arm in a sling, his tattered coat across his shoulders like a cape. Bolitho reached his side and studied him. The sight of Inch did more than he would have thought possible to control his rising emotion.

He said quietly, 'I believe I ordered you below?'

Inch showed his teeth in a painful grin. 'I thought you would like to know, sir. The commodore was unconscious throughout the battle. But he is astir now and *demanding brandy.*'

Bolitho grasped his good hand, Inch's face suddenly blurred and out of focus.

'And he shall have it, Mr Inch!'

He looked past Gossett's huge grin and the capering, cheering gunners. The ship was mastless and heavy in the water, and he could almost feel her pain like his own.

Then he clapped his hat across the rebellious lock of hair and said firmly, 'We've sailed a long way together, Mr Inch.'

He unbuckled his sword and handed it to Allday.

'Now, if *Hyperion* is to be jury-rigged enough to lead our prizes back to Plymouth, there is a great deal of work to be done.'

He could feel the emotion pricking his eyes but continued in the same brisk tones, 'So what are we waiting for, eh?'

Inch looked at him sadly. Then he replied, 'I'll attend to it *directly*, sir!'

Epilogue

THE WINDOWS of the Golden Lion Inn were no longer sealed against the rain and icy wind, but were thrown open to receive what was little more than a gentle breeze. There were no white horses cruising across Plymouth Sound, and the bright midday sun threw a million dancing reflections from the blue water and played down upon the jostling sightseers along the road and jetty with friendly warmth.

But the telescope on its tripod was still there, and the room exactly as Bolitho had remembered it. And yet it was different in some way, and as he stared down at the slow-moving throng of townspeople below the window he was conscious of the stillness at his back, a quiet emptiness which seemed to be waiting for him to leave. Even now he could hear the landlord shuffling beyond the closed door, no doubt still wondering at Bolitho's strange request and fretting with impatience for him to depart so that some new guests could take over the room, as he had once done.

Most of the people along the busy waterfront had come for one purpose only. To see the ships at anchor, to display pride or horror at their battle-scarred appearance, as if by watching and waiting they, too, might share in some way the visible evidence of this victory. Any success was welcome in these uncertain times, but to see the spoils of war, and savour the sights and smells of conflict and death were to most people far more satisfactory than some vague account in the *Gazette* or hearing the shouted news from some hard-riding courier on his way to London.

Bolitho touched the brass telescope with his fingers and watched the busy comings and goings of small boats as they carried their paying passengers around the towering shape of the anchored *Tornade*, Lequiller's great three-decker, which within months would be at sea once again under the flag of her old enemy. With a new captain and company, and perhaps her old identity concealed behind some carefully chosen name.

He was thankful that *Hyperion* was not down there for all to see and examine like some grotesque relic. Almost as soon as they had crept into the Sound on the previous morning she had been warped into the dockyard, her pumps still struggling manfully to keep the vengeful sea at bay. One thing was certain. The old *Hyperion* would never fight again. Now, with the unwounded remnants of her company paid off and scattered to the demands of the fleet, she was lying empty and lifeless to await her final fate. At best she might be used as a receiving ship. At worst . . . Bolitho tried again to shut his mind to the possibility, she might end her days in some estuary or river as a prison hulk. He had left her just a few hours earlier, saddened at what he had seen, yet knowing that he could never have left without that final understanding which had grown between them.

As he had walked across the splintered quarterdeck he had thought of the voyage home after the battle. It had taken nearly two weeks, and had the Bay of Biscay chosen to turn on them, the *Hyperion* would be out there now resting on the sea's bottom in peace. At the end of the first week the slow-moving ships had been hit by a sharp squall, and one of the Fernch two-deckers had broken her tow and turned turtle within a few minutes. If the squall had not passed over just as swiftly, it was doubtful if the *Hyperion* would have survived either.

It had meant constant work and effort, and all the coaxing and skill they could muster to survive. Each day had seemed like a week, and every one had been marked by sea burials as yet more of the wounded had given up the struggle.

Then at last they had met with Sir Manley Cavendish's squadron and the burden had eased somewhat. But Bolitho had been too spent and worn out by strain to recall much more than blurred images and disjointed pictures of the events and the suffering which had made this moment in time possible.

Sympathy and congratulations, Cavendish gripping his hand and murmuring hints of recognition and possible promotion, all seemed lost in time and with no real substance.

When he had walked along the dockside, studying the great shot holes in the ship's hull, the smoke stains and patches of dried blood, he had wondered if the ship herself could feel and understand that her life was indeed over.

But when he had reached the bows he had stood looking up at the fierce-eyed figurehead and just for a few moments had imagined he had found his answer. There was no dismay or empty despair there. The Sun God's stare was as steady as ever, and the out-thrust trident still pointed to some invisible horizon with the same indifference and arrogance as ever. Perhaps after twenty-three years of hard service the ship was ready for retirement, and it was wrong to wish her otherwise.

All the way from the dockyard he had found himself wondering what would happen to himself. The rest of his company, willingly or otherwise, would all soon be at sea again, their lives merging and joining with new ships and different worlds almost before they had found time to give thanks for their survival. It had been hard to see them go, to find the words which always seemed so plentiful when it was too late and the right moment had passed. Gossett and Tomlin, and all the others who had shared and done so much. And of course there was Inch, who even now was seeking out the girl he hoped to marry before he, too, was posted to another ship to serve, Bolitho hoped, a captain who might take the time to understand his ways and appreciate his unwavering loyalty.

Many of the *Hyperion*'s survivors had luckily been sent straight to Herrick's ship to replace some of the many casualties, and they, too, would be at sea in a matter of weeks. For if the *Impulsive*'s human losses had been great, her actual damage had been incredibly light.

Even Pelham-Martin seemed strangely satisfied. Perhaps the thought of resting on the laurels of his wound, with the added prospect of receiving the massive portion of prize-money which would come his way from the blood of others less fortunate, would disperse his earlier threats of charges for insubordination. Bolitho found that he neither hoped nor cared.

The door opened a few inches and the landlord called anxiously, 'Beg pardon, Cap'n, but I was wonderin' how long you was intendin' to stay?' He coughed as Bolitho turned to look at him. 'There be another seafarin' gen'leman an' his

lady comin' very soon, an' . . .' His voice trailed away as
Bolitho picked up his hat and walked to the door.

'I have done, thank you.'

The landlord knuckled his forehead and watched him cross
to the stairs with obvious relief.

Bolitho guessed that the man did not even remember him,
and why should he? Yet he could recall exactly the moment of
that last parting here. Seven months ago. He quickened his
pace and had to forcibly stop himself from turning to look back.
As if he expected to see her there on the landing, watching
him go.

He almost collided with a young commander and bright-
eyed girl as they hurried up the wide stairway towards him.
He watched them pass. He could have been invisible to their
eyes. Their time, as his had once been, was too precious to
share, too valuable to waste beyond their private happiness.

At the foot of the stairs he paused and studied himself in
the wall mirror. It had been a mistake to come here. Or was
it merely one more method of delaying what he must do? He
thought he heard the sound of wheels and hoofs on the roadway outside and swung away from the mirror with something
akin to panic.

Back to Falmouth, but to find what? Would the house really
seem so empty, or could there still be some lingering presence
which he could hold and share with no one? He felt a sudden
stirring of hope, a strange power which moved him beyond
imagination.

He stepped out into the blinding sunlight and touched his
hat as some passers-by gave him a cheer, and one even held
up his child to see him better.

The coach was indeed waiting, and Allday stood beside it,
his eyes slitted against the sun as he idly watched the sightseers,
his tanned features showing little of the strain which he had
endured over the past weeks.

Bolitho asked quickly, 'Is everything ready?'

Allday nodded. 'All stowed.' He gestured with his thumb.
'What about him, Captain?'

Bolitho turned and saw the boy sitting on a bollard studying
the small ship model which Bolitho had been given at St Kruis.

He said, 'Come here, Mr Pascoe!'

317

As the boy walked towards him Bolitho felt both sad and strangely moved. More than that, he was suddenly ashamed. For thinking only of his own loss and hurt when others, many others, had so much to bear with less to sustain them through it. And Hugh was dead, too. Buried at sea with all the rest. Yet this boy, who had faced sights and deeds more terrible than he could have imagined existed, had known nothing of his true identity.

Pascoe stood looking up at him, his eyes clouded and tired.

Bolitho reached out and rested one hand on his shoulder. 'We've not got all day, you know, Adam.'

'Sir?'

Bolitho turned away, unable to watch Allday's pleasure or the boy's obvious gratitude.

He said harshly, 'We're going *home*, so get in, will you!'

The midshipman snatched up his bag and scrambled after him.

'Thank you, Uncle,' was all he could find to say.